The Property
of

Mr AE Hanna
c/o 15 Northfield close
Tetbury
Glos

The
Badminton
Tradition

BARRY CAMPBELL

The Badminton Tradition

MICHAEL JOSEPH
London

First published in Great Britain by Michael Joseph Ltd
52 Bedford Square, London WC1
1978

Filmset in Great Britain by
BAS Printers Limited, Over Wallop, Hampshire
and printed in Great Britain by
Redwood Burn, Trowbridge

Contents

List of Illustrations   vii

Acknowledgements   ix

Introduction   xi

Part I: Badminton—the Farm of
Beadmund's People   15

Part II: Noble Lords and Ladies All   35

Part III: The Blue and the Buff   93

Part IV: A Most English Occasion   159

Bibliography   225

Index   227

List of Illustrations

1 The Beaufort coat of arms

2 The 1st Duke of Beaufort

3 The 1st Duke of Beaufort's wife

4 Badminton House from the east

5 The Great Hall, Badminton House

6 The Sporting Sweep of Chipping Sodbury

7 The 9th Duke following hounds by car

8 Lawn Meet at Westonbirt, 1922

9 After the meet at Tetbury Market

10 The 9th Duke of Beaufort with his son, the present Duke

11 The 10th Duke of Beaufort, Master of the Horse

12 Brian Gupwell, Huntsman to the Beaufort Hunt

13 Frank Weldon riding Kilbarry

14 Lucinda Prior-Palmer with Killaire and George

15 The 10th Duke of Beaufort riding Apollo

Acknowledgements

I should like to express my gratitude to His Grace, the 10th Duke of Beaufort, KG, PC, GCVO, MFH, for his permission to write this book.

I should also like to express my gratitude to Lieutenant-Colonel Sir Peter Farquhar, DSO, for his kindness in contributing the appreciation of His Grace, the Duke of Beaufort, which appears on page 133 and also to Lieutenant-Colonel F. W. C. Weldon, MVO, MBE, MC, for his advice and generous assistance.

My grateful thanks are extended to the following people, for generously allowing me to quote from their works.

Lady Clodagh Anson—*Victorian Days* (Garnstone Press/Geoffrey Bles);

E. W. Bovill—*English Country Life, 1780–1830* (by permission of the Oxford University Press);

Mr Michael Clayton—for permission to quote extracts from articles printed in *Horse and Hound*;

T. F. Dale—*The 8th Duke of Beaufort and the Badminton Hunt* (Constable Ltd);

Mrs Horatia Durant—*The Somerset Sequence* (Hughes & Sons Ltd., Pontypool);

H. P. R. Finberg—*The Gloucestershire Landscape* (Hodder & Stoughton Ltd.);

Mr Jack Ivester Lloyd—*Hounds of Britain*;

Miss Daphne Moore—*In Nimrod's Footsteps* (J. A. Allen & Co. Ltd.);

Mr James Archibald Morrison, FCA, MH(Retd.)—"Loppylugs" articles published in *Horse and Hound*;

Lieutenant-Colonel F. W. C. Weldon for permission to quote from the Badminton Horse Trials programmes.

P. Whitwell Wilson (ed.)—Excerpts from *The Greville Diary* (Doubleday & Co. Inc.);

Lord Willoughby de Broke—*The Passing Years* (Constable Ltd.).

World Badminton (H. A. E. Scheele—editor)

For their interest, assistance and generosity in helping to supply information used in this book, I am indebted to the following: Mr Charles Balch, Mrs M. Barker, Mr David Bartlett, Mr S. Bywater,

Miss Patricia Biden, Major R. J. G. Dalls, Reverend T. T. Gibson, Mr Jim Gilmore, Major Gerald Gundry, DSO, Mr Brian Gupwell, Mr A. Hutchinson, Mr E. M. Mitchell, FRICS, Mr A. L. Rochester, Mr John Shuter, Mr Charles Smith, Lady Caroline Somerset, Mr David Somerset, MFH, Mr Wally Trotman, Major A. G. Wakeling, Mr B. L. Watkins, Mr Michael Whitbread.

I should also like to thank all those people who wrote to me in response to my appeal for information, especially the following: Mr M. Bousted, Mr R. S. Bray, Major-General H. H. Evans, Mr R. Ford, Mrs Yvonne Gunn, Mr R. Huggett, Miss Ruth K. Hynes, Mrs E. Knight, Mrs Anne Long, Miss J. Moore, Mrs F. B. Shepperd, Mr W. F. Lisle Taylor and Miss J. A. Young.

With the exception of photograph no 8, all the photographs in this book were taken and supplied by Mr Peter Harding of Tetbury, to whom I am indebted for his interest and cooperation.

Last, but not least, I should like to thank my wife, Janet, for all her assistance.

Introduction

"Those gentlemen who make a profession of writing live chiefly in town, and consequently cannot be supposed to know much of hunting; and those who know anything of it are either servants who cannot write, or country gentlemen who will not give themselves the trouble."

(Peter Beckford, 1740–1811)

In May 1976 I paid my first visit to Badminton with the Huntsman of the Monmouthshire Hunt, David Bartlett. David had some business at the Badminton Kennels and I was able to accompany him.

Prior to that visit, I had been aware of Badminton, through the pages of *Horse and Hound* and other sporting journals, as the venue of the annual Badminton Horse Trials and as the headquarters of the Duke of Beaufort's Hunt—a place somewhere in the Cotswolds where the best foxhounds were bred.

My own experience of foxhunting had been of the foot-following variety, as well as through the pages of the great sporting writers, such as R. S. Surtees, Peter Beckford, "Nimrod", and so on. It was, therefore, with some trepidation that I first entered the marvellous Kennels at Badminton.

We were received with great friendliness by the Duke of Beaufort's Huntsman, Brian Gupwell, who treated us to a tour of the kennels and also showed us the hound puppies which were shortly to be displayed at the annual Duke of Beaufort's Puppy Show. Finally, and perhaps most exciting of all, we were invited to walk out with the Huntsman and Whipper-In, as some seventy couple of the best foxhounds in the world were being exercised.

To walk through the beautiful park, with herds of deer in the distance and Badminton House in the background, was to take part in a ritual which has been going on for hundreds of years. The mundane world of traffic congestion, mindless noise, inflation, constant political crisis, and all the other horrors of modern life, might never have existed. For anyone not at all interested in hunting, it would have been a pleasant excursion, but to a hunting enthusiast it was a tremendous pleasure, certainly the highlight of a holiday, and it was an experience which left a lasting impression.

As we drove away from Badminton, David Bartlett said: "Well, you've seen the best." Indeed, we had.

During the months which followed, the memory of that visit to Badminton was reinforced by constant references in magazines and old sporting books to the Beaufort Hunt, the Estate, the Horse Trials. Then a chance conversation with a publisher, plus a move of house to Gloucestershire, brought about the idea of writing a book concerned with Badminton and its sporting associations. A somewhat hesitant letter to the Duke of Beaufort, resulted in His Grace very kindly giving permission for work on a book to go ahead.

In order to ascertain the type of material available, before actually starting work in the Badminton area, I placed a letter in the correspondence column of the *Daily Telegraph*. This resulted in a shower of letters from all over the country, from all types of people, some of whom had worked at Badminton, or who had visited the House, or who had, in some way, come into contact with the Duke of Beaufort.

Reading these letters, one thing soon became apparent, and that was the tremendous affection which the present Duke of Beaufort seems to inspire in everybody. This was certainly not just snob value (for we all know that the British "dearly love a Lord"), but it was a genuine respect and affection. Perhaps His Grace, with his dedication to the English countryside and his great love of field sports, has come to represent for a great number of people a better, or at least a different, way of life.

It is true that His Grace is the descendant of a long line of well-to-do noblemen, and he does own a large country estate, and no doubt the "faceless men", who wish to see England turned into one glorious heap of concrete, will find the idea of a rich nobleman devoted to country pursuits utterly abhorrent but Badminton House, with its park, its stables and its Kennels, does exist and has done so for hundreds of years.

It is one of the last of the really big estates, and it represents a way of life which is fast disappearing, as more and more land is carved up and parcelled out in the name of progress.

It seems to me, therefore, that it is important to create (in however small a way) some record of Badminton from the material which is available. Perhaps, in one hundred years from now, some socially orientated young people will read about it and exclaim: "Did such a place really exist?" Perhaps it will still exist, and Lord Willoughby de

Broke's words will have proved to be prophetic: "At Badminton, the stud and the park are integral portions of the establishment. Like their masters, they did not come there yesterday, and they will not be gone tomorrow."

So, whether the idea of one family owning a great estate, with all its sporting associations, excites, interests, or angers you, Badminton does still exist and, as such, is the subject of this book.

PART I

Badminton—the Farm of Beadmund's People

"There is no place in the British Isles where the spirit of the chase breathes so naturally as at Badminton"
Lord Willoughby de Broke in *The Passing Years*

The village of Great Badminton is situated in fine woodland and hill country, adjacent to the grounds of Badminton House, the Palladian mansion home of the Dukes of Beaufort. The village lies in the upper division of the hundred of Grumbolds Ash, nine miles south-west of the town of Tetbury, six miles north-east of Chipping Sodbury, and twenty-eight miles south of Gloucester. It is bordered on the north by Little Badminton,* to the south by Acton Turville, to the east by Alderton, and to the west by Old Sodbury. According to Samuel Rudder, in his *A New History of Gloucestershire*, published in 1799, at Badminton "the air is healthy and the soil more suitable to corn than pasture. There is no river nor stream of water running through it. It hath been asserted of the village that no adder, snake, nor lizard hath ever been found in it notwithstanding they are frequent in the neighbouring places."

Concerning the etymology of the name Badminton, Rudder is uncertain—"wherefore I decline giving as my own an explanation of it. Some people, however, have conjectured that it is comprised of two Anglo-Saxon words, Bedan to pray, and Moign, a monk, and so make it signify the name of priest's town. But the ancient manner of writing it Madminton (Madmintune) as it is in the Domesday Book, is an argument against that notion."

According to the official guide book to Badminton House—"for nearly a thousand years there has been a village community at Badminton, 'the Farm for Beadmund's People'. A Saxon Charter of 972 calls it Badimyncgton, but by 1200 the spelling had become Badmintun. The Domesday survey, which was compiled by William the Conqueror's orders, issued in the Cathedral Chapter House at Gloucester, gives the population of the village as twenty-four, including a priest." Today, the population is approximately three hundred and twenty-five, including a vicar, the Reverend T. T. Gibson, Vicar of Badminton. In seven hundred years only two families have owned Badminton. From the thirteenth century it was owned by the Boteler family. Then in 1608, the Manor of Badminton was purchased by Edward Somerset, 4th Earl of Worcester (1549–1627), and the Somerset family has continued to live at Badminton until this day.

In July 1935, Eleanor Knight travelled to Badminton to join her husband, who had recently been appointed Head Gardener to the 10th Duke of Beaufort. Over forty years later, she wrote: "Being

*Little Badminton, in the upper division of Grumbolds Ash, is described by Rudder as "being merely a small place". No mention is made of it in the Domesday Book. Some of the cottages in the village date from Saxon times, while the dovecote is supposed to have been built at the time of the Battle of Hastings, when only landowners were allowed to keep pigeons and doves.

driven the last mile from the station at Acton Turville I had a curious feeling of having come home.''

It is interesting to speculate just how many thousands of people must have experienced exactly the same feeling as Mrs Knight when first visiting Badminton—that feeling of having come home, for there is an atmosphere of peace and tranquillity and a quality of permanence about Badminton and the surrounding countryside which is to be found in few places elsewhere. Indeed, in these days of high-speed jet travel, motorways, high-rise flats and all the bustle and stress of modern life, to stroll through the park and the village at Badminton is almost to enter another world—a world of stability, where there is time to consider other matters besides the latest industrial dispute or the problems of inflation. It is almost another world, yet, apart from the antiquity of its buildings, there is nothing "olde worlde" about the village. Its inhabitants are just as aware as the rest of us of national and world events. They watch the same television programmes and eat the same brands of pre-packed food. The village is the centre of a major farming operation; every year in April over a hundred thousand people gather at Badminton for the Horse Trials, while throughout the summer months tourists from all over the world are shown over Badminton House. So Badminton and its population can hardly be said to be "other-worldly" or out of touch, and yet there is no doubt that the place does have a certain feeling of tranquillity about it.

The Vicar of Badminton, the Reverend Mr T. T. Gibson, suggests that this is probably the result of continuity.

"It has got something special, which is based, I think, on the people. Because, in spite of the fact that quite a lot of people come in here, you have got a hard core of the families who live in Badminton and round about who have been here for goodness knows how long. I was looking through old registers at the school and going back to when it was first started—about 1690—and there has always been, without exception, a Salt boy or girl at that school. And the Salts still live here. You can pick out about five family names in the parish which have been here since the Beauforts.''

Despite the thousands of visitors who pass through the village each year, Badminton cannot be said to be a tourist village. There are no "tea shoppes", no antique shops, and there isn't even a public house! This, according to Mr E. M. Mitchell, Agent for the Badminton Estate is "in modern times by design. We have an excellent village club, which has all the facilities of a pub, but it is a place where the locals have a chance to drink and where they are not kept out by visitors.''

And visitors, tourists, or what you will, can and do create problems, as one resident of the village explained. "It's very much a country village until you get something happening here, and then we get in a terrible muddle—jam-packed, treble parking, sometimes four or five hundred cars in the main street.''

Originally, the Estate Office was an hotel—The Portcullis, named after the Beaufort coat of arms—where people used to stay when they went hunting with the Duke of Beaufort's hounds, but eventually this was closed down.

As regards the actual date of the closing of the public house at Badminton, Mr A. L. Rochester, one-time Station Master at Badminton Station, and a former Steward of the Badminton Club, thinks that this came about in 1904—''when they were building the railway line from London to Wales. They were digging the cuttings in the tunnels and there were hundreds of Irish navvies around here, and they made such a nuisance of themselves that the Duke at that time, the father of the present Duke, closed the pub, and it didn't open again for several years and then only as a club.''* The club used to be on the site where the Post Office is now; later it was moved to the site of the old Portcullis Hotel and is housed in the same building as the Estate Office.

The village of Badminton consists of one hundred and nineteen houses and cottages (including council houses), the Hunt Kennels, the village hall, a village green and the vicarage. The church, though essentially a parish church rather than a family church, is part of Badminton House.

The original church at Badminton being ''very ruinous'',† the 5th Duke of Beaufort built a new church in 1783. It was designed by Charles Evans of London and was attached to the south side of Badminton House. The original church was sited at the front of the west door of the present church, with the old chantry and altar having been sited under the present tower. The new church was built of Cotswold stone, quarried from the Badminton estate, and the timber used was grown in Badminton Park. The foundation stone was laid in April 1783 and in October 1785 the new building, dedicated to St. Michael and All Angels, was consecrated by the Bishop of Gloucester.

At Badminton it is impossible ever to get far away from foxhunting, and in the porch of the church there is a memorial to one Dr Robert Penney, a hunting Vicar and one-time encumbent of Badminton Parish. The porch also contains a memorial to the twenty-seven men of Great Badminton who gave their lives in the two world wars.

*However, there seems to be some confusion about this since the Ordnance Survey sheet of 1903 does not show a public house in Badminton village.
†Badminton Parish Register.

The somewhat plain exterior of the church belies its extremely attractive and comfortable interior, which is beautifully proportioned and well appointed. It is, in fact, rather like a small intimate theatre, even having a gallery at the back—a gallery which has always been the subject of much curiosity.

It is known as the Tribune and is the Duke of Beaufort's family pew. It is called the Tribune by virtue of its raised position in the west gallery of the church. The Tribune is directly connected to Badminton House by means of a passage which leads to the Library. There the entrance is concealed by a door disguised as part of the book shelving. This is thought by many people to be a secret passage, a notion which Lady Caroline Somerset rejects: "There was no question of secrecy about it. It was just that another door would have looked ugly, so they concealed it."

The family pew has also caused much comment because it is furnished with large leather armchairs as well as a splendid fireplace. Lady Clodagh Anson has recorded* that, in the 8th Duke of Beaufort's time, "It had a fireplace with a huge fire in it in the winter and the most comfortable armchairs to sit in, enormous prayer books at the front where we stood or knelt, so that that was the only time the clergyman could see if anyone was in the gallery at all, which was very convenient, as all the men used to creep out before the sermon. In those days it was always considered that 'women should be religious', this being apparently unnecessary for the male of the species."

The church at Badminton contains many attractive features. There are, for example, monuments to all previous nine Dukes of Beaufort, the most interesting being those which were erected in memory of the 2nd and 3rd Dukes by the Flemish sculptor, Michael Rysbracht (1694–1770) and, on the north side of the chancel, the large monument commemorating Henry, 1st Duke of Beaufort. This monument was the creation of Grinling Gibbons (1648–1721) and was "one of only two works he did in stone". It was originally placed in St. George's Chapel, Windsor but, in 1875, Queen Victoria requested that it should be moved to Badminton as she wished to make room for a memorial to her husband, Prince Albert. According to the present Vicar of Badminton, "They [the Beauforts] didn't know where to put it because the church, at that time, ended at the present chancel arch. After a lot of discussion, however, they managed to get Queen Victoria to pay for the extention to the church in order to house the monument."

The aisle windows of the church are of plain glass, with leaded

* *Victorian Days* by Lady Clodagh Anson who was the daughter of Blanche, the 8th Duke's only daughter and who married 5th Marquess of Waterford.

panes, but are decorated with small stained glass panels depicting the Beaufort coat of arms together with heraldic borders in blue and gold. These windows are dated 1846. The stained glass east window is very beautiful and depicts the miraculous healing of the lame man (Acts of the Apostles, chapter 3). Other features of interest in the church include the original oak box-pews, which are four foot six inches in height. The dado in the nave is of panelled oak as is the pulpit, which is embellished with some Adam-style carving.

In 1908, the 9th Duke of Beaufort provided the present altar, communion rail, organ and choir stalls, as a memorial to his mother (Georgiana, Duchess of Beaufort) and his sister, Blanche, Marchioness of Waterford. The two-manual organ, dated 1908, is also of carved oak. The original church organ was blown by water-power, which was brought from the lake in the park through an underground conduit, and then over a wheel, thus providing an unusual source of power.

In 1954, the Duchess of Beaufort erected a Portland stone memorial—"The Archangel Michael victorious over the dragon"—in memory of her brother Lord Frederick Cambridge, who was killed in action in Flanders in May 1940.

Two standards have been laid up in the church—the King's Colour of the Royal Horse Guards, in which regiment the present Duke served as a young man, and the standard of Badminton and District Branch of the British Legion, presented by Louise, Duchess of Beaufort, wife of the 9th Duke.

The church has three bells which were re-hung in 1914. The tenor bell weighs eight and a half hundredweight. It is inscribed, "The most noble Henry, Duke of Beaufort" and is dated 1690 (this was presumably hung in the original church). The two other bells, both dated 1784, are also inscribed: "The most noble Henry, 5th Duke of Beaufort".

The Parish Registers at Badminton were opened in 1538, while the church plate includes a communion cup and paten cover of silver-gilt, dated 1675.

The houses and cottages at Badminton are, for the most part, built of beautiful, soft grey-coloured Cotswold stone, although the majority of them are faced with a light ochre-coloured lime and sand compound (stucco) which takes on a golden colour in sunlight. Some of the houses in the village have stone slated roofs as well as mullioned windows, and many of them look as though they have grown where they stand rather than having been built.

The ages of the buildings in the village cover a wide range of dates. At the eastern end of the village, for example, is the school, which is in the middle of a row of almshouses, and dates from the beginning of the eighteenth century. The school was founded by Mary, Duchess of Beaufort, widow of the 1st Duke, in 1705, and it remained open as a school until 1975. A contemporary plan to turn this building into two almshouses for retired estate workers has had to be abandoned owing to Government planning restrictions. One particularly attractive feature of the almshouses, and of some other houses in the village, is the number of beautifully carved ducal crests which adorn them.

The Post Office block in the middle of the village is dated 1860, while at the far end "The Cottage" dates from 1780. "The Cottage" is, in fact, rather a misnomer for a really beautiful twelve-bedroomed house, where the present Duke of Beaufort's mother lived when she was the Dowager Duchess. It is now the home of the Duke's heir, Mr David Somerset, and his family.

Beyond "The Cottage", at the far end of the village, are a number of small cottages which date from 1680. Some of the residents of Badminton think that the village has become rather shabby, that it "wants a million pounds spent on it to bring it into line with some of the 'Best Kept' villages, such as Castle Combe". No doubt there are some buildings much in need of improvement—some, for example, still have outside privies—but any superficial attempt to smarten the village would reduce Badminton to the level of just another pretty village thereby losing much of its unspoiled charm.

On the fringe of the village is a vicarage built, according to its present incumbent, by the Duke's father in 1922. There is also a singularly unattractive village hall, dating from 1919. The village has a Post Office and two shops (general stores), and it also has the Horse Trials Office, which is housed in one of the old buildings. At one time there was a butcher's shop and a draper's shop.

Approximately twenty percent of the villagers are employed on the Badminton Estate, and many of the retired Estate workers live in the village houses and cottages, paying only nominal rents. Seventy-five percent are people that have worked.

The stables at Badminton, adjacent to the house, are magnificent. The entrance to the enormous courtyard is reached after walking from Badminton House through the archway (dating from 1841) and through another smaller arch. At one end of the courtyard, set high in the wall of the surrounding building is a pigeon-loft, which is surmounted by a weather vane—which, of course, is a fox. The stables surround the courtyard, and a wall at the far end bears yet another ducal crest. Inside, the stables are beautifully appointed and they are kept in superb order. The dozens of large, airy boxes are set inside the stone buildings with heavy wooden partitions, all with highly-polished brass fittings to them. During Horse Trials week, the competitors' horses are kept in the stables. During normal times, the stables house some thirty-five hunters.

Because Badminton is, or has been, a working village, it has not had to assimilate (as have the majority of villages in England) an influx of townspeople buying property to which to retire, or rich businessmen acquiring properties as week-end cottages. This is perhaps another reason why it has kept its character. It is, however, an "old" village or, rather, its inhabitants are, for the most part, elderly. The Revd. T. T. Gibson said that "The Duke, of course, has never put any widow out of any house—widows of the people that have worked for him—and so you've got a village of old people living in what really are family houses. This makes it difficult to get outside people to come and work here, since there's nowhere for them to live."

It is true that there are not many children or young people in the village and this does pose several questions concerning the future of the village and, indeed, its surrounding area. The local school, at Acton Turville, which takes in pupils from Badminton, Little Badminton, Acton Turville and part of Tormarton, still only has thirty-six pupils.

At one time, Badminton used to have its own Fire Brigade, complete with a horse-drawn engine—two horses being kept especially for the purpose. The Brigade dealt with any fires (mostly hay and straw fires) in and around Badminton village and estate, providing a very useful service in the area. An interesting relic of the Badminton Fire Brigade is one of the original fireman's helmets which is still kept in the Estate Office. During one period, the written orders for the Brigade were also kept in the Estate Office, when a previous agent for the Estate, Mr Markham, was also the Chief Fire Officer.

Unfortunately, enquiries as to the exact origins of the Fire Brigade have proved fruitless. After the Brigade was disbanded—some time between the wars—the Duke of Beaufort presented the fire engine to the Bristol Museum. Two letters and two telephone calls to the Museum produced the information that the Museum had no details of any kind about the Fire Brigade and would be grateful for any details which could be passed on to them!

The villagers of Badminton are well used to Royal and other distinguished visitors. Her Majesty the Queen and the Royal Family are frequent visitors to Badminton House—the Queen is said to be especially fond of Badminton, having spent much time there as a child—and regularly attend the Badminton Horse Trials. It has not been unknown for a visit from Queen Elizabeth, the Queen Mother, to coincide with the National Hunt Festival at nearby Cheltenham.

The Royal visits to Badminton are happy occasions. As the Revd. Gibson said, "There has been of latter years, since Queen Mary stayed here, a very real and strong connection with the Royal Family. For example, they came to the opening of the Church—when it was restored—the whole lot of them, and when they do come down here, they are really relaxed and it is super."

Remarkably, the village and its inhabitants have been quite unaffected by this influx of Royalty "Hasn't had its head turned"—and the Reverend Mr Gibson believes that "this must be put down to the Duke and to the Duchess. You see, he knows everybody here, every single person. He's been brought up here since he was a boy, and he knows every nook and cranny of it and of the surrounding countryside, and so he knows all the people and all the tenants. And it's not just a question of knowing them in a formal sort of way. He knows them very well, and he remembers little things about them . . . and the Duchess is the same, and if ever anything goes wrong and she can possibly help in any way, she does so."

The villagers of Badminton are quick to resent any suggestion that they live in the shadow of the "big house" and to assert that any feudal aspect of Badminton village life is a thing of the past. The villagers, and indeed the people in the surrounding area, do have a genuine affection for the Duke and Duchess and, remarkably, during the time spent in working on this book, not one nasty or even unkind remark has been passed about them.

As for life in the village, apart from high days and holidays, Royal visits and the Horse Trials, it is very much the same as life in most old-established villages. One resident suggests that this is gradually changing. "Probably because before the war the majority of the inhabitants either worked on the Estate or for local farmers. Now the younger generation tends to work outside the village, and therefore, the old close community will, I think, gradually die out."

Even so, newcomers to the village can still be made to feel that they are "outsiders". Charles Smith, who is eighty-one and who has lived in the village for most of his life, thinks that "sometimes, especially if they come from other villages, they're taken to right away. Others are strangers all their lives. A stranger has only to say one wrong word in the village and he is out of favour for years." And even in these liberated times, newcomers feel this. For example, one young couple of shopkeepers in the village—comparative newcomers—refused to record an interview, "having their position in the village to think of"!

During World War II, Queen Mary* lived at Badminton House. Her immediate arrival was a time of some upheaval, it seems, and she

---

*Queen Mary was the Duchess of Beaufort's aunt, being the sister of her father, the Marquess of Cambridge.

arrived with so many in her entourage that chaos ensued for a time. Although several of the entourage were men, not one was entirely fit for the services. They were pretty disgruntled at being hustled out of London, and apparently several of the existing staff in the House left. The first morning, a maid coming downstairs thought she had switched on a light, but it was the stable bell, which was to act as a danger warning. The poor Queen was roused and taken down to a specially strengthened ground floor room. Of course, the entire village was alert to the false alarm as well.

Queen Mary was held in great affection by the villagers and by the Service personnel who were stationed in and around Badminton at that time. Many of them still treasure their favourite "Queen Mary" stories as, for example, Major Arthur Wakeling who went to Badminton to deal with an unexploded bomb following a German air raid in 1940.

"Queen Mary was living with the Beaufort family at the time, and we were instructed, like the villagers, not to acknowledge her in the village. One day, wishing for something to do, the Queen took secateurs and was trimming some ivy, watched very critically over the wall by an old Estate worker who, at last, said, 'Oh, the old Duchess wouldn't have done it like that.' The family was much amused when the Queen related this at dinner that evening."

Queen Mary took a lively interest in everything that went on at Badminton, and was always looking for "something to do". Major-General H. H. Evans remembers vividly how the Queen used to attend the lectures which were laid on for the troops who were stationed at Badminton as a guard for her. "These lectures took place in a white-washed room in the stables at Badminton, and Queen Mary, accompanied by Lady Airlie, used to sit at the back. If the subject of the lecture dealt in any way with current affairs, Lady Airlie used to bring an atlas. On one occasion, the lecturer became so nervous that he broke his map-pointer and then dried up completely."

Queen Mary later discussed the matter with Major-General Evans. "Queen Mary suggested that I could improve the quality of the lectures, and she offered to write to Lord Cranborne at the Colonial Office. I was horrified; the men really preferred much simpler topics. So I said, in a careless moment, 'But, Ma'am, I do not think that these men would appreciate the presence of a big-shot.' She rounded on me in a flash. 'Big-shot, Mr Evans? What is a big-shot?' Thrown off balance, I replied lamely, 'Well, you are, Ma'am.' 'Bless my soul, what an odd expression,' was her reply."

On another occasion, Queen Mary, who enjoyed walking in the grounds, discovered that one of the soldiers had cut his hand. The

Queen immediately bound up the wound with her handkerchief. Several weeks later, much to the consternation of the Commanding Officer, Queen Mary asked for her handkerchief back. The handkerchief, meanwhile, had been laundered, and was hanging in the soldier's home in a frame. On being told this, Queen Mary said, "Please tell him to keep it as a souvenir,"—much to everyone's relief.

Queen Mary also spent much of her time at Badminton sorting through and cataloguing much of the great mass of historical documents to be found in the Muniment Room, often inventing her own form of classification. There is, for example, one bundle of documents which is clearly marked in her own hand-writing with the title "Interesting Things".

Opened in 1903, Badminton Station, with its red-carpet waiting-room and its ducal crest, has always figured large in the history of the Estate during the early part of this century, by virtue of the fact that the "non-stop" South Wales express often did stop at Badminton in order to set down parties of visitors—much to the amazement of the other passengers. This was, in fact, a concession obtained by the 8th Duke of Beaufort in return for allowing the Great Western Railway to cut through his Estate. The castellated air-vents of the Sodbury Tunnel can still be seen on the Estate. (Two reporters covering the 1977 Horse Trials spent much time debating whether or not these were "follies" or whether the Duke of Beaufort had a private, underground railway.)

In the days when trains used to run on time, certain letters against the name Badminton in George Bradshaw's famous *Railway Guide* denoted that some of the South Wales Express trains would stop at Badminton to set down and pick up first class passengers on prior notice being given to the officials either at Paddington Station or at Badminton. Richard Ford, a former resident at Badminton, has pointed out that "this not only benefited the hunting people, but was also a matter of great convenience to those people living in the surrounding area. While serving in the Royal Navy during the war, when coming home on leave, I would board a South Wales Express and travel direct to Badminton at commendable speed."

Ronald Bray, son of a former Station Master at Badminton, recollects "that during Queen Mary's residence at Badminton, during World War II, the Royal Train was available at Badminton Station and the Station Master's office was often converted into a Royal waiting-room."

Concerning the Royal Train at Badminton, Mr Rochester tells of a nice little piece of railway protocol when Royal personages arrived at the station. "There wouldn't be any fuss, no red carpets, but you had to pull up the train reasonably near the entrance so they wouldn't have to walk too far, but as long as you kept the platform clear it was quite simple. When the present Queen and Princess Margaret were children, we had the Royal Train here often, and we had to measure the exact distance in feet and inches from the front of the train to the carriage door they stepped out of, and we had to put up a white post where the engine driver could see it so that he knew exactly where to stop."

While on the subject of station masters at Badminton and its environs, Lady Dorothy Neville, a relative of Horace Walpole, has recorded* the following delightful story concerning the Station Master at Chippenham Station who, on seeing a gentleman smoking on the platform, told him that it was forbidden.

"The gentleman, however, continued to smoke, upon which the Station Master repeated his behests more peremptorily than before. A third time the order was repeated, accompanied with the threat that if the obstinate sinner did not obey he would be handed over to the tender mercies of the porters. The stranger took no more heed than before; and so at last the Station Master pulled the cigar out of the smoker's mouth and flung it away. This violent act produced no more effect than commands and threats, and the peripatetic philosopher continued his walk quite serenely.

"Presently a carriage and four drove up—an equipage well-known to the Station Master as that of the Duke of Beaufort. To his inconceivable horror, the refractory smoker entered the said chariot and drove off to Badminton, nor was he at all relieved when he was told that the stranger was the Prime Minister, Lord Palmerston. Fearful of the consequences, the poor man at once ordered a chaise and drove off to Badminton, and urgently requested an interview with Lord Palmerston.

"His Lordship soon appeared, when the Station Master began a most abject apology for having 'so grossly insulted His Lordship'. The Premier heard the Station Master out; then looking down upon him sternly, and with his hands in his pockets, said, 'Sir, I respected you because I thought you were doing your duty like a Briton, but now I see you are nothing but a snob.'"

Badminton Station finally closed down in 1968, as did so many other country railway stations under the Beeching Plan, although not without considerable opposition from the 10th Duke of Beaufort.

Despite Samuel Rudder's statement to the effect that "at Badminton the land is more suitable to corn than to pasture", the 2,000-acre

* *The Reminiscences of Lady Dorothy Neville.*

farming operation (which is, incidentally, one of the largest in south Gloucestershire) is now primarily concerned with dairy farming.

At Castle Farm, adjacent to the village, there is to be found one of the oldest Shorthorn herds in the country. There is also a large herd of Friesians at Little Badminton, and a Jersey herd at West Kington. Corn is not entirely neglected, however, since the Estate does plant somewhere in the region of 900 acres. It also has 300 breeding ewes. All this has nothing to do with the numerous tenant farmers, but is land which is farmed directly from the Badminton Estate Office in the village, in conjunction with the Duke of Beaufort who, according to his Agent, Mr Mitchell, keeps a pretty sharp eye on all aspects of the operation.

"Naturally, we have a Farm Manager who does all the day-to-day business, but the decisions are taken ultimately by His Grace, and he knows all that is going on. For example, it's more than our life is worth to cut down a tree unbeknownst to him, because he will notice within a very short time. It's an incredible fact, but he is the eyes and ears and everything of Badminton, a large part of Wiltshire and a hell of a lot of Gloucestershire!"

The Estate Office is also concerned with the administration of the Duke of Beaufort's Hunt, as well as providing a first-class knackering service—that is, collecting the carcasses of sheep, cattle and horses from farms in the surrounding countryside, which are then used to feed the hounds.

Lord Willoughby de Broke in his book *The Passing Years* writes of "foxhounds walking about at Badminton with a self-satisfied air of proprietorship", and until comparatively recent times the Beaufort hounds did have the run of the village.* According to one senior resident of the village, this could cause problems. "They used to kill the cats, chase the dogs and bite the boys' legs." While another resident found himself on the receiving end of some hostile attention from the hounds: "I was chased; I had to stand with a bicycle between me and a hound—Woodbine, I think she was called. But since this new huntsman's been here [Brian Gupwell] he's kept the hounds well under control compared with what they were."

The Badminton Estate also rears pheasants and, being controlled from one central office, the Badminton farming, hunting and shooting interests all exist happily together side by side, the whole thing working by the simple law of give and take. In addition to being responsible for the cattle and sheep at Badminton and on its adjacent farms, the Estate Office is also concerned with the large herd of deer which roams in

*Bitches in whelp.

Badminton Park. "Nimrod", while on a visit to Badminton in 1838, described Badminton Park as being "one of the largest in England [it was then ten miles in circumference] and the herd of deer, perhaps the greatest of any; it consists of about 1200 fallow deer and 300 red deer. The number of the latter is, I believe, quite unequalled."

Since that time the size of the park has been much reduced. During World War II, for example, much of it was turned over to food production. Today it covers an area of 360 acres and is famous throughout the world as the venue of the Badminton Horse Trials. The deer herd still inhabits the park and these beautiful animals are often to be seen grazing near the lake at the north front of Badminton House. Nowadays there are about 340 red deer and 75 fallow deer.

Samuel Rudder's claim that there "is no river or stream of water" running through Badminton is not quite accurate since, although it is true that no "twelve-month" stream runs through it, two of the reputed sources of the River Avon rise quite close to Badminton Village, while the Park Pond is, incidentally, spring-fed.

Rudder's other claim concerning snakes, or the lack of them, is also to be doubted, although it would be nice to think that St. Hubert, the patron saint of hunting, had performed the same service for Badminton that St. Patrick did for Ireland by banishing them. But at least one resident of Badminton has certainly seen grass snakes on the Estate and "has heard tell of adders".

Motorists driving along the main Tetbury to Bristol road are often surprised when they see an ornate and magnificent building standing, to all intents and purposes, completely isolated some few hundreds of yards off the road. Many people mistake it for a folly. It is, in fact, Worcester Lodge. On a visit to Badminton in 1754, Bishop Richard Pocock (1704–65) noted one of the most attractive features of Badminton Park—Worcester Lodge. "On the highest ground of the park, it is the design of Kent and is a grand gateway. Over it is a grand room where the Duke often dines in summer."

Situated some three miles in a direct line from Badminton House at the northern entrance to the park, Worcester Lodge provides a magnificent view of the House, although, as Mrs Horatia Durant* has pointed out, the view of the lodge from the house is equally imposing. "It might have puzzled people to decide which was the finest sight— the great house from the lodge or the lodge from the great house."

When the Duke of Beaufort's hounds meet at Worcester Lodge, the view from inside the lodge gates, as the procession of Master, Hunt servants and hounds proceeds along the main ride from Badminton

---

* *The Somerset Sequence* by Horatia Durant, who is a member of the Somerset family.

House towards the lodge is a memorable one, and on a clear day with the "great house" standing majestic in the background, it is not hard to imagine that everyone has somehow been projected into an early hunting print.

The "grand gateway", Worcester Lodge, was built for the 3rd Duke of Beaufort by William Kent in 1735. Its curving walls end in pavilions, and the great height of the building is emphasised by the tall archway and the tall windows above it. On the first floor is the summer dining-room, which has five fine windows and a balcony, the principal feature of the room being its beautifully moulded ceiling.

Another of the features of Badminton Park is the number and the variety of trees to be found in it. Successive Dukes of Beaufort have always pursued a far-sighted policy of planting trees for the benefit of future generations, a policy which is continued today. As Mr Mitchell has pointed out: "We are always planting trees, much more obviously nowadays from the point of view of remunerative forestry rather than from the purely aesthetic point of view. We are just beginning to refurbish the park after elm disease. We lost practically every elm we had, and so the avenues have got to be started again, and we have discussed carefully what we are going to plant in their place." After much consultation with the experts, the answer seems to be oaks, beeches, poplars and limes.

The great avenues, cut through the trees and plantations of Badminton, were one of the great features of the place in the days when remunerative forestry was not of such prime importance. Indeed, such was the 1st Duke of Beaufort's passion for long vistas that he even persuaded his neighbours to plant their land and cut their trees to fit in with his scheme of things. "Divers of the gentlemen cut their trees and hedges to humour his vistos, and some plant their hills in his lines for compliment."

At that time, the lantern on the roof of the house was the centre of an asterisk of avenues cut through the woods eventually losing themselves in the distance. When she stood on the leads and looked away to the horizon in 1699, Ceilia Fiennes* counted twelve of these. "Ye may stand on ye leads and look twelve ways down to ye parishes and grounds beyond all through glides or vistos."

Modern writers on the subject of landscape gardening have, however, expressed doubt as to whether the avenues at Badminton did, in fact, extend beyond the boundaries of the Estate. The formal gardens at Badminton during the time of the 1st Duke of Beaufort were

---

*Ceilia Fiennes (1662–1741) an English gentlewoman who travelled throughout Europe and England during the seventeenth century.

magnificent. An engraving dating from 1772 shows a central avenue of two and a half miles which is surrounded by fruit gardens, kitchen gardens and pleasure gardens. The latter included a grove divided into four plots with four pathways and a circular space with a fountain in the centre.

R. Blomfield in his book *The Formal Garden in England* has described these plots in detail. "Each of the plots was planted with close growing trees laid out as mazes and trimmed close and square for a height apparently of some fifteen or twenty feet from the ground. Opposite the central alley was a semi-circular bay divided into quadrants; each quadrant had a basin and fountain and great square hedges trimmed to the same height as the rest of the grove. The whole of these immense gardens were walled in, with the exception of a fence round the grove. Wide gates were set at the ends of all the main paths and from these, as points of departure, avenues were laid out in straight lines radiating and intersecting each other in all directions. These avenues and rides were an attempt to manipulate the face of an entire countryside. During the time of the 3rd Duke of Beaufort, the formal gardens were, for the most part, sacrificed to Capability Brown's concept of landscaping."

The huge kitchen gardens at Badminton remained. However, there has been some comment concerning the size of the kitchen gardens when compared to the actual size and accommodation of Badminton House but, in addition to the actual members of the family, the gardens supplied not only the indoor staff but also the out-workers as well. As late as 1935, Eleanor Knight, wife of the then Head Gardener (at that time, there were sixteen gardeners), remembers, that, "Our cottage was in the gardens and really nice, having a sitting-room, dining-room, big kitchen and scullery with a pantry about 9 feet square. There had been four bedrooms, but the smallest one was converted into a bathroom for us. This was one of the perquisites, with one ton of coal and a load of logs each month. A boy called each morning to see what vegetables and fruit we needed, and a man was paid a little extra to clean our shoes, windows and sweep the ground around us, and the place had been painted and decorated to our taste."

One curious construction to be found in the park at Badminton is the Hermitage. According to Mr Mitchell, its correct title is the "Hermit's cell". It is a one-roomed house built of pieces of "rustic" timber of varying sizes and has a thatched roof (all now, alas, in a sad state of disrepair). Miss Stinchcombe of Chippenham has stated that "this was once the abode of a hermit who lived there for seven years". However, it does not appear to have been in splendid isolation since "his meals were taken to him by an underground passage from Badminton House".

Lady Caroline Somerset agrees that the little dwelling was actually occupied by a hermit, but denies the existence of any underground passage. "In the old days there was a real hermit. Apparently, you advertised for hermits and you got them, and you paid them so much a year. That was in the 1700s, but the present Duke recalls that when he was a child there wasn't a real hermit, and the Second Footman was made to go up and put on a beard and people used to go and peer at him. There is no underground passage from the house, and apart from the fashionable days of hermits, it was always the Second Footman."

Lady Caroline Somerset owns a print which shows the Hermit's Cell in the days when it was fashionable to have a hermit in the grounds, and it gives the name of the Badminton hermit at the time as Urganda.

Another feature of Badminton Park, on the western edge, is the house built in 1703, which is known as Swangrove. Originally a one-roomed dwelling with a kitchen underneath, Swangrove was designed as "a dining place for hunting and pleasure parties". Mrs Durant states that "the 3rd Duke added an upper room and adorned it with the careful taste that suggests a very favoured occupant." Swangrove Covert is a large mixed, primarily hardwood area, described as being "of great antiquity".

In addition to hunting, the Park at Badminton is used for a variety of other sporting activities. The Badminton Horse Trials are, of course, held there each year, while in July the Beaufort Hunt Supporters hold their annual Terrier Show.

At one time, indeed until five or six years ago, cricket was a regular feature at Badminton, and matches were played on what the 9th Duke of Beaufort referred to as "the lawn", which is to the north of the house. The present Duke of Beaufort was a very fine cricketer himself. He is also President of the Gloucestershire County Cricket Club. At Badminton a "house" team used to play against a Gloucester County team. These matches were held on a Sunday, and were invariably for somebody's "benefit".

Mr B. L. Watkins, a former Gloucestershire wicket-keeper, who now lives at the Post Office in Badminton village, remembers when "crowds of anything from ten to fifteen thousand used to gather to watch world-class cricketers, such as Walter Hammond, Don Bradman, and many others. These were usually 'benefit' matches and could be worth somewhere in the region of £500 or so to the players concerned."

Mr R. K. Parsons remembers that "upon these occasions, hay wagons were drawn up around the boundary. Bales of hay served as seats, and the rich voice of John Arlott echoed round the ground, directing wit and friendly criticism towards all the participants. This was always a great day out, with local scrumpy available and the beer tent well patronised."

This was all very much part of a strong cricketing tradition since, during the time of the 8th Duke of Beaufort, the great W. G. Grace played at Badminton. His brother, Alfred Grace, was family doctor to Badminton House and was also a member of the Duke of Beaufort's Hunt.

As regards cricket in the village, Mr Mitchell recalls that "it was only after the war that cricket became an established thing within the village, but I believe that the Hunt used to run a team. There was great rivalry between Badminton and the local villages, and the 'blood' match was always against Didmarton."

Another sporting association which Badminton has is, of course, with the game which bears its name. "Badminton—a game similar to tennis with the substitution of shuttlecocks for tennis balls." The game of badminton was invented one wet afternoon in the entrance hall of Badminton House about one hundred and thirty years ago. The dimensions of the original badminton courts were those of the entrance hall at the house. The game was evolved by the great-aunts of the present Duke of Beaufort and their house guests, one of whom, according to *World Badminton Magazine*, was John Loraine Baldwin, one of the founder members of the I Zingari Cricket Club.

Credit for the invention of the game, or at least for the formulation of its early rules, is given to John Baldwin, who was described by *Vanity Fair* as a friend of the then Duke of Beaufort. Baldwin, who was born in 1809, was educated at Oxford where his interests were cricket and dramatics. Later he became interested in "all manner of relaxations". He was a recognised authority on many card games and was the founder or co-founder of many London social clubs, so much so that he later became known as "the King of Clubs". According to *Vanity Fair*, "for more than half a century, indeed, his voice was the voice of a master in Clubland, to which none listened without respect, and he has never been equalled as a draughtsman of club rules and a general referee in all matters of doubt and detail."

Baldwin seems to have attracted more than one nickname. In the latter part of his life, when he lived near Tintern Abbey, he became known as "The Bishop of Tintern". Baldwin died in 1896 at the age of eighty-seven. A photograph taken of him in 1858 shows that he looked remarkably like Oscar Wilde. Baldwin died just three years after the formation of the Badminton Association.

Today, top-class badminton is a matter of hard-fought international competition, far removed from the rainy afternoon's activity of the Beaufort family and their friends all those years ago. The racquets used in those early games are still at Badminton House.

PART II

Noble Lords and Ladies All

"You, if you are what you ought to be, are in my
eye the great oaks that shade a country, and
perpetuate your benefits from generation to
generation."
Edmund Burke to 3rd Duke of Richmond, 1772

The Somerset Lineage

EDWARD III—1312–1377 = PHILIPPA OF HAINAULT—
d. 1369

JOHN OF GAUNT—1340–1399 = KATHERINE SWYNFORD—
d. 1403

JOHN BEAUFORT, EARL OF SOMERSET—c. 1372–1410 = LADY MARGARET HOLLAND
dau. of 2nd Earl of Kent—d. 1440

EDMUND BEAUFORT, DUKE OF SOMERSET—c. 1406–1455 = LADY ELEANOR BEAUCHAMP
dau. of 5th Earl of Warwick—d. 1467

HENRY BEAUFORT, DUKE OF SOMERSET—c. 1436–1463 = JANE HILL or
DE LA MONTAIGNE

CHARLES SOMERSET, 1st EARL OF WORCESTER KG—d. 1526 = LADY ELIZABETH HERBERT
dau. of William Herbert, Earl of Huntingdon—d. 1500

HENRY SOMERSET, 2nd EARL OF WORCESTER—c. 1496–1549 = 2ndly, ELIZABETH BROWNE, dau.
of Sir Anthony Browne—d. 1565

WILLIAM SOMERSET, 3rd EARL OF WORCESTER KG—c. 1527–1588 = HON. CHRISTIAN NORTH, dau.
of Baron North

EDWARD SOMERSET, 4th EARL OF WORCESTER KG—c. 1549–1627 = LADY ELIZABETH HASTINGS
dau. of 2nd Earl of Huntingdon KG—d. 1621

HENRY SOMERSET, 5th EARL AND 1st MARQUESS OF WORCESTER—1577–1646 = HON. ANN RUSSELL, dau. of Lord Russell—d. 1639

EDWARD SOMERSET, 2nd MARQUESS OF WORCESTER—1601–1667 = ELIZABETH DORMER, dau. of Sir William Dormer—d. 1635

HENRY SOMERSET, 3rd MARQUESS OF WORCESTER AND 1st DUKE OF BEAUFORT KG—1629–1699 = HON. MARY CAPEL, dau. of Baron Capel and widow of Lord Beauchamp—1630–1715

CHARLES SOMERSET, MARQUESS OF WORCESTER—1660–1698 = REBECCA CHILD, dau. of Sir Josiah Child—1666–1712

HENRY SOMERSET, 2nd DUKE OF BEAUFORT KG, PC, DCL—1684–1714 = 2ndly, LADY RACHEL NOEL, dau. of Earl Gainsborough—d. 1709

HENRY SOMERSET, 3rd DUKE OF BEAUFORT—1707–1745 (d.s.p.) = FRANCES SCUDAMORE, dau. of Sir James Scudamore

CHARLES NOEL SOMERSET, 4th DUKE OF BEAUFORT—1709–1756	=	ELIZABETH BERKELEY, BARONESS BOTETOUT, dau. of John Berkeley—1719–1799

CHARLES NOEL SOMERSET, 4th DUKE OF BEAUFORT—1709–1756 = ELIZABETH BERKELEY, BARONESS BOTETOUT, dau. of John Berkeley—1719–1799

HENRY SOMERSET, 5th DUKE OF BEAUFORT KG, DCL—1744–1803 = ELIZABETH BOSCAWEN, dau. of Admiral the Hon Edward Boscawen—1747–1828

HENRY CHARLES SOMERSET, 6th DUKE OF BEAUFORT KG—1766–1835 = LADY CHARLOTTE LEVESON-GOWER, dau. of 1st Marquess of Stafford—d. 1854

HENRY SOMERSET, 7th DUKE OF BEAUFORT KG—1792–1853 = 2ndly, EMILY CULLING SMITH dau. of Charles Culling Smith—d. 1889

HENRY CHARLES FITZROY SOMERSET, 8th DUKE OF BEAUFORT KG, PC, MP—1824–1899 = LADY GEORGIANA CURZON dau. of 1st Earl Howe—d. 1906

HENRY ADELBERT WELLINGTON FITZROY SOMERSET, 9th DUKE OF BEAUFORT—1847–1924 = LOUISE DE TUYLL, dau. of W. H. Harford and widow of Baron Carlo de Tuyll—d. 1945

HENRY HUGH ARTHUR FITZROY SOMERSET 10th DUKE OF BEAUFORT KG, PC, GCVO—b. 1900 = LADY MARY CAMBRIDGE, dau. of 1st Marquess of Cambridge—b. 1897

LORD HENRY SOMERSET—1849–1932 = LADY ISABELLA COCKS, dau. of 3rd Earl of Somers—d. 1921

HENRY SOMERSET—1874–1945 = LADY KATHERINE BEAUCLERK dau. of 10th Duke of St Albans—d. 1958

HENRY SOMERSET—1898–1965 = BETTINE, dau. of Major Charles Malcolm

DAVID ROBERT SOMERSET—b.1928 = LADY CAROLINE THYNNE, dau. of 6th Marquess of Bath—b. 1928

HENRY b. 1952   ANN b. 1955   EDWARD b. 1958   JOHN b. 1964

BADMINTON.

THE great centre-piece of the Park at Badminton is, of course, the home of the Duke of Beaufort—Badminton House—with its magnificent architecture in the Palladian style and its artistic and historic treasures. It is a stately home which is not just a museum but a real home. "Commend me to the solid comfort of Badminton", once remarked a certain Mr Chapman,* and anyone who has ever visited Badminton House will appreciate that "solid comfort" is indeed, a most apt description.

Only two families have owned Badminton in seven hundred years: the Botelers and the Somersets.

In 1608, the 4th Earl of Worcester purchased the Manor of Badminton from one Nicholas Boteler, whose family had been settled there since the thirteenth century and since then Badminton has been the country home of the Somerset family (Dukes of Beaufort since 1682).

Having purchased Badminton, the 4th Earl of Worcester bestowed it upon his third son, Thomas, who later married the wealthy Dowager Countess of Ormonde, and was subsequently created Viscount Somerset of Cashel (in 1626). Thomas and his wife had one daughter,

---

*Lord Willoughby de Broke (*The Passing Years*) quotes Lord Ribblesdale, who describes Mr Robert Chapman "as a man who for many years supplied the Badminton Stables with a succession of conspicuous weight carriers".

Elizabeth, who did not marry and so, when she died in 1655, she bequeathed Badminton to her first cousin (once removed) Lord Herbert (Henry Somerset), the son of the 2nd Marquess of Worcester.

In 1657, Lord Herbert married Mary, Lady Beauchamp, the wealthy widow of Henry Seymour, Lord Beauchamp, the daughter of Lord Capel and a sister to the Earl of Essex. In 1667, Lord Herbert succeeded to the title of 3rd Marquess of Worcester and on 2 December 1682 he was created 1st Duke of Beaufort by Charles II. It was Henry Somerset, the 1st Duke of Beaufort, who was described by the diarist John Evelyn (1620–1706) as "a person of great honour, prudence, and estate", who began the work of transforming Badminton from a "Faire Stone Howse"* into the palatial residence that we know today.

Henry Somerset (3rd Marquess of Worcester) was eleventh in the male line from Edward III through the King's third son, John of Gaunt† (Duke of Lancaster) by his mistress, Katherine Swynford, whom he later married as his third wife. John of Gaunt had several illegitimate children to whom he gave the name of Beaufort. The eldest son was created Earl of Somerset. Charles, the illegitimate son of Henry Beaufort (3rd Duke of Somerset) adopted his father's title as his surname. He was created Earl of Worcester by Henry VIII. The 5th Earl of Worcester was made a Marquess by the ill-starred Charles I, and his eldest son, Edward, was the father of the 1st Duke of Beaufort.

Edward Somerset, 2nd Marquess of Worcester: 1601–1667

Edward Somerset (styled Lord Herbert), who afterwards took the titles 2nd Marquess of Worcester, Earl of Glamorgan, and Duke of Somerset and Beaufort (hereafter referred to as Edward Somerset) was a man of considerable originality, and he is credited with the invention of the steam engine. He described this as "an admirable and most forcible way of driving up water by fire" ("A Century of Inventions",‡ written by Edward Somerset, Marquess of Worcester, in 1655).

To say that Edward had an eventful life would be to understate the case. An ardent Royalist and Catholic, he has been described as "almost a soldier, almost a scholar, almost a statesman, almost a genius

---

*It was so described by a passer-by in 1644.

†In the Library at Badminton House, there is a portion of a doublet worn by John of Gaunt.

‡Actually entitled: *A century of the names and scantlings of such inventions as at present I can call to mind to have tried and perfected, which (my former notes being lost) I have, at the instance of a powerful friend, endeavoured now, in the year 1655, to set these down in such a way, as may sufficiently instruct me to put any of them to practice.*

... who never more than attained a splendid failure in each department". (T. F. Dale in his *The 8th Duke of Beaufort and the Badminton Hunt.*)

Edward was born in 1601 and, as a young man, he studied in France and Germany. Later he married Elizabeth Dormer, daughter of Sir William Dormer and a sister of the Earl of Carnarvon. The couple had three children—a son and two daughters. Edward and his family lived quietly at Raglan Castle, the home of his father the 5th Earl of Worcester * (later 1st Marquess of Worcester), and here Edward set up a laboratory and workshop in order to carry out his numerous inventions and his scientific experiments into such matters as flying and the power of steam.

In 1635, Edward's first wife died. Following her death, he spent a great deal of his time in London, working upon his experiments at Vaux Hall. Then, in 1639, he married Lady Margaret O'Brien, daughter of the 5th Earl of Thomond.

In the Muniment Room at Badminton House there is a copy of a letter which suggests that Edward was in Paris in 1641, where he met one Salomon de Caus, author of *Les Raisons des Forces Mouvantes avec Diverses Machines*, published in 1615. Salomon de Caus was credited by the physicist François Arrago (1786–1853) with the invention of the steam engine. The letter at Badminton (which appears to be a copy of a translation) is from Marion de Lorme to the Marquis de Cinq Mars, and is dated Paris, 7 February 1641.

It begins: "I am at present doing the rounds of Paris with your English Lord, the Marquis of Worcester", and continuing, it sheds an interesting light upon Edward's character: "He is remarkable for never being satisfied with any explanations which are given him and he never sees things in the light in which they are shewn to him." This letter goes on to describe a visit to the Asylum at Bicetre, where Edward spoke to Salomon de Caus. "De Caus, it seems, had come from Normandy to present to the King of France "the use of steam from boiling water".

At first Cardinal Richelieu sent him away without listening to him and later had him committed to the Asylum at Bicetre. Marion de Lorme continues: "He [de Caus] calls out to every visitor that he is not mad. Worcester spoke to him! He is mad now. You have confined the greatest genius of the age. Since then he has done nothing but talk of Salomon de Caus. He imagined he had discovered a genius in a madman."

Mrs Durant, in her excellent history of the Somerset family (*The*

---

* Long before the Dukedom was created, the Somersets were a powerful family in Wales and on the Welsh border. The 5th Earl of Worcester was one of the richest men in the Kingdom.

Somerset Sequence) mentions de Caus at some length, and states: "It will be seen that Lord Herbert took de Caus's fountain some steps further and turned it to practical use." The inclusion of the de Lorme letter is in no way meant to detract from Edward Somerset's great invention, but is merely included as a fascinating historical sidelight on the bizarre meeting of two such men of genius. It is also the only reference which appears to authenticate the meeting of these two men.

In 1639 Charles I determined to raise an army to quell the Scots. He appealed for support, and Edward's father immediately offered a generous donation as well as the services of his son. Thereafter, and throughout the Civil War, the 5th Earl of Worcester and his son poured substantial amounts of money into the Royal coffers, to the eventual tune of some hundred thousand pounds—and this in the seventeenth century.

Randolph Churchill, in an article published in a magazine pointed out that, "Throughout history, the Somersets have given service to the Crown. Indeed, they have, and none more so than the 5th Earl. Charles I must often have wished for more such loyal and generous supporters."

In 1642, the 5th Earl was created 1st Marquess of Worcester as a reward for a gift of £10,000. In an envelope at Badminton, the letter conferring this honour is still to be found. Dated 21 October 1642, Killingworth, it begins: "I salute you Marquesse" and ends, "your most assured friend, Charles R."

In the same envelope* are two other letters, one from James I, dated 1605, and another from Charles I, dated 2 December 1642. This latter begins: "Woster, No subject has done that ye have for me" and holds out a promise of the Order of the Garter (no doubt in exchange for yet more generous support).

It continues: "I have commanded your son Herbert to tell you what will complete the businesse and as a testimonie of my harty acceptance I have given you the style of Marquis [the name whereof, when ye will shall be changed]. So now and doe by him send you the assuerance of the Blew Riben the whch though for the present I thinke not fitt that it should be delivered yet I leave that to your discretion and in all things will keep promis with you and be still Your most assuered constant frend, Charles R."

Although the Somersets were prepared to support the Royal cause they were by no means foolish where their money was concerned. The 5th Earl is reported to have said: "Since I was a Marquess I am worse

---

*There is so much of historical interest at Badminton that such things are treated almost casually. These letters were in a dilapidated envelope stamped 'Royal Aeronautical Society' and dated 1946.

by one hundred thousand pounds, and if I should be a Duke I should be an arrant beggar."

During the Civil War, Edward Somerset served on the Royalist side (Henry Somerset, later 1st Duke of Beaufort, was at his father's side during the Royalist Siege of Gloucester). Then, in 1644, Edward Somerset was made Earl of Glamorgan. Later that year he was sent by Charles I to Ireland to undertake secret and somewhat delicate negotiations with certain Irish Catholics in order to gain support for the Royal cause. Alas, Edward Somerset, like so many others, became embroiled in Irish affairs. His "secret" negotiations were revealed and he was suspected of treason. He was arrested and committed to the custody of the Constable of Dublin.

Later, however, he was released. The King's disavowal of him on this occasion said, "I believe it was his misguided zeal more than any malice which brought this great misfortune on him and on us all". In 1646 Charles I sent Edward a warrant for the title of Somerset and Beaufort.* Edward Somerset continued to support King Charles with the utmost loyalty and never ceased in his efforts to raise an army for him.

In England the Civil War was running its course, and in August 1646 Raglan Castle was captured, the walls being breached by cannon sited on the old Monmouth point-to-point course. Later the castle was ordered to be demolished. Edward's father, the 5th Earl and 1st Marquess of Worcester, was taken as a prisoner to London, where he died in captivity in 1646. Money from the Somerset estates was awarded to Oliver Cromwell as a reward for his services, and Charles I was beheaded on 30 January 1649.

Edward Somerset remained in Ireland until 1648, when he and his family went to live in Paris as poverty-stricken exiles. In 1650 his son, Henry Somerset travelled to England, where he skilfully and successfully petitioned Parliament for the grant of an income (£1,700 per annum) the revenue from a portion of the family estate which had been bestowed upon Cromwell.

In 1652 Edward Somerset returned to England, where he was arrested and committed to the Tower of London. Later, he was released on bail, thereafter devoting himself to his diverse scientific

---

*In 1660 the question of the Patent of the Dukedom of Somerset, granted by Charles I, came before Parliament. This Patent was then in the hands of Henry Somerset (later 1st Duke of Beaufort) though his father claimed the title. The Seymour family also laid claim to the Dukedom, and to them it was adjudged to belong (T. F. Dale— *The 8th Duke of Beaufort*). In 1660, also, Parliament decreed that such of his properties as had not been sold should be returned to Edward Somerset, 2nd Marquess of Worcester.

experiments, producing his Century of Inventions in 1655). In April 1667 Edward Somerset died, his last years having been spent in virtual poverty. Both he and his father had more or less beggared themselves in their support of Charles I.

It was left to Henry Somerset, 3rd Marquess of Worcester (afterwards 1st Duke of Beaufort) to restore the Somerset family fortunes.

Henry Somerset, 3rd Marquess of Worcester and 1st Duke of Beaufort: 1629–1699

Henry Somerset (Lord Herbert, 3rd Marquess of Worcester in 1667, and 1st Duke of Beaufort in 1682) was born in 1629. As a boy he lived through the upheavals of the Civil War. Twice he accompanied his father to war—once at Oxford and once at Gloucester. Henry Somerset must have been a man of great determination and ability, for not only did he regain the Royal favour for himself and his family but, within a few years, he was possibly the richest subject in the kingdom.

Soon after his return to England in 1650, when he had petitioned for the restoration of part of the family estates, he became a Protestant, which cannot have pleased his father, an ardent Catholic. T. F. Dale tells us that Henry and his father were never on good terms. A letter from Edward Somerset to the Lord Chancellor (Clarendon) in 1660 contains the line: "My son Lord Herbert's underhand working by false suggestions . . ." On the other hand, the Lord Protector, Oliver Cromwell, the recipient of part of the Somerset estates, must have been gratified to witness this change of faith on the part of a member of one of the great Catholic and Royalist families.

In 1655 Henry was bequeathed Badminton by his cousin, Elizabeth. Then, in 1657, he married Mary, the extremely wealthy widow of Lord Beauchamp. Following his accession to the title of 3rd Marquess upon the death of his father, Henry lived for a time at Worcester House in London, which stood upon the site of the present Savoy Theatre.

According to T. F. Dale, "Cromwell liked him personally and soon admitted him to some degree of friendship. At this time he was known as 'Mr Herbert' and as such he sat in the Long Parliament." (In fact, there is no authority for this latter statement, and it has been suggested that it was probably Henry Herbert of Colebrook who represented Monmouth in the Long Parliament.) However, he was the Member of Parliament for Monmouth from 1660 to 1667. There is no doubt that Henry Somerset did make his peace with Cromwell, who allowed him £25,000 per annum out of his parental estates.

In 1659 Henry suffered a set-back when he was arrested and committed to the Tower of London, being suspected of some degree of involvement in an abortive Royalist uprising. This imprisonment was only a temporary inconvenience, however, and in 1660 Charles II, "The Merry Monarch", returned to his crown and kingdom.

Henry Somerset was one of twelve commoners deputed in May 1660 to invite the return of Charles II. He was also a member of Monk's Convention Parliament and a member of Charles II's escort from Breda. (The Monk referred to is George Monk, Duke of Albermarle who, when Oliver Cromwell died in 1658, marched to London with 6,000 troops and who, after careful negotiations, brought Charles II back to England.)

With the return of the Monarchy, diverse appointments were bestowed upon Henry Somerset, who became Lord Lieutenant of the Counties of Gloucestershire, Hereford, and Monmouth. In 1663, he entertained the King and Queen at his country home at Badminton.

It was soon afterwards that Henry Somerset began to enlarge and improve Badminton House and its environs, thus transforming the "Faire Stone Howse" into the palace which it was eventually to become. During the next thirty years, he continued to introduce innovations and improvements at Badminton. He also enlarged and improved the family property, Troy House, in Monmouthshire.

His wife also, it seems, took a great interest in the re-building of Badminton. In 1666 we find him writing to her as follows: "The painter says he has more oil and colours at Badminton than are to be had in the whole town." Sixteen years later, he wrote to inform his wife that he is glad that "she walks about among the workmen".

Lord Guildford's observations,* made during a visit to Badminton, suggest that the Duchess (as she was by then) was well qualified to ensure that the workmen went about their business in a proper manner during her husband's frequent absences: "If the Duke or the Duchess—who concerned herself much more than he did for every day of her life in the morning she took her tour and visited every office in the house and so was her own superintendant—observed anything amiss or suspicious, as a servant riding out or the like nothing was said to that servant but his immediate superior or one of a higher order was to enquire and answer if leave had been given or not. If not, such a servant was straight turned away. No fault of order was passed by."

According to the official guide book to Badminton House, the name of the architect who carried out the original alterations to Badminton House will never be known, "nor who was to blame for the loss of all the building plans". Some information, however, is available as

Lives of the Norths, Hon. R. North.

regards the work which Henry Somerset had carried out. It was he who arranged for the building of the beautiful oak staircase "which ascends to the top of the house" and also for the Dining Room, employing the celebrated wood-carver of the time, Grinling Gibbons (1648–1721), who created some marvellous decorations above the chimney-piece and between the windows.

Mrs Durant considers that the present south face of Badminton is more reminiscent of Henry Somerset's time than any other. "The Church, which was re-built in 1785, adjoins it on one side and on the other is the immense servants' hall, designed to hold two hundred persons. The Marquess incorporated much of the former house into the present wing."

As regards paintings and other works of art, Henry Somerset seems to have lacked the expertise of Henry, 3rd Duke of Beaufort, who returned from Europe with ninety-six cases of objets d'art and pictures, one a reputed Leonardo da Vinci. Henry Somerset seems to have gone in for buying job-lots, and on one occasion bought thirty paintings (plus carriage and frames) for £250, remarking that they were "indifferent good in the judgement of those who understood these things".

In 1672 Henry Somerset was made a Knight of the Garter and a Privy Councillor. He also became Lord President of Wales and Lord Lieutenant of North and South Wales. But in 1682 there came the greatest honour of all when Henry Somerset was created a Duke, choosing the title Beaufort. His Duchess, however, does not seem to have been entirely happy with his choice: "Family letters crossed and he was to find that he had not 'lit on the title' his wife would have chosen."

Lord Guildford, who was related to the 1st Duke of Beaufort by marriage, has left an account of his visit to Badminton, in which he comments upon "the princely way of living that the Duke and his family enjoyed, above any other, except crowned heads that I have notice of in Europe, and in some respects greater than most of them, to whom he might have been an example . . ."

After describing the Duke's interest in horses and breeding,* Lord Guildford goes on to describe the Duke's household: "He had about two hundred persons in his family all provided for, and in his capital house nine original tables covered every day; and for the accommodation of so many a large hall was built with a sort of alcove at one end for distinction, but yet the whole lay in view of him that was chief, and who had power to do what was proper for keeping order among

---

*Like all the Somerset family, the 1st Duke enjoyed hunting and we are told that he was one of the Duke of York's favourite hunting companions.

them and it was his charge to see it done. The tables were properly assigned as, for example, the chief stewards with the gentlemen and pages, the master of the horse with the coachman and liveries, and under steward with the bailiffs and some husbandmen, the clerk of the kitchen with the bakers, brewers and altogether and other more inferior people under these in places apart. The women had their dining room also and were distributed in like manner."

Lord Guildford has also left us a fascinating description of the way the family and their guests at Badminton spent their time: "As for the Duke and Duchess and their friends, there was no time of the day without diversion. Breakfast in the gallery that opened into the gardens, then perhaps a deer was to be killed, or the gardens or parks with the several sorts of deer to be visited and, if it required, mounting horses of the Duke's brought for all the company. And so in the afternoon when the ladies were disposed to air, and the gentlemen with them, coaches and six came to hold them all. Half an hour after eleven the bell rang to prayers and at six in the evening, and through a gallery the best company went into an aisle in the church."

Lord Guildford seems to have taken a lively interest in all aspects of life at Badminton, describing the dining habits as follows: "The meats were neat and not gross, no servants in livery attended but those called gentlemen only" and "although many a brisk round went about . . ." there was "no sitting at table with tobacco and healths, as the too common custom is."

Regarding the 1st Duke's great interest in improving his country home, Lord Guildford wrote: "The Duke always had some new project of building or walling or planting, which he would ask their advice about; and nothing was forced or strained but easy and familiar."

The Beaufort children, Guildford tells us "were bred with a philosophical care. No inferior servants were permitted to entertain them, least some mean sentiments, or foolish notions and fables should steal into them." They were also, it seems, strongly imbued with a sense of honour, one of them remarking to a judge, who was a friend of the family: "You should make them [criminals] promise upon their honour they will not do so and then they will not."

In July 1684 the 1st Duke of Beaufort, Lord President of the Welsh Council, made a five-week "progress" through Wales. This "splendid cavalcade" was described by one Thomas Dineley,* who travelled with the ducal party, which he says was "attended with shouts and acclaimations of the people, ringing of bells in the neighbouring

* *The Official Progress of His Grace, the Duke of Beaufort through Wales in 1684*, printed in 1888.

villages, various soundings of trumpets, and beating of drums." Elsewhere, he notes that "the streets were strewed with flowers and sweet herbs by the loyal and well-minded people". A triumphal progress indeed, and Dineley further records that at the end of it, "the Duke expressed himself as being 'extreamly satisfyed' with the good order and loyalty he had found to be existing throughout the Principality."

However, there were soon to be "various soundings of trumpets" of a different kind in England, and once again a member of the Somerset family was to be in the thick of things, again in support of the Crown. In February 1684, Charles II died. At his funeral procession, the Duke of Beaufort had been one of the supporters of the Chief Mourner, Prince George of Denmark. Charles II was succeeded by James Stuart, James II of England and James VII of Scotland—a Catholic.

On 11 June 1685 the illegitimate son of Charles I, James, Duke of Monmouth, landed at Lyme Regis, come to liberate the country from the "Papal Tyranny" of his uncle, James II. Once again, England was in a state of arms. When the Duke of Monmouth landed in England, his supporters flocked to join him, although none of the great nobles were to be found among them. The Duke of Beaufort was one of the first to take up arms against the rebels, occupying the key port of Bristol with nineteen companies of foot and four of horse. When the King gave orders that new regiments should be formed, the Devonshire Regiment came into being and was placed under Beaufort's Command.

On 18 June 1685, Monmouth's army marched into Taunton, where they were received with general exultation. On the following day, Monmouth was proclaimed "King". The rebel army then marched through Bridgwater towards Bristol. The attack on Bristol was never made, however, for an already somewhat dispirited army was thwarted outside the village of Kenysham when the Monmouth Horse was routed by a Troop of Lord Oxford's Horse (later the Royal Horse Guards—the Blues) together with two troops of Dragoons, brought from Bath by the Earl of Feversham. Abandoning the attack on Bristol, Monmouth marched towards Bath, meeting with set-backs all the while. Then, on 6 July 1685, the rebel army was completely routed at the bloody battle of Sedgemoor* (five miles south-east of Bridgwater). On 15 July, Monmouth was beheaded and thereafter followed the awful retribution of the "Bloody Assizes", presided over by Judge Jeffreys.

James II's reign was to last for only three years. In 1688, by virtue of

*Shortly afterwards, James II was at Badminton expressing his satisfaction at the Duke's "constant loyalty".

his tyrannical government, he was forced to flee to France, whereupon a group of leading English statesmen invited William of Orange to assume the throne.

In December 1688, William landed at Torbay. Unlike the Duke of Monmouth, William was supported by the great nobles, who hurried to join him. The Duke of Beaufort was not among these, and he immediately called out the Gloucestershire Militia, once again occupying Bristol. The unpopular James II had few such loyal supporters as the Duke of Beaufort, and the citizens of Bristol opened the gates to William's troops when they arrived and the Duke of Beaufort was forced to retreat.

In January 1689 William of Orange and his wife, Mary, were proclaimed King and Queen of Great Britain and Ireland. It could hardly be expected that William would look with favour upon those who had opposed his coming to England, and shortly after his accession to the throne, a new Privy Council was formed. The 1st Duke of Beaufort ceased to hold high office, and virtually retired from public life to his home at Badminton. Lord Macclesfield was made President of Wales in place of the Duke.

The Somerset family, however, were not completely out of favour with the new regime, since Beaufort's son, Charles, Marquess of Worcester (1660–1698) was given a seat on the Privy Council.

In 1696 a plot to kill King William while he was out hunting came to light. The Duke of Beaufort was thought to be involved in the plot. His London house (Beaufort House, Chelsea) was searched and one of the members of his household was arrested. Later an oath of allegiance to William was drawn up, which was signed by the members of the House of Commons and most of the Lords. In effect, this meant that William had the sole right by law to the English Crown. At first, the Duke of Beaufort refused to sign the oath, but later, in 1697, he kissed William's hand at Kensington Palace.

Late in 1699 Henry Somerset, 1st Duke of Beaufort, died of fever at Badminton. He was buried in the Beaufort Chapel at St. George's, Windsor. The 1st Duke was succeeded by his grandson, Henry, for in 1698 his elder son, Charles (then Marquess of Worcester) had been killed in a coaching accident.

2nd Duke of Beaufort: 1684–1714

Henry Somerset, 2nd Duke of Beaufort, was described by Thomas Hearne,* "as a gentleman of very great probity, of a comely personage

*A noted British Antiquary (1678–1735).

and of ordinary good nature". He was born in the Castle of Monmouth in April 1684, succeeding to the title when he was fifteen years of age.

Before he was twenty-eight, he had married three times, two of his wives having unfortunately died in childbirth. His first marriage took place in July 1702 when he married Lady Mary Sackville (daughter of Charles Sackville, Earl of Dorset) at Knole in Kent. A month later the Duke and his new Duchess were entertaining Queen Anne and her Consort at Badminton. The Queen was journeying through Gloucestershire on her way to Bath, presumably to take the waters, since she suffered from gout. Mrs Durant tells us that on this occasion "the Duke of Beaufort prepared a great welcome and led a concourse of gentlemen towards Cirencester to escort the Queen and her Consort to Badminton."

The 2nd Duke was, it seems, extremely fond of entertaining, and it was during his time at Badminton that Swangrove, the pretty hunting lodge on the edge of the Park, was put to good use. Accounts books for the period give some indication of what entertaining at Badminton at that time entailed—"When Badminton was full [in 1705 over six thousand people attended the Lords' table, and the servants' tables], seven hundred and fifty eggs were eaten a week, fifty-three chickens, five geese, sixteen ducklings, eighty-six pigeons, a hundred hares and rabbits, besides quantities of beef, mutton, veal and lamb. The powdered sugar amounted to thirty-three pounds. Canary, white Lisbon and claret were the favourite drinks."

It was while a large house-party was in progress at Badminton, on 14 June 1705, that the Duchess of Beaufort was brought to bed. Four days later, despite the attentions of three doctors, she died "in childbed". She was later buried at Badminton.

And so, at the age of twenty-one, Henry Somerset became a widower for the first time. Later that year he moved to London, where he took his seat in the House of Lords.

On 26 February 1706, at the Chapel Royal, St. James, Middlesex, Henry Somerset, the 2nd Duke of Beaufort, married Lady Rachel Noel, the second and youngest daughter of the 2nd Earl of Gainsborough. Lady Rachel, who had a fortune of upwards of £60,000, was co-heir to the Earl with her sister, the Duchess of Portland. She was described by Thomas Hearne as "a woman of very great virtues". Unfortunately, this marriage was also to be of a short duration, for on the 13 September 1709 Lady Rachel died "in childbed". She also was buried at Badminton. However, she had given birth to one son in 1707—Henry, later to become 3rd Duke of Beaufort—and Charles Noel (1709–1756) who subsequently became the 4th Duke of Beaufort.

In 1710, the 2nd Duke of Beaufort, a confirmed Tory presented himself, with other members of the Tory nobility, before Queen Anne, following the fall of the Whig Government. The Duke had absented himself from Court until the accession of the Tory Ministry in 1710, when he is said to have told the Queen that "he could then call her Queen in reality".

The Duke was later given a seat on the Privy Council and was also made Lord Lieutenant of Gloucestershire and Hampshire. He was additionally honoured by being made a Knight of the Garter in August 1713.

At Wimbledon, Surrey, in September, 1711, the 2nd Duke of Beaufort was married for the third and final time—this time to Lady Mary Osborne, the youngest daughter of the Duke of Leeds. Remarkably, this marriage, too, was to prove of short duration since, on 24 May 1714, when he was thirty years old, the 2nd Duke himself died—"of inflammation caused by drinking small beer in a journey which he had rid in one day". Lord Bathurst, writing of the Duke's death in that same year, states that, "having heated himself shooting, he drank a great quantity of liquor, which made him vomit blood, and he died in three days".

Henry Somerset was buried at Badminton. His widow later married John, 4th Earl of Dundmald.

3rd Duke of Beaufort: 1707–1745

It was Henry Somerset (afterwards Scudamore) 3rd Duke of Beaufort who was responsible for the many fine improvements which were made to Badminton House at the beginning of the eighteenth century. Henry was born in March 1707 and succeeded to the title at the age of seven. He was educated at Westminster School, and later attended University College, Oxford.

At the age of nineteen he embarked upon a "Grand Tour" of Europe, accompanied by a tutor named Phillips. While in Rome, Henry became interested in the collection of pictures and objets d'art, and on his return to England he brought with him many fine pictures to be housed at Badminton. These included a painting attributed to Leonardo da Vinci, two paintings by Claude and two by Poussin. Henry also acquired an antique marble urn—the Alberoni Urn— which disappeared during the time of the 5th Duke, and an expensive Florentine Pietradura cabinet.

Back in England, Henry Somerset successfully managed to combine his love of art with the Somerset family's passion for hunting (he was a keen stag-hunter) by commissioning the artist John Wootton, who has been described as "the first English equine artist of importance", to paint for him. A generous patron, Henry Somerset actually sent Wootton to Rome in order that he might gain the necessary artistic training and experience. On his return, Wootton lived at Badminton for several years, during which time he worked on five large sporting canvases for the Duke. These included "Stag Hunting at Badminton" and "Hare Hunting on Salisbury Plain", both of which may still be seen in the Hall at Badminton House and appear in illustration no. 5.

Beautiful paintings are, indeed, one of the features of Badminton House. In the dining room, for example, there is a portrait of the 1st Duke of Beaufort's mother by Sir Anthony Van Dyck, while in the library is another Van Dyck painting—a beautiful portrait of his patron, Charles I. There are also portraits of the 1st Duke of Beaufort by Sir Peter Lely (1618–1680) and of the 1st Duke and his family by a little-known English painter, Captain Stephen Browne. In the Oak room there is a portrait of the 2nd Duke by Thomas Hudson, a West Country painter and one-time Drawing Master to Sir Joshua Reynolds. There is a portrait of the 3rd Duke by Sir Godfrey Kneller and one of the 4th Duke, again painted by Thomas Hudson.

There are two magnificent views of Badminton painted by Antonio Canaletto—one of them is of the house and is shown on the jacket of this book, and the other is of the Park. These paintings were commissioned by the 4th Duke. There are also portraits of Admiral Boscawen, father-in-law of the 5th Duke of Beaufort, painted by Sir Joshua Reynolds and of the 5th Duke himself, again painted by Reynolds. There is a magnificent portrait of Georgiana, wife of the 7th Duke, painted by Thomas Lawrence. In addition to the hunting and sporting paintings by John Wootton, there are dozens of hunting and sporting pictures to be found all over the house, painted by a variety of known and unknown artists during the last two hundred years.

The original Hall was re-designed and re-decorated in order to accommodate the Wootton pictures, and this work (including the frames for the pictures) was undertaken by William Kent, the architect and painter. Kent, who was born in Yorkshire, started his career as an apprentice coach-builder. Later, he travelled to Rome to study, and there he met one of his future patrons, the 3rd Earl of Burlington, both men being influenced by the work of the Italian architect, Andrea Palladio. When Kent eventually returned to England, he gradually gave up painting to concentrate on architecture. Kent's concept of buildings in their surroundings was largely responsible for the introduction of the landscape style of garden which was later fully realised by his friend and student, the famous "Capability" Brown, who was also to work at Badminton during the time of the 3rd Duke.

In 1730, Henry Somerset engaged Kent to undertake the enlargement and improvement of Badminton House.* It was also Kent who built Worcester Lodge (see page 29). Kent transformed the North Front of Badminton House, adding a pediment containing three Oeils de Boeuf and two cupolas, as well as building two long low wings ending in massive pavilions. He completed the West Front of the house, adding a pediment, and he added a third storey to the East Front. Kent was also responsible for the magnificent entrance with its pediment and portcullis.

While the Duke of Beaufort's Gloucestershire home was being enlarged and improved, his home life, it seems, had much room for improvement. In 1729 he had married a Miss Frances Scudamore, the daughter of Sir James Scudamore (an Act of Parliament enabled the Beauforts to take the surname and arms of the Scudamore family). Miss Scudamore was apparently of a shrewish disposition and also seems to have had other faults, since it later came to light that she had had an affair with Lord (William) Talbot—a married man.

In March 1744, the Duke of Beaufort obtained a divorce (as well as the right to marry again—by Act of Parliament). Alas, he never did marry again, for shortly afterwards, on 24 February 1745, he died "worried by a complication of disorders". There had been no children.

Mrs Mary Delany† wrote, somewhat uncharitably, of the 3rd Duke a month or so after his death: "His death is not to be lamented; he was unhealthy in his constitution, unhappy in his circumstances, though possessed of great honour and riches. His brother [Charles Noel] is qualified to make a better figure and *his* wife I *hope* will prove an able and virtuous Duchess of Beaufort."

Mrs Durant, commenting upon Mrs Delany's remarks, defends the 3rd Duke of Beaufort, stating that he was a "man who was renowned for upright dealing in the House of Lords and generosity in private life, and later generations can point to a lasting memorial to his good taste in the development of Badminton and the priceless treasures he collected there".

4th Duke of Beaufort: 1709–1756

Henry Somerset being without a son, was succeeded by his brother, Charles Noel Somerset, who became the 4th Duke of Beaufort in 1745.

---

*Although William Kent is credited with the work on Badminton House, it has been suggested by Mr Mervyn Bousted that the work could, in fact, have been carried out by one James Gibbs or his master-builder, Francis Smith of Warwick.
†Mrs Mary Delany, 1700–88, author of *Autobiography and Correspondence*.

Incidentally, Charles Noel was the only Duke of Beaufort not to be named Henry. Like his brother, Charles was educated at Westminster School and later studied at Oxford University, where he gained a degree as Master of Arts in 1727. The 4th Duke was Tory Member of Parliament for the County of Monmouthshire from 1731 until 1734, and for Monmouth Borough from 1734 until 1745.

Charles Somerset was described by Matthew Tindal* "as a man of sense and spirit and activity, unblameable in his morals but questionable in his political capability". Questionable, presumably, because Charles Somerset was an avowed Jacobite, a supporter of the House of Stuart and of Bonnie Prince Charlie, the grandson of the deposed James II. In 1749, after riots had taken place at Oxford, Charles Somerset "publicly praised rebellion against the government". In 1750 he was among those present at a supper party in Pall Mall, when Bonnie Prince Charlie (the "Young Pretender") paid a visit to London.

In May 1740 Charles Somerset married Elizabeth Berkeley, the daughter of John Berkeley of Stoke Gifford and the sister of Norborne, Lord Botetout, to whose barony she succeeded. Horace Walpole's letters suggest that Elizabeth Berkeley was fonder of London than of the country, while T. F. Dale suggests that it was Elizabeth's influence which prevented Charles Somerset from devoting so much time to hunting as his predecessor had done or as his own son was to do later.

An epitaph for Elizabeth Berkeley described her as having "in her veins the blood of Berkeley and Botetout, in her démarche the greatness of the Queen of Sheba". However, Horace Walpole, who lived next door to the Somersets in Berkeley Square, once said that Elizabeth's presence had turned his card party into the semblance of a Quaker Meeting.

In 1741 Elizabeth gave birth to a daughter; in 1742 yet another daughter was born. Then, in 1744, she had a son, Henry (later to become the 5th Duke of Beaufort), followed at intervals by three more daughters.

Despite his Jacobite sympathies, Charles Somerset seems to have led a tranquil and, for the most part, uneventful life. He does, however, seem to have been a man of taste, especially where pictures were concerned. It is thanks to him that we have such a delightful record of the exterior of Badminton House during the middle of the eighteenth century, for in 1748 he commissioned the great Venetian painter, Antonio Canaletto to paint the two pictures of Badminton—one showing the north front of the house (see cover) and the other a view

*A writer on religious topics, 1656–1739.

looking towards Worcester Lodge. Charles Somerset was also, it seems, appreciative of the Chinese work of Thomas Chippendale, the Worcestershire cabinet-maker.

The Bishop of Ossary, who visited Badminton in 1754, was much taken with the Chinese Room, with its gilt and lacquer furniture, its bamboo-decorated wallpaper and its bed.* "Nothing in the bedroom could have been so impressive, not to say terrifying as the bed itself, with four dragons at the corner of the canopy—a strange device at its apex, and stalactites all around the cornice."

The 4th Duke died on 28 October 1756, aged forty-seven, and was buried at Badminton.

5th Duke of Beaufort: 1744–1803

Popularly credited with the "invention" of foxhunting in 1762, Henry Somerset, 5th Duke of Beaufort from 1756, was born at Hanover Square, London on the 16 October, 1744. As a child he did not enjoy the best of health, but is said to have recovered from a supposedly nearly fatal illness and to have strengthened his weak constitution by virtue of having eaten boiled mutton.

Henry Somerset, who succeeded to the title when he was twelve years old, was educated at Westminster School and later at Oriel College, Oxford. Like his uncle, the 3rd Duke, he then embarked on a "Grand Tour" of Europe, in order to round off his education.

In July 1765 his mother wrote to him concerning certain alterations which were currently being carried out at Badminton: "The house is very much improved within doors. The ceilings, chimney-pieces, doors being all very elegantly fitted up by Mr. Adams, the Architect. The upper row of windows in the Great Room are taken away and light sufficient remains without them. It will be a good room when finished. The outside of the house, large portis, vast stables, must ever remain as proof of the late Lord's desire of greatness . . . I had almost forgotten to tell you that I have examined the front of the house and it looks very well. It cost over £200 to paint anew and do up. Really, such a sum cannot be spared. Wherefore there are any cracks they shall be repaired."

This letter ends with the warning—". . . there will be no ready money for you when you come over and to increase your debts will be deplorable".

There is also at Badminton a curious letter from a correspondent in Gibraltar concerning a report which was circulating in London at the

*Bought by the Victoria and Albert Museum in 1921.

time, to the effect that the 5th Duke of Beaufort had died abroad.

The letter, which is dated February 1765, reads:

"My dear Lord Duke, I have known you to be a man of gallantry. I can never believe your passion for it strong enough to induce you to run these risks which, by our letter accounts from England, the world has given themselves the liberty to suppose. It took its rise from a young nobleman of great distinction on his travels being rash enough to enter a convent in France in women's clothes for the conveniency of carrying on an intrigue with a nun. That he was discovered by the priests and immediately flung from a window into the streets and killed on the spot. It was likewise added that, by the accident, the title became extinct. By the packet succeeding that which brought the above account, a letter was shown by an officer in the garrison acquainting him that the report was spread in London of the death of the Duke of Beaufort abroad. This, my Lord, affected me very much, as you may imagine. The last mail, however, absolutely contradicted the above report and added the agreeable news of your being perfectly well and happy."

If the 5th Duke was not the "young nobleman" in question, some of his conduct while abroad most certainly led members of his family to be seriously concerned for him, as witness the postscript to a letter, dated August 1765, addressed to the Duke of Beaufort in France, and signed H. Somerset (Henrietta, the Duke's sister):

"Remember, Mama sees your letters. Therefore, don't be a fool!" (this last being heavily underlined).

On 2 January, 1766, at St. George's, Hanover Square, the 5th Duke of Beaufort married Elizabeth Boscawen, the sister of George Evelyn (Boscawen), 3rd Viscount Falmouth, and the daughter of Admiral the Hon. Edward Boscawen (1711–1761)—a distinguished naval officer known as "Old Dreadnought" for his fearlessness in battle.

When the Duke married Elizabeth, her father had been dead for five years. His widow, "who never wholly recovered her joy" after his death, seems to have been a model mother-in-law. Three years after their marriage, the young Duchess of Beaufort suffered a serious accident when her carriage overturned. She broke a leg and was left permanently lame. The Duke, who was described by Mrs Boscawen as "the best and most judicious nurse", did everything he could to assist and amuse his wife during her convalescence. Mrs Boscawen, who was a frequent visitor to Badminton, wrote that while the family were walking in Badminton Park, the Duke tried to cheer up the Duchess by "chasing a hare with some little dogs". She added—"I saw it and I wished it well."

From 1768 until 1770 the Duke was Master of the Horse to Queen

Charlotte, but it has been suggested that he resigned the office in order to have more time to devote to nursing his wife.

The Duchess, having recovered from her accident, continued to produce healthy children at fairly regular intervals during the next few years, and by 1787 there were seven: these included Henry (later the 6th Duke), who was born in December 1766; Lord Charles, who eventually became Governor of the Cape of Good Hope; Lord William, who not only became a clergyman but also a good whip; Lord Edward (Robert Edward Henry), who achieved distinction by leading the charge of the Household Brigade at the Battle of Waterloo; and, in 1788, the Duchess gave birth to her last child, Lord FitzRoy, later Lord Raglan, of Waterloo and Crimea fame.

The Beaufort family at that time, including the Duchess's mother, Mrs Boscawen, seems to have been a very close-knit one, and the 5th Duke of Beaufort was never happier than when he was at Badminton where he entertained lavishly, to the delight of his country neighbours.

"A great lover of the country", he was, of course, extremely fond of hunting and also of racing, an interest not shared by his mother-in-law. She wrote a letter to a friend following a visit to Tetbury Races:

"In weather like this (July) it does require a considerable share of patience and good humour to hold out through the venison dinner, the broiling, tedious races and the stewing stifling Balls, doing the honours of all, and smiling and smirking through the day."

In 1770, the 5th Duke had taken over the Heythrop hunting country from Lord Foley and continued to hunt this as well as his own Beaufort country for many years. Each year, after cub-hunting, the Duke and his family, complete with an entourage of servants, attendants and friends, set out for Heythrop House in Oxfordshire, where they remained for a period of some two months.

In 1783 he decided to carry out various alterations and improvements at Badminton. It was at this time that he decided to pull down the original church and to replace it with another one further to the east of the house which was connected to the house by a long passage.

In 1771 the Duke was made Lord Lieutenant of Gloucestershire (he was, at various times, also Lord Lieutenant of Breconshire, Monmouthshire and Leicestershire).

In 1786 he was created a Knight of the Garter, and on 11 October 1803, at the age of fifty-nine, he died of "gout in the stomach", and was buried at Badminton. Shortly before his death in 1803, he obtained confirmation that he could add the Barony of Botetout to his titles, the title being up until then in the possession of his mother.

His widow lived on until 1828, and saw nearly eighty of her descendants with the name of Somerset.

6th Duke of Beaufort: 1766–1835

Henry Charles Somerset, the 6th Duke of Beaufort, succeeded to the title in 1803. He was born on 22 December 1766, and was educated at Westminster School and at Trinity College, Oxford, where he obtained his degree of Master of Arts in 1786.

Described by Mrs Durant as "the first of his family to pay heed to party politics", Henry Somerset was Tory Member of Parliament for Monmouth from 1788 until 1790. He was Member of Parliament for Bristol from 1790 until 1796; for Gloucestershire from 1796 until 1803.

He was popular with the electorate and was much concerned with education and welfare. According to a footnote in *Burke's Peerage*, the Duke was a "man of generous disposition, plain and straightforward in his dealings, and of strict integrity. He was kind and open in his manner, very benevolent in his character and always willing to oblige." "Nimrod" (Charles Apperley) thought that he looked exactly as a duke should look, but it has been suggested that, although he was a handsome man, he was lacking in the more attractive qualities possessed by his brothers.

On 16 March 1791, Henry Somerset married Charlotte Sophia, the daughter of Granville (Leveson-Gower), 1st Marquess of Stafford at Lambeth. Apart from Henry Somerset, later the 7th Duke, they had eight daughters and another son. After succeeding to the title in 1803, he was created a Knight of the Garter in 1805.

Worthy but dull would seem to be an apt description of the 6th Duke's reign, at least as far as certain of his relatives were concerned. Perhaps they weren't dedicated fox-hunters. For example, the Duchess of Beaufort's brother, Lord Granville, who married Lady Harriet Cavendish in 1809, describes the life at Badminton in a letter to a friend written shortly after his marriage:

"We occupy ourselves, all of us, the whole evening playing chess. Our days are all alike. We breakfast about twelve. I read while Harriet instructs my sister's girl upon the harpsichord till past two, when the post comes in. We then walk till near dark; then Harriet and I read the 'Nouvelle Heloise' together till dressing for dinner; after dinner play at chess; go to bed between one and two."

Lord Granville was also, it seems, rather put out concerning the number of children at Badminton at that time: "It is such an incessant rattling of spoons, plates and chatter that it quite stuns me." Lady Granville also seems to have found life rather dull at both Badminton and at Heythrop—"The Duke, Henry and Plantaganet Somerset are breakfasting with us in overalls. Their underalls make Heythrop terribly dull. . . ."

However, the Duke did have some admirers. Baron von Naumann thought that he was the perfect "grand Seigneur", while it is recorded that the Duke's political opponents both liked and respected him.

Imbued with the Somerset love of building, he was responsible for the commencement of work to restore Raglan Castle, in order that it might be opened to the public.

The 6th Duke of Beaufort is perhaps best remembered for his part in the "Harriette Wilson affair", when his son, then Lord Worcester became involved with this notorious woman. Harriette Wilson, who was often referred to as "the little Fellow" or "Harry", was the daughter of a Mayfair shopkeeper. She was, at various times, the mistress of Lord Cavendish, the Duke of Argyle, and of a great many others. One commentator even went so far as to describe her as "a veritable Queen of Tarts".

Sir Walter Scott once wrote of her: "I think I supped once in her society at Mat Lewis's in Argyle Street, where the company chanced to be fairer than honest. She was far from beautiful, but a smart, saucy girl, with good eyes and dark hair, and the manners of a wild schoolboy."

In 1825 Harriette Wilson was to create a sensation when she published her *Memoirs*. She had announced the intended publication well in advance, doubtless in order to enable any of her ex-lovers who wished to do so to "buy themselves out" before publication. Among those mentioned in the *Memoirs* was the Duke of Wellington. "The Duke of Wellington was now my constant visitor—a most unentertaining one, heaven knows." The Iron Duke, it seems, had been one of those who refused to "buy himself out" of the work— "Publish and be damned!" being his famous retort to Miss Wilson's demands.

In 1825 when the *Memoirs* were eventually published—"I shall not say how or why I became at the age of fifteen the mistress of the Earl of Craven"—a special barrier had to be erected in order to hold back the crowds of potential purchasers, who stood ten deep in the Haymarket in front of the offices of Stockdales, the publishers.

It was this woman who, in the early 1800s, became the object of Henry Somerset's infatuation. At that time, Harriette Wilson was living with Lord Leinster and it was he who introduced the young couple to each other at the Opera. Later, when Leinster went off to the wars in Spain, Harriette turned her attention to Henry Somerset, then the young Lord Worcester—"a long, thin, pale fellow with straight hair".

When the 6th Duke and his wife got to hear of the matter, they were extremely angry, as they had every right to be. If, as Miss Wilson claimed, "Worcester daily swore to make me his wife", then there was every chance of the next Duchess of Beaufort being little more than a prostitute. There was certainly no love lost between Harriette Wilson and Henry Somerset's parents and she, described by the Duchess as "this vile, profligate woman", rails against them in her *Memoirs*, using such phrases as—"His Grace was determined to separate us", or "Those worthy wiseacres, the Beauforts". She also writes of the Duchess opening her letters to Lord Worcester, and of the 6th Duke "doing nothing but write and torment Lord Worcester to leave me".

According to Miss Wilson, the Duke arranged for Henry to join Lord Wellington, who was then fighting the Peninsular War in Spain. She, it appears, was to have an allowance "paid quarterly" in order to console her for the loss of her lover. However, the Duke of Beaufort was somewhat tardy about paying this allowance to her. "The Duke perhaps hoped to starve me into putting up with the first man I could find."

On one occasion the Duke sent a Mr Robinson to Harriette in order to obtain from her Worcester's letters. Playing for time, she consulted her solicitor in order to find if she had a case—no doubt for breach of promise. Her solicitor's advice being favourable, it is somewhat surprising to note that Miss Wilson did eventually return the letters. One would have thought that a lady of her enterprise would have known how to make vast capital out of them, at some later date.

Eventually, the 6th Duke and his son's mistress met, when she called at his house in Grosvenor Square, London. This meeting must have been somewhat embarrassing to both parties, the Duke telling Miss Wilson that "she was a fool ever to suppose that she could marry his son". According to Miss Wilson's account of the affair, the atmosphere had thawed considerably by the time she took her leave, the Duke of Beaufort even going so far as to shake hands with her, saying, "I only wanted to observe to you that such unequal marriages are seldom, if ever, attended with happiness to either party."

Finally, the matter was settled by a payment from the Duke of £1,200, but not before there had been talk of Miss Wilson taking the family to court and of her joining Worcester in Spain, together with hints of letters in her possession "worth £20,000".

Perhaps the best and easiest solution to the whole business would have been to have adopted the course suggested by Henry's uncle, Lord William Somerset (as recorded by Miss Wilson herself):

" 'My brother is a fool,' said Lord William Somerset one day to us. 'I could have cured you both in less than a month and made Worcester hate you most cordially.' 'How, pray?' I enquired. 'Why,' continued Lord William, 'merely by shutting you up in one of my country houses together, making it my request that you never left each other an instant to the end of your lives.' "

Eventually, however, Harriette married a Mr Rochfort and went to live in Paris, leaving the Beaufort family in peace.

In 1831 the Duke bore the crown of the Queen Consort at the Coronation of William IV. By 1834, however, the Duke's health had begun to fail, and in 1835 he took his hounds from Heythrop to Badminton for the last time for, on 23 November of that year, he died at Badminton, and was buried there.

In *Bell's Life*, dated 3 January 1836, "Nimrod" wrote an appreciation of him:

"The object of these lines is to pay a short but sincere tribute of respect to the memory of the last departed of these worthy men, whose remains are now scarcely cold in the grave and, not merely as a Master of Foxhounds, but as a conspicuous member of society . . . The Duke, as I said in one of my tours, 'looked like a Duke', and his servants looked like servants of the very best description of their line. More civil or generally well conducted men were never born."

7th Duke of Beaufort: 1792–1853

Since the time of the 2nd Duke of Beaufort, the succeeding Dukes had preferred the role of country landowners and hunting men to that of adepts in London political and Court circles. The 7th Duke of Beaufort, however, was of a somewhat different type.

Once described as a "man who moved more in the world than his immediate predecessors", Henry Somerset, 7th Duke of Beaufort, was born in 1792. He was a man of many talents—soldier, politician, amateur actor, amateur coachman, and socialite. Although he moved in wider circles than had the previous Dukes of Beaufort, he was, nonetheless, equally devoted to country pursuits and, in his later life, to his Badminton home and to his family. *The Gentleman's Magazine* described him as "an excellent landlord, and a great patron of the sports of the field".

As has been previously described, Henry Somerset had been involved in a first-class family row when, as a young undergraduate at Oxford and while he still bore the title of Lord Worcester, he became involved with the notorious Harriette Wilson. According to Miss Wilson, it was the 6th Duke who arranged for Lord Worcester to be sent to the war in Spain. According to Colonel R. S. Liddell (in his *Memoirs of the 10th Royal Hussars*, published in 1891) Lord Worcester "then held a commission in the Monmouth and Brecon Militia. His father having refused to put him in the regular army, Lord Worcester shipped himself and three horses on board a marine ship proceeding to

Lisbon. On arrival in Tagus, he at once joined Lord Wellington, who placed him on his staff, and in this position he was present at the Battle of Bosaco. In August 1811 he received a commission in the 10th Hussars, but the regiment being still at home, he remained on the staff of Lord Wellington."

T. F. Dale has described the 10th Hussars (the Prince of Wales' Own) as "that brilliant band of soldiers, sportsmen, and dandies, known in society as 'Elegant Extracts' and officially as the 10th Hussars. Many officers of this regiment distinguished themselves in war, sport and politics." There were others who were less well disposed towards the 10th Hussars (also known as "The Chainy 10th") and at one time they were lampooned for having, in thirteen years of war, never seen an enemy or having travelled further than the Isle of Wight. In their rather flamboyant uniform of yellow boots, red breeches and heavily laced jackets—a uniform especially designed by the Prince Regent himself in a moment of boredom—the 10th Hussars were often held to be figures of fun. However, they fought well enough when they had to in the Peninsular War, and finally earned their place in military history when they broke the squares of Napoleon's Old Imperial Guard at the Battle of Waterloo.

When the 10th Hussars landed in Lisbon in 1813, Lord Worcester joined them and took part as a Regimental Officer in all the operations of that and the following year. On one occasion during 1813, near Morales del Toro (described by Wellington as "a handsome little affair") Lord Worcester was in charge of the leading squadron. The 10th Hussars then charged the French Dragoons so fiercely that they were completely routed. "It then became a chase across country over the prickly-pear hedges, the pace being so good that the whole of the enemy's Dragoons were destroyed or taken prisoner." It is interesting to note that of all sports "the 10th has at all times placed foxhunting before them all". What better regiment for a member of the Somerset family to belong to. The 10th Hussars regarded foxhunting "not only as the king of sports but as one of the best calculated to give those acquirements most essential to a cavalry officer—a quick eye, knowledge of country, the requisite dash and going straight."

The Duke of Wellington, incidentally, was an intrepid foxhunter himself, and neither heat, wet, cold, or even war were allowed to interfere with his sport. Throughout the Peninsular campaign he kept a pack of foxhounds at his headquarters. Doubtless there were some Beaufort hounds in his pack since there is a receipt at Badminton which records that the Duke of Wellington purchased from the Duke of Beaufort "nine and a half couple of hounds (19), for which he paid £31".

In June 1813 the 10th Hussars were engaged in another action at Vittoria, again distinguishing themselves in a charge led by the young Lord Worcester. In the spring of 1814, he was taken prisoner by the French when crossing a ford between Bordeaux and Toulouse, but his period of captivity proved to be of short duration since, with the capture of Toulouse in April of that year, the Peninsular War came to a close.

In 1814, after approximately four years of military service, Lord Worcester returned to England. In that same year, on July 21st, at a ball given by the Prince Regent at Carlton House, his engagement was announced to Georgiana FitzRoy, the niece of the Duke of Wellington, and a favourite companion of the Prince Regent's daughter.

According to Mrs Durant, Georgiana was actually present on the famous occasion when the Prince publicly 'cut' Beau Brummel. This occurred at a Dandy Ball given by Lord Avenly at the Argyle Rooms, the Prince being the guest of honour. Beau Brummel, who had incurred Prinny's displeasure by slighting Mrs Fitzherbert was quite deliberately ignored by the Prince, and countered by loudly asking Lord Avenly: "Avenly, who is your fat friend?"—a remark for which he was never forgiven and which was to cost him dear.

The Iron Duke was very fond of his niece, Georgiana, and so approved of the match that he undertook to give the bride away at the wedding, which took place only four days after the Carlton House Ball, at the house of Charles Culling Smith in Upper Brook Street, London. Following the wedding, Henry and his bride went to Paris as guests of the Duke of Wellington.

A contemporary description of the evening dress worn by Henry Somerset at a ball in Paris at about this time is as follows: "It consisted of the Beaufort Hunt evening coat of blue lined with buff, an embroidered silk waistcoat, tight light blue silk web pantaloons, white silk stockings, shoes brodes à jour, and a cocked hat."

It is interesting to note that the Beaufort hunt buttons which he wore on his coat were made of brass and bore the initials G.P.R., as a tribute to the Prince of Wales. Today, of course, the Hunt buttons bear the initials B.H.

If Henry Somerset's costume sounds somewhat outlandish when compared with our modern ideas of dress, it must be remembered that his costume was perfectly in accord with the fashions of his time. In fact, Lord William Lennox once remarked that Henry Somerset "never looked overdressed". For those were the days of the dandies and of high fashion, when that arbiter of elegance, Beau Brummel, invented the stiffened cravat. When he first appeared in it in public it was said that not only were the dandies struck dumb but a washerwoman miscarried!

During the 6th Duke's lifetime, Lord and Lady Worcester had a house in Upper Brook Street, London, where, being fond of society, they often entertained. Lord Worcester, at this period, divided his time between politics, drama and sport, being interested in both coaching and racing. A consistent supporter of Conservative politics, he was Member of Parliament for Monmouth from 1814 until 1831 and from 1831 until 1832. He was also Member for West Gloucestershire from January to November 1835 (when he succeeded to the title). He was a noted patron of the stage and was one of the founder members of the Garrick Club (founded in 1831). He was reputed to be an actor of some talent with a flair for light comedy. He once appeared in amateur productions of *Othello* (as Cassio) and *Matrimony* (as O'Clogherty) at the Tottenham Court Theatre, and in doing so earned the displeasure of the Duke of York for having appeared before a paying audience.

Henry Somerset was also responsible for the founding of another famous London Club—Pratt's. When Crockford's gaming club was closed, Henry was distressed because "the only gentleman's servant I know is Pratt at Crockford's and now I shall never see him again". Later, acting upon friends' advice, he set Pratt up in a club of his own.

Henry Somerset's charm and good manners made him one of the most popular men in London, and he seems to have inherited the family gift of being able to put men from all walks of life at their ease without condescension. Indeed, so highly did most of his contemporaries speak of him, that it comes almost as a relief to find that not everybody liked him. Lady Granville (the wife of the 1st Earl of Cavendish and sister-in-law to the wife of the 6th Duke of Beaufort) wrote that she left Woburn Abbey with a sigh of relief "having been compelled so often to sit next to him at dinner".

On the subject of Lady Worcester, Lady Granville seems to have had mixed feelings. In 1820 she described her as "being in great beauty improved beyond anything, giving herself no airs and with enough quickness to adorn society". A month later, however, Lady Granville wrote: "If Lady Worcester had had an education as good as it was bad, she might have been a delightful person."

The Worcesters' marriage was to last for only seven years. On 3 May 1821, Lady Worcester attended the King's Birthday Ball. At that time she was staying at Apsley House, Piccadilly, famous as the home of the Duke of Wellington. The day after the Ball she felt ill and had a cold bath, which set up an internal inflammation. After terrible suffering, she died on 11 May. They had two daughters, but no heir.

Lady Worcester does not seem to have been as popular as her

husband. Following her death, a Mrs Calvert (described by Mrs Durant as "an Irish beauty") recorded in her diary—"Lord Worcester, I hear, is in great dispair, but he will soon console himself, and his family will not much regret her." In Charles Greville's diary it is stated that "she has been snatched away from life at a time when she was becoming every day more fit to live, for her mind, her temper, and her understanding were gradually and rapidly improving. She had faults, but her mind was not vicious, and her defects may be ascribed to her education [shades of Lady Granville] and to the actual state of society in which she lived."*

Mrs Calvert's prophesy, "he will soon console himself" seems to have been an accurate one, for after the prescribed period of mourning Lord Worcester was married again, this time to Emily Culling Smith, his wife's half-sister. The wedding was a very private affair, taking place at St. George's Church, Hanover Square, on 29 June 1822. Henry Somerset seems to have had some doubts as to the propriety of marrying Miss Culling Smith as, immediately after the wedding, he hurried off to consult FitzRoy Somerset† on the matter.

There was good reason for concern as the marriage was definitely within the proscribed degrees of affinity and might have been declared void by an ecclesiastical court. When the news of the wedding was made public, the closeness of the relationship gave rise to much comment. The new Marchioness was first cousin to Lady FitzRoy Somerset and her beautiful sister, Lady Bagot. Sir Charles Bagot wrote to Lord Binning in July 1822:

"I heard by the last post of Worcester's marriage with Emily Smith. What a complication of folly, and I should fear eventual of misery. He never was and never can be steady to any one thing or person, and is, I should suppose, utterly ruined. Does not the marriage, too, fall within the proscribed relationships, or do you cease to mind these matters?"

In 1835 an Act of Parliament, known as Lord Lyndhurst's Act, was passed whereby marriage between persons within the prohibited degrees of affinity, which were solemnised *before* 31 August 1835 cannot be annulled for that cause; but such marriages (as well as those within the prohibited degrees of consanguinity) solemnised *since* that date are absolutely *void* and the issue consequently illegitimate. Since Lord Lyndhurst (Attorney-General in 1819 and three times Lord

* *The Greville Diary* (Charles Cavendish Fulke Greville)
†FitzRoy Somerset (later Lord Raglan) the youngest son of the 5th Duke of Beaufort, was the Duke of Wellington's Military Secretary. He distinguished himself at the Battle of Waterloo, where he unfortunately lost an arm. Later he became Commander-in-Chief of the British Forces in the Crimean War, and was thus responsible for the Light Brigade débâcle.

Chancellor of England) was a friend of Henry Somerset, it has been supposed that "the desire to give indisputable validity to this important alliance contributed not a little to the passing of the Act".

In February 1824, Lady Worcester gave birth to her only son in Paris. He was followed by six girls, so that the 6th and 7th Dukes of Beaufort had eight daughters apiece. All but one of the sixteen girls were eventually married, and their dowries must have been a heavy strain on the family resources.

It was also in 1824 that Lady Granville met the new Marchioness, whom she described thus: "She touches me. She looks careworn, with her sad eyes and thin projecting nose."*

The political climate in England during the early 1830s was far from being stable, and in December 1830 there were riots throughout the country. The 1830s saw a number of significant legislative and social changes, which were eventually to alter the lives and circumstances of the landed gentry. The Reform Bill was passed in 1831, the Game Act in 1831, and, of course, this period saw the beginnings of the great railway networks. It is interesting to note that the Duke of Cleveland successfully opposed one railway project on the grounds that it would disturb his fox coverts.

Greville records that "London is like the capital of a country desolated by cruel war or foreign invasion, and we are always looking for reports of battles, burnings and other disorders. Wherever there has been anything like fighting, the mob has always been beaten and has shown great cowardice. They broke into the Duke of Beaufort's house at Heythrop, but he and his sons [including Henry Somerset] got them out without mischief and afterwards took some of them. On Monday, as the field which had been out with the King's hounds were returning, they were summoned to assist in quelling a riot at Woburn, which they did."

Following the attack upon Heythrop House, Newport—in his Monmouth constituency—begged Henry Somerset to support a petition for reform, but this he refused to do, with the result that "four months later the Newport crowds gave him a rough time, and it was Frost [John Frost, the chartist] who saved him from an involuntary plunge into the river". In 1831 the Reform Bill was passed, and in the following year Henry Somerset lost his seat in the election.

During the 1830s, it was not uncommon for gentlemen to drive coaches, acting as or in the capacity of coachmen, and Henry Somerset was amongst the best of them. He was physically very strong and had the gift of "hands" where horses were concerned. He often drove the

*Lady Granville's husband was Ambassador to France at that time.

Oxford, Bath, Portsmouth and Somerset coaches, and the story is told that once, when driving a party of friends back from Brighton after the races, one of the passengers lost his nerve and shouted: "You had better put the skid on the wheel." "I think not", Worcester replied, "it would probably cause the hind wheels to strike and in that case we should be floored with this heavy load." Later Henry told Charles Apperley: "I never let them know that we were going down a steep hill and all went well."

Henry Somerset was also a keen supporter of racing, and did much to improve the quality of British bloodstock. He was greatly respected on the Turf, giving great pleasure to the public, and had a reputation for honesty.

Lord William Lennox wrote that he spent the best day of his life in the Marquess of Worcester's company, setting out for Newmarket Races at 7 o'clock on a July morning, driving a phaeton the first stage and posting the rest of the way. They breakfasted at Chesterfield and dined there on the way back. Lord Lennox claimed that as much as he enjoyed the racing, he enjoyed Worcester's conversation even more. T. F. Dale suggests "that these two old comrades [they had been on the Duke of Wellington's staff together] amused each other by telling stories of the Peninsular Campaigns". Whatever they talked about, their perfect day finished with an hour in the green room of Covent Garden Theatre.

In 1835 Henry Somerset, Marquess of Worcester, succeeded to the title as the 7th Duke of Beaufort at the age of forty-three, and thus his parliamentary career came to an end. Some time later he applied for an Embassy but was refused that of Vienna and, in turn, refused that of St. Petersburg.

In 1838 "Nimrod" paid a visit to Badminton, when he noted with amazement that "there are one hundred and sixteen rooms, and the distance from my bedroom to the Billiard Room can be little short of the eighth of a mile." In the following year, "Nimrod" returned to Badminton for the celebrations which marked the then Lord Worcester's (later the 8th Duke) fifteenth birthday. These were the days of the great Lawn Meets at Badminton, when "members of the hunt and inmates of the house breakfasted in the Great Hall with a full attendance of servants, all in their evening costume; when Mr Vizard, the sporting sweep rode out with the Beaufort Hunt, and carriages filled with ladies and gentlemen from Bristol and Bath turned out to enjoy the spectacle of the Beaufort Hunt meeting in the magnificent setting of Badminton House and Park." "Nimrod" also notes that at one such Meet, some three hundred people (riders) attended.

If the 7th Duke's boyhood affair with Harriette Wilson had caused his father some distress, he, in his turn, was to find the romantic adventures of two of his own daughters equally trying. One of them, Lady Rose Somerset, eloped with a handsome "Life Guard", Francis Lovell, when she was seventeen, while the other daughter, Lady Augusta Somerset, was the central figure in a scandal which swept through Europe.

In November 1842, the year in which the 7th Duke was made a Knight of the Garter, Greville wrote: "I have been engaged these last few days in devising means of stifling the scandalous stories which have gone all over the world about Prince George of Cambridge and Lady Augusta Somerset. The story is that he got her with child, that he did not object, but that the Royal Marriage Act stood in the way and the Queen was indisposed to consent."

Prince George was the son of the Duke of Cambridge, and the Royal Marriage Act (still applicable today) meant that the Sovereign had to give approval before any member of the Royal Family could marry. The rumour was, in fact, untrue, and was based upon the fact that Lady Augusta and Prince George had enjoyed a mild flirtation at Kew in the previous year—a flirtation, wrote Greville "such as is constantly going on, without any serious result, between half the youths and girls in London".

Greville was very much concerned in the whole business for, on the 7th Duke of Beaufort's behalf, he went to the Editor of *The Times* in order to get a "formal contradiction into their paper". The contradiction was published, but to little avail since the scandal was far too good to be dropped so quickly.

The was also a further complication in that Queen Victoria believed that the rumour was true and forbade the Court to speak to or even to acknowledge Lady Augusta—"that 'very ill-behaved girl, ready for anything that her caprice or passions excite her to do'." And this, despite Prince George having given his word that there was no truth whatever in any of the rumours. In February 1843, Prince George's mother, the Duchess of Cambridge, visited Windsor Castle, bringing with her Lady Augusta Somerset. According to Lady Georgiana Bathurst, "none of the ladies would take the least notice of her". After the visit, Greville notes: "the Queen broke out with great violence, said she knew the stories about Lady Augusta were all true, and that it was very wrong of the Duchess of Cambridge to have brought her, and that she was only brought there for the purpose of getting rid of the scandal".

The Duke of Beaufort was extremely angry about the whole affair, and wrote to Sir Robert Peel, demanding an audience with the Queen. The Duke of Wellington, however, told the Beauforts that Peel was so afraid of the Queen that he did not think he would venture to speak to her. The upshot of the whole business was that Sir Robert Peel finally wrote to the Duke of Beaufort, on behalf of the Queen, saying that "she was now entirely satisfied and she begged there might be no further discussion on the subject".

The Duke could not forget the incident and when in August of that year Prince Albert proposed that the 7th Duke's son, Lord Worcester, should be appointed as a Lord-in-Waiting, the Duke angrily refused the offer.

At the age of fifty-two, the 7th Duke suffered a serious fall from his horse while riding in Hyde Park. He was badly shaken and, as he suffered from gout—which Mrs Durant describes as the Somerset "family enemy"—a condition which was aggravated by an accident of this kind, he was eventually forced to give up riding altogether and had to be content with following his hounds in a phaeton.

He died on 17 November 1853, and was succeeded by his son, Henry Somerset.

8th Duke of Beaufort: 1824–1899

Sometimes known as the "Old Blue 'Un" or the "Old Duke", and one of the most popular noblemen of his day, Henry Somerset was born in Paris on the 1st February, 1824. He was to become the best-known sporting figure in England, popular with every class. In Gloucester-shire, men said that they would rather be sworn at by the Duke than spoken to civilly by other folk. In Monmouthshire, where he owned 27,000 acres, his tenants called him "Uncle".*

As a small boy, he was sent to a school in Brighton, which could well have been modelled on Dickens' Dotheboys Hall. Later in his life he was to recall this unhappy period: "Early in November, 1833, I being then nine years old, had committed the high crime and misdemeanour of ending a pentameter with a three-syllable word, for which the usher caned me . . . At 5 o'clock the Doctor came in. I think he must have been served two writs that day. His eye fell upon me—'Have you been caned today?' 'Yes, sir.' 'What for?' I told him. 'Go and fetch my cane.' The usher was a good fellow, and passionate, and said: 'I caned him severely for it.' 'Never mind,' said the Doctor. 'He will remember two thrashings better than one.' His hand was on my throat and I was writhing under his blows for fully three minutes. As he went from the room, he turned and said: 'After prayers tomorrow morning you shall have just such another thrashing.'"

* *The Somerset Sequence.*

The unfortunate victim of this assault tried to run away from the school, but was eventually brought back. Later, however, things improved when he was sent to Eton.

While undergoing his formal education, Henry Somerset, like all the young Somersets, also learned the ways of the hunting field. Later, his own children were not allowed to hunt more than three days a week until they were five! He also became a "fair coachman" by the time he was fifteen. He sometimes drove the London to Brighton coach, "The Age".

Having left Eton, Henry Somerset embarked upon a military career, and in 1843 he was a Lieutenant in the 1st Life Guards. On 1 February 1845, there were lavish celebrations at Badminton to mark his coming of age. (He became Marquess of Worcester in 1835 when his father succeeded to the title after the death of the 6th Duke of Beaufort.)

It is difficult for us today even to imagine the style in which the rich aristocrats of the mid-nineteenth century lived for, with social changes over the years and as the result of two world wars, the standards of the aristocracy have declined as those of the rest of the population increased.

In the modern world of inflation and supermarkets, it is difficult even to speculate upon the extravagant way in which things were done at Badminton during this period. The 7th Duke of Beaufort marked the coming of age of his eldest son and heir in the grand manner, entertaining both the tenantry and the local inhabitants of Badminton.

The *London Gazette* of 8 February 1845 informs us that: "The carcases of no less than six oxen were given away, besides an immense quantity of other viands, and twenty hogs heads of strong ale."

The distinguished visitors who assembled at Badminton two days before the Marquess's birthday, included His Royal Highness, the Duke of Cambridge, the Marquess and Marchioness of Normanby, Earl Howe, with his son Viscount Curzon and his daughter Lady Georgiana Curzon, Earl Bathurst, Lord Alvanley, Count Esterhazy, and a host of others. The Duke of Cambridge, as guest of honour, was received by the 7th Duke of Beaufort in the entrance hall and was then led to the drawing-room. Here he was "presented to the distinguished circle there assembled". Later, the guests sat down to a "sumptuous Banquet" at a table almost covered with gold and silver plate.

On the following morning, the Duke of Cambridge, attended by Henry, Lord Worcester, the Earl of Barrington, Viscount Curzon, and others, went shooting in Swangrove Covert (the Duke of Beaufort being obliged to attend a Magistrates' Court). At 4 o'clock in the afternoon the carcase of an ox, trussed and spitted and decorated with blue ribbons, was drawn on a sledge through the village before being roasted in the Park. Later in the afternoon two hundred of the tenantry (a drawing representing the occasion shows them to be all men) sat down to dinner in the Servants' Hall, which had been specially decorated for the occasion with banners, flags and "festoons of every colour".

The bill of fare included a baron of beef, weighing 300 lbs., six haunches of venison, six necks of venison, loins of veal, four hams, two rounds of beef, six dishes of boiled owls—(I don't think we are to believe the *London Gazette* and this must be a misprint, for the next item is)—six dishes of roast fowls, forty pheasants, twenty hares, four boiled legs of mutton, four roast shoulders of mutton, and six venison pies. Twenty jellies, sixteen apple tarts, eighteen plum puddings, and sixty-five desserts. To this excellent fare, it is noted, "the guests did ample justice". Later that evening, the whole of the "distinguished company" in the mansion proceeded to where the tenantry were seated, and "at the entrance of the party, every man rose simultaneously, and the vaulted roof of that fine old hall reverberated with cheers of affectionate welcome".

Again, later that night, when the distinguished company had concluded yet another sumptuous banquet, the 7th Duke and his son returned to the Hall, where they were toasted. "The health of the Marquess was received with nine times nine rounds of applause, and the well-known 'View Halloo' of the Beaufort Hunt." The Marquess thanked the company, "expressing a hope that he should meet those present in the field for years to come". Following a visit from the Duke of Cambridge, the tenantry were then entertained by a song composed in honour of the occasion and sung by "a gentleman".

> His stately halls where welcome smiles
>   on Peasant and on Peer,
> Whose lawn supplies old English Sport, his
> Larder good old cheer.
> Long o'er his hospitable gates, his scutcheon proud may rear,
> And there his ancient motto stand—
> —He scorns all change and fear—
> Does this fine old English Nobleman—all
> of the Beaufort line.

On 3 July that same year, Henry Somerset married Georgiana Charlotte, the daughter of Richard William Penn, 1st Earl Howe. Lady Clodagh Anson, a grand-daughter of the 8th Duke of Beaufort, has left an account of the circumstances surrounding this wedding.*

Lady Georgiana Curzon was staying at Badminton when she and the young Henry Somerset fell in love. A thunderstorm had started and she was so frightened that she went and hid between one of the great double doors, but he found her there and proposed marriage to her. "Lord Howe wouldn't do anything about the wedding; he was so angry with her for leaving him. But they married at some little Royal Chapel, at Bushey, I think. Grandpapa, who was then in the Blues, was very much annoyed at Lord Howe's behaviour, so he bought a huge wedding-cake himself, cut it up with his sword, and gave it round to all the soldiers of his troop."

A keen soldier "whose regret was deep that no opportunity of active service was open to him",† Henry Somerset was a captain in the 7th Dragoons (1847) and by 1858 he had become a lieutenant-colonel. At one time (1842) he was aide-de-camp to the Duke of Wellington.

Early in his military career, and shortly after his marriage, Henry Somerset lived a normal soldier's life. At one time, after being posted to Ballincolig in Ireland, the couple had four rooms for themselves, two baby boys and their nurses, and a corner of the sitting-room had to be screened off as a dressing-room.

Lady Clodagh Anson has recorded that on another occasion they were quartered in Dublin, "and had two tiny houses, with another one in between, so that they had to run backwards and forwards into the street when they wanted to get dressed or fetch anything. I think these Irish years were the happiest time of their lives."

Having left the army, Henry Somerset embarked upon a political career. He was Conservative member of Parliament for East Gloucestershire from 1846 until 1853. Then, in 1853, the 7th Duke died, and he succeeded to the title, becoming the 8th Duke of Beaufort, and settling at Badminton.

Unlike many of the great families of England, the Somersets preferred to pursue their equestrian activities in the hunting field rather than on the Turf. While it is true that the 8th Duke's father was well-known in racing circles in his day, the Dukes of Beaufort are not thought of in the same light as, say, the Roseberys, the Lonsdales, or the Derbys. The one exception, however, was the 8th Duke, whose racing colours—"blue with white hoops and a blue cap" which were registered when he succeeded to the title—were as well-known as anybody's in his day.

As early as 1854, when he was thirty years old, the Duke was elected a member of the Jockey Club and was honoured and popular on the

Victorian Days.
†T. F. Dale.

Turf. He took an active part in the government of racing, and was a founder member of the National Hunt Committee. Although he was a keen racing man, the 8th Duke was "far too honest and open in his racing dealings" and was "sometimes made use of by unscrupulous and designing persons".*

The Duke's horses were trained by "Honest" John Day at Danebury. Day also trained for the Duke of Newcastle and the luckless Marquess of Hastings (Harry Hastings), both of whom were later to be ruined by gambling, while John Day, who proved to be anything but honest, eventually went bankrupt. Subsequently, the Duke's horses were trained by the "Wizard of Manton", Alec Taylor, a man of independent mind, who could "throw his tongue" on occasions. On one occasion, for example, when the Duchess of Montrose (who raced under the name of Mr Manton) asked Taylor what he thought was the chief danger to one of her horses, he replied: "Damned to hell if I know, your Grace." However, Alec Taylor seems to have had a great respect for "that most courtly of gentlemen, the Duke of Beaufort".

The Duke's involvement with racing was not without success. In 1865, his filly, Siberia, won the One Thousand Guineas. In 1867 he won the Two Thousand Guineas with Vauban, which later started favourite for one of the most famous Derby's ever run—"Hermit's Derby", which cost the Marquess of Hastings well in excess of £100,000. Hermit came up to win with a late run, relegating Vauban to second place, and thus thwarting one of the Duke of Beaufort's greatest ambitions—to win the "Blue Riband" of the Turf.

In 1869, the 8th Duke again won the One Thousand Guineas, with his filly, Scottish Queen. In 1887, he won both the One Thousand Guineas and the Oaks with Rêve d'Or. In 1880, he won the Two Thousand Guineas again, this time with Petronel.

On one occasion, he also had a surprise winner in the Goodwood Stakes. The story was later told by Alfred Watson,† who was working as Assistant Editor for *The Badminton Library of Sport* series.

"I was accompanying the Duke to the meeting, going down every day from London. We had a fly to meet us at Drayton Station, and on arriving at the stands on the Stakes day, the driver leaned down from his box and asked whether he should back Winter Cherry. 'The flyman wants to tout you, Duke,' I said. Should he have his half-crown on the filly? our driver enquired; he had a great fancy for her, he said. The Duke replied that he could not understand how the fancy had arisen, and strongly advised him to keep his half-crown in his pocket as the

*T. F. Dale.
†*A Sporting and Dramatic Career*, 1918.

filly had no sort of chance. While we were walking to the stand, the Duke told me that Winter Cherry was only being started to make the running for the then Lord Hartington's Sir Kenneth. When the flag fell, Winter Cherry, who had only 5 stone 7 lbs. on her back, jumped off in front and led the whole way. Wood on Sir Kenneth delayed his effort, apparently under the impression that the other would come back to him; but the boy on Winter Cherry stuck to his work, and to the dismay of her owner and friends she just beat Sir Kenneth by a short neck. The flyman looked very reproachfully at us when we took our seats to drive back to the station, the winner having started at 20 to 1, which would have yielded him a crop of half-crowns. On reaching Drayton, however, the Duke consoled him with an extra sovereign and a quite earnest assurance that the result had been totally unexpected."

The 8th Duke of Beaufort was a man of considerable zest and energy. He spent a great deal of time in London—according to Lady Clodagh Anson, the Duchess of Beaufort hated London and would hardly ever leave Badminton—often playing cards at Pratt's until well into the early hours of the morning; "then he would drive to Paddington, sleep in his brougham, take the train to Chippenham, and drive the ten miles to Badminton. Then he changed and hunted all day, sometimes returning to London that night."*

He was rarely punctual, which often infuriated his wife. Lady Clodagh has recorded how on one occasion the family were kept waiting on the Duke's return from London. ". . . we waited and waited and felt sure that he must have missed his train, when three-quarters of an hour later the carriage lamps appeared. Granny was almost dancing with fuss by this time; we collected in the hall as usual, waiting for the carriage to drive up, and after he had been duly hugged by us all in turn, we demanded to know what had kept him."

In fact, the Duke had been performing one of those acts of kindness which caused people to refer to him "as the most charming man I know".† Arriving at the station late that night, he had discovered what Lady Clodagh Anson describes as "a poor little woman from a 3rd Class carriage" and her three children stranded on the platform. He had put their luggage on the top of his brougham and had driven them home.

Although on this occasion the Duchess "was almost dancing with fuss", and bearing in mind that she hid during a thunderstorm before her marriage, there is no doubt that she could and did show tremendous sang-froid when the occasion demanded—as for example on the occasion when she was attacked by a lunatic: "He was the head-

* *Victorian Days.*
† *Victorian Days.*

cook there at the time and suddenly went raving mad; he appeared with a revolver in one hand and a huge kitchen knife in the other, and told Granny he was going to kill her. But she was very brave and also had an extraordinary dominating look in her eyes which she could summon to her aid in any emergency. She sometimes used it on us when we were naughty, with great effect. Anyhow, it defeated the cook, because when she looked at him and said, 'Leave the room'. He went quite quietly, and they were able to disarm him and take him away to the asylum without much trouble."*

In addition to his social and sporting activities, the 8th Duke also had the obligations required of him by his numerous public appointments. In 1854 he was made High Steward of Bristol, an office he held until his death in 1899. In February 1858 he became a Privy Counsellor; from 1858 until 1859 and again from 1866 until 1868 he was Master of the Horse to Queen Victoria. In 1867, he was created a Knight of the Garter. In 1867 also he was made Lord Lieutenant for Monmouthshire where, in 1868, the celebrations for the coming of age of his heir, Lord Worcester (later the 9th Duke of Beaufort) were held. A public dinner, races, fireworks, shoots, were all arranged at Monmouth. Two thousand five hundred loaves of bread, a ton and a half of beef and an ox were given away, which was paraded through the town to the accompaniment of music.

Towards the latter end of his life, the 8th Duke of Beaufort suffered from intermittent attacks of gout. He also had to contend with family matters which caused him great sorrow. Two of his sons were involved in a scandal, and then the Marquess of Waterford, the husband of his only daughter, Blanche, suffered a fall while out hunting which left him severely crippled. Later, when the Marquess discovered that his wife had developed an incurable illness, he took his own life.

It was during this period of his life that the 8th Duke found consolation in working on *The Badminton Library* series of sporting books (see page 128).

Following the Marquess of Worcester's marriage in 1895, the 8th Duke decided to hand over his estates† to his son, in order to avoid heavy succession duties, and so he and the Duchess went to live at Stoke Park (Stoke Gifford) near Bristol. They still continued to attend numerous official functions, the Duchess often being greatly embarrassed when brass bands at local bazaars played "God Save the Queen" when she arrived and departed.

---

* *Victorian Days*.
†Family Estates: These, in 1883, consisted of about 27,300 acres in Monmouthshire, about 16,600 in Gloucestershire, 4,000 in Breconshire, 1,200 in Glamorgan (the last valued at above £4,000 a year), and about 2,000 in Wiltshire. Total 51,085 acres, valued at £56,226 a year.

On the 30 April 1899, when he was seventy-five, the Duke of Beaufort died of gout, and was buried at Badminton.

The 8th Duke of Beaufort was the last of the Dukes of Beaufort to live in a really grand manner and who was really able to afford to entertain on a truly magnificent scale. There were many of the famous Lawn Meets at Badminton, when over one thousand people sat down to breakfast and five hundred or so came to lunch.

A soldier, politican, huntsman, hunting man, coachman, clubman, and a great gentleman (although he was not without his 'little affairs and dissipations'*) Henry Charles FitzRoy Somerset seems to have been liked and respected by all who ever came into contact with him. Of all the complimentary things written and said of him, perhaps the nicest was written by Lady Clodagh Anson: "He was a most charming and delightful companion."

Establishment of his Grace, the 8th Duke of Beaufort, Badminton Park, Glos., in 1836 †

No.

CHAPLIN
Revd. H. Randolph   1

LAND AGENTS
Francis Wedge, Esq., 1st Clerk, Mr. R. Salter   2

HOUSE
House Steward, Butler, Groom of the Chambers, French Cook   4
2 Under Butlers, 2 Ushers of Servants Hall, and Footmen   9
Steward's Room Boy, 2 Coal Carriers, Man to attend to lamps   4
Man to attend to Heating of rooms by steam, do. fire flues   2
2 Men to pump water, 2 House carpenters, Painter and
Guilder   5
1 Brewer, 1 Maltster, 1 Baker, 2 Odd Men for sundry work   5
1 Housekeeper, 4 Lady's Maids, 1 Sempstress, 4 Housemaids,
  and 3 Charwomen, 2 Still Room Maids, 4 Nurses and
  Assistance in Nursery, 2 Dairymaids, 4 Laundry do. and 4
  Washerwomen, 5 Women in Kitchen, Clerk of do., Butcher
  and Man, Knife Boy   38

STABLE
1 Head Groom, 1 Coachman, 1 Second Coachman, 2
  Postillions, Pad Groom, 33 Stablemen and Helpers, 1

Victorian Days.
†This list appears exactly as it was produced in 1836—mistakes included.

Carriage Washer   39
Carriage Horses, Hunters, Hacks, Poneys, etc., 119

KENNELS
1 Huntsman, 2 Whips, 4 Kennelmen   7
Hounds (Hunting) 120, Breeding, Pups, Pointers, etc., 40

GARDEN
1 Head Gardener, 1 Second do., 1 Florist, 12 men in Kitchen
    Garden, 5 Women do., 6 men in flower garden and pleasure
    grounds, 3 Women   29

GAME
Park Keeper, Game do., and Assistance   14
Head of deer, 14 hundred fallow deer, 4 hundred Red
Cost of deer in 1837 for 16 weeks for hay, beans, etc., £70 per
    week

FARMING BAILIFFS
1 Head Bailiff, 1 Second do., 12 men   14
4 teams of mules 4 each, 3 teams of oxen, 4 do., 2 horses for
    sundry work (with 2 men)   2

TRADESMEN
1 Clerk of works, 1 second do., 4 carpenters, 3 cabinet makers,
    4 rough carpenters, 2 painters, 2 plumbers and glaziers, 3
    blacksmiths, 2 wheelwrights, 4 sawers, 2 men attending
    timber yard   28
6 woodmen, 12 men cutting timber, and other work in park,
    etc.   18
20 boys and 1 man to superintend them on roads, 20 men on
    roads and sundry work, stone digging on the estate   41
6 men living at different lodges, old men after their work was
    done that had lived for large numbers of years in the Family   12
do. men and women (in place called the Hospital with
    house)   14
Firing, food, etc., found therein
Nursery (fruit trees, evergreens, etc.) 2 men, 1 woman   3

    Total
    men and women 271

9th Duke of Beaufort: 1847–1924

Henry Adelbert Wellington FitzRoy Somerset (the 9th Duke of Beaufort from 1899 until his death in 1924) was born on 19 May 1847. He was educated at Eton and, at the age of twenty, he joined the Royal Horse Guards as a Cornet, attaining the rank of Captain in 1869.

In 1877 he retired from the Army, and later became Honorary Colonel to the Gloucestershire Yeomanry. He was Hereditary Keeper of Raglan Castle and High Steward of Bristol and Gloucester, and at the Coronation of King George V and Queen Mary, in 1911, he bore Curtana, the Sword of Mercy.

Five years before he succeeded to the title, however, in October 1895, he married Louise Emily, the widow of Baron Carlo de Tuyll. She was the youngest daughter of William Henry Harford of Oldown in Gloucestershire. In the 9th Duke of Beaufort's obituary, published in the *Wiltshire Standard* on the 29 November 1924, it was noted that the Duchess fully shared the Duke's love of hunting "and the three children of the marriage have followed hounds from earliest childhood". One of these children, the present 10th Duke who was born in 1900, is still regularly following hounds at the age of seventy-eight!

It is impossible to record anything of the life of the 9th Duke of Beaufort without mentioning foxhunting. The Somerset family have always had a great love for the chase, but the 9th Duke had a passion for hunting which precluded almost everything else.

Villagers in and around the Badminton area all know of and have memories of the 9th Duke as a great hunting man, but few could provide any information beyond this fact. The 9th Duke of Beaufort was a retiring, unassuming man, who loved his Badminton home, where he lived the life of a country gentleman. He was never happier than when he was out hunting. He was popular, both as a landlord and as a Master of Foxhounds, and children, it seems, were especially fond of him. He also, on occasions, drove a coach, and was a member of the Committee of the "Four in Hand Club", of which his father was President.

Until the death of his father in 1899, Henry Somerset (then Marquess of Worcester) was not the titular head of the Beaufort Hunt. However, his father had for many years, especially in later life when he was troubled by ill-health, left the entire management of the hunting establishment to his son, who showed a keen interest in the hounds from his childhood and who first hunted the hounds on the retirement of the professional Huntsman, Tom Clarke, in 1868. It was on 22 February 1871 that Henry Somerset achieved lasting fame in the annals of foxhunting by virtue of his famous "Greatwood Run", which ranks as one of the most famous of the historic hunts of the nineteenth century (see page 121.).

During the 1880s, the Beaufort hounds hunted five days each week. However, as if this was not sufficient, Henry Somerset often used to round off the week by hunting with the adjacent V.W.H. Hunt (Vale of the White Horse). Later, when the Beaufort hounds passed into his possession, he used to hunt six days each week. He hunted the largest hunting country in England, and sometimes found it necessary to have two packs of hounds out on the same day in different parts of his country.

A man of gentle, simple nature, the 9th Duke could, on occasions, be a stern disciplinarian, especially in the hunting field. On one occasion he even went so far as to take his hounds home in order to teach some rather too enthusiastic members of his field a lesson.

Although he was a good horseman, the 9th Duke was little given to jumping fences, and although he was always very well mounted, he preferred observing good hound work to galloping wildly across country. Remarkably, he never lost touch with his hounds, and always managed to provide the members of his Hunt with first-class sport. Unlike his father, the 9th Duke took no interest at all in racing, nor, indeed, in shooting, his hounds taking up the greater part of his time when he was not actually hunting.

This all-consuming interest in hunting left him little time for other activities, although he did at one time take up polo when the sport was in its infancy in England, playing both at Lillee Bridge and Hurlingham. The ninth volume of *The Badminton Library* series on *Polo*, gives the following description of his prowess on the polo ground, where he "displayed all those qualities which have since characterised him as a huntsman, being very enthusiastic, quick and hard-working. His great height, however—he was 6 foot 4 inches—told somewhat heavily against him, but he was always there or thereabouts in a 'bully', and his quickness of observation, besides his good horsemanship, made him a formidable antagonist."

The 9th Duke of Beaufort was apparently a man of few words, with a dislike of appearing in public. Indeed, he had little time for social activities, other than those affairs, such as the annual Farmers' Dinner, where he regularly presided over his friends, the hunting farmers of the Beaufort country. Like his predecessors, he held strong Conservative opinions, which he could, on occasion, express forcibly in a practical manner and with a great deal of common sense but, unfortunately, these utterances were seldom recorded.

The Duke's appearances in the House of Lords were infrequent, and when he did attend it was to give a silent vote. He also took little interest in politics, either national or county, his all-consuming interest being hunting.

On 27 November 1924, after some weeks of failing health, the 9th Duke of Beaufort died "of complications following an attack of gout". For two generations he had hunted the Beaufort hounds and had become perhaps the greatest figure among English foxhunters.

In his obituary, it was written that 'the death of the 9th Duke of Beaufort is indeed a loss to English foxhunting which may well be recorded in the West of England as almost irreplaceable". Almost irreplaceable, but not quite—for the 9th Duke's son and heir, the then Marquess of Worcester, was to prove every bit as passionate a foxhunter as his father had been.

10th Duke of Beaufort, b. *1900*

Henry Hugh Arthur FitzRoy Somerset, 10th Duke of Beaufort, was born on 4th April, 1900. He was educated at Westminster School, Eton, and the Royal Military College at Sandhurst. In 1921, while still a subaltern in the Royal Horse Guards, he hunted the Beaufort hounds for the first time. Within a very short time, he was recognised as the best amateur huntsman in England.

In 1924, in addition to his title and estates, the Duke of Beaufort also inherited eighty couple of the best foxhounds in the world and a family reputation in the hunting world which was second to none. For the next forty-three years he hunted the hounds himself, and by virtue of his hunting and sporting activities (he is interested in both fishing and shooting, and as a young man frequently rode in point-to-points) he became the best-known sporting nobleman in England.

In January 1930, the Duke of Beaufort was created GCVO (Grand Cross of the Victorian Order). In October 1936 he was sworn to the Privy Council, and in May 1937 he was created a Knight of the Garter. He has also been the recipient of numerous honours from overseas, including the following: The Grand Cross of the Legion of Honour (France); the Grand Cross of Leopold (Belgium); the Grand Cross of the Order of Faithful Service (Rumania); the Grand Cross of the Order of the House of Orange (and Grand Officer of the Order of Orange Nassau) (Netherlands); the Grand Cross of the Order of St. Olav (Norway), the Grand Cross of the Order of Dannebrog (Denmark), the Grand Cross of the Order of the North Star (Sweden); the Grand Cross of the Order of Menelik II (Ethiopia), and the Grand Cross of the Order of Christ (Portugal).

His Grace is an Honorary member of the Masters of Foxhounds Association of America, and many of the American foxhound packs can boast that they own draft hounds from the Beaufort Kennels or that their breeding pattern is based on Beaufort hound blood-lines.

One of His Grace's many trips abroad led to a curious report in a Toronto newspaper. Whilst foxhunting in Canada, the Duke and Duchess of Beaufort were allowed to "go first", i.e., to lead the field. The local newspaper, however, came up with the startling piece of information that "His Grace had led the fox". On this particular visit to Canada, His Grace met a great many expatriates from Gloucestershire, all of whom were anxious to learn how the hunting was going at home—proof that Beaufort Hunt supporters are to be found all over the world.

It was once said that members of the Duke's hunting field have always regarded themselves as a sort of chosen people amongst foxhunters—and they have every reason to do so, for it has been the Duke of Beaufort who has set the standards of hound breeding and hunting in Great Britain as well as abroad. His Grace is known affectionately as "Master" and has now become so much a part of the Gloucestershire countryside that it is sometimes known as "Beaufortshire". However, as his Agent, Mr E. M. Mitchell, once remarked, "His Grace's activities in the hunting field are only a part of His Grace as a countryman." For the Duke is also a farmer and takes an active interest in the farming and management of his 52,000-acre estate. He is extremely knowledgeable concerning forestry and, of course, takes an active part in the organisation and administration of the Beaufort Hunt.

The Duke also attends most, if not all, of the Hunt and Hunt Supporters' Club business and social events. A man of seemingly inexhaustible energy, at seventy-eight years of age, he still hunts on at least two days a week, answers his own letters, and carries out a wide variety of public and social engagements, which would exhaust most men of half his age.

He is known to millions of television viewers as the "tall man who escorts the Queen and the other members of the Royal Family around Badminton" during the Badminton Horse Trials—an event which he instituted in 1949, and which has done so much both to improve and to popularise equestrian sports in England as well as laying the foundation for British success in the Olympic Games.

The list of associations and societies with which His Grace has been, and in some cases still is, actively concerned is seemingly endless. These include his duties as Master of the Beaufort Hunt, President of the Federation of Boys' Clubs (he is especially fond of boxing: his godfather, incidentally, was Lord Lonsdale of the Lonsdale Belt fame and, while at Sandhurst, His Grace was taught boxing by the champion boxer, Jimmy Wilde), President of M.C.C., President of Gloucestershire County Cricket Club, President of the British Olympic Association, President of Bristol Rovers' Football Club (although he confesses that he does not get time to watch as much football as he would like as he is usually busy on Saturday afternoons during the hunting season), President of the Masters of Foxhounds Association, President of the British Field Sports Society, President of the British Horse Society, President of the Royal Agricultural Society, as well as many other organisations too numerous to mention.

His Grace has also been President of the Battersea Dogs' Home, and as an example of his interest he once took a stray dog from the Home to live at Badminton. "I felt so sorry for it that I brought it home. We call it Tory. It came here at the same time that Mr Heath got in."

As well as taking part in these seemingly endless outside activities, the Duke of Beaufort also takes a keen interest in the more parochial aspects of Badminton. He is, for example, the longest-serving church warden in Gloucestershire, and is on the Badminton Parish Council and the Committee of the Badminton Social Club.

However, these are only some of the many calls upon his time since there are also His Grace's public offices and appointments, many of which call for his special attention. For example, he was Master of the Horse for over forty years before he resigned the office in 1978—the longest-serving holder of this office. He is also High Steward of Bristol and Tewkesbury, and Lord Lieutenant of Gloucester and Bristol.

On the 14 June, 1923, the Duke of Beaufort (then Marquess of Worcester) married Lady Mary Cambridge whom he had met whilst out hunting. The wedding took place at St. Margaret's, Westminster, and was very much a Royal occasion, numbering among the guests King George V and Queen Mary, as well as Queen Alexandra. The Duchess of Beaufort is a niece of Queen Mary, who was the sister of the Duchess's father, the Marquess of Cambridge, and is a direct descendant of George III. As can be seen from the family tree, the Duke of Beaufort is descended from John of Gaunt, the son of Edward III.

In the August of 1923 the young Lord and Lady Worcester returned to Badminton, where they received a tremendous welcome. The Reverend T. T. Gibson, Vicar of Badminton, has pointed out that during the 1920s the Duke of Beaufort was virtually a "king" at Badminton, and contemporary accounts* of the homecoming of the

---

* *The Wilts. and Gloucestershire Standard*, 1923.

newly-wed Marquess and Marchioness of Worcester would certainly seem to bear this out.

"When it was known that the young Lord and Lady Worcester would arrive early on Monday evening by train, arrangements were immediately set on foot to give them a reception good and hearty. The village streets were gaily bedecked with flags, and emblems and streamers spanned the roads leading from the railway station. There were several very effective designs—one particularly striking: it was a broad strip of the Beaufort Hunt Cloth bearing a fox's mask in the centre and a couple of [fox] brushes on either side. The village was agog with excitement as the time for the train's arrival—6.40—drew near. Hundreds of people assembled at the station where the Station Master was master of ceremonies. A limousine with its hood down drew up at the exit from the platform and to it were attached two long ropes. As the train entered the station, a score or so of detonators proclaimed the occasion, and the appearance of Lord and Lady Worcester was the signal for a burst of cheering and the waving of hats and handkerchiefs. The young couple were then escorted to the waiting limousine and, the Marquess having taken his place behind the wheel, thirty of the oldest hands on the Badminton Estate manned the ropes and in the good old style dragged the young couple to the house. [Badminton House was approximately one mile from the station.] On the bonnet of the car was a large black cat and the headlamps were decorated with the family Hunt colours, the Blue and Buff."

At Badminton House, the procession was greeted by the 9th Duke of Beaufort, the Duchess of Beaufort, and Lady Diana Somerset (Lord Worcester's sister). Then "the car was pulled along the drive to the front of the house, and in response to repeated cheers Lord Worcester expressed his and Lady Worcester's appreciation". The festivities were kept up well into the night and there was dancing on the lawn in front of the house "to the strains of the Chipping Sodbury Quarry Band".

While on the subject of dances and dancing, there is a delightful account * of a Beaufort Hunt Ball, which took place at Chippenham in January of the following year. "Over five hundred people attended and the scene was a brilliant one. The hall and precincts were lavishly decorated. The interior of the room was draped with Blue and Buff, and the floor was covered with Oriental carpets, while lounges and settees were provided in Blue to match. The dances included waltzes and foxtrots to various tunes, including 'Broadway Blues', 'Toot-Toot-Tootsie', 'Cat's Whiskers', 'Runnin' Wild', 'Ten-Ten-Tennessee'—

* *The Wilts. and Gloucestershire Standard*, 1924.

ending with a One Step and Gallop to the tune of 'John Peel'. The guests included Her Grace, the Duchess of Beaufort, the Countess of St. Germans,* Lady Diana Somerset, and the Marquess and Marchioness of Worcester."

In November of that same year, 1924, the 9th Duke of Beaufort died of the "family enemy"—gout. He was succeeded by his only son, whom he had watched since 1921 developing into a first-class huntsman, and it no doubt gave him pleasure in his last years to know that the Beaufort Hunt and hounds were in such capable hands.

The present Duke of Beaufort has, during his lifetime, seen more social and technological changes than his nine predecessors saw in almost 250 years. He has had to adapt to continually diminishing standards, for as the standard of living of the rest of us has steadily improved, that of the aristocracy has correspondingly decreased. This is the way of the world and, for the great mass of the people, it is no doubt a good thing, but for a young man, born into great riches, inheriting a dukedom as well as vast estates at the age of twenty-four, a virtual "king" in his own country, the gradual acceptance of new standards must have been difficult.

As the Vicar of Badminton comments, "At that particular time— the twenties—he was a very powerful person, and the whole class structure was very much more definite. Ordinary mortals dared not even approach him, and now he has had to adapt to complete and utter change. To drive your own motor car and not to have fifty servants in the house was unthinkable."

In 1836, as shown on page 76, there were sixty servants of one kind or another actually working in the house. During the Golden Wedding celebrations of the present Duke and Duchess, in 1973, Her Grace, commenting upon the changes she had seen at Badminton, and recalling that there used to be sixteen housemaids on duty at Badminton when she first went there, said: "Now we have only four excellent dailies to look after this large house."

Nowadays, as His Grace recently commented, there is a very small staff. "We have the butler and an under-butler with him, and the rest is done by the housekeeper and the ladies in the village who come up every day. Of course, when we have the Queen coming to stay and other members of the Royal Family, we have to increase the staff." However, as Lady Caroline Somerset has pointed out, "Not many people have a butler these days, let alone a footman and odd-job man so, by today's standards, there are plenty of people." She does add, though, "By the standards of the old days, it is incredible how few there are."

*Formerly Lady Blanche Somerset, the 10th Duke's eldest sister.

Badminton House, although by comparison with other stately homes not really a very big house, does have to be kept in first-class order, since not only are the Queen and other members of the Royal Family frequent guests, but the house is also open to the public on every Wednesday throughout the summer months (from May until September), attracting visitors from all over the world. Although Badminton House is open to the public, it is by no means a museum and is, in fact, the only country house of its size in England today which is lived in the whole year round.

It is a friendly, comfortable house, and when being shown over it, visitors are always likely to meet either the Duke or the Duchess walking through a room or a corridor, as often as not accompanied by their dogs. There are many homely touches which would seem out of place in some stately homes, but at Badminton they only tend to enhance the feeling that this is a house which is lived in. For example, in the Library, next to a portion of the doublet of John of Gaunt, there is a collection of Beatrix Potter animal figures, while an open copy of Kenneth Clark's *Civilisation* lies on an armchair near the chimney-piece. In an upstairs bedroom, two beautiful Georgian china urns live side by side with three little china ornaments of crinolined ladies which were bought at a local bazaar, and there are always attractive arrangements of flowers everywhere in the house.

Lady Caroline Somerset, who lived at Badminton House for some time, has described her own feelings about it as follows:

"It is a home first—a stately home second. It is very much a home, more so than any other house I know. It has never been 'done over' by a decorator, and its character has remained, with slight additions, during each generation. Somebody has acquired a new picture, somebody has hung new curtains. Family possessions have just accumulated. Sometimes things that aren't very pretty—'We keep that because old Aunt Enid was fond of it'—that sort of thing. Of course, one takes pride in the Grinling Gibbons and in admiring the beautiful pictures, but it is *not* a museum."

Colonel Weldon, Director of the Badminton Horse Trials, has paid tribute to His Grace's intrepidity when riding across country, but even the best horsemen must come to grief occasionally. The Duke is no exception, and he has suffered dozens of falls during his long riding career. He does, however, seem to possess remarkable powers of recovery. For example, as a young man, when riding in a Beaufort Hunt point-to-point, he suffered a crashing fall, damaging his sciatic nerve. A contemporary report of the incident concluded, "an unfortunate accident which will keep him out of the saddle for several days".

In 1957, whilst out hunting, he was thrown over his horse's head, landing heavily on his back, and suffered neck and back injuries. He was taken to hospital, where he was examined by a spine specialist who described his condition as "being generally satisfactory", and it was thought that "no bones were broken".

In 1967, at the age of sixty-seven, the Duke of Beaufort regretfully decided to give up hunting the Beaufort hounds himself, although remaining as Joint-Master. *The Wilts. and Gloucestershire Standard*, commenting upon this decision, was careful to point out that it had "nothing to do with a recent fall in the hunting field when the Duke broke two ribs and cracked another when he was kicked in the chest by a horse". Following this incident, the Duke was soon out hunting again (see page 140). Major Gerald Gundry, Joint-Master of the Beaufort Hunt from 1951 until 1978, who has hunted with His Grace under all sorts of conditions, has described him as "a very tough man indeed".

The Duke is never happier than when he is out hunting, and like his father, grandfather and great-grandfather, he will find an alternative means of transport if he is unable to ride in order to follow the Hunt. On one occasion, having been discharged from hospital following treatment for a damaged knee, he was told not to ride for a while. He did ride, however, and damaged the knee again while out cubbing. Much incensed, he ordered a pony to be harnessed to a little Victoria and, with David Somerset as his navigator, he kept up with the field in a remarkable manner. One member of the field commented, "I didn't know whether to watch the hounds or 'Master'; it was great fun."

To many people, the present Duke of Beaufort *is* Badminton. His Agent once described the Duke as "the eyes and ears and everything of Badminton". The Vicar of Badminton thinks that "he has blended into the background to such an extent that he has become part of the place".

It is true that little escapes his notice. It is also true that however busy he may be, he always has time to help people in trouble. One elderly villager remembers that when his wife died "the Duke was the first one to come and offer his sympathy". Recently, one of the grooms at Badminton was kicked in the face by a horse, and as soon as the Duke heard about it, he dropped everything, got straight into his Land Rover, and went down to see the man. "There's no nonsense about him," said the Vicar.

His Grace is always prepared to take part in village activities, especially those connected with the raising of money for charity. On one occasion he attended a fancy dress ball, in aid of the Church funds, dressed as a brigand; the Duchess accompanied him, dressed as an able-seaman. Major Gundry went as a clown. During the Silver Jubilee year, His Grace campaigned vigorously in order to raise money for the Silver Jubilee Fund. One of the many fund-raising activities was an auction which was held at Badminton House at which several of His Grace's own possessions were sold.

Since it is impossible for any one to go through life without making some enemies, the opponents of foxhunting—described by one Master of Foxhounds as "the sort of fellows who wear plimsolls"—would no doubt have a lot to say on the subject of the Duke and the Beaufort Hunt. Amongst hunting and country people, particularly in Gloucestershire and Wiltshire, it is very rare indeed to find anybody who criticises "Master". That is not to say, of course, that he does not come in for his fair share of affectionate abuse—what Master or Huntsman does not? There is, for example, the story of one tenant farmer who was talking to some friends at a horse show, when the Duke's name was mentioned. Asked his opinion of His Grace, the farmer replied: "He's a wonderful man—a great sportsman, a charming man, and a great gentleman, but when he gets that green coat on, he's the biggest devil in creation." And yet on one occasion, while wearing "that green coat", he noticed a small boy in difficulties trying to mount his pony. Immediately His Grace went to the boy's assistance, holding the pony while the boy re-mounted.

Mrs Marjorie Barker, who for many years has hunted with the Beaufort, is convinced that it is because of dozens of little acts of kindness such as this that the Duke is held in such great affection by the people who know him. "His behaviour is an object lesson to many younger Masters, because he takes the trouble to help a small boy, or to stop and chat to a chap mowing his lawn, or to recognise and acknowledge an old friend or hunting acquaintance whom he hasn't seen for many years."

On one occasion, for example, Mrs Barker, who had been living in North Devon for a time, met His Grace when he travelled to that part of the country to address a Hunt Supporters' Club. Mrs Barker expressed a wish to have a day out with the Beaufort Hunt. The Duke replied, "Yes, do—we are always glad to see old faces." After a pause, His Grace said, "Oh, dear, perhaps I shouldn't have put it quite like that."

The Duke of Beaufort's Hunt has a tradition of welcoming genuine foxhunters from whatever station in life. In an article he wrote, dealing with Masters and Huntsmen,* the Duke explained: "Those who support hunting are welcome, whether mounted and in a red coat, on

---

* *In Praise of Hunting*, edited by David James and Wilson Stephens.

foot, or sedentary in a motor car. Country folk feel a pride in their local packs, talk of 'our hounds' and everybody feels a proprietary interest which soon becomes infectious."

The members of the Beaufort Hunt and those country people in the surrounding areas are proud of His Grace, talk of "our Duke", "Master", and lately even speak of him as "Father". They take a great interest in the Duke and all he stands for.

To many people, especially those who live in towns and who know nothing of the ways of the countryside and of hunting, the Duke of Beaufort must appear to be something of an anachronism—a man of title and property, who hunts his hounds to please himself. "Something like a General Postman, riding about the country, surrounded by dogs, whooping, halloaing, and blowing a horn."* What they do not always see is the other side of the coin—the great tradition of public service he represents and the public duties he fulfils. For the Duke is a man who, having no *need* to work, works that much harder than the rest of us and invariably for somebody else's benefit.

In 1965 it was announced that the Duke of Beaufort was to become Chancellor of Bristol University. At the time, there was much criticism of the appointment and the inevitable student demonstrations took place. Undeterred, the Duke fulfilled his term of office and proved to be one of the best and most popular chancellors that the university has ever elected. Not for nothing is the family motto "I scorn to fear a change".

At seventy-eight years of age, the Duke of Beaufort is still carrying out his numerous public engagements and still hunting as often as possible during the season. Long may he continue to do so!

MASTER OF THE HORSE

On Friday, 11 June 1976, on the evening before the annual Birthday Parade and Trooping the Colour, Her Majesty the Queen and the Duke of Edinburgh held a reception at Buckingham Palace. The reason for the reception was to celebrate the fortieth anniversary of the Duke of Beaufort's appointment as Master of the Horse, an appointment which he had held between 1936 and 1978.

To mark the occasion, Her Majesty the Queen presented the Duke of Beaufort with a specially commissioned portrait, painted by Mr Terence Cuneo. The picture, which was commissioned following subscriptions collected from two hundred persons associated with the Royal Household, shows the Duke of Beaufort wearing the full ceremonial dress of the Royal Office and mounted on Quebec, a 17-hand grey police horse. Her Majesty and Prince Philip, dressed in their

Handley Cross by R. S. Surtees.

uniforms ready for the Trooping the Colour ceremony, are also to be seen as they descend some steps from Buckingham Palace into the Courtyard.

Mr Cuneo, incidentally, is well-known for his habit of "signing" his pictures with a small mouse, and this portrait is no exception. A careful study of the picture, which is reproduced as illustration no. 11, will reveal a tiny mouse, dressed in the uniform of the Crown Equerry, Colonel Sir John Miller.

In earlier times, the duties and responsibilities of the Master of the Horse were far greater than they are today. "To him is committed the charge of ordering and disposing all matters relating to the king's stables, races, breed of horses as he had anciently of all the Posts in England. He hath the power of commanding all the equerries and all other officers and tradesmen employed in the King's stables." Today, the duties are somewhat less onerous, the details being attended to by the Crown Equerry, who is responsible for the smooth running of the Royal Mews. However, this is not to say that the office is purely a sinecure.

According to the present Duke, "The duties are chiefly ceremonial. They do, however, include being on duty with Her Majesty on a number of occasions. I very much enjoy being Master of Horse. The Queen is a very good and knowledgeable judge of horses and a very good rider and, therefore, she knows what's what, and that makes it all the more interesting and I do my best to make everything as comfortable for her as it is possible to do."

The present Duke of Beaufort was the seventy-fifth holder of the Royal Office of Master of the Horse. He held the office for forty-two years, longer than any of his predecessors. The previous longest serving Master of the Horse was Robert Dudley, Earl of Leicester, who served from 1558 until 1588, this appointment having been made by Queen Elizabeth I on her succession to the Throne.

The Royal Officer of Master of the Horse is one of the three great Offices of the Royal Household—the other two being that of the Lord Chamberlain and of the Lord Steward. The Office dates back to the reign of Edward III, and it was at the time of the Duke's great ancestor, John of Gaunt, that the Office of Keeper to the Royal Stables became known as Master of the Horse.

The present Duke of Beaufort was not the only member of his family to hold this great office. The 4th Earl of Worcester, was for a time (1597–1601) Master of the Horse to Elizabeth I, and actually led the State Palfrey at her funeral in 1601. The 5th Duke of Beaufort was Master of the Horse from 1768 until 1770 to the Queen Consort, Charlotte, the wife of George III.

The present Duke's grandfather, the 8th Duke of Beaufort, was Master of the Horse to Queen Victoria, a position which, according to Lady Clodagh Anson,* was not without its problems. "Grandpa Beaufort told me that when he was Master of Horse to Queen Victoria it was often rather difficult to arrange. Some footman would contrive to upset a few coals when the Queen was in the room, and then proceed to apologise most humbly, thus getting into conversation with her. The Queen would graciously ask him after his family, and he promptly began by saying that his brother, or nephew, was hoping so much to be able to serve her, the result being that she would express a wish to Grandpa that this man should be taken on as one of the coachmen. In vain he suggested that the man did not know how to drive. The Queen waved that away, and just said she wished it."

The 8th Duke fell foul of the Queen's famous Scottish servant, John Brown, on a State occasion which Lady Clodagh Anson has described, as follows: "One day he [the 8th Duke] was arming Queen Victoria into her carriage when John Brown pushed by him and tried to take his place. However, he did not succeed, and later on Grandpa got a rather rambling message from the Queen saying that John Brown was a very old and privileged servant and so on, and he noticed that for some time after this incident her manner was rather cold towards him."

High office, it seems, often brings unexpected problems and the phrase "however, he did not succeed", conjures up delightful visions of these two most faithful servants of Queen Victoria in silent struggle for possession of the Royal arm.

In addition to his own ancestors' association with the Office of Master of the Horse, the present Duke of Beaufort has another link with it, for Her Grace, the Duchess of Beaufort is herself descended from an earlier Master of the Horse, being the grand-daughter of the 1st Duke of Westminster, who held the Office from 1880 until 1885.

A delightful tribute to the Duke of Beaufort's forty years as Master of the Horse took place in July 1976, at the Royal International Horse Show at Wembley (an event which His Grace has presided over for thirty years). A special pageant, depicting some of the most famous holders of the Royal Office, was arranged by Mr Dorian Williams, MFH. Many famous personalities in the horse world took part in the event. Among the Masters depicted were the Duke of Richmond (surely the youngest ever Master of the Horse)—a natural son of Charles II, he was appointed to the Office at the age of ten; the Duke of Monmouth, who led the rising against William of Orange; George Villiers, Duke of Buckingham; Sir Thomas Tyrell, and many others.

**Victorian Days.*

The part of the 8th Duke of Beaufort was played by Edward Somerset, son of the present Duke's heir, Mr David Somerset.

On Sunday, 4 September 1977, a special celebration—"A tribute to the Master of the Horse"—was held at Badminton, all the proceeds going to the Queen's Silver Jubilee appeal fund. Thousands of people from all over Great Britain attended, including a variety of famous people connected with horses of every kind. There were representatives from ten hunts, as well as hundreds of people from riding clubs and schools all over the country. Following a short service held by the Vicar of Badminton, the Reverend T. Gibson, on the lawn in front of Badminton House, some three hundred riders paraded past the Duke of Beaufort in an affectionate tribute to the man who has perhaps done more to encourage equestrianism in Great Britain than anyone.

The impressive programme produced for this occasion had on its cover a beautiful photograph of the Duke of Beaufort (taken by Mr Peter Harding) in the uniform of the Master of the Horse—a red tunic slashed with gold, with gold epaulettes, white breeches and gloves, long black riding boots with gold spurs, and a cocked hat with white plumes. On his chest, the Duke is wearing the Order of the Garter as well as many other decorations and medals.

To those people who attended the event, it would have seemed inconceivable that barely six months later the Duke of Beaufort would no longer hold the Office of Master of the Horse. Sadly, this was to prove the case, for in March 1978 it was announced that his Grace was to relinquish the office for reasons of health. There is no doubt that the Silver Jubilee year must have imposed a great strain upon the Duke, the Office requiring the Master of the Horse to attend as senior personal attendant to the Sovereign on all State occasions when horses are used.

When the Duke of Beaufort's numerous other commitments, in his capacity as Privy Councillor, Lord Lieutenant of Gloucestershire (and those living in the county can testify that no one has worked harder to raise money for the Silver Jubilee appeal fund) are considered, it was indeed a remarkable achievement for someone approaching his seventy-eighth birthday, to have undertaken the duties of Master of the Horse in Silver Jubilee year. He has been succeeded in the Office by the Earl of Westmorland, who lives in the Beaufort country and who hunts with the Duke of Beaufort's hounds. Lord Westmorland, who competed in the first Badminton Horse Trials in 1949, is the third member of his family to hold the Office.

PART III

The Blue and the Buff

"You will see the werry finest pack of hounds in all England: I don't care where the next best are: and you will get as good a turn-out as ever you saw in your life, and as nice a country to ride over as ever you were in."

R. S. Surtees in *Jorrocks' Jaunts and Jollities*

"THERE is no place in the British Isles where the spirit of the chase breathes so naturally as at Badminton": an observation which is as true today as it was when it was first written by Lord Willoughby de Broke in 1924. For Badminton is to foxhunting as Newmarket is to racing—"the Headquarters"—and few foxhunters would deny the present Duke of Beaufort the title of "Britain's Number One Foxhunter", which was bestowed upon him by Michael Clayton, editor of *Horse and Hound*. (Incidentally, one of His Grace's cars bears the number plate MFH 1.)

In fact, one of the first impressions which any visitor to Badminton receives is of the large number of foxes—real and otherwise—which inhabit the place. The weathervanes on both the Kennels and the Stables are cut-out foxes; two models of foxes stand at the entrance to the Kennels; in the entrance hall of Badminton House the supporters on the decorative wall panels are foxes; in a small sitting-room a fox brush hangs from a fox mask and bears the inscription "His Grace's 5,000th fox"; in the same room are several model and toy foxes; there is even a signed photograph of the puppet, "Basil Brush"! All of which bring to mind John Jorrocks's remark: "It aren't that I loves the fox the less but that I loves the 'ound more." Indeed, the fox could well be the symbol of Badminton and, according to one source, at one time any employee, either direct or indirect, was obliged to raise his cap or touch his forelock to any fox sighted on the Estate, under threat of disciplinary action.

"A fox living in hunting country is fortunate indeed", wrote Jack Ivester Lloyd,* and in these days, when the opponents of hunting tend more and more to acts of senseless violence, it is perhaps worthwhile to include the rest of his paragraph. "The chance that he will meet a miserable end together with whatever other creatures may be in the same earth are less likely than in a district where no hounds are kept. It is to be hoped that he will not have his limbs mangled by traps, nor die of festering gunshot wounds. Nor I hope will he perish agonisingly by poison or with a snare round his neck."

The exact date when foxhunting actually began in Great Britain is a matter of some speculation. Popular belief has it that it all started during the middle of the eighteenth century, ("Cecil", pseudonym of the sporting writer, Cornelius Tongue, gives the date as 1762), when Henry, the 5th Duke of Beaufort, returning one day to Badminton after a disappointing day's stag-hunting, threw his hounds into Silk Wood, where they found a fox which gave them such a good run that thereafter the Duke decided to hunt the fox exclusively. Popular belief, however, is not always strictly accurate.

Hounds of Britain

Mrs Horatia Durant, in her book, *The Somerset Sequence*, points out that "One Thomas Coke, Great Uncle of Coke of Norfolk, deliberately planted fox coverts twenty years before the Fifth Duke (of Beaufort) was born." And in a letter to *Horse and Hound* in 1968, Mrs Durant wrote of a letter which she had discovered at Badminton, written by the 3rd Marquess of Worcester (created 1st Duke of Beaufort by Charles II). Apparently the Marquess was complaining in a letter to his wife in 1667 that he had been told nothing about the foxhounds by Drake (presumably the huntsman). He goes on to say: "I wish I had enough to spare the Prince of Orange some for he is mighty desirous to get a good pack."

Miss Daphne Moore, a leading authority and writer on hounds and hunting, in her *Book of the Foxhound*, states that ". . . in 1743 the list includes thirty-two couple of deerhounds and one couple of foxhounds. This is the first mention of foxhounds in the Duke of Beaufort's Kennel, and is some twenty years prior to the classic and widely quoted story of the Fifth Duke."

Jack Ivester Lloyd writes that: "Records of the Goathland Hunt go back to 1650" and that "another pack, the Bilsdale, claims to be the oldest purely foxhunting establishment in Britain".

Volume VII of the *Lonsdale Sporting Library* quotes a writer in the *New Sporting Magazine* (1832) who unearthed from "the accounts of the Comptroller of the Wardrobe to Edward I for the years 1299 to 1300 some facts and figures" from which he concludes: "We may form some estimate of the small degree of repute in which foxhunting, if indeed hunting it can be called, was held at that period. The fox destroying establishment of that Monarch consisted of twelve 'fox dogs (terriers not unlikely) with one man and two boys. The master of these fox dogs and his two assistants were allowed sixpence per day and three pence a day for a horse to carry the nets, while one halfpenny per day was allowed for the keep of each of the dogs'. The writer opined that the whole concern savoured of rat-catching, and it certainly bears little relation to the matter of serious foxhunting." Even so, it is an interesting description of an early hunting "establishment", and might perhaps account for the high opinion which terriers have of themselves, in view of the fact that they have probably been at the business longer than anyone else.

No doubt the question of how and when the whole thing started will remain a matter of argument and conjecture for as long as men and women continue to hunt the fox. As T. F. Dale wrote in his book, *The 8th Duke of Beaufort and the Badminton Hunt* (1901): "There is, in fact, no period at which we can positively say that foxhunting began; the sport as we know it grew up as the result chiefly of the decay of staghunting, owing to the increase of enclosures. No doubt the fox has been hunted occasionally from an early date, and by no family earlier than the Somersets." And, certainly, no one has pursued the fox with such single-minded devotion and enthusiasm as have the successive Dukes of Beaufort since the time of the 5th Duke.

It is difficult to decide whether foxhunting was invented for the benefit of the Dukes of Beaufort, or whether the Dukes of Beaufort were invented to hunt the fox.

Although it is highly likely that foxes were hunted at an earlier date than the Silk Wood episode, it was from this time—the middle of the eighteenth century—that foxhunting began to develop into a national sport. There were a number of reasons for this. In the first place, changing agricultural methods and the enclosure of common tillage and pasture land resulted in more fences, field boundaries, hedges and walls—hence more obstacles to be jumped. Also, the importation some fifty years earlier of Arabian stallions had resulted in a better breed of horse. Riders to hounds, therefore, required a somewhat faster quarry than the deer or the hare, and the fox was ideally suited to the purpose by virtue of its speed, cunning, and elusiveness. As Colonel John Cook wrote in 1826: "What makes foxhunting far superior to others is the wildness of the animal you hunt and the difficulty in catching him."

Not all the hunting men of the time, however, were in favour of the new style of sport which was gradually developing. The Hon. John Byng complained, in 1781, that "Gloucestershire was spoilt for hunting by virtue of the new stone walls", while a contemporary of his commented that hunting would become a "hopping in and out clever sort of thing all day".

But foxhunting has a curious way of adapting to changing circumstances and conditions, which is no doubt why it has lasted for so long. As packs of hounds which had been more used to hunting the deer or the hare took to hunting the fox, it soon became apparent that there was still one other element required before hunting could develop properly. This was, of course, a hound which could match the fox for speed, for foxhunting in its infancy was a slow business. Indeed, hounds would meet at the break of day and follow the overnight trail of a fox. In order to do this, long open tracts of country were necessary (another argument against the Enclosure Act). The Victorian novelist, Anthony Trollope, wrote of this early style of foxhunting: "It may be doubted whether men who think that the cream of hunting is to be found only in a fast run almost without a check, and with a kill in the open, would enjoy the sport as it existed. Even at the end of the last century, hounds had not been trained to run with the speed which is now attained, nor had the profession of hunting produced men skilled in casting when the hounds were at fault as is done now. There was no great crowd, and the fox had a better chance when there were few or none to halloa him. The hounds were obliged to puzzle out their own quarry; men were more patient than they are now."*

To those who especially enjoy watching hounds work, it sounds most attractive, and one wonders what Trollope would have made of today's hunting, with its squadrons of attendant motor cars, ever ready to head foxes, block gateways, and commit all sorts of nuisance.

As for halloaing, it seems almost an impossibility for the majority of people to view a fox without making some sort of noise. The 8th Duke of Beaufort was constantly troubled by this, and his hunting diaries are full of remarks, such as: "Mr S. . . . (confound him) halloaed us on to a fresh one"; and, again: "The longer I hunt the more I value silence on the part of everyone in the field except the huntsman".

The first man to breed hounds for speed as well as nose was Hugo Meynell of Quorndon Hall in Leicestershire, who hunted from 1753–1800 in what is now known as the Quorn country. So successful were his methods that soon other Masters followed suit, not the least being the successive Dukes of Beaufort. T. F. Dale wrote about the Beaufort hounds in *Country Life*, dated October 1913: "The history of the pack at Badminton is that of the development of the English foxhound. We can trace (whereas in others we can only guess) the influence of the various lines of blood which have resulted in the blend we know as the modern foxhound."

Since foxhunting began, there have always been those who saw its continued existence as being threatened, and yet it has always managed to adapt itself to new and changing circumstances and conditions, such as the introduction of enclosures, canals, railways, motorised transport, road and motorway networks. One of hunting's great strengths is, of course, the fact that of all sports it is one of the most democratic and, as such, it is part of the very fabric of English country life.

And yet, foxhunting is often criticised because it is thought to be the exclusive pastime of the very rich and of what used to be known as the Upper Classes. However, as anyone with even a little experience of the sport knows this is nonsense. Lord Willoughby de Broke, describing this aspect of hunting, wrote: "If foxhunting had been based on exclusiveness, it would have deservedly perished long ago."

Any countryman is well aware that a hunt is made up of a wide range of types, classes and professions. Anthony Trollope wrote: "The non-hunting world is apt to think that hunting is confined to country gentlemen, farmers and rich strangers, but anyone will find that there

British Sports and Pastimes edited by Anthony Trollope, 1868.

are in the crowd attorneys, country bankers, doctors, maltsters, millers, butchers, bakers, innkeepers, auctioneers, graziers, builders, stockbrokers, newspaper editors, artists and sailors." Trollope doesn't mention parsons or clergymen in this list, although elsewhere he has written: "I own that I like the hunting parson. I generally find him to be about the pleasantest man in the field." Of course, it has been known for hunting parsons to come in for a certain amount of criticism from time to time, but one Prelate is said to have stated that he didn't mind his clergy hunting as long as they didn't "tally ho!"

E. W. Bovill, the historian, has pointed out one of the advantages which field sports and the like give the countryman over the townsman. "The simple social structure of the countryside was held together by the sharing of common interests; the love of land, of field and of pastimes, of the village green, in all of which every class could play a part. The far more complex structure of the towns lacked, as it has always lacked, the humanising influence of common interests which override social differences."

The familiar caricature of the red-faced, red-necked choleric and brutish aristocrat riding roughshod over the peasantry in pursuit of his quarry is, therefore, very much a fiction. This is not to deny that there have been such men, as witness Lady Palmerston's description of Lord and Lady Euston: ". . . a nice bouncing milkmaid married to a hunting brute little better than his dogs".

But these are individuals and not types representative of the whole hunting field. "By and large", as one member of the V.W.H. Hunt was heard to remark after being introduced to a writer, "all sorts come out hunting".

The Beaufort Hunt has always enjoyed a reputation for being democratic. "The hospitality at Badminton and each Duke's devotion to the sport gradually gave it a special place in English life. The hunting there was a democratic institution that noblemen and chimney sweeps enjoyed together, equally welcome provided they were good sportsmen. Somersets, in fact, were democratic before the word was on everybody's lips."*

The bracketing together of "noblemen and chimney sweeps" might prove puzzling to anyone unfamiliar with the history of the Beaufort Hunt. But in the 1830s, a certain Mr Vizard, a chimney sweep by profession, often hunted with the Beaufort, and became quite famous as "the Sporting Sweep of Chipping Sodbury—wot 'unts with the Duke". According to one source, Mr Vizard was always certain of a mount from the 7th Duke whenever he wanted one.

There is a famous engraving of Mr Vizard by R. B. Davis which

* *The Somerset Sequence.*

shows him on horseback carrying his sweep's brush under his arm. Legend has it that one day, as they were returning from a great run, the Duke of Beaufort asked the sweep if he had been in at the death. "There are strong symptoms of it," Vizard is alleged to have replied, "for your Grace may perceive that I have got the brush."

"Nimrod", the sporting writer, whilst on a visit to Badminton during the latter part of the eighteenth century, witnessed a lawn meet attended by some three hundred foxhunters, and noted "none were more welcome than Mr Vizard".

There is also a splendid engraving by Henry Alken depicting Mr Vizard addressing a politician. This bears the legend: "To tell you the truth, gemmen, I can't vote for you 'cause I 'unts with the Duke." (see illustration no. 6).

In addition to Mr Vizard, there was also a sporting tailor of Cheltenham who regularly hunted with the Beaufort at about this time, while Mr Ralph Lambton's field in Durham included a hairdresser. "No man ever turned out a horse with a finer mane or tail."

It must be remembered that when Mr Vizard and others were out hunting, social distinctions were far from what they are today; there was at that time an extremely rigid class distinction. Indeed, Robert Surtees, creator of that great hunter, John Jorrocks, often allows his characters to abuse one another with "trade descriptions"—for instance, Lord Scamperdale in *Mr. Sponge's Sporting Tour*, is a master of the invective: "Oh, ye barber's apprentice! Oh, ye draper's assistant!"

The great John Jorrocks, himself a grocer, also abuses on occasion: "Old 'ard, you 'air-dresser on the chestnut 'oss!"

"Hair-dresser, sir? I'm an Officer in the 91st Regiment!"

"Then you hossifer in the 91st Regiment, wot looks like an 'air-dresser, old 'ard!"

Of course not all foxhunters of the eighteenth century were inclined towards democracy in the hunting field, some even drew the line as to which hunts they would be seen with. There was, for instance, the distinguished soldier of Whyte-Melville's acquaintance who, when asked by a mild stranger whether he had ever been out with the Crawley and Horsham Hunt, thundered in reply: "No, sir! I have never hunted with any hounds but the Quorn or the Pytchley, and I'll take damned good care I never do!" This story is related in the *Hunting* volume of *The Badminton Library*, written by the 8th Duke of Beaufort, who commented upon it as follows: "An expression of opinion which, it may be here observed, the narrator of the story by no means subscribes to."

However, even the crack Shire hunts, such as the Pytchley, had their more humble riders to hounds, and it is recorded that in 1842 a pauper in actual receipt of outdoor relief from the guardians of the County Union went out with the Pytchley on an aged horse and in still older clothes.

But, by and large, as "Nimrod", who was himself a great snob, has it: "Fox hunting links all classes together."

"Tell me a man is a foxhunter and I loves him at once" is still indicative of the great freemasonry which is to be found amongst hunting people. Charles Balch tells the story of another Beaufort follower—a scrap metal dealer from Wootton Basset, who, in 1916— ". . . bought knacker horses for which he gave we young farmers one pound. His name was Ernest Camden and he only had one leg but that did not stop him hunting. He lived in a gypsy caravan on the Bushton Road, where the Bushton, opening Meet was held, and as if it was only yesterday I can see the old Duke, Will Dale, huntsman, and Tommy Newman, 1st Whip, going past that caravan and Ernest Camden, complete with his crutch, mounting a £1 knacker as if it was Golden Miller . . . and he followed those hounds, half a leg one side and the whole leg the other and went as straight as any member of the Hunt. Several years ago I told the present Duke this story by letter, and he replied: 'Yes, and they still call that Camden Lane'."

Mr Camden's story brings to mind that of Tom Jones, a whipper-in in Hugo Meynell's service who, it is said, suffered from two things, a cork leg and a thirst. Often he would wake up on a hunting morning and be unable to remember where he left his leg the night before!

As always, of course, there are objections to every rule, and the story is still told in at least one Gloucestershire pub of the lady who, because she was unable to join the Beaufort Hunt, re-named her hostelry "The Snooty Fox". There was also the vet who remarked, "Well, of course, nowadays it pays the Beaufort Hunt people to be polite", presumably meaning that it was necessary purely as a public relations exercise.

However, by and large, hunting is and always has been a very democratic sport, with the field, car followers and foot followers enjoying a country pastime which has gone on for over two hundred years, and which continues to grow in popularity, with somewhere in the region of half a million people, of all sorts and conditions, taking part in it each week. Everyone who is prepared to observe the rules of the game, which are framed to ensure the greatest sport to the greatest number of people, is welcome in the hunting field, and this is as true of the Duke of Beaufort's Hunt as of any other hunt.

Masters

"First of all I'll explain to you what I means by the word Master.
I means to ride with an 'orn in my saddle." R. S. Surtees—*Handley
Cross*

The 5th Duke of Beaufort	1786–1803
The 6th Duke of Beaufort	1803–1835
The 7th Duke of Beaufort	1835–1853
The 8th Duke of Beaufort	1853–1899
Mr. Wemyss (Joint Master)	1896–1897
The 9th Duke of Beaufort	1899–1924
The 10th Duke of Beaufort	1924–
Mr. H. C. Cox (Joint Master)	1930–1935
Captain F. Spicer (Joint Master)	1935–1941
Major G. Gundry (Joint Master)	1951–1978
Mr. David Somerset (Joint Master)	1974–

Huntsmen

"If you would learn the business of a huntsman, go and hunt with one
of good repute and exercise all your intelligence and common sense in
explaining to yourself, the why and the wherefore of the various things
you observe him do." *The Badminton Library*, 1899.

Will Crane	⎫
Thomas Ketch	dates
Thomas Alderton	uncertain
John Dilworth	⎭
Philip Payne	1802–1826
William Long	1826–1855
8th Duke of Beaufort	1855–1858
Thomas Clarke	1858–1868
Lord Worcester (later 9th Duke)	1869–1914
Will Dale	1896–1910
George Walters	1910–1915
Thomas Newman	1915–1936
Fred Brown	1936–1938
10th Duke of Beaufort	1921–1967
Bert Pateman	1937–1967
Reg Holland	1938–1941
Ted Reade	1946–1952
Major G. Gundry	1951–1974
Brian Gupwell	1967–

5th Duke of Beaufort: Master 1786–1803

Although there is strong evidence to suggest that foxhunting took place, in some way or another, prior to the middle of the 18th century when the 5th Duke of Beaufort threw his "coarse staghounds of many colours" into Silk Wood, in or about the year 1762. Whether the fox was first hunted at Badminton earlier than 1762, or a little later, there is no doubt that foxhunting in the area was soon on a properly organised basis, as witness an item taken from the Duke's personal account book, dated 5th July, 1777—"Pay earth-stoppers at Badminton £25.16s.6d." (today the figure would be somewhere in the region of £500).

There is a painting of the 5th Duke of Beaufort's hounds in Wychwood, near Cornbury, painted in 1786 (the horses and hounds were painted by F. Sartorius, while W. Tomkins and Edmund Estcourt were responsible for the landscape and the figures, respectively). The picture shows hounds, horses and riders gathered round a tree watching a whipper-in suspend a dead fox from a branch. The 5th Duke and Lord Charles Somerset look on, while in the background is Dr Penney, the Somerset family's chaplain (who, according to "Druid", had a pad from the very first fox caught in Silk Wood mounted and attached to his bell rope). This ritual—known as treeing a fox—has long since died out. It was intended, according to Peter Beckford, to "make the hounds more eager and to let in the tail hounds".* The body of the dead fox was hung on a branch for the hounds to bay at before it was eventually thrown to them.

Although the fox provided better sport than the stag, and so eventually became the principal beast of the chase, there were not many to be found in the area of Badminton at that time and so, in 1770, the 5th Duke took over the whole of the Heythrop country (which had previously been hunted by Lord Foley). In 1779, he also took over the North Cotswold country (which had previously been hunted by Mr Fretwell). At that time, the Badminton hounds and horses would move to Heythrop House, in Oxfordshire, at the end of the cub-hunting season, remaining there for two months.

According to T. F. Dale, many of the Gloucestershire and Wiltshire riders followed the Duke, and lived a jovial life at one of the inns, hunting by day and drinking "more claret and port than was good for them when the day's amusement was over".

Dale's censorious "more than was good for them" brings to mind Anthony Trollope's outrage in 1868, when he described as follows:

---

* *Thoughts on Hunting.*

"We took up the other day a volume of a modern sporting magazine, and found bound up with it as a frontispiece a picture of sundry men in top boots, sitting or lying round a dinner table—and all of them apparently drunk. This picture of a drunken revel was intended to be characteristic of a hunting man's delight."

The annual "pilgrimage" to the Heythrop country was not without some discomfort. In addition to the Duke and his household, many of his neighbours joined the cavalcade, staying at inns and rented houses en route. On one such occasion, Mrs Boscawen (mother of the 5th Duke's wife) complained that all the beds except her own and her daughter's were nothing but old velvet rags.

As well as members of the ducal household, a large contingent of servants also went from Badminton, and Sir William Beach Thomas tells us in his *Hunting England* (published 1936): "Of course everything went by road in those days, and everyone who could get on a horse had to ride one of the hunters. Footmen, chefs, bottle-washers, and even some of the housemaids, and the whole cavalcade rode on grass all the way, which says something for the country they crossed."

There is a letter at Badminton from a chef, complaining of soreness after his long ride.

The Beauforts continued to hunt the Heythrop country until 1835 when the 6th Duke, owing to ill-health, decided to confine his hunting to Badminton, and so the present Heythrop Hunt came into being. "Cecil's" *Hunting Tours* (1924) states that: "It was supposed in those days that the two countries could not individually contain foxes sufficient for two packs of hounds, and much difficulty existed, but a Committee was eventually formed and the requisite funds raised. The management being invested in Mr Langston, aided by the powerful influence of Lord Redesdale."

The Heythrop took its name from Heythrop House.

During the time of the 5th Duke, the Badminton Hunt servants were dressed in green plus livery with gilt buttons, the members of the Hunt being dressed in the famous blue coats with the buff collar facings. To this day, the Heythrop Hunt servants still wear the Badminton green (as, of course, do the Beaufort Hunt servants). Indeed, until recently, the then Master of the Heythrop, Captain Ronnie Wallace, MFH, carried the horn himself and also wore the green coat.

From the very beginning of its existence as a separate hunt, the Beaufort has always maintained the friendliest relationship with the Heythrop. On November 1st, 1935, for example, the present Duke of Beaufort took his hounds to a joint meet at Lower Swell, to open that season and to mark the centenary of the Heythrop Hunt. We are told that: "Good humour and feeling prevailed throughout".

Again, on 5 April 1977—the day following the Duke's Birthday Meet at Hawkesbury Upton—the Duke attended, in his capacity of Patron, a unique point-to-point, held at Stow-on-the Wold: unique because it marked the end of a quarter of a century's Mastership by Captain Wallace. The highlight of this occasion was a parade of a mixed pack of the Heythrop hounds (led by the present Huntsman, Tony Collins), together with ten Huntsmen and other Hunt servants from nine adjacent Hunts—the Warwickshire (Mr Stephen Lambert, MFH, with Clarence Webster); the Bicester and Warden Hill (Captain Ian Farquhar, MFH) the Vale of Aylesbury (Jim Bennett); the Old Berkshire (Mr Colin Nash, MFH); the V.W.H. (Sidney Bailey); the Cotswold (Mr. Tim Unwin, MFH); the North Cotswold (Captain Brian Fanshawe, MFH); the Berkeley (Tim Langley); and, of course, The Duke of Beaufort's Huntsman, Brian Gupwell. The Master of the Whaddon Chase, Mr Dorian Williams, MFH, was the commentator as the hounds and huntsmen paraded before the Duke of Beaufort and Captain Wallace. The parade was watched by somewhere in the region of 20,000 people who had come from all over the country to see this unique spectacle. The Beaufort-Heythrop ties are, therefore, as strong as ever, and on this occasion also "good humour prevailed".

The 5th Duke of Beaufort hunted and bred hounds at Badminton for forty seasons. Together with his Huntsman, Will Crane, he was one of the great founders of foxhunting, and by the end of the eighteenth century the Beaufort hounds were among the very best in England.

The 5th Duke's hunting activities seem to have caused his wife some apprehension. At Badminton House, there are a number of letters written by her from Grosvenor Square, addressed to the 'Duke of Beaufort, near Woodstock, Oxfordshire', advising him to take care of himself.

"Pray remember me to all your party, and above all things think of me yourself when you are hunting that I may be a preservative against leaping or any imprudence of any kind whatsoever."

And again:

"I can only say that when I think of the daily risks you run, my blood is chilled so that if you think of me you cannot fail of taking all imaginable care of yourself. The [name illegible] horse is at present my object of terror and brooks and leaps of all kinds. I trust that you are past the age of showing off."

The 5th Duke's Huntsman, Will Crane, was generally acknowledged to be the best huntsman of his day. Indeed, the Beaufort Hunt has always had a tradition of employing the very best Huntsmen and Hunt servants. Crane was a powerfully-built, heavy man but, being a strong horseman, was always able to keep up with his hounds.

The great Peter Beckford, whose *Thoughts on Hunting* (1781) is one of the classic books on the sport, once asked Crane how his hounds behaved. "Very well, sir," replied Crane. "They never come to a fault but they spread like a sky rocket." Beckford adds: "Thus it should always be."

According to one source, Crane's retirement was brought about by "too great a love of the bottle".* He was succeeded by Thomas Ketch, whose only fault seems to have been that he was "a little rough with his tongue" (a fault more readily condoned in Masters of Foxhounds than in Huntsmen). He was, however, a good and devoted huntsman, and remained in this employment until old age caused him to retire.

Ketch was succeeded by Thomas Alderton, who was promoted from Whipper-in and, as is sometimes the case, although a first-class Whipper-in, he did not prove to be a great success as a Huntsman. He therefore requested that he might be allowed to return to "his old place". This was agreed, and John Dilworth was appointed as Huntsman. Dilworth, a first-class Huntsman in the field proved to be less of a success in the kennels. It is recorded that he "served as long as he could, and retired with a pension".

Dilworth was succeeded, in 1802, by one of the great Beaufort Huntsmen, Philip Payne. "A Huntsman whose hounds loved and trusted him and flew to horn or voice." K. W. Horlock, who wrote upon hunting matters using the nom de plume "Scrutator" tells us in his *Recollections of a Foxhunter* (1861) that: "It was highly amusing to see old Philip Payne, the celebrated Huntsman to the Badminton pack, drawing his favourites for inspection, and the rush with which they would spring out of the lodging room nearly knocking him off his legs. But he bore these onsets or outsets with the most imperturbable good humour, patting their heads all the while, they apparently venting threats both loud and deep against their venerable master. Poor old Philip—a better judge of breeding or hunting hounds never existed or a cleverer or kinder Kennel Huntsman."

Payne, who had previously been in service with the Earl of Durham (Raby) and the Earl of Lonsdale (Cottesmore) was a wonderful hound man, and possibly the best breeder of hounds of his time. The following story which Payne used to tell is an example of Dilworth's slackness and Payne's efficiency where hounds were concerned.

After he had been installed as Huntsman, he was preparing to walk hounds in the Park one day when the Whippers-in appeared loaded

* *T. F. Dale.*

with couples (a double collar used to run hounds in pairs). "What are these for?" asked Payne. "To put on the hounds, sir," replied a Whipper-in, and went on to explain that they were accustomed to couple hounds when exercising them for fear of their running riot among the deer. "Stuff and nonsense!" Payne replied. "T   von't run the deer while I'm with them." And this proved to be the case.

When Philip Payne became Huntsman to the 5th Duke of Beaufort. the staghound origins of the pack were still very much in evidence. Payne found the hounds to be somewhat splay-footed and heavy of shoulder. By careful breeding and crossing with carefully chosen hounds from the Cottesmore and from Cheshire, Payne succeeded in doing away with the heavy-shouldered type of foxhound, and thus produced a type of hound which was much better suited to the faster type of hunting which was then coming into fashion.

During Payne's time at Badminton, there was one hound in the kennels which was to become the most famous foxhound in English literature. This was the Beaufort Justice, immortalised by R. S. Surtees in *Mr Sponge's Sporting Tour*.

His Lordship resumed reading the letter. "'I think I have a hound that may be useful to you . . .' The devil you have!" exclaimed his lordship, grinding his teeth with disgust. "Useful to *me*, you confounded haberdasher! You hav'n't a hound in your pack that i'd take. 'I think I have a hound that may be useful to you . . .'" repeated his lordship.

"A Beaufort Justice one, for a guinea!" interrupted Jack; adding, "He got the name into his head at Oxford, and has been harping upon it ever since."

"'I think I have a hound that may be useful to you . . .'" resumed his lordship, for the third time. "'It is Old Merriman, a remarkably stout, true line hunting hound; but who is getting slow for me . . .' Slow for you, you beggar!" exclaimed his lordship; "I should have thought nothin' short of a wooden 'un would have been too slow for you. 'He's a six-season hunter, and is by Fitzwilliam's Singwell out of his Darling. Singwell was by the Rutland Rallywood, out of Tavistock's Rhapsody. Rallywood was by Old Lonsdale's . . .' Old Lonsdale's!—the snob!" sneered Lord Scamperdale. "'Old Lonsdale's Palafox, out of Anson's . . .' Anson's! curse the fellow," again muttered his lordship . . . "'out of Anson's Madrigal. Darling was by old Grafton's Bolivar, out of Blowzy. Bolivar was by the Brocklesby; that's Yarborough's . . .' That's Yarborough's!" sneered his lordship, "as if one didn't know that as well as him—'by the Brocklesby; that's Yarborough's Marmion out of Petre's

Matchless; and Marmion was by that undeniable hound, the . . .'
the . . . what?" asked his lordship.

"Beaufort Justice, to be sure!" replied Jack.

"'The Beaufort Justice!'" read his lordship, with due emphasis.

"Hurrah!" exclaimed Jack, waving the dirty, egg-stained
mustardy copy of *Bell's Life* over his head. "Hurrah! I told you so."

The Beaufort Justice was not, in fact, bred at Badminton, but went
there as an unentered draft hound. He was by Mr Nicholls's New
Forest Justice, who was by Jasper, who was by Lord Egremont's own
Justice, and was bred by Sir Thomas Mostyn out of his Hopeful.

Philip Payne was succeeded by the most famous of all the Beaufort
Huntsmen, William Long, who was born and brought up at
Badminton, where his father was a stud groom. Long began his career
as post-boy in the village, and was later employed to school horses in
the hunt stables. Will Long, who estimated that during his service at
Badminton he had handled three thousand foxes and ridden more
than a million miles across country, served under four successive Dukes
of Beaufort (the 5th, 6th, 7th and 8th).

In 1807, he was appointed Second Whipper-in to Philip Payne,
and in this capacity he gave excellent service for ten years, on one
occasion causing the 6th Duke to remark that, "If the young pack
enter as well as the young Whipper-in, there won't be much the matter
next season."

Later, Long was put on as First Whipper-in, a position he was to
hold for eight years.

The lot of a hunt servant at Badminton at that time was by no means
a sinecure, and Long has left a description of the many hours of
arduous work that were required of him.

"During the whole time I was whipper-in, I did first of all two horses
every morning, and then went hunting, and assisted for an hour and a
half in cleaning my horse, be the hour what it might when we got
home. On our hunting days, I did earth-stopping, dressing my horse
when I returned, with the addition of having all my hunting clothes,
boots, etc., to clean. But, being fond of hunting, it so stimulated me or I
could not have got through the work."

In 1826 Will Long was appointed as Huntsman to the Beaufort
hounds, and in this capacity he served until 1855.

When Long first took over from Payne there was some doubt
amongst certain members of the Hunt as to his capabilities as a
huntsman, but this is almost always the case when a new huntsman
takes over from one who is well-established in a country. However, any
doubts there may have been as to Long's promotion from Whipper-in

to Huntsman were quickly dispelled, for he proved to be a superb huntsman, and was described by the 8th Duke as "a man of singular intelligence. One who reasoned and turned over in his mind all things connected with hunting."

As a horseman, Long was also the recipient of much praise from his contemporaries. "He is unrivalled. I invite all lovers of the chase to see him ride. The finest seat, with such hands as are rarely in use. He rides without jealousy and takes the country as it comes."*

It has been recorded that Long had eight horses for his use at Badminton, his favourite being Milkmaid, which he rode for seventeen seasons.

Described as "a little spare, wiry figure with a quick sharpness of manner", Long was possessed of a most musical voice. He was, however, "very quiet with the pack, till his quick eye saw that the moment had come to act, and then he would rouse every hound to activity with a rousing cheer". Like Payne before him, Long was an advocate of big hounds, and introduced fresh blood from the Brocklesby, Belvoir and Milton Kennels.

6th Duke of Beaufort: Master 1803–35

When the 5th Duke of Beaufort died in 1803, he was succeeded by a man "who did not care for town life" and who increased the size of the kennels and hunted the country even more thoroughly than his predecessor had done.

It was the 6th Duke who instituted the custom of awarding silver cups to those tenants who reared the best hound puppies—a custom which is still upheld today, the presentations being made at the annual Badminton Puppy Show, that "annual assemblage of the cognoscenti to inspect the entry of young hounds for the ensuing season, in whom so much of the huntsman's fondest hopes are centred". ("Cecil", 1924).

The 6th Duke also inherited the Heythrop country, which he continued to hunt until shortly before his death in 1835.

"Nimrod" (Charles Apperley), the great sporting writer, and even greater snob, visited Heythrop in 1825. He later recorded many of his impressions in a notice of the 6th Duke, which was published in *Bell's Life* in 1836.

"Yet it is as a Master of Foxhounds that it is in my province to speak of the late Duke of Beaufort; and, from the many seasons experience I had of His Grace in the field, I feel myself in some measure competent for the task. I need scarcely say I was always an admirer of his hounds,

*T. F. Dale.

although I could not like his country. The greatest improvement I saw in the former, in defiance of all the disadvantages of the latter, convinced me that there was a system at work highly worthy of my consideration." (Not for nothing did R. S. Surtees dub "Nimrod", "Pomponious Ego—that man wot makes obserwations on M.F.H.s, their packs, their 'osses, their 'untsman, their everything in fact.")

"Nimrod" continues his description of the 6th Duke:

"But whence this directing hand I was a long time unable to discover. I doubted it being the Duke, not from mistrust of his capacity, but because I had reason to believe the numerous avocations of his station prevented his attending to the minutae of the kennel, although I did not consider His Grace a sportsman of the first class in which his hounds certainly stood. I doubted it being that of Philip Payne, for to appearance a duller bit of clay was never moulded by nature."

"Nimrod" goes on to say that we should not judge by appearances and that he lived to confess his error since there was "about Philip Payne a steady observance of circumstances which, increasing with the experience of their results, was more useful to him as a breeder than all the learning of a Porson." (Richard Porson, 1759–1808, was an eminent Greek scholar and a prodigy of learning.)

"Nimrod" also writes elsewhere that Payne "is allowed on all hands to have more skill in the breeding of hounds than any other huntsman of his day".

Of the Beaufort hounds of the time, "Nimrod" was enthusiastic.

"The first thing which strikes a stranger is the cleanliness and brightness of their skins . . . hence we may infer that these hounds are in good condition, which the stoutness of their running also establishes. In one respect, the Duke of Beaufort's hounds stand pre-eminent and that is in the persevering manner in which they carry a cold scent over a cold country." (The Heythrop country is well-known for being a cold-scenting country, although anyone who has seen Captain Ronnie Wallace's bitch pack in full cry might doubt it.)

"Nimrod" then went on to earn the undying enmity of generations of Badminton Hunt servants in his description of the Hunt uniform:

"The establishment was perfect, all but the green plush coats on the men, the regular thistle-whipping colour [a term usually applied, often derisively, to harriers] which, to my eye, was offensive." However, in mitigation, "Nimrod" did go on to say that: "The Duke, as I said in one of my tours, looked like a Duke, and his servants looked like servants of the very best description of their line."

Concerning the Blue and the Buff coats of the Hunt members, "Nimrod" wrote: "The effect is sombre, if not livery-like, and certainly has not so sporting or so lively an appearance as scarlet." He describes

the demeanour of the 6th Duke of Beaufort in the hunting field in what
T. F. Dale has called a "thoroughly Nimrodian manner".

"But how did His Grace carry himself in the field?"
"Why, here he was like a Duke because he was like a gentleman."
"But was he not difficult of access?"
"Certainly not to such as had a right to address him."
"Did he not blow up his field and swear at them as his father did?"
"No, at least, not half as much as they deserved, for no man's
hounds were more over-ridden at one time than the Duke of
Beaufort's were."

"Nimrod" also says of the 6th Duke: "If he were a competent judge
of what his hounds were doing, he kept it very much to himself."*

Indeed, it is not hard to imagine His Grace's reticence when faced
with "that man wot makes obserwations on M.F.H.s."

7th Duke of Beaufort: Master 1835–53

The 7th Duke of Beaufort, on his accession to the title in 1835,
succeeded to the Mastership of the Badminton country only. However,
he also inherited a hunting territorial dispute with K. W. Horlock,
("Scrutator"). This dispute had come about as follows:

In 1828 Mr Horlock had begun to hunt part of West Wiltshire
(including the present Avon Vale country). While the 6th Duke of
Beaufort was still hunting the Heythrop country, he had permitted Mr
Horlock to draw certain of the Badminton coverts. When the
Heythrop country was relinquished in 1835, the 6th Duke, not
unnaturally, expected to resume hunting all his old country. Mr
Horlock, however, thought otherwise and refused to give up the
Badminton coverts.

This dispute dragged on until 1839 and, according to T. F. Dale:
"There was a division in the country of rather a serious nature."

Eventually, the following announcement appeared in the *Sporting
Magazine*. "The differences between the Duke's Hunt and Mr Horlock
have been amicably settled, the Badminton Hunt giving the country
claimed by Mr Horlock, while he, on the other side, relinquished
several small coverts near the Duke's Kennel, the hunting of which was
a constant source of annoyance to His Grace and his party."

Incidentally, since Mr Horlock was a writer upon hunting matters,
it is interesting to read his estimate of the Badminton pack at that time:
"To affirm that the Badminton pack are the best pack of hounds in

Bell's Life 1836.

England would be claiming for them an invidious, though I am inclined to think not an unfair distinction. But when I consider by whom they have been kept and by whom hunted, they have a right to stand second to none in the kingdom. Their noble masters have been invariably good sportsmen and excellent judges, both of hounds and hunting."

Mr Horlock seems to have been of a somewhat contentious nature, though, since some time later he was also involved in a minor dispute with the 8th Duke of Beaufort, when he wrote to *Bell's Life*, criticising the Duke's current Huntsman, Thomas Clarke ("Sagacious Thomas") for having refused him admittance to the Badminton Kennels. The Duke was quick to reply, pointing out that since Mr Horlock had seen fit to turn up uninvited with Will Long (then the ex-Beaufort Huntsman), it was his own fault. "I was quite prepared to show him every possible courtesy, but my hounds are not public property and I do not like to be treated as he treated me, and I resented it accordingly."

In 1838 the indefatigable "Nimrod" (then in his sixties) paid a visit to Badminton. Unable to hunt owing to bad weather, he filled in the time as best he could by examining the kennels and the stables.

"It may be supposed that I made the acquaintance of the pack by walking and riding with them every now and then when at exercise in the Park, and this I must say—the more I saw of them the more I admired them."

Of the stables, he remarks that "they are very conveniently placed, being within one hundred yards of the back entrance to the mansion. (The interior) exhibits a splendid stud, and this composed of every description of horse." There were in the stables at that time "thirty-four regular hunters" and another ten "that are able to go a-hunting". "I much like the style of horse for the Duke's own riding, of which he has twelve . . . Will Long has likewise eight first-rate horses for his use, leaving fifteen well-seasoned hunters for the Whips and other purposes."

A first-class Master of Foxhounds, the 7th Duke was renowned for his kindness and consideration in the hunting field, often putting up with a great deal of nonsense from over-keen young undergraduates from nearby Oxford University. He could, on occasions, however, display that wrath for which Masters of Hounds are justly famous.

On one particular occasion, a lawyer from Bath halloaed the hounds on to a hare when they were, in fact, already running a fox, and it is recorded that the Duke had never before been heard to "throw his tongue so loud". Later, however, he despatched a neck of venison to the offender. This was kindness indeed, considering the circumstances.

Later during the 7th Duke's reign as Master, "Nimrod" paid another visit to Badminton, and this time he was able to go out with the Hunt. Incidentally, "Nimrod" throws an interesting light upon the social conditions of the time, when describing his journey to Badminton.

"The postboy who drove me to Badminton told me that which very much surprised me: but all that he did tell me was afterwards confirmed by the Duke. He said so numerous had been the highway robberies lately in that part of the country that the farmers riding home from market carried either pistols or life-preservers, and that even the waggoners going for lime or coals, were knocked down and robbed of the money taken to pay for them."

"Nimrod" also gives an interesting description of the 7th Duke of Beaufort's keenness to get to the Meet: "I have often gone a good pace to cover, but never I think as fast as on this day."

Preparing for his day's sport, "Nimrod" was warned that he "had better make a start. The Duke is going to ride Mayflower, and he puts her along at a terrible pace." And so it proved. "Nimrod" records that:

"Although we took it gently till His Grace and his other friends overtook us, we were only 32 minutes from the time I mounted at the stable door, going seven miles over a very indifferent cross country road. The old mare slips along at an extraordinary speed, although not appearing to be doing beyond 8 miles in the hour."

Mayflower, who had a reputation for being somewhat skittish, was at one time offered to Queen Victoria as a gift, an offer which, it seems, was declined. Just as well perhaps, since one can hardly imagine Her Majesty cracking along "at a terrible pace".

"Nimrod's" visit to Badminton coincided with the Marquess of Worcester's fifteenth birthday, and he tells us that so loudly did the bell-ringers ring the changes to celebrate the occasion that the Duke was eventually forced to send word that the louder they rang the less they should have to drink—a cunning, and no doubt effective, piece of labour relations.

"Nimrod" also informs us of one Mr William Wray who, despite having hunted with the Beaufort Hunt for more than twenty seasons, could only remember the names of two of the hounds—"One because his name is Wellington and the other because he has but one eye instead of two".

It was during the 7th Duke's time as Master that Mr Vizard, the sporting sweep of Chipping Sodbury, hunted with the Beaufort, and indeed the Duke must have held him in high regard, since he was always sure of a mount from the Badminton stables whenever he wanted one.

In 1849 there were 75½ couple of hounds in the kennels at Badminton, and the country was hunted four days a week. Later this was increased to six days a week.

At the age of fifty-two, the 7th Duke suffered a bad fall from his horse whilst riding in Hyde Park. He was at that time liable to attacks of gout, and as a heavy blow or fall was likely to bring on an attack, he thought it wiser thereafter to cease jumping hedges and to confine his jumping to timber and walls. Eventually, however, he was forced to give up riding to hounds altogether, and took to following the pack in a light phaeton drawn by a pair of piebalds, with an outrider in attendance to open gates and occasionally to lower a wall. In this manner, the 7th Duke was able to see much of the hunting, often accompanied by his grandson (later the 9th Duke).

On 17 November 1853, the day of two magnificent runs, the 7th Duke of Beaufort died.

8th Duke of Beaufort: Master 1853–99

"Nimrod", on one of his visits to Badminton, was most interested in the development of the then Marquess of Worcester (8th Duke). "Will he do?" he had asked. "He will, if they don't spoil him," was the reply he received. However, neither "Nimrod" nor his informant need have worried, for when the 7th Duke died he was succeeded as Master of the Beaufort Hunt by one of the best-loved and respected of all of the Dukes of Beaufort—the 8th Duke of Beaufort, sometimes known as the "Old Duke" or the "Old Blue 'Un"—and one of the best-known sporting personalities of his day. As Lord Worcester, he had already acted as Master in the field during the later years of his father's life, and soon after his succession to the title he was to hunt the Beaufort hounds himself.

This came about as follows:

In 1855, following a disagreement with the 8th Duke, Will Long retired from service. T. F. Dale, in his book *The 8th Duke of Beaufort and the Badminton Hunt*, has described the incident as follows:

"The last entry in Long's diary, 18 October 1855. 'The Duke sent Nimrod home for striking the hound, Piper, and that same evening sent for me and Nimrod to his room, and after some little talk I gave him notice that Nimrod and myself would leave the service' and, being a man of his word, this he did. An entry in the Duke's diary, dated 20 October, 1855, refers to the matter as follows: 'The Huntsman, Bill Long, having retired and Nimrod Long, his son, the First Whipper-in, leaving me also, I take to the hounds myself with the Second Whipper-in, Bill Walker, and a boy, Tom Goddard to whip in.'"

This must have been a sad parting on both sides. The Duke had written of how he had "been brought up under Bill Long", while Long, with his record of excellent service to the Dukes of Beaufort, must have remembered that his present Master had been a baby of only two years old when he (Long) was first engaged as the Beaufort Huntsman. However, there appears to have been no animosity on either side, and Long, who retired on a pension, often returned to the kennels to see the hounds.

When the great Will Long left his service, the 8th Duke of Beaufort undertook to hunt the Beaufort hounds himself. To take over a pack of hounds which have been regularly hunted by another huntsman is no small task. Hounds come to rely upon and to recognise their huntsman's voice and manner, and will sometimes refuse to work for a new huntsman. In the Duke's case, this must have been a doubly hard task since he was following one of the greatest huntsmen of his time. However, he had, as he said, been brought up with Bill Long, and had hunted since an early age and so, on 20 October 1855, the Beaufort hounds met at Shipton Lodge (between Badminton and Malmesbury) with the Duke carrying the horn.

Luck was with him, and he has recorded:

"Find in the first Spinney on the left of the approach to Estcourt House. A beautiful find—fox crossing in view to the other side of approach. After two hours good work and hard running with pretty rings over the open and park, ran into him in the lake between waterfall and bridge near Keeper's house."

The Duke's hunting notes are from his own hunting diaries, which are quoted in T.F. Dale's life of the 8th Duke and they show that he was an extremely observant and often humorous huntsman.

"3 November 1855, went to West Park. Found. The Fence—took a flying leap clearing the fenced brook below West Park on going away. The prettiest thing I ever saw."

Again, and for those people who would have us believe that all huntsmen are blood-thirsty brutes:

"I might have killed a fox in the withy bed and they [the hounds] very near had him. I could have turned him into their mouths, but refrained and let him go. Very good behaviour for a huntsman, I think."

"On 8 January 1856 at 5 o'clock, just as we were coming home, a most curious meteor fell, which Captains Berkeley and Baillie, Colonel Edward Somerset, Mr Granville Somerset, Lord Suffolk, Mr John Bailey, and several others, including myself, saw. It was like a large ball of fire, as big as one's head. It fell perpendicularly, leaving a column of light on its course, which lasted two or three minutes, and then apparently turned into smoke, which was visible for a quarter of an hour."

"It is delightful to hear hound-singing as it rises and falls, and seems as if each hound had studied his notes; it is also a beautiful sight to see them sitting up with heads in the air enjoying their chorus. At Badminton, ever since I can recollect, it has been the practice not to interfere with them and to let them have their song out. They sing much more in summer, and when they are fresh, than in the hunting season; still, they will do it at all times, but more or less according to how fresh they are, and with regard to the state of the weather. Fine weather induces them to sing. I am sure it is much better for them to enjoy their music."

Although the Duke, with his great love of the countryside and of hunting, thoroughly enjoyed his period as huntsman, it was by no means always plain sailing, and his diaries are peppered with remarks relating to the behaviour of both the Hunt followers and the Hunt servants, particularly those who could not keep quiet.

"Oh that the field would stand still!" is one heartfelt entry.

Obviously little has changed in that respect during the past one hundred and twenty-three years, although what the 8th Duke would have said of some of today's car followers is perhaps better left to the imagination.

Cecil Aldin, in his invaluable book, *Ratcatcher to Scarlet*, commented upon silence in the hunting field as follows: "Every man should be silent in the hunting field and every woman should wear a scold's bridle—a cheery field, but wouldn't hounds be able to catch foxes!"

Wouldn't they indeed? And there can't be a Huntsman or a Master in the country who would not agree with the idea of a "scold's bridle" (Lady Masters, of course, always excepted). Perhaps it is just that the women's voices being pitched higher, carry further. (There was, for example, the memorable occasion when a female hunt follower whispered to her friend—in a whisper which must have been heard in at least three counties—"If we stay here and keep quiet, nobody will know we are here.")

Another habit of hunt followers which greatly incensed the 8th Duke was that of people halloaing. It is a remarkable thing that ninety-nine people out of a hundred must make some sort of noise upon seeing a fox. It seems to be a reflex action which they simply cannot control. If only they would emulate John Jorrocks and count up to twenty first. The 8th Duke was particularly plagued by this tiresome habit—"They ran him up to within 60 yards of the Bell Farm. A man in the field, I believe, turned him short right but, unfortunately, a fellow halloaing forward tremendously at the moment I went to him. I believe the man was drunk. He certainly had never seen a fox."

Or again: "It is wonderful, but not uncommon, that a man when he sees a fox never knows where he is gone to or can distinguish his head from his brush."

Again: (and this time in respect of the Hunt servants): "We could not have failed to kill him [the fox] if the Whips had kept quiet."

Indeed, Whippers-in were frequently the cause of the Duke's wrath.

"Are Whippers-in intended as a trial to our patience, or are they a naturally stupid race?"

Nowadays, of course, the Beaufort Hunt Whippers-in carry whistles (introduced by the 9th Duke), a rather more humane practice than one the 8th Duke had in mind for them. "I have known several Whippers-in—all good men in their own way—I should like to have taken out with the muzzles on."

Towards the end of his first season of hunting the hounds, His Grace recorded on 8 March 1856:

"This day Worcester (later the 9th Duke) put on his first B.H. jacket and waistcoat"—and thus the great tradition was to continue.

Lord Worcester was at that time aged nine, but he was already an accomplished horseman. All of the 8th Duke's children learned to ride at a very early age, although they were not allowed to hunt more than three days a week until they were five!

In all, during his first season, the 8th Duke hunted on 102 days and killed 123 foxes (including the 60 Will Long had handled during cub-hunting). The 8th Duke carried the horn for three seasons, during the first two of which he enjoyed good sport.

On 2 May, at the end of the second season, His Grace recorded: "Good finish to the season. May we have a good one next year. Vivat Regina." This was not to be, however, for his last season as Huntsman proved to be a disappointing one, being a very bad scenting season.

In addition to hunting, His Grace's racing and political activities were taking up a great deal of his time. There was also the problem of ever-increasing size of fields. On one occasion the Duke recorded in his diary "a merry day's sport, though not quite a brilliant one—500 people out—many of them to meet me."

However, his third season began with an amusing incident. On 18 August 1857, he commenced the season in Silk Wood at 4.30 a.m.

"A black horse I bought kicked at President, a young Trojan dog, which ran home to his old walk at Sopwith. On the following Saturday, President, the dog that was kicked last Tuesday, ran home to his walk directly we found, and oddly enough his brother, Pilot, went home to Badminton. I suppose his brother had told him."

In all that season, the hounds hunted on 147 days, killing 113 foxes.

During this third season, the Duke was assisted by one Heber Long, who was the son of Charles Long, a Whipper-in under Will Long. When asked by the Duke how he had come to name the boy Heber, Charles Long answered: "Well, Your Grace, I came across the name of Heber the Kenite in the Bible and at the same time I was reading some sermons by Bishop Heber, so I thought I could not do better."

Heber Long later became Huntsman to the South and West Wilts Hunt.

In 1858, the 8th Duke, finding that his public duties were taking up so much of his time (he was appointed as Master of the Horse in that year) decided to engage a professional Huntsman. He engaged Tom Clarke, who had formerly been in the service of Mr James Morrell in the Old Berkshire country. An excellent Kennelman, Clarke was also an expert Huntsman, of whom the Duke wrote:

"It was a pleasure to hunt with him. He was wonderfully cheery and fond of a good gallop. I learnt many wrinkles from him, enjoyed many good days sport, and saw him kill many a good fox that would have beaten a less expert huntsman than Sagacious Thomas."

On the other hand, however, Clarke's love of a good gallop also earned the Duke's disapproval: "I think he spoilt my hounds by his anxiety to get away for a gallop."

His Grace also disapproved of Clarke's policy where his Whippers-in were concerned, and considered him rather less intelligent and less observant than Will Long. Overall, therefore, the Duke seems to have had mixed feelings about Clarke, but then the position of a Huntsman following on from a Master who has hunted the hounds himself and yet remains Master cannot be an easy one.

In all, Clarke remained at Badminton for eleven seasons, before retiring to take on the running of an inn at Chipping Sodbury. Before that time, however, he was to have many excellent seasons as Huntsman to the 8th Duke. He was succeeded by the young Marquess of Worcester in 1868.

In 1861 the 8th Duke of Beaufort wintered abroad (the hounds were placed under the management of Sir William Codrington and Colonel Kingscote). The Duke went to Gibraltar, taking with him some of the Beaufort hounds as a gift to the Master of the Calpé Hunt, Colonel Powlett Somerset (a cousin of the Duke). Then, in 1863, the Duke started upon what must have been one of the most extraordinary expeditions ever to be undertaken by a Master of Foxhounds, when he embarked at Folkestone with 25 couple of hounds and a party, which included the Marquess of Worcester and Tom Clarke, in order to go wolf hunting.

The master (Officier de Louveterie) of a wolf-hunting pack in Poitou had written to the Duke as he wished to purchase some hounds. The Duke, in return, wrote offering a couple of hounds as a gift, and expressed an interest in wolf hunting. This led to an invitation to hunt in France, and the following remarkable piece of journalism appeared in the *Journale de la Vienne*:

"An English Sportsman. The Duke of Beaufort has just passed through Paris with two hundred dogs intended to destroy the wolves which are here the terror of the shepherd and of the inhabitants of lonely dwellings. It may be said of the Peer that he is a sportsman by profession. He has inherited a rental of 1,000,000 Frs., on condition that he shall always maintain three packs of hounds and shall hunt six days a week. Another clause in the Will binds him to expend 250,000 Frs. a year on his hunting establishment. There are collaterals always on the watch who would cause the bequest to be revoked in case the conditions are not carried out. These noble eccentricities are to be found only in England."

At first, it seemed that the English foxhounds would have nothing to do with the sport of wolf hunting but later on, having seen French hounds kill, they did take to the scent, with the result that the Duke returned to Badminton with a wolf "trophy", which used to be on display in a glass case in the dining room at Badminton House.

The Beaufort Hunt, during the time of the 8th Duke, was once described as a sort of open air club, with the hunting field free to all, although the right to wear the coveted Blue and Buff hunt uniform could only be given by the Duke. Indeed, everything was done in the grand manner. On hunting days, a coach-load of guests would be driven to the Meet, either by Lord Worcester or by the Duke himself. At the end of the day, guests would find a change of clothes and a meal awaiting them at a nearby inn. Later, they would be driven back to Badminton. The Lawn Meets at Badminton were remarkable enough during the time of the 7th Duke, with fields in the region of three or four hundred, but Hunt members only had been entertained.

During the 8th Duke's term as Master, it was not unknown for him to provide breakfast for a thousand people and lunch for four or five hundred. In 1860, according to the writer "Cecil", 2,200 horsemen, in addition to a vast line of carriages, attended a Lawn Meet. While in 1863, no less than five thousand people assembled. According to Mrs Horatio Durant, visitors wandered through the house at will. As the result, however, of disappearing trinkets, eventually the general public had to be excluded.

In 1867, the Prince of Wales (later Edward VII) paid a visit to Badminton, bringing with him nine horses. It is recorded that he enjoyed a remarkably good run with the Beaufort Hunt.

The Duke of Beaufort had a great respect for His Royal Highness, and dedicated the famous *Badminton Library* series (see page 128) to him as "one of the best and keenest sportsmen of our time".

These visits made by royalty who enjoy hunting at Badminton have become very much a tradition. Wally Trotman, terrier-man and earth-stopper to the Beaufort Hunt for some nineteen years, remembers the occasion when he met another Prince of Wales (later Edward VIII) in the hunting field.

"There were three of us boys, and the Duke came over and said: 'Stay here for a little while and you might see the Prince of Wales.' Well, we stopped there and nobody came, so off we went after the Hunt. Anyway, a little later on we saw a fox, running left-handed, and, of course, we started to shout, and then across the field we saw this horseman riding towards us, and it was the Prince of Wales, and he shouted out: 'Shut up!' he shouted: 'We don't want every . . .—. . . to know I'm out!'"

Nowadays, of course, it is virtually impossible for every . . .—. . . not to know that a member of the Royal Family is out with the Beaufort Hunt. In November 1976, for example, HRH Prince Charles, together with Princess Anne and her father-in-law, Mr Peter Phillips, were out hunting with the Beaufort, when a flock of reporters, photographers and television cameramen suddenly appeared in the hunting field. They made such a nuisance of themselves, that it required a Royal request, delivered by a detective, before they would retire to the sidelines. It was reported upon this occasion that there were plenty of foxes about and that Prince Charles, looking completely at home in the saddle, enjoyed some vigorous gallops.

Perhaps in earlier days, royalty and other visitors were attracted to Badminton not only for the splendid sport shown there, but also in order to view the great beauties of the Gloucestershire countryside, that is, if *Bailey's Magazine* is to be believed. In April 1874, it published the following remarkable passage:

"The Duke of Beaufort's and the V.W.H. fields are largely patronised by ladies, well mounted and accomplished horsewomen, and some of them in the neighbourhood of Tetbury are endowed with such superlative fascinations that nothing short of the mythology of Mount Ida, with its aphroditean specialities, has been deemed sufficient for their description." (What hunting man could resist those "superlative fascinations"?)

In 1871, the Beaufort hounds enjoyed a run which has become famous in the annals of foxhunting, and which was to be commemorated by a special gathering of foxhunters at Badminton House one hundred years later. This was the Greatwood Run (see next page)—a distance of some twenty-seven miles as hounds ran (fourteen miles from point to point), with one eight-minute check during the course of three and a half hours.

The Greatwood Run took place on Wednesday, 22 February 1871, the Meet being at Swalletts Gate. Lord Worcester, who was riding his horse, Beckford, was hunting hounds ($17\frac{1}{2}$ couple of dog hounds), with Heber Long as First Whipper-in. What follows is an account of the run which appeared in *Bailey's Magazine*:

There was a long draw, nor was it till they reached the east end of the Wood that hounds found their fox. Comparatively few people heard the whistle. The wind had chopped round to the south-west. Lord Worcester and Heber Long, with a few followers only, got away. Hounds settled down to run, but before they reached Brinkworth Brook the fox was headed and swung round again to the Wood. A bold fox like this one always makes his point if he possibly can and, entering the Wood on the opposite side to that from which he had left it, he went through without stopping. The splendid chorus of the hounds through the covert put those who had been left once more on terms. They little knew that the loss of that first ring was a blessing in disguise. Those who were, as they thought, out of the fun, merely saved themselves three miles of stiff going.

This time the fox was fairly away, but there lay before the pursuers the Brinkworth Brook. Some charged it; some refused; and some went in. Lord Worcester and a few followers saved their horses a little, and obtained a slight pull by going over the bridge. Of those who were weeded out at the brook, few saw hounds again. At the village of Brinkworth, hounds threw up their heads. Giving them time to make their own cast, Lord Worcester watched them closely, and then with a low whistle quietly cast them on. Steadily, and without flash, they settled on the line again, and now were running hard for Somerford Common, a famous covert, well-known to followers of the V.W.H. Hounds never paused or wavered on the Common, for the fox had gone right through. Those who had eased their horses found themselves in the rear.

Either because he felt hounds too close, or perhaps meeting some obstacle, the fox twisted about here, but hounds (led by Sexton, Sentinel—then in his fifth season—and Ganymede, while Galloper strove hard to the front, for the credit of his Yorkshire blood he was by Lane Fox's Gainer out of Stately) were never off the line. From this point onward, the fox disdained the shelter of coverts.

Over the Tadpole Vale hounds ran hard, and horses began to

flounder and fumble at their fences. Everyone felt by this time that he was in for a great run, and all were riding resolutely, silently, and making every effort to save their horses.

Cricklade was passed and the waters of the Isis were in front. Lord Worcester's quick eye saw a cattle drinking-place on the opposite bank, and he plunged in, getting out with a scramble ere the tail hounds had scattered the drops from their coats and were straining away in pursuit of their comrades. The foremost hounds, now running mute, had a long lead; but as the line was parallel to the Canal, the towing path gave the huntsman a relief.

Once more the river was crossed, but this time the bridge at Castle Eaton helped the wise ones, though two rash and eager spirits, Messrs. Candy and Byng, tried to swim it again and were nearly drowned for their pains. At Castle Eaton the hounds came close to hunting, and Hamblin's [Charles Hamblin, the Kennel Huntsman] good work at their condition told, for where many packs would have been unable to hunt on for sheer weariness, Hannibal and Nathan led the pack through gardens and a farmyard, while Lord Worcester and Messrs. Alfred Grace [brother of the great cricketer, W. G. Grace] and Candy were reduced to running on foot, Mr Pitman following with poor old Beckford in tow.

Now, luckily, the pace was slow and the end was at hand. Mr Hynam lent Lord Worcester a good stout cob to finish on. Hounds marked the fox to ground in a rabbit-hole in a meadow belonging to a brewer, near Highworth Street. When Heber Long, who had gone well on a Badminton-bred grey—a descendant of the famous old Lops—counted over the hounds, but one couple was missing.

It was a very small group at the finish: Colonels Ewert and Dickson, Messrs. Tom Wild and Pitman, Captain Candy and Mr Byng, as well as Mr Jenkins, who went through the run—omitting the first ring—on a horse named Gifford, belonging to Mr Walter Powell of Dauntsey. About a quarter of an hour later, the Duke, riding Dyrham, a favourite, stout-hearted bay, arrived, so did Lord Arthur and Mr Granville Somerset. The heavyweights, of course, missed their second horses.

Hounds and horses went by train from Swindon to Chippenham. They were thirty-five miles from home when they left off. Lord Worcester went on to Town to be ready for his regimental work the next day.

As the Master of one of the finest, if not the finest, pack of foxhounds in the country, the 8th Duke was often asked to take his hounds to Meets

THE
GREATWOOD RUN
WITH THE
BEAUFORT HOUNDS.
FEB 22 1871

HIGHWROTH

The Run
Railways
Rivers & Canals
Roads
Coverts
Scale same as Ordnance Map

GREAT WESTERN RAILWAY

RIVER THAMES

SEVERN CANAL

CRICKLADE

in other countries. In 1874, he and Lord Worcester visited Stetchcombe, and in April 1875, they embarked upon an excursion to the New Forest where, T. F. Dale tells us: "It was something of a trial to Lord Worcester, for, as is usually the case in the New Forest in the Spring, there were several Masters present." These included Sir Reginald Graham of the New Forest, who features in one of the best hunting stories ever told. In his *Foxhunting Recollections*, Sir Reginald tells us that "the hounds ran on for another five minutes, then threw up suddenly in the middle of a fallow field, and never touched the line again. There was no one in sight, so after a time, with all the confidence of youth, I proceeded to hold the hounds down the wind and then in other directions. No doubt I must have thought it encouraging to the pack to wave my right arm with energy as I took them along with that action of the hand which is so much in vogue on poultry farms. All in vain. They never touched the line again. I looked round once more; what did I see? Fifty yards behind there stood Lord Henry [Bentinck] himself, the Messrs. Chaplin, Chandos Leigh and Charley Hawtin. Would that the earth could have swallowed me up at that moment! Slowly, step by step, the cavalcade approached! I heard a smothered hush and yet another pause! At last, Lord Henry, in slow, measured tones, almost hissed out, word by word: 'Sir Reginald, when you have quite done feeding your chickens, perhaps you will allow *my* huntsman to cast *my* hounds!'"

Stories of Masters of Foxhounds "throwing their tongues" are, of course, legion, and the 8th Duke of Beaufort was by no means lacking in this respect. On one occasion, an obsequious gamekeeper approached the Duke and told him that the hounds would be sure to find in his area as he had "been taking so much care of the foxes". "Thank you," was the reply. "If only you would leave them alone, they would be sure to take care of themselves."

It was his grandfather, however, the 6th Duke, who once delivered what must have been one of the most cutting rebukes ever made in the hunting field. Tired of having his hounds ridden over by visiting undergraduates from Oxford, the 6th Duke rode up to an offender on one occasion and, raising his hat, said: "Sir, I have to thank you and I beg every gentleman will follow my example and take off their hats to you and thank you for spoiling a very good day's sport."

Alfred Watson, a writer (joint editor of *The Badminton Library* series) and hunting enthusiast, visited Badminton in 1877. "I had never been what may be called 'behind the scenes' of a great hunt, and looked forward most eagerly to the Badminton expedition. The nearest station, when I paid my first visit, was Chippenham, eleven miles off, and the Duke used to have several pairs of carriage horses kept exclusively for station work. Soon after my arrival at the house, I had the treat of going through the stables, and before dinner remember asking the Duke how many horses they contained. He said that, had I enquired five minutes earlier, he should not have been able to answer, but he had just had the return and that evening there were one hundred and forty-seven. The hounds were then hunting five days a week. Two of his sons, besides Lord Worcester, were at home; the Hunt servants, of course, wanted a great many mounts, and there were always abundant reserves. On the occasion of my first visit, I stayed over Sunday; the Church at Badminton is reached by stairs from the drawing room, and after the service I was taken to the Kennels, where the Duke was accustomed to spend much of his time."

Watson was concerned as to what sort of figure he would cut in the hunting field "in a strange country on a strange horse". After all, the Beaufort Hunt was a "crack" hunt, and he might have found himself up against some stiff opposition. As it transpired, his fears proved to be groundless.

"I soon found there was no ground for apprehension. At the stone walls, which had looked not a little formidable, the Duke never rode until they were reduced to what he called 'walking places'. Indeed, owing to what I understand to have been an accident, he never jumped and his sons did so rarely. I remember once, however, looking down into a covert at Lord Worcester, who hunted the hounds himself, and wondering how he was going to get out of it, for there seemed no way except over a really big fence. This he rode at, and cleared unhesitatingly. I fancy it was on my second day that I took note of a hound closely following Lord Worcester's horse, wherever he might chance to go, as we rode to the Meet, and I commented upon it to the Duke. 'It is strange', he observed, 'she always sticks to the heels of the huntsman's horse, and what makes it more remarkable is that her mother and her grandmother used to do exactly the same thing.' Here is a little problem in heredity, the solution of which is utterly beyond me."

The 8th Duke of Beaufort had a reputation for kindness and consideration to everybody, and Alfred Watson found him to be the perfect host.

"The morning I left, he bustled about to cut me sandwiches and make sure that my flask was filled, though the journey from Chippenham to London is not a long one and, to my great delight, he had fixed the day for a repetition of my visit. The Duchess, too, was the kindest of all possible hostesses. When I came down to breakfast the first morning, I found her scooping out the crumbs from little rolls and filling them with a mixture of minced chicken and ham with cream.

Worcester, she said, did not like 'kitchen sandwiches' and, thus, she supplied her guests with lunch to take with them.

"I was hunting at Badminton on almost the last day of the season—I think it must have been in 1877—and had some little difficulty with my horse, which I endeavoured to explain away by saying that I was not accustomed to plain flapped saddles. Soon after hunting began the next season, I went down [to Badminton] by the newspaper train, and we drove to the Meet. 'That's your first horse', he said, pointing to the animal destined for me. 'I've got you a padded saddle; I remember you said you didn't like plain flaps.' A little incident typical of his kindly thought. When he was suffering from gout, and it must have been painful for him to move, I have often seen him go round with a match to someone who had an unlighted cigarette in his mouth in the billiard room, to which we used generally to adjourn after dinner.

"Many as the days were I was privileged to spend at Badminton, I only remember one, excluding Sundays, of course, when I did not hunt. We must, I suppose, have been stopped by frost."

Another memory which Alfred Watson carried away with him from Badminton was of the Duke's remarkable instinct where the run of a hunted fox was concerned.

"The Duke had, as I gradually found out, an extraordinary presience of the run of a fox. I have sometimes sat on a hillside with him, seen the pack off on a hot scent, and grown nervous lest we should be left behind, and doubtless shown signs of anxiety. The Duke would say 'Just wait a minute' and, when we had so waited, would set off in what, at first, seemed to me a hopelessly wrong direction; but I think I may say that we never failed to nick in, and though he did not jump, he had the knack of making his weight carriers gallop at a great pace."

In that same (1878) G. J. Whyte-Melville, the famous sporting writer, who was killed whilst out hunting with the V.W.H. (and who is commemorated every week on the cover of *Horse and Hound*) also wrote of the 8th Duke of Beaufort's ability to judge a run.

"There is an intuitive perception, more animal than human, of what we may call 'the line of the chase' with which certain sportsmen are gifted by nature, and which I believe would bring them up at critical points of the finest and longest runs if they came out hunting in a gig. The Duke of Beaufort possesses this gift in an extraordinary degree. When so crippled by gout, or reduced by suffering as to be unable to keep to the saddle over a fence, he seems, even in strange [hunting] countries, to see no less of the sport than in the old days when he could ride into every field with his hounds. And I do believe that now, in any part of Gloucestershire, with ten couple of the "badger pyed" and a horn he could go out and kill a fox in his bath chair."

Indeed, nowhere is there a more indicative example of the successive Dukes of Beaufort's passion for hunting than in the fact that in later life, after a lifetime of hunting hounds and when no longer able to ride, they have still managed to follow hounds in other ways. T. F. Dale relates that the 8th Duke in his later years "came out on a cob to view hounds, even though age, cares and gout had left him but a remnant of the gay vitality that had so long distinguished him". The 9th Duke had his first view of hounds when a child from the hood of his grandfather's carriage and he, in his turn, when an old man, used to follow hounds in a chauffeur-driven open car, accompanied by his terrier, Johnnie (see illustration no. 7).

In 1888, as a result of the agricultural depression, the Beaufort Hunt's hunting days were reduced to four a week (the Wiltshire side of the country being loaned to Captain Spicer of Spye Park, to whom the Duke also loaned some hounds).

It was at this time, also, that a subscription was raised amongst the Hunt members, although the hounds remained the Duke's own property. However, according to one source, the members of the Hunt had been contributing to the Poultry Fund for years, although this information was kept from the Duke, for fear of hurting his feelings.

In 1896, Will Dale was engaged as professional Huntsman to the Beaufort hounds. Dale began his career as a Whipper-in with the V.W.H. Hunt and was later Huntsman to Lord Galway (Grove Hunt). In 1873, he went to the Fitzwilliam, and in 1884 to the Brocklesby, where he remained for twelve seasons. Will Dale must have been a man of incredibly good health and fitness, for he came to the Beaufort Hunt when he was sixty and remained there, hunting two or three days a week (alternately with the then Marquess of Worcester) for fifteen seasons, before retiring in 1910.

Claude Luttrell, in his *Recollections of a Younger Son*, described Dale as a man who "combined all the essential attributes to make hunting with him a real pleasure. His kennel management and knowledge of hound breeding were unrivalled and, in his prime, he was the best huntsman I ever had the good luck to hunt with. He was always cheery and good-tempered and, in short, deserved the testimonial contained in what I once overheard the Duke say of another famous Huntsman—'He is the nicest man I know except Will Dale'."

In 1899, one year before the birth of the present Duke, the 8th Duke of Beaufort died, aged seventy-five. It was a great pity that he did not live to see his grandson, who was to become the greatest foxhunter of all the Dukes of Beaufort.

A good landlord, a great sportsman, the 8th Duke's reign as Master covered what was perhaps the most magnificent period in the history of the Beaufort Hunt, in what must have been the "golden age" of foxhunting, with superb foxhounds, hunted over unspoilt country, by enthusiastic and knowledgeable foxhunters.

In his later years, the 8th Duke was very much occupied with the foundation of *The Badminton Library*, which was, in its time, the standard authority on most forms of sport then being enjoyed.

THE BADMINTON LIBRARY

In 1882 Alfred E. T. Watson was asked to assist His Grace, the 8th Duke of Beaufort to edit a series of books dealing with a wide variety of sports and pastimes. This series, which ran into some twenty-eight volumes, was to prove highly successful, and was known as *The Badminton Library*.

Longmans, the publishers, had persuaded the Duke of Beaufort to act as general editor of the series, a position which Alfred Watson assumed would be purely nominal. He reckoned without the Somerset thoroughness, however.

"I had an idea", wrote Watson, "that the real work would fall upon me. I soon found out, however, that he (the Duke) had every intention of doing the work he had undertaken in the agreement between the editor, assistant editor (Watson), and the publishers, which was signed in 1885."

Watson goes on to give an example of just how thorough the Duke of Beaufort could be when it came to research.

"In an early volume of the *Library*, reference was made to a lately deceased nobleman as having served in the Grenadier Guards in the Peninsular [War]. 'I don't think Lord — was in the Grenadiers,' the Duke wrote to me when he returned the proof. 'I have searched in every book I can think of at Badminton as likely to furnish the information, but I shall be going to Bristol in a day or two and may find one there. If not, when I am in London, I can doubtless ascertain.'"

Alfred Watson thought this rather an excess of care, and replied: "Do you think it really matters? Let us say he was in the Guards. That would cover the point. Or, indeed, why mention any regiment? Would it not be enough to say Lord —, who did excellent service in the Peninsular? Nothing turns on his having been a guardsman."

But this did not satisfy the Duke, who replied: "No, let us be right. My impression is that he was in the Coldstream Guards, and it is just as well to make sure if we can."

As it transpired, Lord — had been in the Coldstream Guards. "And though I considered the matter unimportant," wrote Watson, "it showed me the spirit in which *The Badminton Library* was to be written. I understood that our work in its most trivial details was to be as

1 The Beaufort coat of arms.

The 1st Duke of Beaufort was eleventh in the male line from Edward III (1327–77) through the King's third son, John of Gaunt, Duke of Lancaster. By his mistress, Katherine Swynford whom he married as his third wife, John had several illegitimate children and he gave them the name of Beaufort. The eldest son was created Earl of Somerset. Charles, the illegitimate son of Henry Beaufort, 3rd Duke of Somerset, adopted his father's title as his surname, and thus was founded the family of Somerset. He was created Earl of Worcester by Henry VIII. The 5th Earl was made a Marquess by Charles I, and his eldest son (1629–1700) was the father of Henry Somerset, the 1st Duke of Beaufort.

2/3 The 1st Duke of Beaufort and his wife: portraits by Sir Peter Lely

4 Badminton House from the east

5 The Great Hall, Badminton House

THE SPORTING SWEEP,
To tell you the truth, Gemmen, I can't vote for you, 'cause I hunts with the Duke.

6 The Sporting Sweep of Chipping Sodbury: picture by Henry Alken

7 The 9th Duke following hounds by car: picture by Lionel Edwards

8 Lawn Meet at Westonbirt, 1922. The 9th Duke and Queen Mary are on the extreme left.

9 The Beaufort hounds being led through Tetbury after the meet at Tetbury Market. The 17th-century market house is in the background.

10 The present Duke of Beaufort as a boy,
with his father, the 9th Duke.

11 The 10th Duke of Beaufort as Master of the Horse: painting by Cuneo.

12 Brian Gupwell, Huntsman to the Beaufort Hunt, with hounds in front of Badminton House.

13 Frank Weldon riding Kilbarry, winners of the Badminton Horse Trials in 1955 (at Windsor) and in 1956.

14 Lucinda Prior-Palmer holding the Whitbread Trophy after her third win in 1977, with Killaire (left) who was third and George (right) who was first.

15 The 10th Duke of Beaufort riding Apollo.

accurate as care could make it. That if critics thought proper to differ from our conclusions, they were not to be allowed to disprove our asserted facts."

Alfred Watson need not have worried about the critics, however, for when the first volume of *The Badminton Library* appeared in 1885 it was an immediate success. This first volume which, naturally, dealt with hunting, was dedicated to the then Prince of Wales and, in a brief introduction following the dedication, the editor stated the purpose of the series:

"There is no modern encyclopaedia to which the inexperienced man who seeks guidance in the practice of various British sports and pastimes can turn for information. Some books there are on hunting, some on racing, some on lawn tennis, some on fishing, and so on; but one Library, or succession of volumes, which treats of the sports and pastimes indulged in by Englishmen. . . . and women is wanting. *The Badminton Libarary* is offered to supply the want."

The Badminton Library series covered a very wide range of subjects, including *Racing and Steeplechasing* by the Earl of Suffolk; *Shooting* by Lord Walsingham; *Driving* by His Grace, the Duke of Beaufort; *Yachting* by Lord Brassey, and so on. There was even a volume devoted to the *Poetry of Sport. Athletics* and *Football* were also covered, while Viscount Bury produced a volume on *Cycling*!

In 1902 a volume was published on *Motors and Motor Driving*, a subject which most people today would barely classify as a sport or pastime, as they wait in traffic jams. And it is tempting to wonder what the Duke would have thought of the road system which has carved up so much of his beloved hunting country.

9th Duke of Beaufort: Master 1899–1924

In 1868 when the Huntsman, Tom Clarke, retired, the Marquess of Worcester carried the horn with the Beaufort Hunt so that when he succeeded to the title as the 9th Duke of Beaufort in 1899, he had already hunted the hounds for some thirty seasons. He was, in the words of Major Gerald Gundry, recently retired Joint-Master of the Beaufort Hunt, a man "who absolutely lived for hunting—six days a week—and that was his life."

On his succession, the 9th Duke took back the Avon Vale country from Captain Spicer, and hunted it until 1904 when it was loaned to the South and West Wilts (it became the Avon Vale in 1912, under Colonel Fullerton).

The 9th Duke was extremely popular throughout the country, especially with children. Although he was a strict man in the hunting field, Charles Balch, who as a young farmer hunted with the Beaufort Hunt, says of him—"The discipline the Duke kept in the hunting field would have done credit to a Sergeant Major in the Grenadier Guards." He adds, however: "He was respected by all and sundry, and would stand no nonsense from anyone. My memory of him is of a perfect aristocrat of the very best traditional type—the perfect English gentleman."

In 1901 there occurred another fine run from Greatwood, as recollected by Claude Luttrell, in his *Recollections of a Younger Son*:

"Of the four best runs I saw in the Duke's country during sixteen years' hunting, three were over the Dauntsey and Bushton Vales—the other was over the walls. Very curiously, two of these runs started by hounds hitting the line of a travelling fox when going on to another covert to draw. The last of the four best runs was from Greatwood on 31 October 1901. We had met at Greatwood for the last day's cub-hunting, and the Duke had given orders that hounds were not to be halloaed away except on to a tired cub. Anyhow, one of the Hunt second horsemen viewed this fox away on the lower side of Greatwood, and assured Dale [the Huntsman] that it was a very tired cub; so Dale blew hounds out of covert, and thus started as fine a hunt as anyone could wish to see."

The following account of this hunt appeared in *The Field*:

THE DUKE OF BEAUFORT'S HOUNDS. These hounds had a very fine run on 31 October. They met at Greatwood and, after hustling a strong litter of cubs, were halloaed away on to an old fox at the bottom end of the covert at about 11.30. Leaving Meux Gorse on the left, this good fox crossed the Brinkworth Brook close to the withy bed, and was headed by navvies on the new railway but, turning left-handed, soon made his point and crossed the railway and the Wootton Bassett Road near Brinkworth. From here, he set his head straight for Braydon Pond and, as everyone knows, it is a grand line across the best of the V.W.H. country. Just short of Braydon, our fox was again headed, and hounds swung back and into Somerford Common. Here the small field who had been lucky enough to be with hounds up till now, were glad enough to take a pull at their horses, but hounds never hesitated, and drove their fox straight through Somerford Common and away to Webb's Wood, through this big wood and on to Lydiard Plain. Dale now, for the first time, had a view of this gallant old fox as he ran the road towards Lydiard and Swindon, but hounds were screaming along, and needed no lifting. Turning out of the road by Flaxlands, this bold fox set his head for the Duke's country again, but hounds were pressing him so hard that he had to turn short back from the Wootton Bassett road and, catching a view, they coursed him across the big fields to Webb's Wood, and rolled him over within a few yards of the main earth which, being in the V.W.H. country, was, of course, open. It was exactly 1 o'clock when they killed, and I do not expect there was a happier man in England at that moment than Will Dale. It was a grand performance on the part of hounds; they were hardly touched all the way but, needless to say, Dale was always with them, cheering them on and ready to keep them to their hunted fox. It was, of course, a great piece of luck to run through these big woodlands without having another fox on foot but, thanks to Dale's kennel management, every hound was up when they first touched the woods, and every hound was helping to drive a sinking fox to his death, instead of hanging about and trying to have another hunt on her own (for it was the lady pack).

Hounds never crossed a ploughed field, and as they ran, it must have been a long 10 miles. One could not help feeling sorry that such a gallant fox was dead, but when one thought of the triumph of Dale and the hounds it was quite sufficient compensation for the death of as bold a fox as ever made his kennel in Great Wood.

In 1910, Will Dale retired and was succeeded by George Walters, with Tom Newman and Fred Pittaway as Whippers-in. Walters hunted a mixed pack on Mondays and Thursdays, while the 9th Duke hunted the dog hounds on Tuesdays and Fridays, with occasional days when both packs were out in different parts of the country.

One final word on Dale from a distinguished Huntsman: "Will Dale was a big man and the [present] Duke's father was a big man, so progress must have been just a little bit slow, and that is why the country, particularly around Badminton is so well gated—sometimes scores of gates in a field." (According to Lady Caroline Somerset, His Grace seldom jumped anything.)

Charles Balch also remembers the 9th Duke by virtue of his size:

"The Duke's father used to have a special train to bring the hounds to Wootton Bassett and I have told the present Duke I can well remember his father, who was an imitation of Henry VIII, and woe betide Mr Tett, the Station Master at Wootton Bassett, if a pair of steps were not ready to allow his Grace to mount his 18-hand horses."

Commenting upon the 9th Duke's hunting ability, Major Gundry says:

"He must have been a very fine Huntsman indeed. He knew the line of every fox throughout the country, and there are many people in the country today who remember him as the tremendous hunting man he was. And, remember, that although good sport was easier to come by, it was a very much harder way of life—there were no motor horse boxes and horse box trailers in those days, and he did hunt a very much larger part of the country. He hunted the Avon Vale as well as the present-day country. Hounds went great distances to the meet, and he had to do the same himself [on horseback]."

During the 1914/18 War, hunting at Badminton was severely cut back. However, a pack of thirty couple was maintained, and the country was hunted two days a week.

According to the present Beaufort Huntsman, Brian Gupwell, there is a unique, and often unnoticed, memento of the 9th Duke's passion for hunting at Badminton:

"All the weather-vanes I know of point to the direction the wind is in. If the wind is in the north, the weather-vane points to the north and tells you that's where the wind is. The Duke's father thought this was ridiculous, because the fox hardly ever goes into the wind—he goes downwind—so the weather-vanes at Badminton are weighted the other way round, so that you have to look at the fox's brush to see which direction the wind is in."

The 9th Duke also carried his enthusiasm for hunting into a debate in the House of Lords. Winston Churchill had, on one occasion in 1904, told the Lords that he would be "quite content to see the battle joined between representative government and a miserable minority of titled persons who represent nobody". (Hard words indeed from the son of a duke!) In the subsequent debate, the 9th Duke of Beaufort said that he would like to see both Lloyd George and Winston Churchill in the middle of twenty couple of dog hounds.

The 9th Duke of Beaufort was Master of Foxhounds for twenty-five seasons. When in later life, he was no longer able to ride to hounds, he followed in a car, and it is reported that he "kept in touch with the hounds in an amazing way". When he died in 1924, he was succeeded by his son, the present Duke of Beaufort who, as Lord Worcester, had been hunting the Beaufort hounds since 1921. He was to carry on the Beaufort hunting tradition in a magnificent manner and to become, in Daphne Moore's words—"the greatest Nimrod of them all".

10th Duke of Beaufort: Master 1924–   : Foxhunter Extraordinary

There is an Eastern proverb which states, in effect, that Allah does not count to a man the years spent in the chase, and this would indeed seem to be the case as far as the present Duke of Beaufort is concerned.

At the age of seventy-eight, he is still hunting as enthusiastically as ever, as well as managing to cope with hundreds of official and unofficial engagements. Indeed, at times, it seems as if there must be two or three Dukes of Beaufort—hunting, attending functions and official engagements, and farming all at the same time.

There is a photograph, taken in 1909 (see no. 10) which shows the present Duke as a boy standing outside Badminton House with his father, both of them dressed for hunting. To anyone interested in foxhunting, the boy's stance and the unquestionable air of authority leave one in no doubt that here is a future Master of Foxhounds.

Sir Peter Farquhar, a close friend of the Duke of Beaufort, former Master of the Bicester and Warden Hill Foxhounds, and one of the greatest living authorities on hound breeding, very kindly wrote the following appreciation of His Grace as sportsman and foxhunter in August 1977:

"'Master', as he is affectionately known throughout the sporting world, is one of my oldest and best friends, and one for whom I have the very greatest admiration. Many people think that he is known as 'Master' because of his prowess as a Master and Huntsman of Foxhounds. In fact, this is not so, but dates back to his childhood. His father kept a pack of harriers for him to hunt during his school holidays and, when hunting them, his two elder sisters and others who helped, made a point of addressing him as Master, and this has stuck ever since in the form of a nickname.

"Descended from a family who had always been dedicated to all forms of field sports, he started hunting his father's bitch pack in 1921; in 1924, after the death of his father, he assumed the dual role of Master and Huntsman, which continued until 1967 when, having sustained one or two nasty falls at the age of sixty-seven, he very wisely, though very reluctantly, handed the horn to his professional huntsman.

"Besides having been a brilliant huntsman, he is also a very talented breeder of foxhounds. Whilst maintaining the old, tough Badminton female lines, he has introduced wise outcrosses from Wales and elsewhere, and today the standard of his kennel is second to none.

"Ever since the last war, he has taken every opportunity to help any keen Masters of Foxhounds by making his stallion hounds available to them, or by giving them proven bitches from which to breed.

"The present very high standard of foxhounds, throughout the country, owes a great deal to his generosity in this respect.

"Perhaps one of his greatest contributions to the sporting scene was in introducing 'Eventing' to this country when, in 1949, he inaugurated the Badminton Three-Day Event, which has continued annually ever since and set a pattern throughout the land.

"Apart from his fame in the hunting world, Master is also an accomplished horseman, a very fine shot and a talented fisherman. In this last respect, I am reminded of a day just after the war when we were fishing together in Ireland on the river Slaney. The beat we were fishing was owned by a friend whose foxhounds were kennelled a few hundred yards from the river. Before starting out that morning, Master had told me that this was a very important day for him as it was the hundredth anniversary of his father's birthday—a father of whom he was very fond and who was also a great foxhunter and sportsman.

"On the opposite bank of the river was a wood in which there was a litter of fox cubs and, on this particular summer day, one of the brood bitches from the kennels decided to leave her whelps for a short time and give the vixen a bit of exercise! Just as Master hooked his first fish of the day, he heard the old bitch "open" and, looking up, saw the fox, closely followed by the foxhound, pass by along the opposite bank. He cheered her on and a few minutes later landed his fish.

"Between the wars, his hounds hunted six days a week, and he sometimes, very kindly, asked me to bring my hounds to Badminton for a week's early cubhunting. On these occasions we used to fit nine days hunting into the six-day week, taking out one pack at 5.30 in the morning and another at 5.30 in the evening. I seem to remember that we had but little trouble in getting to sleep on the Saturday night!

"Now, at the age of seventy-eight, Master still follows his hounds regularly two days a week, and seemingly finds little difficulty in riding across the country he knows so well; although he sometimes complains of feeling a little stiff! There can be no doubt that he will go down to history as a very great foxhunter and very great sportsman."

In addition to the Beaufort title and estates, when the present Duke succeeded in 1924, at the age of twenty-four, he also inherited sixty horses and eighty couple of foxhounds, and well and truly had the Somerset family's passion for hunting.

The Duke began hunting as a child: "I've done it ever since I can remember—on a donkey, on a pony being led about. My father used to hunt hounds five or six days a week."

When he was nine years old, as Peter Farquhar has already said, he had his own pack of harriers:

"My father gave me a small pack of harriers, to hunt hares. At the Meet, the people who used to come out hunting with me used to come up and say, for a joke: 'Where are you going to draw today,

Master?'—much the same as they said to the Master of the Foxhounds with a big pack. It came to be a joke. Everybody used to say, when they met me, 'Master', and somehow the name stuck.''

Later, His Grace gained further experience of hunting with the Eton College Beagles. As has been said, he was hunting the Beaufort Hounds by the time he was twenty-one, and he continued to do so until 1967 becoming, in those forty-seven seasons, the finest amateur huntsman in England as well as being the recognised "champion" of fox hunting.

In addition to his achievements in the hunting field, the Duke of Beaufort has also been active in other spheres associated with hunting: he is recognised as an outstanding judge and breeder of foxhounds. During the past fifty seasons, the Duke has bred a pack of hounds which are second to none, and which epitomise the modern foxhound at the very highest peak of its development. Beaufort hounds have been consistent winners at the Peterborough Show, the "mecca" of hound breeders, and the number of rosettes on display at the Badminton Kennels has to be seen to be believed.

The Duke's foxhounds have also influenced hound-breeding, not only throughout the British Isles, but also in America and other countries. Major Dallas, Honorary Secretary to the Beaufort Hunt, has pointed out how very generous the Duke is when it comes to drafting hounds.

"It's a very fine pack of hounds, and the Duke will always let any other Master of Foxhounds use his blood lines. Lots of people write to him from other hunts—'If you are drafting any hounds, will you please consider me'—and he *gives* them the hounds. Well, a lot of people sell their draft hounds . . .''

As far as his own preference for hounds is concerned, His Grace has described this as follows:

"As regards make and shape, I like a fair sized hound. A dog hound: strong, muscular, with good neck and shoulders, good ribs, straight legs; he mustn't knuckle over too much. Good hind legs, and strong quarters; I don't like a curly stern. As regards hunting qualities, I like a hound that has plenty of tongue, can gallop and jump, and has a good nose. Those are the two most important things—nose and tongue. It's no good having a good shaped hound if he hasn't got nose and tongue. Some packs in England conform entirely to our more old-fashioned hounds—English without any Welsh cross—but I have crossed mine with Welsh hounds, and I do believe that it has given them more cry, which I think is most important.''

With over fifty years' experience as Huntsman and Master combined, the Duke of Beaufort has no doubt as to what it takes to make both a good huntsman and a good Master of Foxhounds:

"A good huntsman requires good health. He needs to be a good horseman. He loves his hounds and his hounds love him. He has to have a very good knowledge of where a fox is likely to go, and so he has to know his country well. He also has to have a good voice and horn— very nice to hear. A good Master, if he's well-known in the country, it makes things easier for him. A Master has to learn about all parts of the country and what is going on. He has to get on well with his neighbours and the landowners and farmers in the country. As to whether good Masters are born or made, I think they are made, probably. It's something new to start off with, if you haven't been a Master before, and you have to be willing to listen to the advice of former Masters of the country, and so on, and that all helps, but I'm not sure that huntsmen aren't born—the really good ones, that is . . ."

When His Grace first succeeded to the Mastership in 1924, he hunted the hounds four days a week. Later, this was reduced to two days, the professional Huntsman taking over during the rest of the week. However, on one occasion when his Huntsman, Tom Newman, was injured, the Duke hunted the hounds for six days a week over a period of six weeks.

Tom Newman began his career as a boy, whipping-in to his father in the Hambledon country. He was later put on as second Whipper-in to Will Dale, who was then the Beaufort Huntsman, and was subsequently promoted to first Whipper-in. In all, Newman served for sixteen years before being engaged as Huntsman, in 1915. Newman has been described as "one of those professional huntsmen who are sportsmen and lovers of hounds first".

In 1930, the Duke of Beaufort invited a Joint Master to assist him— Mr. Cox of Malmesbury—who remained with him for five seasons. Then, in 1935, Captain Spicer became Joint Master (Captain Spicer's father had hunted the Avon Vale country, by permission of the 8th Duke, during the late 1880s).

Tom Newman retired in 1936, after twenty-one years as Huntsman and thirty-six years in the service of the 9th and 10th Dukes of Beaufort. He was succeeded by Fred Brown, who came to Badminton from the adjacent V.W.H. Hunt. Unfortunately, Brown died in only his second season, as the result of a bad fall. He was succeeded by Reg Holland, formerly Huntsman to the Cattistock.

Prior to the outbreak of the Second World War, the Beaufort Hunt was hunting six days a week, with the present Duke and Reg Holland dividing the hunting of hounds between them. During the war years, hunting was again severely reduced, although the country was hunted as much as was possible under the circumstances. In 1941, Captain

Spicer relinquished his Joint Mastership of the Beaufort Hunt (to take over the Avon Vale), and Reg Holland was called up to serve in the army in the same year.

After the war, hunting in the Beaufort country was soon back to normal and, in 1946, Ted Reade, first Whipper-in, was put on as Huntsman. Reade once gave a splendid piece of advice to David Knight, the young son of Rupert Knight, a former Head Gardener at Badminton. David Knight wrote of Ted Reade as follows: "A good friend of mine was the Chief Whip, Ted Reade. With him I used to go to the meets, holding my crop in the approved huntsman style. From whom I learnt many a piece of wisdom. One I always remember: when hunting take three things—a piece of string to tie any trophies to the saddle, a knife to cut off the trophy, and a shilling to buy a pint for the Huntsman."

During Reade's time as Huntsman, the Beaufort hounds hunted four days a week, with Reade and His Grace hunting hounds two days each. By 1949, they were hunting five days each week.

During the 1951/52 season, hunting was being carried on six days a week, with the Duke hunting the bitch pack, Major Gerald Gundry hunting a mixed pack, and Ted Reade hunting the dog hounds. In 1952, Ted Reade retired, and Major Gundry continued hunting the hounds alternately with His Grace. Bert Pateman was the Kennel Huntsman at that time.

In the old days at Badminton, the hounds used to have the run of the village and, according to Mr Charlie Smith, a long-time resident of Badminton, there wasn't a cat to be seen there. Mr Les Rochester remembers the time when he had to fend off a large dog hound for ten minutes, using his bicycle as a shield.

Brian Gupwell tells the story of one hound which, in Bert Pateman's time at Badminton, leapt through the window of the Huntsman's cottage, breaking the glass in her efforts to get inside.

"It was after a Puppy Show, and old Woeful, a very famous old brood bitch, was wandering about outside—I suppose it would be a June night. They had the windows open, and old Woeful was jumping in the window, and they were giving her a sandwich, and out she would jump again—in and out—in and out. When it got a bit cooler in the evening, they shut the window, and later old Woeful came back. I suppose she had been on her rounds to see her pups. When she came back, it was dark and the light was on in the sitting-room here, and crash, straight through the window Woeful came—straight through and broke all the glass."

For two hundred years now, people have been predicting the end of foxhunting for one reason or another, and yet it still survives. Before the last war, of course, Badminton was a foxhunters' paradise. Today, however, heavy traffic and the vastly increased number of roads across the country make it slightly less so. The M.4, for example, cuts right across the Duke's Badminton Estate, dividing the country.

Another change which has come about is the amount of ploughing which is carried out by the farmers. As His Grace said, "In the old days, we used to be on grass all day." Even so, His Grace is optimistic.

"I think the future of hunting looks pretty good. There are more people hunting now than ever before, and there are more packs of hounds than there used to be. Roads, railways and the development of building land make an area a good deal less attractive for hunting, but I think that, apart from where it has become too overgrown with buildings, it will continue."

One notable feature during the Mastership of the present Duke of Beaufort has been the "birthday meets". For hunting people living in the Beaufort country, His Grace's birthday meet is always a special occasion, but three birthdays in particular, which deserve special mention, have been recorded by Daphne Moore in her book, *In Nimrod's Footsteps*.

1950. On the Duke's fiftieth birthday, 5 April 1950, it had been arranged to hold an unofficial point-to-point for the Royal Gloucestershire Hussars prior to a day's hill hunting from Starveall, a few miles from Badminton. In all, there were thirteen starters, including the Duke himself, and the race took place over natural country, chiefly walls. There was an enormous crowd, both of foot people and those who had come out to hunt later. I counted no fewer than eleven masters of Foxhounds and ex-masters later in the day. The Duke was leading over the initial part of the course, going great guns, and finishing not far behind the winners John White and Gregory Phillips (both of the V.W.H.) who reached the winning post in what was practically a photofinish.

1960. No memoirs of Badminton would be complete without mention of two historic meets which took place in 1960 and 1970, respectively; the first to commemorate the Duke's sixtieth birthday, the second to mark the occasion of his seventieth. The scene of Barraud's well-known painting of 1840—"The Lawn Meet at Badminton"—was the setting in 1960, the first Badminton Lawn Meet to be held there since the war. Never, perhaps, has a more important occasion been acknowledged at a Meet of foxhounds, for this not only marked the Duke's sixtieth birthday, but also forty years of hunting hounds. He had for so long been known as one of the greatest amateur huntsmen of all time that the whole country, it seemed, turned out to greet him. Though it was nearing the end of the season, there were nearly two hundred horsemen, chiefly members of the Hunt in the traditional "Blue-and-Buff", and a crowd on foot close on five hundred strong. On the roof of the great house, the Duke's personal standard fluttered in the light north-easterly wind, and the splendid old building towered majestically above the wide sweep of gravelled drive and the Deer Park beyond. The late Major-General Sir Stewart Menzies, the oldest member of the "Blue-and-Buff", who had started to hunt with the Duke's father in 1912, made the presentation from the Hunt, in the form of a Minton breakfast service, a replica of one which has been used at Badminton for at least one hundred years and embodying the Beaufort badge of a portcullis. The residue of the total sum was to be used towards the purchase of the best hunter that money could buy. A total of eighty-four years between father and son as Master and huntsman can seldom have been equalled, and Sir Stewart remarked that, could the Duke's father have been present, it would surely be the happiest day of his life to see his illustrious son, now his successor, the 10th Duke. "In years to come", he went on, "those hunting today would proudly recall that they had had the privilege of hunting with the greatest huntsman of all time. His hard work, too, on non-hunting days, to ensure good sport on the morrow; his care and thought in breeding the pack, and his many successes at Peterborough, made up a record never equalled." The presentation took place "with affection, admiration, and gratitude for wonderful sport".

The Duke replied with a characteristic and entertaining speech, in which he referred to the forty years of hunting his own hounds as "a labour of love". He felt just as great a thrill today when hounds left kennel as he did forty years ago—and this was his 2,285th day on which he hunted hounds. To him there was never a bad day's hunting; some were just not as good as others. A good day's hunting ensued, and a birthday fox was killed.

1970. Ten years later, a great day's sport followed the 1970 anniversary, when the Meet was at Worcester Lodge, at the north end of Badminton's splendid Deer Park. An afternoon fox provided a flying hunt, which ended at the very gates of the kennel, where hounds rolled over their tired fox at the very feet of the Duke himself—a fitting finish to an historic day.

There is no doubt that the Duke of Beaufort is, to put it mildly, an intrepid horseman. Colonel Frank Weldon, Director of the Badminton Horse Trials, once explained what it was like to follow His Grace across country: "He is incredibly brave. You come up to a fence, and you think—he's never going to jump that—but he does, and, of course, one has to go after him." (Remember that that comes from an Olympic Gold Medal winner, who has also won twice at Badminton.)

However, even the best of horsemen suffer falls from time to time, and so it was with the Duke in March 1967, when he suffered a serious fall which left him with cracked ribs and concussion. For most men that would have been the end of the season, but little more than a week later His Grace was out hunting again.

Horse and Hound dated 8 April 1967 carried the following report by "Loppylugs":

I have long held that the Duke of Beaufort is no ordinary mortal, and before I describe the day's hunting upon which I have been privileged to write, let me briefly chronicle the events that led up to it.

On the Monday before Easter, His Grace has a serious fall and is discovered on the ground alone and unconscious. On arrival at Tetbury Hospital, it is diagnosed that he is suffering from cracked ribs and severe concussion. He lies in hospital till the weekend and then, returning home, everyone expects him to convalesce quietly for a couple of months. Two days later, however, he mounts a horse in the Park, though even he agrees that he couldn't hunt hounds. But on waking next morning, when there is an inch of snow lying around, he is advised that Bert, the Kennel Huntsman, has a high temperature and cannot hunt hounds as had been arranged. Without giving a thought to the idea of cancelling the Meet, it seems that the Duke's words were something as follows: "The snow will melt before noon and I'm sure that, in view of the emergency that has arisen, I shall be fit to hunt hounds."

Now, that in my opinion is the first amazing thing—to be able to rise above indisposition when the occasion demands it. I mustn't labour the point, but anyone who knows the difficult Lower Woods, with their great muddy rides, the deep ravines outside, the quantity of foxes, etc., will appreciate the second surprising thing, and that is for a huntsman, in His Grace's state, to hunt only two foxes in two and a half hours and kill the second one. No mean feat.

When I arrive at the Meet in Inglestone Common on March 29th, a penetrating cold wind after the snow is blowing across the common, and with that infectious smile of his, the Duke says quite quickly: "I don't think I'll wait long here, but go and draw Lance Coppice straight away."

His bitches find at once, and a great big chestnut fox comes away across the Hawkesbury Road to the vast Lower Woods. For the next hour, the music of hounds, coupled with His Grace's melodious cheering voice and an occasional exquisite touch of the horn is quite enthralling. Hounds circle Little Wood, Burnt Wood and Upper Wetmoor, and then, on approaching the "Lodge", we see that a dark red fox has ideas of bigger territory, and after running Stonybridge Wood and Boys Wood, the thrilling sound of the Duke's horn blowing "away", encourages my muddy feet to better things, and I am in time (just) to see hounds stream away across the fields towards Wickwar Village and the Berkeley Country.

Fortunately for me, the fox decides to run Bishops Hill Wood and back to Upper Wetmoor; then, for over an hour, those bitches persist on, at times, a quite catchy scent through the chain of Littley, Burnt, Stonybridge and Boys Woods until, crossing Wetmoor Brook, it is "whoo-whooop" and a beaming Duke is saying quite simply: "I think I've really done enough for one day."

In April 1967 the Duke of Beaufort hunted his hounds for the last time. This occasion was also recorded for posterity by the same correspondent—Archibald John Morrison, better known to hunting people throughout Great Britain as "Loppylugs"—hunting correspondent of the *Horse and Hound* magazine. "Loppylugs", who has covered thousands of miles on foot following hounds, described the occasion as follows:

April 15th was the last day of the last season that the Duke of Beaufort had decided he should hunt his bitches personally! Yes, we knew it would come, but somehow we did not quite expect the drama surrounding it. We moved off from the little grass field of Starveall promptly at noon. In front, with $17\frac{1}{2}$ couple of his bitches, was a gay Duke, with a sprig of four-leaved clover (presented, I was told, by a humble well-wisher) in his buttonhole. Riding beside him was the incomparable Sir Peter Farquhar, and, just behind, the efficient Whipper-in, David Goring. Then came his Joint Master, Major Gundry, riding beside his charming wife, and behind a cavalcade of some sixty followers. (Let me remind readers here that this was an unpopular hill hunting Meet when, in the ordinary way, probably only a dozen mounted followers would have turned out.) All these followers, and hundreds on foot besides, had turned out largely as a token of affection and gratitude to "Master" to mark the end of an era of almost fifty seasons of hunting hounds personally. I had prayed for a wet day with a good scent, and I'm afraid I had also asked that I could holloa away the Duke's first fox on his "last day". My first request was not acceded to, for the sun beat down from a cloudless sky, but to my infinite pleasure my second was.

A SHORT HOLLOA

As I stood in the grass field at the edge of Bangel Wood, a huge chestnut dog fox slunk out past me and away over Hennel Bottom. One short holloa and up came the Duke with every hound with him. Pointing across the field, I said: "Looked like a dog fox, Your Grace." "Sounds like a dog fox, doesn't it?" came the instant reply. What experience to know whether your hounds are hunting a dog fox or a vixen—*from the moment they give tongue*. A nice half-hour in and around Miry and Stickstey Woods followed before Sir Peter Farquhar and myself viewed this fox away to Hammouth Hill, but then we soon realised that hounds had changed. What we did not know was that this was the point when a fairy tale hunt was commencing. Throughout several seasons now in the hills, the Duke has pitted his skill against a big, black, bob-tailed dog fox, and always been defeated by bad scent, snow storms or open earths. Now, as hounds circled Barley Ridge and Miry Wood, many of us saw that this old fellow was again the quarry.

FOX HEADED

When the pack crossed the Bangel Bottom, some folk headed the fox on Kilcott Lane. Then three couple split off and went up to the Monument on their own. However, the Duke rallied his pack with infinite patience and got them into Stickstey Wood. All was silent at first, but then, on joy! One lone hound spoke below. His Grace's cheering voice helped the others to join it, and as I dashed out on to the bank above Kilcott, there was Peterborough winner, Posy, leading the pack. Over Clay Hill, across the Splatts and Hillesley, and back to Miry Wood continued the hunt, and exactly ninety minutes from when hounds had changed onto this bob-tailed fox, the Duke was holding up the mask he had wanted to see at close quarters for so many seasons. As he drew round afterwards, information came in that foxes had been seen leaving over main roads, down to the valleys and across to another Hunt country. For the first time that I can remember, His Grace had cleaned the hills of foxes by dint of the music and persistence of his bitches.

As a last tribute, the entire field waited at 5.00 p.m. while the Duke blew for a missing hound. Then came the "thank-you's" for all those fifty-odd seasons of magnificent sport. To my mind, there'll never be another day quite like it, but it is a joy to know that "Master" will carry on in command for dozens of seasons (we all hope).

At that time, there was much speculation throughout the hunting world as to who would (or, indeed, who could) succeed His Grace as Huntsman. The choice fell upon Brian Gupwell, a young, professional Huntsman, at that time with the Eridge Hunt. This was a tremendous fillip to professional Huntsmen, since there can be no doubt that His Grace, with his wide knowledge of hunting and hunting personalities, and his contacts throughout the country, must have looked long and hard before appointing his successor.

Brian Gupwell comes from a hunting family. His grandfather was a stud groom at the Old Surrey and Burstow, where his father, Walter Gupwell, started as Second Horseman, before going to the Hambledon, where he was Second Whipper-in for nine seasons. He then went to the Fitzwilliam with a famous Huntsman, Tom Agutter, and in 1936 he was engaged as Huntsman to the Middleton (the Masters at that time were Lord Grimthorpe and Lord Halifax). When the Second World War broke out, Lord Halifax decided to take his horses into the Yorkshire Hussars with him, also taking his Huntsman with him. After the war, Walter Gupwell spent four years in Ireland with the Galway Blazers before returning to England, where he was appointed as Huntsman to the Fernie for fifteen seasons.

On leaving school, Brian Gupwell signed on as an apprentice jockey to Walter Easterby at Malton, for the princely salary of two shillings and sixpence a week. He remained at Malton for two years, by which time he had become too heavy to become a jockey, in addition to which, he was not particularly impressed with the life of an apprentice jockey at that time. And so, following in the family tradition, he obtained a position in hunt service, as Second Whipper-in to the East Middleton in Yorkshire, where he remained for two seasons. He then went to the Belvoir. "When I got the Second Whipper-in's place at the Belvoir, I was very pleased, but I didn't get on with the Huntsman and I left after only one season. And then, rather stupidly, I joined the Navy."

His mother's side of the family had a tradition of naval service, a tradition which Brian Gupwell was not destined to carry on. "I knew nothing about the Navy, which seemed to me such a romantic life. How wrong I was! They didn't know anything about hunt service or hunting, and I regretted it."

Returning to civilian life, he rode second horse for a year and then became First Whipper-in to the Brocklesby, where he remained for five years before applying for the position of Huntsman with the Eridge, a position which he obtained despite some very stiff competition—for there were some forty-nine other applicants for the job. Brian Gupwell remained with the Eridge for six years before being offered the position of Huntsman with the Duke of Beaufort's Hounds, a position which he has now held for ten seasons. However, Brian Gupwell's initial reaction to being offered what is perhaps the most coveted job in hunt service was not what one would expect.

"Well, honestly, I was quite happy where I was, and when they first came to me and said that the Duke of Beaufort was giving up hunting his own hounds and is looking for a Huntsman, well, I thought that they were trying to get rid of me. Anyway, Lady Abergavenny said that it was a great honour, and then His Grace drove down and offered me the position. He would obviously have looked down the list at every other Huntsman in the country, because nobody loves his hounds or hunting more, and it really was a big boost to every professional Huntsman that he had chosen a professional to succeed him."

Brian Gupwell was succeeded at the Eridge by John Cooke, whose reaction to Brian's new appointment was much more what one might have expected from a professional Huntsman: "'By Gum!' he said to me. 'You're a brave man, Brian!' I said: 'Why?', and he said: 'You're going to the Beaufort.' 'Yes', I said, 'but why am I a brave man?' 'Gum!' he said. 'Have you ever seen that crowd up there and the Kennels up there?' You see, I didn't know; in my ignorance I didn't know. But many times I've thought afterwards about that. He knew, you see, that it was a hard and demanding job at Badminton."

And a hard and demanding job it proved to be, since Brian Gupwell was taking over from one of the foremost huntsmen of his time, and not only hunting over the same country, but also accepting the responsibility of looking after the most famous pack of foxhounds in the world.

The first thing he noticed was the quality of his new employer.

"His Grace is incredible. He knows every hound. He knows every fox in covert, and he knows if you haven't got a certain hound out hunting. He is the most fantastic man to observe everything, and it can be very, very off-putting."

Brian's comments are borne out by another professional Huntsman, who once exclaimed, "If you tread on a blade of grass at Badminton he [the Duke] knows it!"

As Huntsman to the Beaufort Hunt, Brian's job involves "looking after sixty-five to seventy couple of the best hounds in the country, and His Grace expects them to be looking sound and well the whole time. Of course, we hunt four days a week, and that says a lot in itself."

Brian Gupwell is also responsible for the running and organisation of the Kennels and for the staff—two Whippers-in and two Kennelmen, although he does not engage the staff himself. During the summer months there is kennel maintenance to attend to, hound exercise, Puppy Shows to attend, and the new entry to be educated.

"I think probably the most work for me is educating the young hounds—about 25 couple of young hounds—young hounds, a year old. And, if you think about it, one has to take them into the Park, and they're not on leads, and they haven't got to look at or chase a cow, a sheep, a cat, or anything—things which are natural and normal to young puppies. These hounds haven't got to do that. And you've got to take them out, and tell them, 'That's not on', and that they are not to do this or that, and it takes a lot of time and a lot of patience to get them steady, so that eventually they can go across country with their blood up and only chase what they are supposed to."

To see Brian Gupwell on duty at one of the more formal Beaufort Hunt Meets, flanked by his two Whippers-in, and in perfect control of his hounds, is a truly splendid sight. "As the Duke's Huntsman, one is always on display." He has the look of the classic Huntsman, and at times resembles a huntsman in a nineteenth-century hunting print. Resplendent in his green hunt coat with brass buttons, well-cut breeches, and highly-polished boots, he looks every inch "the Duke's Huntsman". It is, therefore, comforting to know that he is actually subject to the same afflictions as lesser mortals, and that the Beaufort hunts do not always go as smoothly as one imagines. This is borne out by the following two stories, both of which Brian tells against himself.

"Hunting these hounds, one has got to be very much on the ball. You have to be one hundred per cent fit. Well, one particular day, we were meeting here at the Badminton Kennels. I must have had a cold or 'flu coming on. Anyway, I felt like absolutely nothing on earth. It was several years ago now, and I think there were about three hundred people out hunting that day. On the way to the covert, His Grace said to me: 'You don't want to kill a vixen, and we don't want to go away with a vixen'—a pretty tall order and, as I say, I felt like nothing on earth. Luckily, things went well, and we found a fox in Allangrove, and away he went towards Sherston. I came off at the first fence. Very few people saw me because I was up quickly, but I knew I wasn't feeling as I should be. Another fence, I lost a stirrup, and I knew I wasn't feeling right. Anyway, there was a five-mile point to Colonel Whitbread's at Farleaze, and we lost this fox.

"So the Duke said to me: 'We've got to go back to Badminton'— as there was nothing stopped. Well, this meant a five-mile hack back, and I felt absolutely awful. Anyway, people kept coming up to the Duke with flasks—'Would you like a drink, Master?', or 'Would you like me to drive you to Badminton?', and he would say, 'No, thank you'. Well, by then, I was dying for a drink, and I knew it would put me right. I know the date because it was just after decimalisation day. I felt in my pocket, and there was a fifty-pence piece. As I rode along towards

Fosse Lodge, going by all the car followers, I didn't stop my horse as there were about three hundred people behind me. Well, I said to a chap I know, 'Here's fifty pence. Get me a miniature whisky. We are going to draw the Verge.' Just like that. And I looked at my watch, and thought—this fellow's got time to get to the pub at Sherston before closing time and then get back to the Verge and give me the whisky.

"Well, I never saw the chap at the Verge. We found a fox, and then lost him, and then we went to Luckley Break, found a fox, and had quite a decent little hunt. I was beginning to feel a lot better, and I had forgotten all about this chap and the fifty pence.

"The following Wednesday, the Meet was at Lower Woods. Very few people were out. There was His Grace, Major Gundry, myself, two Whippers-in, and a few more, and when we were at Lower Woods, I suddenly spotted this fellow I'd given the fifty pence to, and he put his hand up and waved good morning, and I waved good morning, and I thought, Thank God he's not going to come over now with a miniature whisky and embarrass me. Well, we got into Lower Woods—hundreds of acres of woods and rides—and suddenly I saw this chap on his own on a ride. He was on his own, and I was on my own, and I thought, now's the magic moment when he gives me my whisky. And as I rode up to him, he said: 'Thank you very much for that drink, Brian. It was very nice of you. Thank you very much!'"

The second story is concerned with Brian Gupwell's most embarrassing moment in the hunting field during the ten years that he has been with the Beaufort Hunt.

"I suppose it was about seven years ago. The Meet was at the Monument, at the end of April, after the Horse Trials. We had just got over the A46, the main road leading to the Monument, when a car came along, and the driver said to me: 'Do you know you have left some hounds on the other side of the main road?' Well, I swung round to look for the Second Whipper-in, but the motorist had already told him, and he had gone back like a scalded cat to the main road. Well, I didn't know what to do. The First Whipper-in counted them, and found that we were two couple short, and I began to wonder how on earth we could have lost two couple of hounds in such a short time. So I said to the Whipper-in: 'Get into the first car that comes along and go back along the A46 and watch those hounds come safely over the road', and then I went along to the Meet. Well, eventually the Whipper-in caught us up, got back on his horse, and said that there were no hounds to be seen. So I began to think, was I right about the count? Was it 17½ couple I had? Was it less? All these dreadful doubts. Then, to my horror, in front of me there was the Duke, and he said to me: 'Brian, you are some hounds short.' So I said: 'Yes, Your Grace.'

'How many?' he asked. So I said 'Two couple.' 'Two couple,' he said. 'Two couple! What—can't you get the hounds to the Meet with two Whippers-in to help you?' etc., etc. Well, I felt like nothing on earth, still not knowing how to explain this thing. Well, we went down the road, and I was still churning it over in my mind, because you just can't lose two couple of hounds going to a Meet.

"When we got to the Meet, Mervyn Barrat, the Keeper, was there, and the Duke said to him: 'You go back and find these hounds they've lost, Mervyn.' 'What are their names?' asked Mervyn. 'Names!' said the Duke. 'Names! I don't know! Even these silly . . . don't know!' And off Mervyn went, and got the hounds back.

"Now, what had happened was this. We were on our horses outside the kennels, and the kennelman let the hounds out to us, but he didn't let them all out. He walked in front of the hounds and the door blew to, leaving two couple behind. But when we'd gone, he realised what had happened and let the two couple of hounds come out behind us. It was the worst thing he could have done, because they hit the line of another horse and away they went up the Avenue. And that really was the worst day of my life."

Like all huntsmen, Brian Gupwell is never happier than when he is showing or talking about his hounds. In July 1977, the Beaufort hounds scored another tremendous success at the Peterborough Hound Show, and on the following Sunday afternoon, Brian, together with His Grace, showed the prize-winning hounds to the hundreds of Beaufort Hunt Supporters who had come to the Badminton Kennels for the annual Terrier Show. As the hounds were brought out and shown, there could not have been two happier men in England than the Duke of Beaufort and his Huntsman.

Brian Gupwell is quick to respond to any suggestion that the Beaufort hounds are bred purely to win prizes at shows. "We definitely do not breed for show. We breed for hunting. But, if you are going to have a pack of hounds to hunt a fox, you might just as well have a good-looking pack as an odds and sods pack. They all hunt, and that is why they are the best in the world."

"They are very intelligent hounds, and every huntsman that has ever had hounds from the Duke, during my time or, indeed, years before, and I meet them at the Peterborough Show or elsewhere, and they all say: 'Have you got any hounds to draft, Brian, because the hounds we've had from Badminton before are the best we've ever had. They all hunt.' And that is why they are the best in the world— because the Duke breeds them, and he drafts them, and it is very hard work drafting hounds, and you have got to think very hard and find faults with hounds, so that the hounds you are left with are all super hounds. And this is why they are the best. Because we breed a lot, and we give quite a few to other packs, and we're left with the very, very best."

The Duke of Beaufort once expressed the idea that good huntsmen were born rather than made. Brian Gupwell has his own list of the qualities needed to make a huntsman.

"He has to be blessed with good health, good hearing, good eyesight. To be a fairly sober man. To be able to talk to people and to know when to be tactful. He also has to be a good horseman to keep with his hounds. He has to love his hounds, and not be afraid of hard work. Without those things he just can't get by."

Brian also has quite definite ideas as to the attraction of hunting, as far as he himself is concerned:

"When you have hunted hounds, and if you've hunted hounds, you obviously love hounds. It is the best love of all, really, hunting and it is a marvellous thing to watch hounds and to be one step ahead and see what they'll do. They'll turn and put their noses down, and you'll hold them round a field, and you think a fox must have gone over a wall, and you're waiting for them to reach the wall and as soon they reach it, they'll put their noses down away they'll go. And, by gum, it's really something! It's the most marvellous feeling to put them right and to see them work.

"We are like our grandfathers, but we can rarely see it because by the time we're here, they're often dead. But with hounds, you can see that this bitch, say, is like her mother or her grandmother, or her sisters, and you can see these characteristics coming out during your years in the kennels. It's fascinating. And you say, oh, isn't she like her mother or her father? And they work like them—perhaps got the same tongue, walk the same way, are shy or bold. Marvellous!"

The range of hunting expertise at Badminton is indeed formidable. In addition to the Duke of Beaufort and his Huntsman, Brian Gupwell, there is yet another first class huntsman, and that is Major Gerald Gundry, DSO, who became Joint Master in 1951, and who hunted the Beaufort dog hounds for twenty-three seasons.

Major Gundry, who originally became Hunt Secretary in 1938, comes of a well-known Dorset hunting family. His grandfather, Parson Jack Milne, had the hounds at Cattistock, and he is a nephew of the great Selby Lowndes, master of the East Kent Hunt for thirty years. Major Gundry's brother, Mr. E. F. Gundry, was at one time Joint Master of the Cattistock.

Major Gundry began hunting when he was very young. He was Master of the Eton College Beagles and was also Master of the

Goathland Hunt for a time. During the war, he commanded the 16/5th Lancers. Afterwards, he resumed his position as Beaufort Hunt Secretary, eventually becoming Joint Master in 1951.

Major Gundry is one of the best-known figures in the Beaufort country. At a recent Hunt Supporters' Club Terrier show, he was an enthusiastic starter of the childrens' races. Prior to the start of the races, there was an announcement to the effect that all those wishing to take part in or watch the races should form up near Major Gundry. Almost immediately, some two hundred people began to make their way in his direction.

At the same show, he entered the ring with his terrier. When asked later how he had fared, he replied: "I didn't come anywhere, but I put the wind up the judge!" And, in some quarters, Major Gundry does have something of a reputation for "putting the wind up" people.

One professional Huntsman has said of him: "He's got an eye like a hawk, and if you get in his way, he'll let you know it." However, this Huntsman also said of him: "He's a foxcatcher." High praise indeed from a professional.

Major Gundry, like his relative, Selby Lowndes, also has a great reputation for the tremendous amount of work which he puts in outside the hunting field on behalf of the Hunt, especially where the farming community is concerned.

"We are extremely fortunate," Major Gundry said, "and I say this with the greatest sincerity, with the number of what are known as 'non-hunting farmers' [a farmer who does not ride to hounds is always known as a non-hunting farmer]. In this country we've got hundreds of these, who perhaps only farm a small acreage, and they are always most hospitable, and who would do anything to help the Hunt, and without their valuable support things would be very difficult. Of course, His Grace owns the hounds and is senior Master, but he really doesn't have the time to spend on the administration and organisation of the country, which involves keeping in touch with all the changes, such as farms changing hands and so on, keeping the country as "rideable" as possible, visiting the farms, particularly through the summer months, organising one's wire field area managers, making sure that when an earth-stopper retires or dies that we can find a replacement, and the hundred and one other things which must be attended to if a hunt is to function efficiently."

Major Gundry is a dedicated foxhunter, and is always concerned with the good name and image of hunting. "The tendency today when most people are so busy attending to their own business affairs, is for people to treat hunting purely as a recreation, without considering their responsibility to the Hunt itself. By which I mean consideration for the farmers over whose land hounds hunt, so more and more attention must be paid to keeping the goodwill of the farming community in the foreground of our thoughts. The person who pays a subscription, whatever that subscription might be and then considers that he or she has a divine right to come out hunting and do and go exactly where he or she likes, creates a very bad image. It is really a question of manners, and if the people who hunt—and they're all very nice people, there's nothing wrong with them individually—would only give this matter a bit of thought, they could perhaps, after a good day's sport, take the trouble to make it known to the farmer over whose land they have enjoyed themselves just how much they have enjoyed themselves. Some simple action like this does so much to keep the wheels well-oiled, and a thank you here and there costs very little."

Major Gundry was instrumental in forming the Registry of Hunt Servants which, under the Master of Foxhounds Association, is of great benefit both to hunt servants seeking employment and to Masters of Foxhounds.

Like Brian Gupwell, Major Gundry is another man who believes that hunting is the best love of all. "I have loved hunting all my life, ever since my childhood. I was fortunate enough to be brought up in a hunting family, and have always been absolutely mad about hunting. The thrill of following a pack of hounds across country is second to none. No day is a bad day, and every day we go out I enjoy it. It's the glorious uncertainty of the sport."

Major Gundry also has his own definite opinions as to what makes a good huntsman. "A good huntsman is bred and gifted to the art of venery. He has got to be dedicated and he must be a man who always tries his best, and he has to be gifted with his hounds. Hounds are very sensitive animals, and if the huntsman is upset, then they sense it. He wants to be quiet, to have a good eye for country and, of course, a knowledge of the run of foxes is a great help to him."

Major Gundry is a keen and knowledgeable "hound man". Once, when showing a visitor in his house a sporting print of Lord Willoughby de Broke with hounds, he not only named most of the hounds in the picture but was quite prepared to discuss their breeding! And, like all those connected with the Beaufort Hunt, he is never happier than when talking about the Beaufort hounds.

"I think that the Beaufort Hunt is looked up to by practically every hunt in the United Kingdom because, first of all, the Duke has a pack of hounds which has been bred continuously in the same family, and we have female tail lines of hounds going back over very many years, and I think that the hounds at Badminton today are as good, if not better, than they have ever been."

Regarding the future of hunting, Major Gundry is optimistic. "Hunting, throughout its history, has overcome difficulties which our forebears predicted would be so detrimental that it would be impossible to carry on. For example, when the stone walls were first erected at the height of four foot six, certain ladies and gentlemen said that they wouldn't be able to cross country. And then the railways were going to be the end of foxhunting and, in more modern times, fast motorways. And though hunting may often be forced to change, it still survives—and we still have tremendous fun. One of the most encouraging things today is the number of farmers and farmers' families that are hunting with us, and this gives strength to the goodwill of foxhunting"—and few people have done more to foster that goodwill than Major Gundry.

Major Gundry retired as Joint-Master of the Beaufort Hunt at the end of the 1977/78 season. Recurring pain from a back injury meant that (acting on medical advice) the Major has had to give up riding altogether. This is a great loss, not only to the Beaufort Hunt, but also to hunting in general, for over the years the Major has become one of the leading personalities of the sport. Although rumour has it that he is to retire to Dorset, it is impossible to imagine that Major Gundry will disappear from the hunting scene altogether.

Another well-known figure in the Beaufort hunting country is Major R. J. G. Dallas, the Honorary Secretary of the Beaufort Hunt, who first hunted with them whilst serving in the Army.

"I was serving in the 3rd Hussars, and my regiment provided the permanent staff of the North Somerset Yeomanry. I was sent there as Adjutant. The HQ of the Yeomanry was in Bath, and so I asked if I might hunt with the Duke of Beaufort's hounds while I was there. I was given permission to do so, and thoroughly enjoyed it. Then, after two years, I returned with my regiment to Germany. About five years later I received a letter from Major Gundry saying that the post of Hunt Secretary was shortly becoming available—the next season—and he and the Duke of Beaufort wondered if I would like the job."

Major Dallas also has a hunting background, and hunted with the Surrey Union when he was only eight years old. As Hon. Secretary of the Beaufort Hunt, Major Dallas is naturally concerned with the economic aspects of hunting.

"Major Gundry acts as the country 'manager', and I assist him in every way possible, and I am responsible to the Hunt Chairman [Lt.-Col. H. T. Brassey] and the Hunt Committee and Treasurer for getting income for the Hunt, and otherwise liaising with the farmers."

It comes as something of a surprise to realise that even today the Beaufort is a committee-run hunt. But this is the case.

"But, of course, His Grace owns the Kennels, and the horses, the hounds, and all the Hunt Servants' equipment and the stable equipment, and it costs him a great deal. We do provide a sort of expense allowance towards these costs, but I don't think we really need go into that."

Enquiries as to the financial aspects of Badminton are always met by a polite but firm refusal. However, the Master of a nearby Hunt recently stated that his Hunt's running expenses were in the region of £30,000 each year, and it may be safely assumed that the Beaufort's expenses are rather more than that. At first sight, the figure of, say, £30,000 seems enormous, but when one stops to consider items such as the wages of full-time Hunt Servants (the Beaufort has five), stable staff, transport, fodder, horses, etc., all of which are subject to the galloping inflation which affects everyone today, then the figures start to become less incredible.

But hunting *is* an expensive business, and even though somewhere in the region of one million people do go out hunting each week, Major Dallas thinks that there is a genuine economic threat.

"I think that the cost of horses is going to be a very great factor in reducing the numbers of people who do hunt. Whereas you used to be able to buy a hunter for, say, £300 to £400, nowadays you're very lucky if you can buy a really good one for somewhere in the region of £1,500 to £2,000, which is a huge difference, and I think that people are finding it harder and harder to find this sort of money to purchase their horses."

Even so, and although the Beaufort fields are perhaps slightly smaller than they were ten years ago, the numbers who still ride regularly to the Beaufort hounds are quite impressive.

"On a Saturday, maybe two hundred and fifty—it depends. Some Meets are more popular than others. And on a Wednesday, between one hundred and two hundred, depending on where the Meet is."

In addition to those riding to hounds, there are, of course, those hundreds of people who follow hounds in cars, on foot, or on bicycles, and a good Hunt Supporters' Club nowadays is literally worth its weight in gold, and can be of inestimable benefit to a hunt.

The Beaufort Hunt Supporters' Club is no exception. First started in July 1958 as an association for people who wished to support and foster goodwill towards foxhunting, rather than as a money-making concern, the Club has gone from strength to strength. Today, with somewhere in the region of six hundred active members, it organises an incredible number of events and fund-raising activities, including terrier shows, dances, skittles matches, clay pigeon shooting, one-day events, sponsored rides, etc., and it provides a useful financial contribution to the Hunt.

"They paid the cost of re-wiring the railway at Badminton Station, where there is a cutting going up to the tunnel, and it is frightfully dangerous unless it is wired. They also bought a flesh lorry. They collected £2,000 towards the cost of fencing the M.4 motorway, and have since contributed to the fence maintenance, which was terribly helpful."

Hunt supporters in the field, as everyone knows, can be a mixed blessing. Major Dallas went on to say: "Obviously, whilst out hunting, a lot of our supporters head the fox and so on with their cars, and are not at times terribly popular. But, on the other hand, they do know the country and the run of the foxes, and they can dash round to where hounds are liable to cross a main road, and sometimes they can get there quicker than we can on horses, and they will often save the situation and prevent hounds being run over—so they are very helpful that way, and I think the Supporters' Club is very worthwhile."

Another great benefit which active foot and car followers of any hunt may contribute is that they can be extremely useful in the event of a rider suffering a bad fall in the hunting field. Perhaps this will be noted by the Recording Angel and weighed against their more obvious faults, such as the heading of foxes, parking across gateways, and leaving their car engines running when hounds are passing.

The Beaufort Hunt Supporters, for some reason, seem to be especially fond of cakes, and their cake stall appears to be an essential feature at many of their activities. Obviously, the ladies in the Beaufort country are still exercising their "superlative fascinations".

David Somerset: Joint Master 1974–

In 1974, David Robert Somerset, a cousin of the Duke of Beaufort, and heir presumptive to the title, became a Joint Master of the Beaufort Hunt. Not surprisingly, as a member of the Somerset family, he had begun his hunting as a child.

"I hunted a little bit as a small boy before the war, in about 1935. My parents lived in Hampshire then, and my brother and I had ponies. We hunted with the Hambledon Hunt. I don't think it was a really great country, but we thought it was terrific, and I enjoyed it very much. I went on riding a pony until just before the war."

During the war years, David Somerset had little opportunity for riding. In 1945 he went into the Army and served in the Coldstream Guards until 1949. In 1950 he married Lady Caroline Jane Thynne, daughter of the 6th Marquess of Bath, who remembers with amusement:

"I'm always told that when we got engaged and I married into this terrifyingly hunting family, the Duke and Duchess, instead of saying— 'Is she nice'—said—'Does she hunt?'. And she didn't! It was rather awful. I took it up later."

David Somerset resumed his interest and hunting when he went to live at Badminton, and was invited by the Duke of Beaufort to go cub-hunting. "I got on to some enormous horse, and felt rather loose in the seat. Of course, I hadn't ridden for about twelve years or so, but when one is young, one is very optimistic, so it didn't seem particularly strange to me when I started again, any more than it has for my children, who started at varying ages."

David Somerset and his wife, Lady Caroline, have four children, one of whom, Edward, took part in the Royal International Horse Show in 1976, when he appeared as the 8th Duke of Beaufort in a pageant celebrating the present Duke's forty years as Master of the Horse.

His interest in hunting having been rekindled, David Somerset found himself enjoying it so much that he began to take riding lessons and, although he had not ridden for some twelve years when he first went to Badminton, it was not very long before he had become sufficiently competent to take part in eventing. He also had some tuition from a brilliant Hungarian rider.

"I was very lucky. There was a Hungarian refugee who came to Badminton, having been released from prison in Russia. I made friends with him, and he soon realised what an appalling rider I was. He helped me enormously and that was how I became really interested. He was a great horseman, having been third in the Equestrian section of the 1936 Olympic Games."

In 1959 David Somerset failed, by one point only, to win the Whitbread Trophy at the Badminton Horse Trials. On Cross-Country day, despite appalling weather conditions, he moved up fifteen places to take the lead. Everything depended upon the final Show Jumping phase.

"I was beaten by Sheila Willcox, who was European Champion at that time. I was ahead of her after the Cross-Country, I think, by 9 marks, and I knocked down one jump, and she went clear. But, still, she was a much better rider than I was. I had a wonderful horse, called Countryman, which was owned by a syndicate of Master [the Duke of Beaufort], the Queen Mother, the Queen and old Colonel Williams, and then, after the Olympics, they very kindly sold it to me."

Although David Somerset has been a Joint Master of the Beaufort

Hunt for some four years, he has, in fact, been Field Master for ten years. As regards the actual administration of the Hunt, he admits that he has not been able to take as great a part as he would like. He runs a fine arts business in London (the Marlborough Galleries) and this involves him in a great deal of international travel.

"Obviously, I go to as many of the dinners and events as I can, and I do know quite a lot of the farmers and people in the country. However, from the point of view of living the life of a Master of Foxhounds, I don't do as much as I would like to. I just haven't the time, and so I can't do the work that Gerald Gundry does. I'm afraid I'm not really a great deal of help to them."

Eventually, David Somerset will become senior Master of the Beaufort Hunt. Following as he does all those great horn-carrying Beaufort Masters, it is interesting to speculate as to whether he will ever hunt the Beaufort hounds himself. He thinks not, however.

"I'm much too old to start hunting the hounds (he is forty-nine) but, obviously, if I'd started it when I was younger, I would have adored to have done it. I can't think of anything more fascinating, but I think it's a full-time job—you can't really do much else."

As senior Master of the Beaufort Hunt, David Somerset will also be following some of the greatest breeders of foxhounds.

"It terrifies me but, obviously, I wouldn't be arrogant enough suddenly to take over the breeding. If I had the opportunity, if it ever came to me, I would ask advice from all the experts. It is a life's work to know the breeding of hounds. I can see how fascinating it is. It is fascinating to breed any animal, anyway, to your own standard of perfection, especially when it happens to agree with the judges at the same time. What is rather exciting about breeding hounds is that you see them so quickly. If you are breeding a horse, you don't get much result for two or three years. But here there are new hounds coming in every year. It is a very quick turnover and I understand it is possible to totally wreck the kennel in one year. I think the quality of the hounds here is absolutely magnificent. I suppose, as conditions change, people always try to breed different hounds to suit those conditions, but I imagine the modern foxhound is pretty well as good as you can get it."

Concerning the Somersets' passion for hunting, David Somerset has his own opinions concerning that "terrifyingly hunting family":

"I must say, my own father was a passionate sailor, and his passion for sailing was only equalled by Master's passion for hunting. I think the Somerset family have, perhaps, been rather one-idea'd about what they were doing. It just so happened that they had the apparatus for hunting, and everything was made for hunting, and they didn't think of doing other things because it was all here, ready made for them. Of course, the 8th Duke was very keen on racing and breeding racehorses. I would like to breed—I have bred a few 'chasers. In fact, I bred a very good horse, called Border Incident, which might win a Cheltenham Gold Cup. I'd love to breed some very good horses, but I don't go racing very much—again, I don't have the time."

As to the future of foxhunting and of the Beaufort Hunt, David Somerset is optimistic:

"I hope, that if I am eventually in charge, that it will continue to flourish, even if in a different way. It is so much better now that farmers and their children hunt. Farmers are rather more prosperous than they were in the days before the war, when many of them could not afford hunting, and I think that this is the great hope for hunting. There is such a tremendous interest in riding in general. I imagine that the greatest danger is finance. The cost will be the danger, but I imagine that people will adapt themselves in time, and perhaps do it in less style— not hunt so many days and not have so many horses. But I feel it will go on."

Whatever the future may hold for foxhunting in general, and for the Duke of Beaufort's Hunt in particular, there can be no doubt that the 10th Duke of Beaufort and his hounds are regarded with great respect and affection throughout the hunting world.

On 4 April 1977, the Duke of Beaufort's hounds met at The Fox, Hawkesbury Upton, a small village some three and a half miles from Badminton House. This was a special Meet, inasmuch as it was His Grace's seventy-seventh birthday.* Unlike those other famous Birthday Meets, so well recorded by Miss Daphne Moore, this time there were no speeches and no presentations. Hunt supporters and country people had come from miles around just for the occasion. One old man had even come on crutches, and it was something of a shock to hear him announce that he was younger than the Duke who, looking fit and well, was sitting on his horse at the door of The Fox, exchanging greetings with friends and well-wishers.

Just as the hounds were about to move off, the entire assembly of villagers, hunt supporters, farmers, and Hunt members, burst into a chorus of "Happy Birthday to You!", and, as the field moved away from the Meet, there were loud cheers.

Those who were determined to celebrate the occasion in style moved back into the bar of The Fox, where His Grace's health was drunk with genuine affection—the general consensus of opinion being put into words by the landlord of the pub, Albert Hutchinson: "Good luck to

*There was no Birthday Meet in 1978.

him! There's no one like him!" Nor is there, and hunting people everywhere owe a great debt of gratitude to "Master"—Henry Hugh Arthur Fitzroy Somerset, 10th Duke of Beaufort and foxhunter extraordinary.

PART IV

A Most English Occasion

"There is no doubt that the event is the greatest possible test of the strength and courage of the horse, coupled with the strength and tact of the rider."

10th Duke of Beaufort in 1949

"The art of designing a good course is to frighten the wits out of the riders on their feet, but not to hurt the horses on the day."

Lt.-Col. F. W. C. Weldon in 1973

THE name "Badminton" has many associations. To some it is a stately home set in the beautiful Gloucestershire countryside. To others it is a game played with racquets and a shuttlecock. To the foxhunter, it is the headquarters of hunting and the home of the famous Beaufort hounds. According to one dictionary, it is a drink—"A summer beverage compounded of claret, sugar and soda water". But since 1949, for the great majority of people, Badminton has come to mean that most English of occasions, the Badminton Horse Trials, an event which, to lovers of equestrian sports, is the equivalent of Cowes Week, Wimbledon and Henley all rolled into one, and one which, with almost Irish contrariness, is a three-day event which takes place over a period of four days (the Dressage Section taking place during the first two days).

Competitive Eventing, Combined Training, or "The Military" has, in fact, been popular on the Continent for many years. Originally a sport which was almost exclusively confined to the military, eventing first figured in the Olympic Games in 1912 but, prior to the end of the Second World War, few people in Great Britain had much idea as to exactly what a three-day event was.

It has been said that many of the spectators who attended the first Badminton Horse Trials in 1949 actually thought that they had come to watch a game of badminton. However, since the poster for the event quite clearly showed a horse and rider jumping an obstacle, it is interesting to speculate whether they thought they were coming to watch mounted games of battledore and shuttlecock!

There is no doubt that many of the twenty competitors who took part in that first "Badminton" (won by John Shedden on Golden Willow) regarded the whole business with some degree of apprehension, while Dressage at that time was looked upon, for the most part, as a lot of newfangled nonsense, and foreign nonsense at that.

Since that first Badminton, however, things have changed drastically. The keen interest taken in the event by Her Majesty the Queen and other members of the Royal Family, together with their regular attendance at Badminton, has meant that the occasion has received world-wide publicity. During recent years, Princess Anne's participation (she was European Champion in 1971) has added an extra zest to the occasion, which has both encouraged and sustained public interest.

Since 1949, British riders have taken to the sport with such flair and determination that, to date, they have not only won nine individual and nine team European and World championships, but also one individual (Richard Meade on Laurieston) and three team Olympic Gold Medals, one Silver and one Bronze Olympic Medals. Today, the

Badminton Horse Trials have become the focal point for the testing and selection of British riders for the Olympic Games.

Badminton is not, of course, confined to British riders. Since 1951, the competition has been an international one and in 1978, for example, riders from France, Ireland, Italy, Spain, Sweden, Switzerland and the United States took part. The fact that Badminton has become a major international equestrian event in such a short time is due mainly to five factors:

The foresight and generosity of the Duke of Beaufort; the Royal Family's interest; the course-building and organisational flair of Lt.-Col. Frank Weldon; the generosity of Messrs. Whitbreads the brewers who, since 1960, have donated both the prize money and the trophies; and last, but by no means least, the determination, patience and courage of competitors, such as Major Laurence Rook, Major Frank Weldon (as he then was), Sheila Willcox, Richard Meade, Mary Gordon-Watson, Captain Mark Phillips, Chris Collins, H.R.H. Princess Anne and many others, including, of course, Lucinda Prior-Palmer, who has achieved the remarkable feat of winning the event on three separate occasions, riding three different horses (1973 Be Fair; 1976 Wide Awake; and 1977 George).

There is also another factor which is often overlooked, and which has contributed greatly to the success of the Badminton Horse Trials, and that is the work put in by the great army of helpers and volunteers from the Badminton Estate, from the Beaufort and adjacent hunts, from the Beaufort Hunt Supporters' Club, and the hundreds of other people who work behind the scenes.

Commenting on the first ever Badminton Horse Trials in 1949, a contributor to *Horse and Hound* wrote: "Nothing of this kind has ever been tried before in this country and it is likely to become the most important event of its type, of very real interest and value."

The accuracy of that prophecy is borne out by a comparison of the attendance figures of the very first and of Badminton 1978. In 1949, the total attendance was in the region of 6,000; in 1978, on cross-country day alone, the figure was in the region of 200,000 spectators.

During the intervening twenty-nine years, organisation, hard work, and improved standards have transformed what was originally a rather happy-go-lucky "county" affair into a highly-organised international event.

Like so many other British "institutions", the whole business came about almost by accident.

In 1947, the British Horse Society decided to enter a team for the Prix des Nations jumping event and for the three-day event at the 1948

Olympic Games. The Olympic Games were the first to be held since the war, and they were to be held in London during July and August, the equestrian events to be held at Aldershot. Colonel Trevor Horn (a founder member of the British Horse Society) was invited to become a member of the Selection Committee for these events and, although he had no great experience where international events were concerned, he was appointed Arena Manager for the Grand Prix des Dressage and also for the three-day event Dressage and Jumping.

Colonel Horn went to Aldershot just two weeks before these events were to take place and "learnt what I could about the practical running of the event". The Duke of Beaufort, then Vice-Patron and Vice-President of the F.E.I. (Fédération Equestre Internationale), having attended the Dressage section, expressed a desire to see the cross-country section of the competition which was to be held near the Royal Military Academy at Sandhurst. Colonel Horn, being by that time familiar with the cross-country course, volunteered to accompany His Grace and his party.

It was during a lunch-time picnic on the day of his visit that the Duke of Beaufort suggested that it would be an excellent idea if a competition, run on similar lines to the Olympic three-day event, were to be held in Britain, in order to give British horses and riders a training ground for the 1952 Olympic Games and other international events. As a venue for such a competition, the Duke offered the use of his Estate at Badminton. This was an extremely generous offer, since the Duke farms on a big scale at Badminton, and must have appreciated the amount of disruption that the setting-up of a three-day event would cause.

Any initial problems in this respect, however, were soon ironed out, and as Mr E. M. Mitchell, Agent to the Badminton Estate, has said: "Nowadays, I think it is fair to say that we farm 'round the three-day event' and the whole thing works very well on the simple law of give and take."

The idea of a British three-day event was an exciting one, and the British Horse Society immediately gave the scheme their blessing. (Incidentally, it is the British Horse Society which receives the profits from the Badminton Horse Trials, which amount to £150,000 to date.)

Colonel Horn, with only two weeks' experience as a dressage official at international level, was appointed Director, and immediately set about the seemingly impossible task of preparing for the first Badminton Horse Trials in April of the following year—1949. To assist him, he had a BHS Committee consisting of The Duke of Beaufort (President); Colonel The Hon. C. G. Cubitt (Chairman of the BHS); Brigadier Bowden-Smith (a former Olympic competitor and trainer of the 1936 British Team); Major Peter Borwick (a competitor in the 1948 Olympic Games); Mr C. Cornell; and Lieutenant-Colonel R. B. Moseley who was appointed Assistant Director. At a later date, a committee of people living in the vicinity of Badminton was also formed.

Anyone who has ever attended the Badminton Horse Trials must be aware of the tremendous amount of organisation required to stage such an event, and so one can only marvel at the enthusiasm and enterprise with which Colonel Horn and his colleagues set about tackling the task and, indeed, at the results that they achieved.

In the first place, there were no written rules laid down for such an event (the first FEI regulations were not published until 1957), and so Colonel Horn and his Committee had to formulate their own rules and, as Frank Weldon has written in the twenty-fifth Badminton Anniversary programme (held in 1976, three trials having been cancelled because of bad weather)—"Where they could not discover the right answers, they made them up, and the whole thing worked admirably."

In those early days, Colonel Horn worked from the piano top in his sitting-room. Later, he hired a room in a cottage at Badminton, and persuaded the owner of the village sweet shop to do his typing. Travelling about the estate with a bicycle wheel measurer, Colonel Horn planned the layout of the course and the design of the fences. It is strange to think that later British successes in International and Olympic competitions, based upon the experience gained at Badminton, should owe so much to Colonel Horn's dedicated wanderings about the Badminton Estate with his bicycle wheel.

However, slowly but surely the first Badminton Horse Trials came into being. From its London office, the British Horse Society dealt with the great mass of paper work which was necessary: entry forms, correspondence, and so on. Nowadays, of course, all this is done from the Trials Office at Badminton.

At Badminton, the Duke and Duchess of Beaufort gave the venture every encouragement, arranging for both the stabling of the competitors' horses and the accommodation of their grooms and other staff. The Duke, in addition to helping with the layout of the course, even went so far as to try out many of the fences which Colonel Horn had designed on one of his own hunters.

In 1949, the event was known as "The Badminton Three Day Event", but later this was changed to "The Olympic Horse Trials, Badminton". Finally, the event was given its present title, "The Badminton Horse Trials" but, to most people, it is simply known as "Badminton".

Over the years, there have been many changes to the event, as gathered experience and altering conditions have determined the shape the trials should take. Originally, for example, both the dressage and the show-jumping sections were held on the lawn immediately in front of Badminton House (see no. 12), but this was low-lying ground and was often at the mercy of weather conditions. Then, in 1959, heavy rain reduced the whole area to a sea of mud, and the subsequent damage took many months to put right. In the following year, therefore, the main dressage/jumping arena was erected away from the house and in the Park on the far side of the lake, where it has been positioned each year since.

Again, in those early days, there were far fewer trade stands, whereas nowadays virtually a small town is erected each year.

The ever-growing number of spectators has also resulted in changes being made on the cross-country course. At first, spectators, within reason, could go exactly where they liked. Later, however, it became necessary to erect barriers around the fences in order to keep the crowds back and, eventually, for the safety of both competitors and spectators, the cross-country course was roped off. But, even today, there is still a great deal of freedom for spectators at Badminton, and on cross-country day, the course resembles Rudyard Kipling's *Grand Trunk road of India*, as thousands of people walk the course or wander about from fence to fence. Marshals with whistles and loud hailers patrol the course on foot and on horseback to ensure fair play for both spectators and competitors alike. The mounted marshals are usually Hunt members and Hunt servants from the Beaufort and adjacent hunts, and are currently under the direction of Major Gerald Gundry, ex-Joint-Master of the Beaufort Hunt.

Since that first Badminton in 1949, the competition has been held annually, with only four exceptions: in 1963, 1966 and 1975 the Trials had to be cancelled because of bad weather; and in 1955, at the request of Her Majesty the Queen, the event took place at Windsor. These 1955 Trials were also a European Championship. That year the British Team easily won the team event, while the title of individual European Champion went to Major F. W. C. Weldon, riding Kilbarry.

Incidentally, one of the pleasures for those regularly attending the Badminton Horse Trials is to watch the development of the younger horses and riders and in trying to spot a future winner.

It was also in the 1955 trials that Miss Sheila Willcox, riding High and Mighty, finished in 13th place in her first three-day event. In the following year, after a terrific battle, Major F. W. C. Weldon, again riding Kilbarry, just managed to win the competition for the second time, by the narrow margin of 1½ marks from Sheila Willcox (again on High and Mighty). But Badminton had by no means heard the last of either Major Weldon (Olympic Team Medallist in 1956) or of Miss Willcox. Indeed, the name "Weldon" has now become synonymous with the Badminton Horse Trials for, in 1965, Colonel Frank Weldon was appointed Director, and it is very much due to his genius for course-building, organisational flair, and shrewdness in matters of Press and Public Relations, that the Badminton Horse Trials are so successful and so popular today. As for Miss Willcox, she went on to win Badminton in 1957 and 1958, on both occasions riding High and Mighty and, in 1959, as Mrs J. Waddington, riding Airs and Graces, she completed the first ever Badminton "hat trick".

The Badminton Horse Trials are today a major international equestrian event as well as being a unique social occasion. In addition to the dressage and show-jumping arena and the sixteen and a half miles of the speed and endurance course, a huge township of trade stands, display tents and club tents is erected in the Park. Throughout the four days of the event, somewhere in the region of 230,000 people from all walks of life and from many countries gather together to watch some of the finest riders and horses in the world compete for the Whitbread Trophy.

The fact that the Queen and other members of the Royal Family attend Badminton each year as house guests of the Duke of Beaufort, adds a special glamour to the occasion but, despite its international flavour, Badminton is in so many ways a very "English" occasion. Indeed, it has sometimes been criticised for its very Englishness, and it has been described as a "snob" event or an affair exclusively for the "upper crust". This is nonsense, of course, since, as Col. Weldon has pointed out, it is clear from the names and addresses of the many thousands who reserve tickets and seats in advance each year, that the majority are by no means upper crust. At Badminton during the Horse Trials anyone with the price of admission is welcome. Considering the quality of the entertainment provided, the prices are extremely reasonable.

Anyone who takes on the job of Director of the Badminton Horse Trials most certainly needs organisational ability, for it is a tremendous undertaking. The fact that it all works so well and so smoothly is proof of the excellent pre-planning and of the hard work put in by the Director and all those connected with the running of the event.

Consider what is involved: entry forms for competitors have to be sent out, and when these are returned, the competitors' and horses' qualifications have to be checked. Accommodation for competitors' horses and for the huge army of grooms behind the scenes has to be arranged. Deer, cattle and sheep have to be penned. Judges, timekeepers, officials and stewards have to be appointed and briefed. Arenas must be marked out and contractors hired to erect all the necessary stands. Applications for trade stands have to be sifted and, as there are always far more applications than space available, these have to be balloted. (These trade stands are very much a part of Badminton, as well as being a useful source of revenue for the BHS funds.) Contractors have to be hired to erect the tents for the one hundred and fifty or so successful applicants. Other aspects which have to be considered are: police arrangements (the presence of the Queen and the Royal Family poses a massive security problem); veterinary services, farriers, medical services, Red Cross facilities; radio and loud-speaker link-ups and radio connections, mounted messengers, course marshals, fence judges, car parking facilities, refreshment and toilet facilities (a massive undertaking when one considers the 200,000 spectators on cross-country day). Then there are the Press facilities to arrange; pre-publicity, results and regular Press information, which have to be supplied throughout the event; advertising, printing, postal bookings, ticket sales, and the hundred and one other details likely to arise when planning for an event such as the Badminton Horse Trials. Few people realise that it now costs upwards of £100,000 to lay on the Event which, especially with VAT to worry about, requires a pretty competent accountant. The Assistant Director, Major Derrick Dyson, does this, amongst a lot of other things.

Of course, much of the work is delegated, but it is the Director who carries the ultimate responsibility, and in this case it is also the Director who lays out the course and designs the fences. And yet, so efficiently does all this work get done at Badminton that one is hardly aware of the fact that the event has been organised—everything just seems to happen in a casual and relaxed atmosphere—and within seventy-two hours of the completion of the Horse Trials, everything is back to normal in the Park.

In 1976 there were one hundred entries for Badminton. In 1977, new and higher qualification standards were introduced, with the result that there were only seventy-two entries. By the final declaration stage—6.00 p.m. on the day before the competition was due to start— there were only forty-seven left in. In 1978, with the higher qualification standards still featured, there were only sixty-three entries, and at the final declaration stage this had dwindled to forty-three, including ten entries from overseas. To the delight of the popular press, H.R.H. Princess Anne was once again competing, only five months after the birth of her baby son. The horses she had entered were Her Majesty the Queen's Goodwill and her own Flame Gun (later withdrawn). Captain Mark Phillips, who had originally entered three horses for the Trials, including the 1977 winner, George, was unable to compete, owing to the fact that none of the horses was considered to be fit enough to take part in the competition. His own horse, Persian Holiday, unfortunately failed to pass a veterinary examination only a week before Badminton 1978 was due to commence. (A fourth horse, offered to him by Mr Bertie Hill, also had to be withdrawn prior to the competition.)

Another well-known rider, Chris Collins, was unable to compete because of an ankle injury he had sustained as the result of a skiing accident, while Hugh Thomas, a member of the 1976 Olympic Team, was also unable to compete.

Before the competition, all the pundits and commentators agreed that this was one of the most 'open' Badminton Horse Trials for years, with any one of a dozen riders in with a chance of winning. With the selectors due to announce the team for the Kentucky World Championships shortly after this year's Badminton, there was no doubt that the competition would be hard-fought.

Among those taking part at Badminton in 1978 was Miss Lucinda Prior-Palmer (the reigning European Champion winning at Burghley in 1977) and three-times winner of Badminton. Miss Prior-Palmer, riding Village Gossip, was bidding for her fourth win as well as a hat-trick. Mrs Jane Holderness-Roddam, who was a member of the winning British Team in the European Championships at Burghley in September 1977, and who, as Jane Bullen, had previously won at Badminton in 1968 riding Our Nobby, competed on Warrior. Others taking part were the Olympic Gold Medallist, Richard Meade, riding Bleak Hills; Diana Thorne, the first woman ever to win a National Hunt race against men, riding The Kingmaker; Jane Starkey, riding Topper Too; while the overseas entries included John Watson from Ireland on Cambridge Blue, and Tomi Gretener from Switzerland riding Camas Park.

The Three-Day Event in General

The three-day event is an equestrian version of the Modern Pentathlon, a comprehensive test of all-round horsemanship, which demands almost every activity of which the horse is capable. Both horse and rider have to be "Jack of all trades", but if they are "master of one", it is at jumping and galloping across country. The competition is scored entirely on a penalty basis. The marks awarded by the Dressage judges are converted to penalties by subtracting them from the maximum number of marks obtainable.

In the second phase's Speed and Endurance Test, which is decided on the basis of time and jumping ability, the time laid down for each phase of the course is calculated on the speeds which, under the old scoring system, would have earned "Maximum bonus" in the case of the steeplechase and the cross-country. Completing the phase within what is now called the "Optimum Time" incurs no penalty. Exceeding the "Optimum Time" is penalised according to a scale which varies according to the type of phase. Any mistakes at obstacles also incur penalties.

The same applies to the jumping test on the final day of the Event, and the winner is the competitor with the lowest total of penalties in all three tests. There can be no tie because, in the case of eventual equality, the best cross-country score is the deciding factor.

The technical requirements of each test are given in each section. In theory, their relative influence should be in the ratio of Dressage—3; Speed, Endurance, Cross-Country—12; Show-jumping—1.

In other words, the second test should have four times more influence on the result than the Dressage and twelve times more than the final Jumping test. In practice, this is difficult to achieve exactly, but it is clear that, if it is to exert such an overwhelming influence, the second test and, in particular, the cross-country, must be difficult enough to give even the better horses and riders plenty to think about. However, there is a technical adjustment allowed for in the rules which at least helps to control the influence of the Dressage test. This is called the "Multiplying Factor", which is decided in advance by the technical delegate, according to his opinion of the severity of the speed, endurance and cross-country tests. It varies between .5 and 1.5; the more severe the cross-country phase, the higher the multiplying factor will be and, therefore, the greater the spread of Dressage penalties between the best and the worst competitor.

A new departure in 1977 and retained in 1978 was that each movement in the Dressage Test was marked from 0–10,* instead of 0–6 as previously. This meant that the maximum number of good marks available was 240 instead of 144, so that if no adjustment were made,

---

*The two changes (0–10 in Dressage and 5 instead of 10 in Show jumping) are *under consideration* by the F.E.I., who paid us the compliment of asking us to try them out to see what effect they might have at a properly conducted international event. They are *not* yet Rules, and perhaps may never be.   F.W.

the Dressage penalty scores would be nearly twice as great. Even more significantly, the difference between the better and worse competitors would be correspondingly wider. In order to exert a similar influence as before, a factor of .6 was automatically applied to all Dressage scores, in addition to the selected multiplying factor; in 1978, the multiplying factor was 1.

Another change in FEI rules is that in the Jumping test, the penalty for a knock-down or a foot in the water, was reduced from 10 to 5 points, although the penalty for refusals or falls remained as before. This helped to ensure that the Jumping did not have too much effect on the final result, but the severity of the course would still depend on what had transpired on the previous day. If few competitors experienced much difficulty, the course would be comparatively simple, but if there were marked fluctuations in competitors' fortunes, then the Jumping course was likely to be made more difficult in order to preserve the correct proportion.

The qualifications for Badminton 1978 were that each competitor was required to pay a £10 entry fee for each horse; owners or horses and riders had to be members of and horses registered with the British Horse Society; the rider's eighteenth birthday had to be before the 1st January, 1978; horses had to have foaled in or before 1971; only Grade 1 horses were eligible.

To enter, horses had to have completed at least one three-day event at Standard or higher level, which could include a junior CCIO (Concours Complet Internationale Officiel). Riders had to have completed at least *two* three-day events, at Standard or higher level, which could include a junior CCIO. In order to start, both horse and rider had to have completed at least one advanced horse trial since the start of the autumn season 1976.

Horses and riders could be exempted from these qualifications only with special permission from the Combined Training Committee. (The above qualifications applied only to British competitors.)

The Badminton Horse Trials competition is conducted in accordance with the FEI (President, the Duke of Edinburgh) three-day event rules, 1975.

Riders compete for the Whitbread Trophy, with four thousand sovereigns added by Messrs. Whitbread and Co. Ltd. The trophy and the first prize are awarded to the owner of the winning horse. There are twelve cash prizes, currently ranging from the first prize of £1,500 (prior to Whitbread's sponsorship, the first prize was £150). Second prize is £1,000 and continues down to a twelfth prize of £50. Replicas of the trophy are awarded to the riders of all prize-winning horses. Twenty-five pounds is awarded to every other competitor who completes the competition, and £10 is awarded to the groom in charge of each horse which completes the competition.

In addition to cash prizes and awards, the Butler Challenge Bowl is awarded to the best placed British rider. A saddle is presented to the winning rider by the Worshipful Company of Saddlers and a plaque is presented to the breeder of the winning horse. Plaques are also presented to all owners whose horses complete the competition, and also to any rider completing the competition who is not the owner of the horse. A special prize of two bronze head trophies and a rosette is awarded by the Hunter Improvement Society to the owner of the most successful horse sired by a Hunter Improvement Society Premium Stallion (provided it finishes in the first twelve places). And, finally, the BBC present the Beaufort Spurs to the British rider with the best cross-country score who is under twenty-five on January 1st of the next year, and who is not entitled to wear the adult Union Jack badge; they also present £100 to the owner of the horse.

Dressage

Dressage—from the French word, *dresser*, to train, to drill—is the term which has been universally adopted by the equestrian world for a series of movements which test a horse's development, state of training, and rapport with its rider.

The Fédération Equestre Internationale gives the following definition of the term: 'The object of dressage is the harmonious development of the physique and ability of the horse; as a result, it makes the horse calm, supple, and keen, thus achieving perfect understanding with its rider. These qualities are revealed by: freedom and regularity of the paces; the harmony, lightness and ease of movement; the lightening of the forehand, and the engagement of the hindquarters; the horse remaining absolutely straight in any movement along a straight line, and bending accordingly without moving on curved lines. The horse thus gives the impression of doing of his own accord what is required of him."

A Dressage test, then, consists of a series of movements, graded in difficulty according to the standard of the competitors, each movement being marked individually by the judges. All tests are judged in an arena measuring 60 × 20 m (66 × 22 yds). See the plan on next page.

At Badminton, and other events, the Dressage competition is scored entirely on a penalty basis. The marks awarded by the Dressage judges are converted to penalties by subtracting from the maximum number of points available. To date, no competitor has ever achieved a perfect score.

The three-day event rider is faced with two problems as far as dressage is concerned. In the first place, his or her horse must be as fit as possible in order to tackle the arduous speed and endurance second phase of the competition, and a really fit, keyed-up horse is less likely to be as calm and as well-behaved as a horse trained purely with a dressage competition in mind. Again, a rider taking part in the Badminton Horse Trials has to train his or her horse for all three phases of the event, and so cannot devote the whole time to dressage.

Time: The time allowed for the test is $7\frac{1}{2}$ minutes, measured from the exact moment after the salute to the judges when the horse moves forward until the horse is brought to a standstill at the end of the test and the rider salutes the judges once more. Time faults are incurred at the rate of half a mark for every second taken over the $7\frac{1}{2}$ minutes.

Marking: Each of the twenty movements in the test and of the four sets of collective marks is awarded from 0 to 10 (normally 0 to 6) good marks by each of the three judges. There are, therefore, 240 (normally 144) good marks which can be awarded by each judge. Any penalties incurred for overtime or errors are deducted from each judge's sheet, and the total marks of the three judges are then averaged. The good marks thus obtained are subtracted from 240 to express the score in penalty points.

Errors of Course: The test must be executed from memory. Errors of course, or wrong sequence of movements, whether corrected or not, are penalised as follows: 1st error—2 marks; 2nd error—4 marks; 3rd error—8 marks and 4th error—Elimination.

Fédération Equestre Internationale, Three Day Event Dressage Test

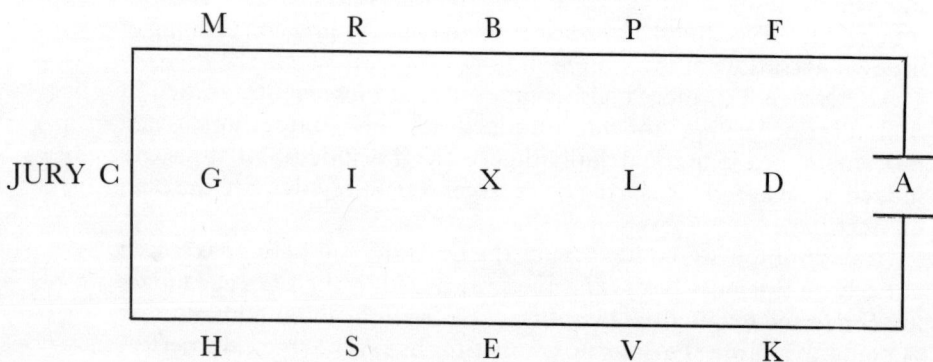

	M	R	B	P	F
JURY C	G	I	X	L	D	A
	H	S	E	V	K

		TEST	MAX. MARKS
1	A X	Enter at working canter Halt—Immobility—Salute—Proceed at working trot	10
2	C S EBE EV	Track to the left Medium trot Circle to the left 20 metres diameter Medium trot	10
3	V A L	Working trot Down centre line Circle to the left 10 metres diameter	10
4	LS	Half-pass (left)	10
5	C	Halt—Rein back 5 steps—Proceed at working trot without halting	10
6	R BEB BP	Medium trot Circle to the right 20 metres diameter Medium trot	10
7	P A L	Working trot Down centre line Circle to the right 10 metres diameter	10
8	LR	Half-pass (right)	10
9	C	Halt—Immobility 5 seconds—Proceed at working trot	10
10	HXF F	Change rein at extended trot (rising) Working trot	10
11	KXM M	Change rein at extended trot Working trot	10
12	C HSXPF F	Medium walk Extended walk Medium walk	10
13	A	Working canter—Circle to the right 10 metres diameter	10
14	AC	Serpentine 3 loops, the first and the third true canter, the second counter-canter	10
15	MXK K	Change rein at extended canter Working trot	10
16	A	Working canter—Circle to the left 10 metres diameter	10
17	AC	Serpentine 3 Loops, the first and the third true canter, the second counter-canter	10
18	HXF F	Change rein at extended canter Working trot	10
19	A L	Down centre line Working canter to the right	10
20	G	Halt—Immobility—Salute	10
		Leave arena at walk on a long rein TOTAL	200

Collective marks:

1	Paces (freedom and regularity)	10
2	Impulsion (desire to move forward, elasticity of the steps and engagement of the hind quarters)	10
3	Submission (attention and obedience, lightness and freedom of the movements, acceptance of the bit)	10
4	Position, seat of the rider, correct use of the aids	10
		240

THURSDAY—DRESSAGE (FIRST DAY)

It has been raining but at 10.30, the rain eases off just as the Dressage phase of the competition begins.

The first to go is Lucinda Prior-Palmer on Village Gossip. She is watched by several hundred knowledgeable and enthusiastic spectators, who appear to be huddling together for warmth in the main stand. A rather drooping Union Jack is hanging from a near-by flagpole.

The competitors enter the arena at ten-minute intervals from the collecting ring and perform a few preliminary exercises outside the actual dressage area. They canter slowly from one side of the main arena to the other, getting their horses used to the crowd on the one side and the Judges' boxes on the other. When the bell is rung, they enter the dressage area at a slow canter through a small gate which is open for them by an official. He removes his bowler hat as each competitor enters to start the dressage test.

Each rider then goes through what appears to the layman to be an incredibly complicated series of exercises, while the Judges' marks for each separate movement are flashed up on three illuminated number boards directly above their booth.

In the trade stands area, the traders are still setting up their equipment. Many of the stands have yet to open. Nothing is yet properly under way except for the competition itself.

In the press tent, reporters and the photographers sign the visitors' book. As well as representatives from the British equestrian press and the national dailies, there are pressmen from America, Paris, Hamburg and Copenhagen. They all stand about in small groups, waiting for something to happen.

Badminton press representative, Jim Gilmore, deals with a variety of queries. A Canadian journalist is anxious to attend any receptions which may have been arranged; a reporter has mislaid his press badge; a photographer wants to know when the Queen will arrive.

The press tent begins to fill up as more and more people sign in. The occupants split into three groups: the equestrian press—the men in tweeds, anoraks, flat caps, mackintoshes, some wearing British Field Sports Society ties; the women in tweeds, anoraks, headscarves. Another group—dressed in driving anoraks, for the most part—are festooned with cameras. It is estimated that somewhere in the region of two hundred photographers will attend the Event, representing magazines, newspapers and news agencies. Many of them are described as "Royal Chasers", whose only objective is to get pictures of the Queen and the Royal Family at all costs. The third group of people consists of the odds and ends—writers, local journalists and photographers—a mixed bunch without the camaraderie of either the photographers or the equestrian press.

All of them shuffle about, waiting for something to happen. The photographers are especially disappointed since it has been announced that Princess Anne, who was to go second in the dressage test on her horse, Flame Gun, has withdrawn him in order to concentrate all her attention on her other entry, Goodwill. As Goodwill is not scheduled to perform the dressage test until late on the following day, this means that most of the photographers have got nothing to do.

In the dressage arena, the competition continues. There are gasps and exclamations at any wrong movements or mistakes in the sequence of the exercises. The foreign spectators take the dressage test very seriously indeed.

There is now a twenty-minute break for coffee, and a few of the spectators make their way to the British Horse Society tent. The Director of the Event, Colonel Weldon, drives past in a Land Rover. He looks grim.

By now the sky has begun to lighten a little—but only a little—and more spectators are beginning to arrive. Those from overseas wear brightly-coloured boots and anoraks. They stand out against the great majority of the English spectators, who wear tweeds, the distinctive green-quilted anoraks, flat caps or headscarves—the recognisable uniform of the English country horsey set, to be seen at the Cheltenham National Hunt Festival meeting, point-to-points, and horse and dog shows all over the country.

In the Press tent, the talk is of a notorious "Royal Chasing" photographer who was ejected from Badminton on a previous occasion. This year, to the great relief of the organisers, he has not shown up.

At this time the previous year, there was a minor sensation in the press tent. Just as Captain Mark Phillips, riding Goodwill, was about to enter the dressage arena, it was noticed that the horse was wearing a noseband of a type not allowed by the rules of the competition. Had Captain Phillips commenced his test, he might have been disqualified. The reporters had become very excited as they asked each other, "What is a Grakle?" and "How do you spell Grakle?" and so on. Had it been any other competitor, no doubt they would not have bothered, but it wasn't just any other competitor, it was "Mark". One could sense the disappointment. There is all the difference in the world between "Mark Disqualified" and "Mark Nearly Disqualified".

However, this year nothing of any great moment has happened, and the reporters sit around despondently. Outside the press tent, groups of damp people trudge along the muddy road between the main arena and the trade stands. Colonel Weldon drives past them in his Land

Rover: this time he is smiling.

In the arena the competition continues. It is cold and wet, and one cannot but admire the stoicism of the spectators who are happy to watch the dressage tests under such conditions, admire too the cheerfulness and the elegance of the competitors as they wait in the collecting ring, wearing cut-away coats, top hats, beautifully tied stocks and highly-polished boots. They look as though they have just arrived to have their portraits painted.

Across the Park, near to the lake, competitors can be seen exercising their horses against the background of Badminton House. It is now almost time for the lunch break, and already spectators are making their way to the various bars and refreshment tents. It is interesting to note that at this, the most English of sporting events, the food this year tends to be of a Continental flavour. In the main catering tent canneloni and pizza are on sale, while in the Yard of Ale bar the delights of bockwurst and bratwurst are available to anyone brave enough to try them.

For most people, lunch being over and the dressage not yet due to re-commence, it is time to investigate the numerous displays and trade stands which have been erected between the main arena and Badminton House.

By tradition, the first two days at the Badminton Horse Trials are devoted to meeting old friends, ordering hunting clothes or boots, and generally doing bits of business or shopping. There is time and there is space. Hunt servants call in at Weatheralls—the most famous suppliers of hunting wear—and over a drink or a fitting, hunting news and gossip is exchanged. In a small tent at the far end of the trade area, Denis Davies, who makes riding boots, is inundated by customers old and new. Again, news and gossip is exchanged as legs are measured and orders are taken.

For the general public, with no particular business to transact, the trade and exhibition stands are well worth exploring. The premises of the various banks look solid, dependable, and extremely well-constructed. One is greeted by a door-opening, smiling official and, business having been completed, one is invited to have some coffee. No wonder bank charges are so high!

The exhibition stands are varied and fun. The Beaufort Hunt Supporters' tent has an exhibition of photographs dealing with all aspects of Badminton. The British Field Sports Society has an informative display on conservation as well as a display of photographs, leaflets and an interesting collection of Hunt buttons. One wonders, however, just who will buy—and wear—a BFSS T-shirt.

The British Horse Society book tent is crowded and remains so for the next three days. In addition to the usual wide range of equestrian books it is possible to buy caricatures of Harvey Smith and David Broome, a jig-saw puzzle depicting Red Rum, a book which explains how to blow a hunting horn, or a guide to collecting horse brasses. This year also there are queues of people wishing to enrol as supporters of the British Horse Society and queues of people wishing to buy Lucinda Prior-Palmer's new book.

One of the most popular exhibitions this year is that which marks the centenary of Her Majesty's Prison Service (1878–1978). Inside a façade built to resemble the outside of a prison, there are displays which show contrasting prison conditions throughout the century. Outside uniformed warders stand smiling and inviting members of the public to be photographed in a pillory and a set of stocks. Almost everyone who stops to talk to the warders expresses the same opinion—"These ought to be in use today."

The commercial trade stands are extremely varied, and offer a wide selection of goods. These range from a Royal Worcester model of Richard Meade riding Lauriston, priced at £650, to Badminton Horse Trials lollipops, priced at 25 pence. The clothing stands do a roaring trade. Anoraks, flat caps, moleskin breeches, headscarves, quilted jackets and waterproof jackets are all being bought. A hunting doctor from Kent tries on a sports jacket. A trade stand owner greets Major Gerald Gundry, ex-Joint Master of the Beaufort Hunt: "Did you have a good season, Major?"

Even though they have been chosen by ballot, the number and range of the stands seems incredible: Asprey & Co. of New Bond Street, Garrard's of Regent Street, Farlow & Co. of Pall Mall, the Lavenham Rug Company, Maclberrys (the knife people), the Rural Crafts Association, Niagara Therapy Ltd., and the Tetbury Furniture Company—which has nothing to do with furniture. It is, in fact, a Joke Shop. A Joke Shop at Badminton!

They all do a roaring trade side by side with the Hunters' Improvement Society caravan, the Hawk Trust, the Shire Horse Society, the Coursing Supporters' Club, Riding for the Disabled Association, and dozens of others. You can buy saddlery, jewellery, soft toys, illustrated poems on horsey subjects, brass buttons with foxes' heads on them, pottery, clocks, furniture, brandy-snaps and gingerbread men, sporting prints and second-hand books (invariably dealing with hunting, shooting and fishing). It is impossible to take in the whole range of the stands first time round.

Exhausted by a preliminary tour of the trade stands, the spectators make their way back to the dressage arena for the afternoon session. By now, there are a great many more spectators, and the whole arena looks less like a beleaguered garrison than it did in the morning.

In the press tent, the atmosphere is reminiscent of a scene in Evelyn Waugh's novel *Scoop*, as a brave body of reporters and photographers prepare to embark on a tour of the cross-country course in a Land Rover. In the Park and all round the lake, there are now hundreds of people. A television camera platform is being erected, and it is obvious that, once again, the lake is going to prove the most popular jump with the spectators. There are now heavy rain showers and the weather is getting much colder. The ground is becoming muddier underfoot, and a few people are already discussing the possibility of a cancellation of the rest of the Event.

In the Yard of Ale bar a few hardy drinkers stand around. An elderly man tries to explain to a young lady reporter why the Three Day Event lasts for four days. He is rather drunk; she is superior, but also rather drunk. They have trouble getting through to each other. A middle-aged reporter tries to interest one of the barmaids in making a tour of the night-spots of Bristol. She had heard it all before, and takes no notice. Next to them two men listen, less than spellbound, while an old man tells them how he used to work for the Co-op.

In the main arena the competition continues. The competitors who are still waiting for their turn to perform, keep their horses on the move in the collecting ring, trying to keep them warm and make them supple enough to do a good dressage test. The riders still manage to look elegant, although they are obviously wet and cold.

The time is now 3.10 p.m., and it is tea-time and once again everyone is on the move. In the Park there is a lovely sight—unnoticed by most of the spectators, and ignored by the photographers. The Duke of Beaufort's Huntsman, Brian Gupwell, is exercising some of the finest foxhounds in the world. A scattering of hardened hunting enthusiasts make a bee-line for them. The hounds then move across the Park and away from the Horse Trials area.

In the press tent it is also tea-time, and while tea and sandwiches are consumed, the word goes round that the Queen and the rest of the Royal party are due to arrive on the following afternoon.

Badminton village at tea-time is almost deserted. In the stable yard, a few people wander about aimlessly. In the blacksmith's shop, an old farrier talks to three ladies: "Yes, the forge was always the place for the children in the old days." The ladies move away, and are replaced by a couple of others. The farrier talks in detail about the quality of this year's Badminton entry, and then goes on to talk of his great love of cricket and of the great days when the Duke of Beaufort's Eleven used to play against a Gloucestershire County team. The farrier is a good subject either for a photograph or a feature article, but no one is interested and, anyway, the Royal party is due to arrive tomorrow.

In the stables, a transistor radio plays pop music. Some horses like music, but here, in these well-appointed, well-lit, beautiful old stables, it seems out of place. A few girl grooms stand about. A young man takes a photograph, not of the girls but of one of the horses. There are polished brass fittings on all the loose-box doors and lots of good luck cards.

Walking through the village and back towards the trade stand area, it is possible, by standing on tip-toe, to look over a wall to where the Beaufort hound puppies are playing in their enclosure.

In the dressage arena, the first day's competition is drawing to a close. Leading at the end of the first day is Clarissa Strachan on Merry Sovereign, with 56.6 penalties. Diana Clapham on Martha has 56.8 penalties, while Gillian Fleming-Williams on Rescator has 62.8 penalties.

In the Yard of Ale bar the old man is still regaling his victims with stories of his days at the Co-Op. Two young men arrive, hung like Christmas trees with expensive cameras. "Has the Queen arrived?" they ask. They are ignored. It is getting colder, and the first cars are beginning to leave the park. Almost unnoticed, the Duke of Beaufort walks slowly back to his house. In Whitbread's caravan, the talk is of sponsorship and of the Beaufort family history. Mr Michael Whitbread talks knowledgeably on both subjects.

In the press tent some reporters telephone their stories through to their offices—"Princess Anne today withdrew her first horse . . ."— and so on. For them it has been an uneventful day. A motor cycle messenger from the Press Association sits sipping a cup of coffee and hopes for better things tomorrow.

For the competitors, those who have completed their dressage test and those who still have to ride on the following day, there is a cocktail party at Badminton House. For many others, there will be a night spent in a caravan where they can keep an eye on their trade stand stock—and, for everyone else who is interested, there is a film of the Montreal Olympics (equestrian section, of course) to be shown later that evening in Badminton Village Hall.

FRIDAY—DRESSAGE (SECOND DAY)
Day two of the Dressage competiton and the sun is shining, but only briefly. Soon clouds appear in the sky and there is a threat of rain. Many people are of the opinion that these conditions will make it hard for today's riders to beat Clarissa Strachan's overnight score of 56.6. The more knowledgeable, however, state that the Dressage scores are always better on the second day.

There are many more people and cars today. The spectators walk about briskly, trying to keep warm. In the press tent, there are many more photographers. They sit about waiting for something to happen. Expensive cameras are lying about on tables and chairs. Still more photographers arrive. "What time is the Queen coming?" they ask, or "How will we know when she's arrived?" One less experienced, or perhaps more naive than the rest, asks, "Where would be a good position to stand on cross-country day in case Princess Anne has a fall?"

Around the main scoreboard people mill about, studying the previous day's results. The Duke of Beaufort walks past; he stops to smile at a small terrier. In the BHS tent the talk is of the refinements of dressage and of the previous day's performances.

Badminton village is almost deserted. A few people watch the puppies over the kennel wall. There are, however, more police in evidence, no doubt in anticipation of the arrival of the Royal party later in the day. In the stable yard, a few competitors and their grooms wander about looking cold. A horse is trotted out for a group of them to inspect. All appears to be satisfactory, and the horse is led back into the stable block.

In the Park, hundreds of people are inspecting the lake jumps. Everyone seems to have brought a dog. Indeed, good-looking dogs are a feature of Badminton, as, indeed, are good-looking young ladies. Some of them manage to look chic wearing flat tweed caps. In the dressage arena spectators wait for the start of the competition. Out in the Park, competitors exercise horses and in the collecting ring a few competitors, looking very cold, make their last-minute preparations.

In the press tent it is announced that the traditional Press Conference with the Director, Colonel Weldon, has been put back one hour. A young lady reporter arrives. She is from a local newspaper and is anxious for information. She asks dozens of questions. Most of the information she requires is to be found in the programme. The Press Association messenger arrives and, having parked his powerful motor cycle outside the tent, he takes up his position next to the coffee urn and hopes for a better day.

The trade stand area is once again extremely crowded, the main attractions on this second day being the Joke Shop (one customer actually asks for an exploding dumpling); the Centenary Exhibition of Her Majesty's Prison Service; the BHS bookstall, and the Whitbread film show of the Montreal Olympics. At the bootmaker's tent a competitor buys boot straps. She has only an hour to go before she takes her dressage test, and is very nervous. The clothing stores do a roaring trade—tweed caps, quilted jackets and green rubber boots being the most popular items.

In the main arena the competition is now under way. The third competitor to go incurs only 53.4 penalties, putting him into the lead. There is a sigh of satisfaction from the knowledgeable ones; the scores are going to be lower than those of the previous day.

Outside the Whitbread Exhibition tent there is a new attraction: two beautifully-appointed drays drawn by two pairs of magnificent Shire horses. For the rest of the day these are kept busy taking parties of children for rides around the Park.

More and more people are arriving; invariably they make straight for the scoreboard to see how the competition is progressing. From the arena there is a burst of applause. There is a new leader.

By now it is nearly lunch-time and the bars and refreshment tents are beginning to fill up. There are numerous police cars in evidence as security preparations are made for the arrival of the Queen and the Royal Family.

At one o'clock the members of the Press gather in the Whitbread Exhibition tent to meet Colonel Weldon. Drinks are liberally dispensed and, as a result, a happy atmosphere prevails. The photographers gather together near to the bar. Colonel Weldon appears and, after a brief exchange of greetings and pleasantries, he stands on a chair and addresses the assembly, talking about the complexities of this year's cross-country course, the dope-testing of horses and about the competition in general. At one point, when describing the difficulty of jumping one particular fence, he falls off his chair. There is a roar of laughter with which he joins in. Indeed, so good is his timing that it is tempting to wonder whether he did it on purpose.

Following his speech there are a few questions. A reporter from *Horse and Hound* makes a good point about the selection of the World Championship Team and, for a moment, Colonel Weldon seems to search for an answer, but only for a moment. He rounds off his talk by introducing a representative from the Police, who addresses the photographers about the facilities for taking pictures of the Queen at the trade stands on Sunday morning. While he "lays down the law", the photographers mutter and joke amongst themselves.

The formal session being over, a number of reporters buttonhole Colonel Weldon for a question session. The previous year, they had been concerned with the dangers of jumping horses over the Badminton fences and with the dope-testing of horses. This year they are only concerned with the dope-testing aspect. They ask the same questions as they did the year before, always probing to know whether or not a Royal horse has been tested.

One reporter is angry when it is suggested that he is asking the same questions as he did the previous year. He defends himself loudly. "It is only by repeatedly asking the same questions that the doping of Event horses will eventually be stamped out," he says. He seems particularly concerned that it should be. Colonel Weldon deals with all the questions easily. He is a competent journalist himself, and since he knows far more about both horses and Eventing than everyone else present does, he gives as good as he gets. Most of the reporters call him Frank, some in the over-familiar way which reporters so often adopt but, for the most part, they do seem to have a great deal of respect and even affection for him.

After the press conference, the photographers make their way back to the press tent, where they are somewhat annoyed to hear that while they have been attending the conference Princess Anne has been exercising Goodwill by the lake in front of Badminton House.

In the Dressage arena during the lunch interval, a military band plays some lively music to no one in particular. After lunch the weather improves and there is a drying wind. The whole tempo of the Event is beginning to quicken. With more than three-quarters of the dressage scores now available, a pattern is beginning to emerge. Interest is now focussed upon the remaining ten competitors still to appear and, with Princess Anne to go in last of all, the tension is likely to increase.

In the press tent more photographers are arriving, and always with the question, "What time is she due to arrive?" They sit around and discuss the main topics of the day—Princess Anne's dressage test and the arrival of the Queen. Indeed, in the press tent, the equestrian press aside, the talk sooner or later always goes back to the same topics. The photographers have a job to do and editors to please, but it does seem that some have been conditioned, like Pavlov's dog, only to react to certain words, such as "Mark", "Anne", "The Queen".

In the main arena, the dressage competition is about to re-commence, and the spectators settle down to watch. In this session, there are only six competitors to perform before the tea interval which is at about 3.00 p.m. The last of these riders, Jane Holderness-Roddam on Warrior moves into second place, with 52.8 penalties.

Tea time. In the BHS tent people drink tea and talk of horses. In a small wooden hut in the Park a group of officials count the programme money. They have a busy time because at Badminton in 1978 somewhere in the region of 35,000 programmes were sold. At the lake thousands of people examine closely the upturned punt jump into the lake and the boathouse and rails jumps out of it.

Outside Badminton House, a crowd is beginning to gather to see the arrival of the Royal Family. In the trade stands it is business as usual, and thousands of people are milling about, some just looking, others buying—buying rocking-horses, wooden toys, dog "nests", raffle tickets, hand-carved house name signs, wine, ties, coats, fishing-rods, corn dollies, and horse blankets. For the more affluent there are magnificent horse trailers, or holidays on offer at "only £685" for the World Championship Three Day Event to be held in Lexington, Kentucky, later in the year.

In the press tent, a few hardy souls drink cold beer. Two lady reporters deep in conversation on some secret subject announce that they are going outside to talk. Nobody cares. The photographers talk of Princess Anne. On the Wednesday before the competition— "briefing day"—she spent some time posing for photographs at the lake.

In the arena, the competition has re-started and there are only four riders left in this the final session of the day. Suddenly, as one man, the photographers move off towards the arena, accompanied by Jim Gilmore. The reason—the last competitor to appear is Princess Anne on Her Majesty's horse, Goodwill. The arena is very crowded now, as is the space between the arena and the collecting ring. The photographers take up their positions, cameras at the ready. Then Princess Anne rides straight through the collecting ring and out into the Dressage arena. She is followed by Captain Mark Phillips who runs alongside the horse until it enters the arena. The photographers go into action and as the Princess circles the arena prior to entering the dressage test area the sound of camera motors fills the air.

Suddenly an almost reverential hush descends upon the crowd as Princess Anne and Goodwill go through the intricate movements of the Dressage test. They incur 57.8 penalties. She rides out of the arena to tremendous applause. Having dismounted in the collecting ring, she talks to Captain Phillips and some friends; a reporter hangs about self-consciously on the fringe of the group, no doubt hoping for some pithy remark to include in his column. Then, as Princess Anne leaves the collecting ring, the crowd begins to melt away—some towards the trade stands, some in search of refreshments, others towards home.

At the end of the second day of Badminton 1978, Jane Starkey and Topper Too are in the lead with 44.2 points; in second place is Jane Holderness-Roddam and Warrior with 52.8 points; while in third place is Richard Meade and Bleak Hills with 53.2 points. Princess Anne on Goodwill is in seventh place, while the reigning European Champion and the winner of Badminton in 1977, Lucinda Prior-Palmer, is in 18th place. But, with two more days to go, anything can happen.

In the press tent there is a sensation. One of the cars carrying the

Royal party has arrived at Badminton with a broken windscreen. Reporters hurry off to investigate. Later it transpires that the windscreen was broken by a stone thrown up by the car in front. No one was hurt, and that was the end of that—but it could have been a story.

By now, many of the crowd are starting to leave and cars are streaming out of the park. In the BHS bar, dozens of enthusiasts discuss the day's events over well-deserved whiskies. "No point in hurrying; let's have another."

In the Park, there are many more policemen and police motorcyclists to be seen, and the Royal Standard is now flying over Badminton House. The Queen, Prince Philip, the Queen Mother, Princess Margaret, and other members of the Royal Family have arrived. The photographers are happy at last, and the reporters are busy telephoning their copy: "Princess Anne today . . ." "A car carrying members of the Royal Family arrived at Badminton today . . .", and so on.

The second day of the dressage is over, and the first phase of the competition has been completed. There are still two more days to go.

Speed and Endurance Phase

There is no doubt that, as far as the majority of the visitors to the Badminton Horse Trials are concerned, it is cross-country day which is the most popular; thousands of enthusiastic people turn up to watch some of the world's leading riders tackling the thirty-four awe-inspiring fences.

For most ordinary mortals, the thought of jumping any of the thirty-four formidable cross-country fences at Badminton is a pretty terrifying one. To see them on television is quite formidable enough, but actually to stand beside one of the trickier fences as the horses and riders negotiate it is impressive to say the least. One feels that every rider deserves the Whitbread Trophy.

It is always interesting, prior to each new Badminton Horse Trials, to discover exactly what that wily course-designer, Colonel Weldon, has up his sleeve. It is interesting, also, to note the casual, almost throw-away style of the pre-Badminton publicity. In 1977, for example, the course was designed to "encourage the riders to be more adventurous". After the Event, many commentators thought that the course had been a relatively easy one. None of the competitors expressed this opinion, however, many of them believing that Colonel Weldon could not design what they hold to be an easy course if he tried.

In 1978, therefore, with the World Championships taking place at Kentucky in September, it was hardly surprising that Colonel Weldon should announce the cross-country course was likely to be a tough one. "Slightly more difficult" was the actual wording in the press handout. It was also stated that one or two of the jumps, such as the Slide and Huntsman's Grave "could well cause some problems".

To the layman, the jumps at Badminton look absolutely enormous, and even to experienced riders when they first walk the course most of the jumps must look frightening. However, Colonel Weldon, with his long experience, both as a top-class international rider and as a course-designer, is well aware of what he is up to, and 1978 was no exception.

The course, which incidentally takes two craftsmen (Alan Willis and Gilbert Thornbury) five months to construct, provided far fewer upsets and spills than most people had predicted and, as usual at Badminton, it resulted in a first-class competition both for the riders and for the spectators who enjoyed every minute of it.

As ever, Colonel Weldon was concerned principally for the safety of the horses, the riders not being *obliged* to take part. With the World Championships in mind, he had "included a few more riders' fences, to put an additional premium on horsemanship, while still encouraging the more confident to get a wiggle on". Certainly, Lucinda Prior-Palmer, showing no lack of confidence whatsoever, romped round the course with almost nonchalant ease.

Colonel Weldon is renowned for his ability to design, year after year, over the same ground, interesting, imaginative, tough, and often controversial cross-country courses, in order to test the skill of some of the best riders and horses in the world, as well as providing the sort of competition which will attract and hold the interest of the spectators— the paying customers.

Some years ago, in an interview, he laid down four principles for successful course-building, and he agrees that these still hold good today. They are as follows:

1. To arrange obstacles so that they fit naturally into the countryside.
2. To make every possible use of natural features. A series of artificial obstacles, however big, set up on flat ground, are boring to ride and ineffective as a means of influencing the competition.
3. To give the rider plenty to think about, without running the risk of hurting the horses if the rider does make a mistake or does not appreciate the problem. This is the most difficult principle to maintain, and some of the best ideas have to be discarded if they conflict with it. In any case, an obstacle where a horse could get "hung up" is always fixed with a rope instead of bolts, so that it can be dismantled quickly with a cut from a hatchet.

4. To build fences that will invite a rider to be bold, bearing in mind that, in addition to courage and jumping ability, speed is an important consideration. Alternative approaches, which reward the skilful rider bent on saving time, are included where appropriate.

It should, of course, be added that all fences are subject to International Regulations as regards height and spread.

Certain of the Badminton fences are designed or re-designed with a view to attracting spectators and to obtain wide Press coverage before the event—not that this makes them any less difficult to jump. Perhaps the most popular obstacle, as far as spectators are concerned, is the Lake and it is amazing just how many people will stand for hours (with riders arriving at approximately five-minute intervals) in the hope of seeing a rider take a ducking. If it is a Royal rider, so much the better.

In 1976 Captain Mark Phillips endeared himself to the crowd, first by falling into the Lake, and then by lying on his back on the bank waving both legs in the air in order to drain the water out of his boots.

Prior to Badminton 1978, most of the equestrian magazines carried copy and photographs relating to the newly-designed fences. In 1977 much had been made of the Lake, which had been decked out like a fishing village, complete with lobster pots and a twelve-foot dinghy named *Scallywag*. In 1978 the motif was the same, but the actual jump was different. For one thing, the course was reversed, and riders had to jump an upturned punt to get into the Lake. Once in, they were given a choice of either jumping out over an enormous set of rails or over the *Scallywag* boathouse.

Very few riders took a ducking in 1978. One who did, however, was former World Champion, Mary Gordon-Watson, riding Speculator II. Another unfortunate rider was the Swiss competitor, Tomi Gretener on Camas Park, who suffered a spectacular fall at the rails. Luckily, and to those who saw it, unbelievably, he was unharmed and, having remounted, he carried on, eventually finishing in 24th place.

In 1978 it was not the Lake which was to be the main subject of speculation, but a number of other wicked-looking obstacles—for example, the pair of brewer's drays which were placed back to back to form a jump, the high side-pieces making it look far more formidable than it actually was. There was much discussion as well as a good deal of criticism concerning this jump, but once again Colonel Weldon scored since not one rider came to grief over it.

A far trickier jump was The Slide, which was described as a cross-country version of the Hickstead Derby Bank. This, again, presented few problems to the competitors. The deep and wide Huntsman's Grave and the re-introduced Irish Bank were among the most difficult of the obstacles in 1978 but, as it transpired, refusals more than spills

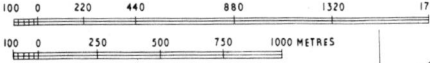

BADMINTON HORSE TRIALS 1978

	METRES	MINS	SEC
PHASE A ROADS & TRACKS	5280	22	—
PHASE B STEEPLECHASE	3450	5	—
PHASE C ROADS & TRACKS	9840	41	—
PHASE D CROSS COUNTRY	6982	12	15

CP CHECK POINT

CAR PARK

were the order of the day. At the end of the cross-country section of the 1978 Trials, eleven riders had completely clear rounds, while twenty-seven out of the original forty-three starters remained to take part in the final stage of the competition.

The overall distance for the second phase of the competition is $16\frac{1}{2}$ miles and takes each rider, on average, about $1\frac{1}{2}$ hours. The object of this test is to prove the speed, endurance and jumping ability of the horse, and the rider's knowledge of pace, and the use of his or her horse across country. The test consists of four distinct and independent phases, which follow one another and are performed at one stretch, with only one halt of ten minutes to allow for a veterinary inspection.

This second stage of the competition is scored entirely on a penalty basis. The Optimum Time for each phase is calculated on the distances and speeds shown in the summary below. Completing any phase within the Optimum Time incurs no penalty, but exceeding the Optimum Time is penalised. In addition, faults at the obstacles are also penalised.

		Distance	Speed	Optimum Time		Time Limit	
Phase	Nature	Metres	Metres per min.	Mins.	Secs.	Mins.	Secs.
A	Roads and Tracks	5,280	240	22	—	26	24
B	Steeplechase	3,450	690	5	—	10	—
C	Roads and Tracks	9,840	240	41	—	49	12
	Veterinary Inspection	—	—	10	—	—	—
D	Cross-Country	6,982	570	12	15	31	2

PHASE A—(ROADS AND TRACKS)

Three and a half miles (5,280 metres) of roads and tracks. The speed demanded is such that the rider has only to maintain a fast trot or mixture of canter and walk. The course is marked with a series of kilometre markers, in order to assist the riders with their timekeeping. There is no advantage at this stage in finishing the course early.

A competitor is penalised one penalty point for each second in excess of the Optimum Time up to the time limit, which is one-fifth more than the Optimum Time. Exceeding the time limit incurs elimination.

PHASE B—(STEEPLECHASE)
For the two-mile steeplechase (3,450 metres) the aim is to complete the course in exactly 5 minutes, which means averaging approximately 26 miles per hour. Again, finishing faster than the time allowed carries no advantage. Indeed, it is more likely to put the horse at a disadvantage in the later, cross-country, stage of the competition. For this phase, judgement of pace is all-important.

A competitor is penalised .8 of a penalty point for each second in excess of the Optimum Time, up to the time limit which is twice the Optimum Time. Exceeding the time limit incurs elimination.

PHASE C—(ROADS AND TRACKS)
At the end of the steeplechase, the second section of roads and tracks follows—this time, six miles (9,840 metres). Following straight after the steeplechase, this phase presents problems for the rider since, again, there are penalties for arriving late. A competitor is penalised one penalty point for each second in excess of the Optimum Time, up to the time limit (which is one-fifth more than the Optimum Time). Exceeding the time limit incurs elimination.

Before the start of the cross-country, there is a ten-minute break, during which each horse, as it arrives, is examined by a panel of experts, made up of a veterinary surgeon and two judges, who decide whether or not the horse is fit to continue. Then comes the most difficult phase of all:

PHASE D—(CROSS-COUNTRY)
Again, judgement of pace is all-important in this phase and, invariably, boldness pays dividends. It is true that the critical factor is the jumping of the thirty-four fearsome fences, but success usually goes to those competitors who, in Colonel Weldon's words, "get a wiggle on", keeping up a gallop over the $4\frac{1}{2}$-miles course (6,982 metres) and using their skill and judgement in tackling the time-saving alternative approaches to many of the fences. It is, if you like, almost a competition between the experience, skill and guile of the course-builder, matched against the skill of the riders and the fitness and quality of their horses. Most of the obstacles at Badminton have been described as "riders' fences"—the object of the whole exercise being that the best-trained, best-ridden horse should win on merit.

On the cross-country phase, a competitor is penalised .4 of a penalty point for each second in excess of the Optimum Time, up to the time limit (which is based on a speed of 225 metres per minute). Exceeding the time limit incurs elimination.

In addition to time penalties, there are the following penalties for faults at obstacles, which only apply if they occur within an area surrounding each fence known as the "Penalty Zone". This is an area surrounding the steeplechase and cross-country fences which extends 10 metres before and 20 metres beyond each fence, at a width of 10 metres from boundary flats at each side. Falls outside the penalty zones are not penalised, except by loss of time.

First refusal, run-out, circle of horse at obstacle	20 penalties
Second refusal, run-out, circle of horse at same obstacle	40 penalties
Third refusal, run-out, circle of horse at same obstacle	Elimination
Leaving the penalty zone before jumping the obstacle	20 penalties
Fall of horse and/or rider at obstacle	60 penalties
Second fall of horse and/or rider at obstacles during the Steeplechase phase	Elimination
Third fall of horse and/or rider at obstacles during the Cross-Country phase	Elimination
Omission of obstacle or red or white flag	Elimination
Re-taking an obstacle already jumped	Elimination
Jumping obstacle in the wrong order	Elimination

(these penalties are cumulative)

Assistance: With the exceptions of (a) catching a loose horse; (b) helping rider to remount after a fall, or to adjust his or her saddlery at any time, provided the rider dismounts, outside assistance is forbidden under penalty of elimination.

When the rider reaches the end of the cross-country phase, he must unsaddle and weigh-in. If he is below the weight, he may include the horse's bridle, but if he is still underweight, he will be eliminated. Dismounting and unsaddling must take place in the unsaddling enclosure in front of the steward responsible for the weighing, and at his order.

SATURDAY—CROSS-COUNTRY DAY

The weather is good, and it is at once obvious that the whole character of the second stage of the competition is going to be entirely different from that of the previous two days. Already, thousands of people and cars are streaming into the Park. Although the second stage of the event does not actually commence until 12 o'clock, by 10 o'clock the Park is already crowded.

Around the scoreboard in the centre of the trade stand area, hundreds of people are marking their programmes with the dressage scores. In a back road, a line of ambulances is drawn up in readiness, and dozens of Red Cross personnel are being briefed on their duties for the day. The Red Cross have one hundred and twelve people on duty, spread all over the area of the course—they are all volunteers.

Near to the ambulances, half a dozen Land Rovers are parked outside the press tent. Driven by farmers and Estate workers (again, volunteers) the Land Rovers have been placed at the disposal of the press, and throughout the day they cross and re-cross the park as they take reporters and photographers to different parts of the course.

In the press tent there is an air of expectancy—the photographers are happy because the Queen and the Royal party have arrived. The big question is: "Where is she going to be?" Later, it is announced that Her Majesty will tour the trade stands at some time during the morning.

At the lake, thousands of people are now inspecting the water jumps against the background of Badminton House. For cross-country day, the crowd is much more colourfully dressed. Reds, blues, yellows abound, and the whole park looks like a gigantic kaleidoscope—the patterns constantly changing as thousands of people walk the course.

The trade stands are doing tremendous business—especially in clothing. Tweed caps, it seems, are especially popular this year. As the spectators stroll through the lanes of tents, every kind of fashion is to be seen; anoraks of all colours, quilted jackets, blue, green and beige, ladies wearing cloaks, country gentlemen wearing appalling tweed knickerbockers.

Groups of young ladies stroll about—they all wear tweed caps. The Joke Shop is doing a roaring trade in sneezing powder, itching powder, powders for all sorts of purposes. A group of farmers stand watching, laughing, as a plastic elephant swims across a bowl of water. Outside the wine traders' tents, groups of salesmen stand about, looking somewhat sinister as they invite prospective customers inside with the promise of a free glass of wine.

There are now thousands of cars in the car parks with rumours of queues stretching right back to the motorway, which lies to the south of Badminton. The windscreens of the incoming cars are plastered with hunt badges, British Field Sports Society badges, Wild Life Conservation badges, Hunt Supporters' Club car stickers. There are dogs to be seen everywhere; several running loose, despite warning notices to their owners. And children—there are children everywhere, queuing for candy floss, lollipops, ice-cream and hamburgers.

In the Secretary's tent, a group of efficient and apparently unflappable young ladies deal with a never-ending stream of queries.

No. 1 FALLEN TREE

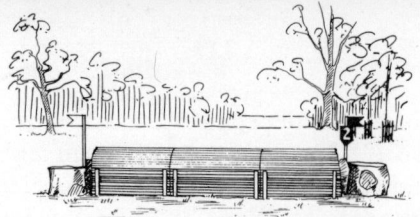

No. 2 WOODPILE

No. 3 PARDUBICE TAXIS

No. 4 CATS CRADLE

No. 5 VICAR'S CHOICE

Nos. 6 & 7 LUCKINGTON LANE

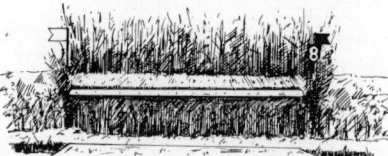

No. 8 BULLFINCH

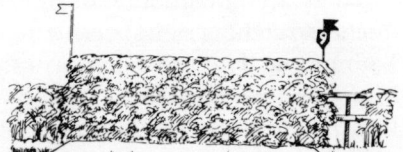

No. 9 BECHERS

CROSS-COUNTRY FENCES, 1978

1 Fallen Tree, 3ft. 10ins. 2 Woodpile, height 3ft. 11ins., spread at base 9ft. 2ins. 3 Pardubice Taxis, hedge and ditch, height 4ft. 3ins., spread at base 9ft. 2ins. 4 Cats Cradle, post and rails, heights from 3ft. 7ins. to 3ft. 11ins. 5 Vicar's Choice, ditch and rails, height 3ft. 9ins. to 3ft. 11ins., spread 7ft. to 8ft. 6ins. 6 Thorn Hedge, 4ft. 6ins. (*Luckington Lane*). 7 Thorn Hedge and Rails, 4ft. 6ins. and 3ft. 11ins. (*Luckington Lane*). 8 Bullfinch, Ditch and hedge, 4ft. 9ins. Bechers, spruce faced hedge 3ft. 11ins. and ditch away.

Nos. 10 & 11 LUCKINGTON LANE

No. 12 PARALLEL BARS

No. 13 VICARAGE VEE

No. 14 STOCKHOLM FENCE

No. 15 IRISH BANK

No. 16 PARK WALL

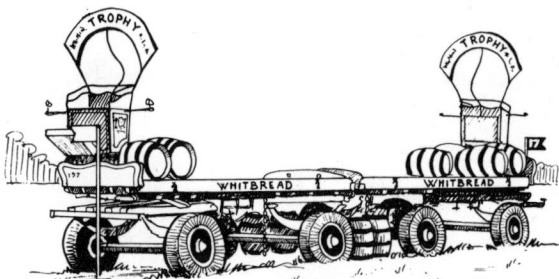

No. 17 WHITBREAD DRAYS

CROSS-COUNTRY FENCES, 1978

10 Stone Wall, 3ft. 11ins. (*Luckington Lane*). 11 Bank, 5ft. and rails 2ft. 6ins. (*Luckington Lane*). 12 Parallel Bars, height 3ft. 11ins., spread 5ft. 11ins. 13 Ditch, 10ft. Post and Rails, 3ft. 9ins. to 3ft. 11ins. (*Vicarage Vee*). 14 Tree Trunk, 3ft. 6ins. over ditch (*Stockholm Fence*). 15 Irish Bank, 8ft. 16 Park Wall, 3ft. 9ins. with ditch. 17 Whitbread Drays, height 3ft. 11ins., spread 5ft. 6ins.

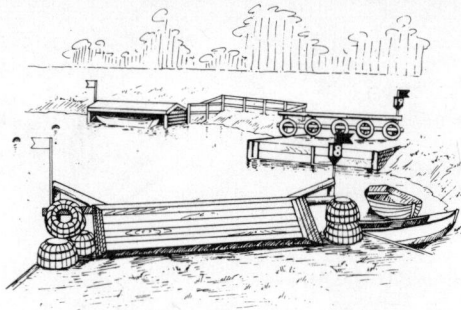
Nos. 18 & 19   THE LAKE

No. 20   NORMANDY BANK

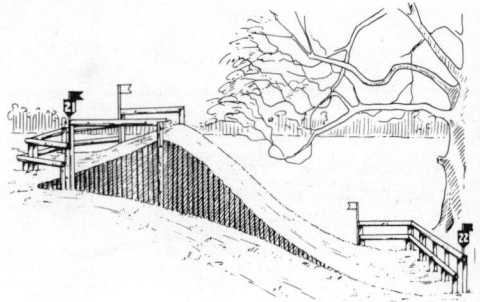
Nos. 21 & 22   THE SLIDE

No. 23   FAGGOT PILE

Nos. 24 & 25   SUNKEN ROAD

No. 26   KEEPER'S RAILS

No. 27   THE QUARRY

CROSS-COUNTRY FENCES, 1978 (contd.)

18 Upturned Punt, 3ft. (*The Lake*).   19 Post and Rails, 3ft. 11ins. or Boathouse 3ft. 10ins. (*The Lake*).   20 Normandy Bank, bank 3ft. 6ins. and rails 3ft.   21 Post and Rails, 3ft. 6ins. to 3ft. 11ins. (*The Slide*).   22 Post and Rails, 3ft. 6ins. (*The Slide*).   23 Faggot Pile, 3ft. 9ins. to 3ft. 11ins. 24 Post and Rails, 3ft. 9ins. (*Sunken road*).   25 Post and Rails, 3ft. 10ins., (*Sunken Road*). 26 Keeper's Rails, height 3ft. 10ins., ditch 9ft.   27 Post and Rails, 3ft. with varying drop (*Quarry*).

No 28 THE QUARRY

No. 29 THE STAR

No. 30 HUNTSMAN'S GRAVE

No. 31 POST AND RAILS

No. 32 ARROWHEAD

No. 33 LAMB CREEP

No. 34 WHITBREAD BAR

CROSS-COUNTRY FENCES, 1978 (contd.)

28 Stone Wall, 3ft. 9ins. (*Quarry*). 29 Combination of Rails, 3ft. 6ins. to 3ft. 11ins. (*The Star*). 30 Huntsman's Grave, ditch 11ft. 4ins. wide. 31 Post and Rails, combination of rails, 3ft. 7ins. to 3ft. 11ins. 32 Arrowhead, angled rails in ditch, 3ft. 11ins. 33 Lamb Creep, thatched roof, 3ft. 11ins. 34 Whitbread Bar, 3ft. 9ins.

The British Horse Society book tent is, as ever, full to bursting, and so too is the Beaufort Hunt Supporters' tent which has a cunningly concealed, and most comfortable bar hidden behind a display of photographs taken by the official Badminton photographer, Peter Harding. Other tents attracting a great deal of interest are the Hunters' Improvement Society, the British Field Sports Society, and Whitbreads' exhibition of inn signs, plus their regular showings of films, including one of the 1976 Olympics in Montreal.

In the stables, last-minute preparations are made by the grooms and riders of those horses which are to tackle the cross-country course early in the competition. Around the officials' tents near the start and finishing area of the cross-country, groups of serious looking men discuss last-minute preparations. Many of them wear bowler hats, and all have the look of ex-Army officers.

All the bars in the trade stand area are packed. Farmers and other gentlemen with the stamp of the countryside about them lounge about, laughing and drinking. Already one or two of them look rather flushed.

In a lane between two rows of trade stands an evangelist, wearing a shabby mackintosh, begins to preach in a loud, high voice. Everyone gives him a wide berth. Most people pretend he isn't there. If he were selling flags or handing out leaflets he would undoubtedly do a good trade, but he is only preaching.

A group of youths walk past. They are wearing denims and football supporters' scarves—they look completely out of place, and come in for some hard looks.

In the press tent there is high excitement as the photographers prepare to venture out away from the cups of coffee and the turkey sandwiches (all laid on by the organisers). They head for the trade stand area, where the Queen is about to commence her tour. Shepherded by Jim Gilmore, the photographers move off in a body. One wonders if they really need all those cameras.

It has been arranged that the photographers are to be given the chance to take pictures of Her Majesty as she visits the first three stands. They form up in a body, watched carefully by a number of plain-clothes detectives. Suddenly the Queen, accompanied by the Duke of Beaufort, appears. The photographers go into action. The crowd immediately realises that something is happening. More and more people are attracted to the scene, and soon a group of uniformed police arrive, having been hastily summoned by two-way radio. They start to control the crowd.

The Royal progress begins. After the third stand has been visited, the group of photographers breaks up. Many try to take some more pictures, but they are discouraged. Their press badges are now a hindrance, since members of the public are producing cameras from all sides in order to photograph the Queen as she walks past them.

A group of women discuss how awful it must be to live a public life and always be stared at and photographed. One woman remarks that in the old days at Badminton it was almost a point of honour not to stare at the Royal visitors. Her companions agree that "it must be awful". Meanwhile, they continue to stare as Her Majesty stops to examine the photographs at the Riding for the Disabled stand. One of the helpers in the stand whispers in panic to a bystander, "What do I say if she talks to me?"

A print and picture seller at another stand is deep in conversation with a prospective customer. He looks up to find himself facing the Queen. He does not know whether to bow, curtsey, nod, say "good morning", or just smile. Panic-stricken, he attempts to do all these things at once.

The procession moves on. More and more people join the crowd. A group of young girls arrive, eating candy floss. "Who's that man with the Queen?" they ask, "Is it Prince Philip?" One of them, better-informed than the rest, announces that it is her bodyguard. It is, in fact, the Duke of Beaufort.

On reaching the far end of the central trade stand area, the procession turns. As Her Majesty passes each trade stand, all the men remove their hats. The Queen continues to smile and to examine each stand and its wares. She is quite unconcerned by the milling crowd around her, and it is curious how, as she passes by, people smile and look happy. Then, suddenly, the tour is over, and the crowd breaks up into small groups to discuss the happening.

The Park is now seething with people—men, women, children and dogs. It is already obvious that this is going to be a record-breaking crowd. (In 1976 there were an estimated 120,000 people at Badminton for cross-country day. The figure for 1978, announced after the Trials, was 200,000.)

All around the lake, thousands of people have gathered in order to get a good position along the wooden fencing which surrounds this most popular jump. Some people even wade into the lake in order to get a better view. By the end of the cross-country phase, later that day, there were so many people around the lake that it was surprising that the competitors could get through at all. Only hard work by the stewards and by the Beaufort Huntsman, Brian Gupwell, acting as a mounted marshal, kept a narrow way open.

Then it is announced that the competition has started, and that the first of the riders (Lucinda Prior-Palmer) has set off around the $16\frac{1}{2}$-

mile course. Hurried calculations are made. The first competitor will arrive at the lake at about 1.30. Thereafter, all being well, the riders should arrive at five-minute intervals.

Everyone decides that it is lunchtime, and hampers and lunch baskets are opened. Most people, if they have any sense, bring their own food and drink to Badminton on cross-country day in order to save time queuing and, indeed, to save money. From the backs of cars and Land Rovers what appears to be an enormous quantity of food and drink is produced and consumed.

In the press tent, the reporters and photographers stand around eating sandwiches and drinking beer or coffee. The talk is of Prince Andrew's forthcoming parachute jump, and of some of the more risqué jokes which are obtainable at the Joke Shop. It has been announced that the Royal party will arrive shortly to watch the competitors from a number of hay carts stationed at the third fence. This is the lull before the storm.

Suddenly, the Land Rovers arrive to take the photographers to their vantage point at the third fence (the equestrian reporters and photographers follow a somewhat different schedule from that of the main body of photographers since they have to cover the whole Event from a technical and much more detailed point of view).

The photographers pile into the waiting Land Rovers. Two French photographers are forced to hang on to the back of the last vehicle to leave. In 1977 these photographers caused a lot of bad feeling by their behaviour when photographing the Queen, and there was even talk amongst the other photographers of throwing them into the lake. This year, however, they are much better behaved. They have gone so far as to purchase English tweed caps, mittens and green rubber boots from the trade stands. They still look exactly like Frenchmen.

The Land Rovers make their way across the park, through the thousands of people walking to and from jumps. The drivers and their companions discuss hunting and farming.

The third fence (the Pardubice Taxis) has attracted an enormous crowd. It has even got its own bar and hot-dog stands. It is an excellent vantage point as once a rider has jumped this fence, it is possible for the spectator to stand on some high ground and see several more fences being jumped in succession.

The photographers emerge from the Land Rovers and stand in a group. At the lake, whistles are blown and the first rider comes into view—Lucinda Prior-Palmer on Village Gossip. There is a tremendous cheer, and one doubts if any Event rider has ever been such a popular favourite with the public. As in 1977, she makes the lake fences seem so easy, and smiling and patting her horse's neck, she rides on to the next obstacle—the Normandy Bank.

In one of the two small annexes to the press tent, a colour television has been installed, and a small group of reporters, notebook and pencil in hand, sit around watching the competition. Watching the televised version of the competition as it is happening outside in the Park is a somewhat curious experience. It is all made so much simpler as the cameras cut from jump to jump, from competitor to competitor. To watch a competitor jumping into the Lake and at the same time to hear the cheers coming from outside the tent has the effect of making one feel slightly drunk. On the television screen, it all seems much smaller and much less exciting, although the amount of information imparted by the television commentators concerning the state of the competition is extremely useful.

At the Pardubice Taxis jump, the photographers swing into action as the Royal party arrive. Three Land Rovers draw up, and the Queen, the Queen Mother, Prince Philip, Princess Margaret, Prince Andrew, Lady Sarah Armstrong-Jones, and Viscount Linley climb up the steps to the hay carts. They are accompanied by the Duke and Duchess of Beaufort. Having taken up their positions, they immediately become the centre of attention as the photographers click away, and a huge crowd gathers.

In the background, the competition continues, and while the Royal party watch with interest from their high vantage point, the crowd and the photographers are, for the most part, staring up at the Royals. The whole atmosphere is like one huge film set.

Eventually the crowd turns its attention once more to the competition, and as each rider flashes over the fence, thousands of people run to the brow of a nearby hill, in order to obtain a better view of the distant fences, such as the Vicar's Choice and Luckington Lane.

The photographers continue to blaze away, one laughingly remarking, "What does it all mean, I ask myself? The same thing, year after year." "Never mind", replies a colleague, "their kids are growing up."

The competition is now well under way, and it is announced that Lucinda Prior-Palmer, having completed her brilliant cross-country round, has covered the entire $16\frac{1}{2}$-mile course without incurring a single penalty.

In the starting box, grooms and riders make hurried last-minute preparations, surrounded by what seems to be an enormous amount of equipment. They are allowed only ten minutes after completing the first roads and tracks section, the steeplechase course and the second roads and tracks section before starting on the cross-country phase itself. An official starts to count down to the starting time. A rider mounts, looking tense. An official calls out "Thirty seconds . . . fifteen seconds . . . ." The rider moves over to the starting position and gets away on time. Over the loud-speakers the commentator describes the progress. At the fifth fence the rider has a fall—at the seventh fence a refusal—at the eleventh fence he retires. In the box his friends look despondent. All that work for nothing.

All over the course, there are thousands of people walking about or standing on high ground and looking down the course—the scene is rather like a rural Lowry painting.

Another announcement: one of the Irish riders, Helen Cantillion, has had a bad fall at the Sunken Road, but although she is injured she re-mounts and hurries on.

Each of the jumps has its own group of spectators. At jump No. 13, the Vicarage Vee, another huge crowd is gathered. The mounted marshal here is the V.W.H. Huntsman, Sidney Bailey. He sits on his horse smiling and talking to dozens of passers-by, some of whom are old friends and hunting acquaintances. Others are strangers and many want to know the name of his horse. As he chats to them, Sidney Bailey carefully watches the course, and at the first sign of an approaching rider he clears his section of the route with that sort of unobtrusive efficiency which professional huntsmen always seem to display.

Across the Park, Pony Club members, acting as mounted messengers, go galloping by, their horses looking stolid in comparison with the "Rolls-Royce" quality of the Event horses. One of the mounted stewards on cross-country day is Colonel Whitbread who, not content with sponsoring the Event (and doubling the prize money for 1978) also turns out as a volunteer helper.

Incredibly, with the competition reaching its final stages, the trade stands are still doing good business. The bars also are not without their supporters, and in the Yard of Ale tent there are roars of laughter as a Welsh lady tells a rude story.

With only three competitors still to go, the main focus of attention is now the Lake.

The Swiss rider, Tomi Gretener comes into view and having jumped into the lake over the upturned punt, he attempts to jump out over the rails. He comes to grief, turning an incredible somersault, and landing flat on his back on the dry side of the fence. His horse, Camas Park, runs loose and is eventually caught by two small girls. Incredibly, Gretener re-mounts and carries on. He is followed by Diana Thorne on The Kingmaker, who negotiates the lake safely. Another announcement is made, this time to the effect that Jane Holderness-Roddam and Warrior have taken the lead.

On the far side of the lake, inside the crowd barrier, the Queen

Mother and the Duke of Beaufort watch the competition. On the side nearest to the trade stand area, a crowd of photographers sits on the grass, also inside the barrier. Suddenly two of them stand up. There are whistles and shouts of "sit down" from the crowd. They sit down. By now there must be somewhere in the region of 10,000 all round the lake, all of them waiting for the last rider to go, Princess Anne on Goodwill. A whistle blows, the crowd parts, and there she is, jumping into the lake. The photographers go into action, the crowd holds its breath. Are they to see a Royal ducking? Unconcerned, Princess Anne takes both fences easily and rides on towards the next fence to a loud cheer.

The cross-country phase is over. Eleven riders have jumped clear, and there are twenty-seven riders left in the competition; the rest have either retired or been eliminated.

In the lead at the end of the cross-country phase is Jane Holderness-Roddam on Warrior, in second place is Lucinda Prior-Palmer on Village Gossip, in third place is Richard Meade on Bleak Hills, while fourth and fifth are Jane Starkey with Topper Too and John Watson on Cambridge Blue (for Ireland). All of these riders appear to have taken Colonel Weldon's advice and "got a wiggle on", especially Lucinda, who has moved up from 18th position to finish the day in 2nd place, and could improve on the final day to take yet another Whitbread Trophy.

In the press tent some reporters are already on the phone. "Princess Anne—A.N.N.E.—today finished in 16th place . . ." and so on. In the BHS tent, old hands settle down to swap stories and drinks with their friends and watch the showjumping in the Whitbread Grand Stakes, while waiting for the worst of the traffic to clear. "Too soon to go yet—let's have another."

Cars stream away from the park in their thousands, and all over Gloucestershire people are making their way home, having thoroughly enjoyed themselves. For a great many of them, there is still another day to enjoy.

Show Jumping

Before the third and final stage of the Badminton Horse Trials, the horses are exercised and then paraded in the Badminton stable yard, for a last veterinary inspection.

Following the sudden death of Wide Awake, winner of the 1976 Event, there was much speculation concerning the advisability of making horses jump round such difficult courses. Charges of cruelty were levelled at Colonel Weldon in his capacity as course-designer, and some "public-spirited" individuals even went so far as to write abusive letters to Miss Prior-Palmer, as if the loss of a well-loved horse were not bad enough. Colonel Weldon is an extremely experienced horseman and course-designer, and though his courses may be tough, they are never dangerous. The veterinary inspections at Badminton are not "for show", but are rigorous and thorough, and any horse which shows signs of distress will be ordered to be withdrawn from the competition.

One final word on the Wide Awake controversy—throughout the 1976 Badminton Horse Trials, there were eight RSPCA inspectors on duty, all of whom agreed that at no time did any of the riders subject their mounts to any cruelty whatsoever.

The final phase of the Badminton Horse Trials is not a show-jumping competition in the strict sense, but rather it is designed to prove that, after the rigours of the speed and endurance tests, the "horses have retained the suppleness, energy, and obedience necessary for them to continue in service".

The final test is carried out over a course of between 700 to 800 metres, with ten or twelve obstacles, at a speed of 400 metres per minute. Competitors are penalised at the rate of a quarter of a mark for every second in excess of the time up to the time limit, after which he or she is eliminated.

The faults at obstacles are as follows:

Knocking down an obstacle, or a foot in the water	5 penalties
First disobedience	10 penalties
Second disobedience in the whole test	20 penalties
Third disobedience in the whole test	Elimination
Jumping an obstacle in the wrong order	Elimination
Error of course not rectified	Elimination
Fall of horse and/or rider	30 penalties

SUNDAY—SHOW-JUMPING DAY

The weather promises to be fine. At 10.00 in the morning, Badminton Park seems to be empty. The only trace of the two hundred thousand people who attended on cross-country day is the litter. It is impossible for such a record number of people not to leave some litter. Even so, the sight of empty Coke tins trampled into the turf in front of Badminton House is an unpleasant one.

The Park, the trade stands area, the main arena, the press tent—all are more or less deserted. The interest this morning is in the magnificent Badminton stable yard, where the veterinary inspection of competitors' horses is in full swing.

The stable yard is crowded and the crowd have formed into two rings. The first impression is that it all looks rather like an early nineteenth-century print depicting a horse sale at Tattersalls. The crowd looks solemn and knowledgeable. The competitors look anxious; to have come so far in the competition and then to have a horse declared unfit would be heartbreaking. It is quite bad enough when something goes wrong before the Trials actually start.

On one side of the yard horses are being walked around with their rugs on prior to entering the actual inspection area. On the other side of the yard a long strip of gravel has been swept clear and the horses, now without their rugs, are being led up and down in turn, watched critically by Her Majesty the Queen, the Duke of Beaufort, Mr David Somerset (Chairman of the Badminton Horse Trials Committee) and the panel of expert judges.

In one corner of the yard the ever-ready group of photographers stand, while above the crowd on a scaffold platform, television cameras scan the scene. Although a few people gawp at the Royal party, the main interest is centred upon the horses.

At last the inspection is over, and the twenty-seven horses left in the competition are all declared sound. There is a sigh of relief when the leading horse, Warrior, is passed fit. Three weeks before the competition he had developed an abscess in one hoof, which had interrupted his training programme. It reflects great credit on Jane Holderness-Roddam and her associates that not only were they able to get the horse fit in time for the competition, but also fit enough to survive the arduous cross-country course (which both horse and rider covered in brilliant style).

While on the subject of veterinary inspections at Badminton, it is perhaps well worth mentioning that throughout the competition there are nine veterinary surgeons in attendance, plus a radiological unit from the Department of Veterinary Surgery at the University of Bristol, who are on hand to keep an eye on the well-being of the horses at all stages.

The inspection over, the crowd dissolves—some to inspect the interior of the stables, others to make their way towards Badminton Church. Others move away towards the main arena, where the Whitbread Spring Stakes have already started.

In addition to the Horse Trials themselves, there are three major jumping events at Badminton: The Whitbread Grand Stakes, which takes place on the Saturday afternoon (with prizes which range from £150 down to £5); the Whitbread Spring Stakes, which takes place on

Sunday morning (with prizes ranging from £100 down to £10); and the Whitbread Championship, which takes place on Sunday afternoon (with prizes ranging from £350 to £10). While the main interest throughout the four days is concentrated on the actual Trials, it is possible, on the Saturday and Sunday, for spectators to enjoy watching riders of the quality and reputation of David Broome, Harvey Smith, Caroline Bradley, Ted Edgar, Derek Ricketts, Marion Mould, as well as many others, competing in the Whitbread show-jumping competitions.

Back in the stable yard, there is a sudden flurry of excitement—the photographers have spotted Princess Anne's detective. Where he goes, she goes—and, sure enough, the Princess has joined a small group of people who are studying the notice which has just been posted on the side of the officials' hut, giving the running order for the final phase of the competition. The photographers sweep into action, and the whirr of camera motors again fills the air.

Inside the stables, it is crowded as people jostle to see the horses in their stalls. There seem to be many more good-luck cards and telegrams in evidence this year, reflecting, perhaps, the openness of the competition. The grooms working on their charges look tired, which is not surprising, since most of them have lived out of suitcases for several days now, devoting all their time and energy to the care and preparation of the horses in their charge.

Already outside Badminton Church, a crowd is beginning to gather. On this particular Sunday, the service is an all-ticket affair, but many people are happy to remain outside, some to catch a glimpse of the Royal party, others just listen to the Service which is relayed over loud-speakers. In Badminton village, people are walking about, enjoying both the weather and the prospect. Here and there, policemen stand about in groups. Suddenly, one constable straightens up at the approach of a party led by a woman wearing a headscarf. He relaxes and laughs. His colleague laughs also, exclaiming, "I was caught like that yesterday." A small group of plain-clothes detectives hold a conspiratorial meeting on the pavement. The volume of traffic entering the village is increasing steadily.

In the trade stand area, many people have gathered by midday, but they are numbered in hundreds rather than the thousands of the previous day. Groups congregate round the scoreboard, bringing their programme score-sheets up to date. Soon the stands are, once again, doing a roaring trade, especially the Joke Shop.

In the press tent, there is a relaxed atmosphere as photographers and reporters wander in and out to inspect the previous day's newspaper coverage—the cuttings being pinned to a notice board.

Pride of place goes to a beautiful photograph of Princess Anne exercising her horse in the Park. Another flurry of excitement erupts as the draw for the last three places in the arena photographers' party takes place.

The policy of restricting photographers in the main arena came about after the 1976 Badminton when far too many were allowed, or managed to get into the arena. This resulted in near-chaos and made a nonsense of the presentation of the awards. In the following year the party was chosen by Jim Gilmore, but there was a great deal of bitterness among those photographers who failed to get into the arena. This year it has been decided that after the generally agreed nine places have been filled (these include Press Agency, official Badminton photographers, etc.) the final places would be decided by ballot.

The names of all those not so far chosen are written on slips of paper which are placed in a brief-case. Shaking this up, Jim Gilmore asks reporters in the tent to take out the names. They do so, and the third person to draw out a name is a young lady reporter. As she puts her hand into the case, a photographer cries out in mock desperation, "Draw mine, for God's sake." Incredibly, his name comes out of the case. There is much laughter and this year there is none of the complaints and anger which followed the choice of the arena party in 1977. This time justice has been seen to be done.

All over the Park people are enjoying their picnics. Many stand, glass in hand, by the open boots of their cars. The whole atmosphere is relaxed and happy, helped by the fact that the sun has decided to make an appearance. In the main arena the Whitbread Spring Stakes is drawing to a close. The winner is Ballywillwill, ridden by David Broome.

In recent years, those competitors in the Horse Trials who are placed lower down in the running order take part in the final phase before lunch. The official ruling is that they should do so if the number of competitors still in the competition exceeds twenty. This year, however, since there are only twenty-seven competitors left in the Event, it has been decided that all of them will jump off in the afternoon. This is extremely popular since those lower in the scoring usually have to perform the show-jumping phase of the competition in front of a very small audience and without very much ceremony. Having put in all the work necessary to have survived so far in the competition, it must come as an anti-climax. In 1978, however, they have the thrill of jumping in front of a full house and before the Queen and other members of the Royal Family.

In the BHS refreshment tent, and in the bars around the Park, lunch is a much more leisurely affair than on the previous day. Old friends greet each other and talk over the results of the competition to date.

Gradually the feeling of expectancy heightens as the time for the main event of the day draws near. With only an hour to go, many people are already beginning to take their seats in the stands, and watch the competitors who are now walking the show-jumping course. Outside, others still wander about the trade stands in search of a last-minute bargain or a last-minute drink. In the Beaufort Hunt Supporters' bar, a group of farmers watch a farming programme on television. They are joined by another group of hunting enthusiasts who have only just discovered (after four days) the existence of this pleasant little bar, and discovered also that the prices are considerably cheaper than anywhere else. Hurriedly, they set about making up for lost time.

As two o'clock approaches, the main arena starts to draw the crowd like a magnet. At the entrance to the ring, a professional Huntsman passes Major Gundry, and hurriedly removes his cap. "Afternoon, Master!" "Afternoon, my boy!" In the centre of the arena the Band of the 2nd Battalion the Royal Green Jackets is playing military music; marching and counter-marching in a curious half-running, half-walking manner. The arena party of photographers enters. They all wear large red badges and are shepherded about by a resplendent Jim Gilmore, who has managed to find time to change into a smart suit.

In the stands which surround the arena, latecomers hurry to find their seats. The remainder of the photographers congregate in the small pen in front of and to the right of the Royal Box

Crowds of people have now gathered in the collecting ring. Princess Anne's baby is being pushed around in a rather shabby pram by her mother-in-law, Mrs Phillips. Competitors' horses are being trotted round either by their riders or their grooms, and there is a tremendous feeling of excitement and tension. Many of the show-jumping fraternity are gathering to watch this last phase of the competition and they discuss the difference in approach between three-day eventing and show-jumping. Some of them who have taken part in the eventing say that it is a much more difficult and demanding sport and they would not wish to devote so much time to it.

Directly in front of the Royal Box, officials are arranging the display of trophies for the presentation. Whitbread's representatives have suddenly all appeared wearing British warms and bowler hats. The tension in the arena mounts as the rumour spreads that the Queen has arrived, or is due to arrive. Plain-clothes detectives take up their positions all around the Royal Box. Many of them are carrying two-way radios.

At 2.30 everything comes to a halt. All are in their appointed places. The stage is set. The band stops playing and, exactly to the second, the Royal party enters the arena in three Land Rovers, which are driven around the arena stopping just in front of the Royal Box. Her Majesty the Queen emerges from the first Land Rover and stands smiling before walking through the gate which leads to the Royal Box.

The photographers are in an ecstasy, and fire off their cameras from a distance of about four feet. Whirrs and clicks are all that can be heard as the Queen and other members of the Royal party, accompanied by the Duke and Duchess of Beaufort, pass through the gate. The Queen, who looks very young, is still smiling, but one senses that she is not altogether happy about the close proximity of the photographers. She enters the Royal Box and, as she does so, the band plays the National Anthem. The crowd stands, and the gentlemen remove their hats.

The Anthem ended, the band departs at its curious jog-trot, and the crowd settles down to enjoy the final stage of the richest ever Badminton Horse Trials.

First comes the parade of the competitors who pass in front of the Royal Box, saluting Her Majesty, the women riders holding their whips in a vertical position and inclining their heads. One competitor performs a creditable piece of dressage in order to salute head-on. A young Army officer gives the smartest of smart salutes.

This year the photographers all remain seated. All, that is, except one who, half-rising, half-turning in his seat, fires away at the Queen. Eventually he is warned by the Stewards and he sullenly puts his camera away.

The competitors jump in the reverse order to their placing in the competition, with the higher-placed riders jumping last. Slowly the field is narrowed down to the last twelve—those in the money. One of the early competitors most worthy of mention is Helen Cantillion who, it is later announced, finished the competition jumping with a broken arm!

Suddenly the cameras whirr again—this time for Princess Anne, jumping twelfth on Goodwill (her final placing is 16th). Once again the delinquent photographer fires away at the Royal Box. Again he is told to stop, and eventually he does so.

Then at last the final stages of the competition have arrived—with the final placings to be decided and the coveted Whitbread Trophy to be won. Richard Meade, who is lying third after the cross-country phase, enters the arena on Bleak Hills, but it is not their day. Having knocked down three fences, they are relegated to sixth place. Then, to loud cheers, the darling of the crowd, Lucinda Prior-Palmer enters the arena on Village gossip, and in almost total silence she jumps a

clear round. As she clears the last fence, there is a great roar of applause
and she leaves the arena smiling broadly.

Now the entire stadium is completely silent as the last to go, Warrior
ridden by Jane Holderness-Roddam (she was placed fourth in 1977),
prepares to jump. The current leader, she can only afford to knock one
fence down. Looking calm and serious, in contrast to the sunny
Lucinda, Jane Holderness-Roddam jumps cleanly and carefully.
Then, as she jumps the second last fence, the tension dissolves. The
crowds cheer and, as she clears the last fence, there is a great roar of
applause, as well as whistles, whoops and holloas. It is all over, and
Warrior and Jane Holderness-Roddam have won the Whitbread
Trophy. Then, with the whole arena still buzzing with excitement, the
competitors enter for the presentations. A broadly-smiling Jane
Holderness-Roddam steps forward to receive seemingly endless
trophies and prizes from Her Majesty the Queen.

Following the prize-giving, the competitors circle the arena again.
Then the winners do a lap of honour to tremendous cheers. Although
so many of the crowd had wanted to see Lucinda Prior-Palmer achieve
her fourth win and her hat-trick, there is no doubt that Jane
Holderness-Roddam is a most popular winner.

There now follows another ceremony popular at Badminton—
the parade of the Duke of Beaufort's foxhounds. There are unlimited
whoops and shouts of joy as the Duke's Huntsman, Brian Gupwell,
circles the arena with $17\frac{1}{2}$ couple of the Beaufort pack. The cheers
reach a crescendo when His Grace, the Duke of Beaufort comes down
into the ring to greet them.

And then, suddenly, it is all over, and the crowds stream out of the
arena. In the BHS tent there is jubilation, and large drinks seem to be
the order of the day. In the Beaufort Hunt Supporters' tent there is also
cause for celebration since Jane Holderness-Roddam is a former
member of the Beaufort Hunt Pony Club. In the trade stand area,
business is still going on. "We shall stay open as long as we are needed"
says one stand owner, as though by taking our money he is providing
some special social service.

Colonel Weldon appears in the vicinity of the Director's tent, deep
in conversation with a friend. Perhaps he is already discussing next
year's event. Already cars and people are beginning to flow out of the
park. In the main show arena, however, the final show-jumping
competition, Whitbread Championship, is already under way and is
won by Sanyo Blender ridden by Harvey Smith.

Jane Holderness-Roddam attends the traditional Press conference
and photographic session at the Whitbread tent, answering the
traditional questions from the reporters. Again it is a source of wonder

that the sort of person who, having spent four nerve-racking days competing in this most demanding event, can cope with a Press conference so easily. Smiling, she signs autographs for a number of children. Other competitors come in unrecognised to collect their prizes. All eyes are on the winner.

And so the 1978 Badminton Horse Trials are over. Once again, Colonel Weldon and his team have skilfully provided the background for an interesting and exciting competition. The competitors and their horses have thrilled the crowds in their attempts to win the generously sponsored Whitbread Trophy. His Grace, the Duke of Beaufort has provided the setting as he has done since he instigated the competition in 1949 and, as the result of the tremendous success of the event and the vastly increased attendance, plus the hard work of all those concerned with the organisation, planning and running of the event, another generous donation will be made to the British Horse Society.

The 1978 Badminton Horse Trials ended with Jane Holderness-Roddam winning on Warrior which she owns in partnership with Mrs S. Howard of America; Mrs Howard gave Jane a half-share in the horse in order to avoid any complications about nationality in the championships. In second place was the reigning European Champion, Lucinda Prior-Palmer on Village Gossip. Although she was not in the first twelve at the end of the dressage phase, her brilliant cross-country round moved her into second place and almost resulted in her bringing off her fourth win at Badminton. In third place was Jane Starkey on Topper Too, whilst in fourth place was Elizabeth Boone on Felday Farmer.

In much the same way that Harold Macmillan must often have regretted his remark "You've never had it so good", so must Colonel Weldon often had cause to regret his famous remark to the effect that "Women should be at home warming somebody's slippers". Whilst it is true that a greater percentage of women are now competing in horse trials, the 1978 result, with the first four places going to the ladies, must have caused many people to remember Colonel Weldon's other remark, made in 1972, to the effect that "girls are less fitted to the strains and stresses of a major competition".* Well, at Badminton in 1978 not only did Jane Holderness-Roddam take a major competition in her stride, but within minutes of receiving the trophy from Her

*"To set the record straight, however, I was answering a question about girls at the Olympic Games, *not* at an individual event like Badminton, where there had already been several female winners. I also said, 'All other things being equal, I preferred men to girls' (for this particular activity). That is to say, provided the horse was equally good and the rider equally proficient." F.W.

Majesty the Queen, she dealt with photographers, reporters, and a host of well-wishers with all the style and confidence of the accomplished veteran that she is.

With the ladies currently sweeping the board, as far as eventing is concerned, perhaps for future Badminton Horse Trials, Whitbreads might like to sponsor an additional trophy—the Weldon Slippers! Not that Colonel would mind in the least, for already he is concerning himself with the World Championships in Kentucky (where he has been chosen to act as one of the three-man Grand Jury) and also with the next two Badminton Horse Trials leading up to the 1980 Olympic Games.

The Badminton Horse Trials are a unique occasion, and a most valuable training ground for British and overseas riders. The Duke of Beaufort, to whom the equestrian world owes a very great debt of gratitude, has every reason to be proud of having instituted the Event.

Just over a week after the completion of the Badminton 1978 Horse Trials, the short list for the World Three Day Event Championships was announced. The list included the first five British riders at Badminton—Jane Holderness-Roddam (Warrior), Lucinda Prior-Palmer (Village Gossip and Killaire), Jane Starkey (Topper Too), Elizabeth Boone (Felday Farmer) and Richard Meade (Bleak Hills)— the remaining places going to Chris Collins (Smokey VI), Diana Thorne (The Kingmaker) and Andrew Brake (Bampton Fair). By the time this book is published, the results will be known.

The Badminton Horse Trials, 1949–1977

1949. The first-ever Badminton aroused a great deal of interest amongst British equestrian enthusiasts. Although this was a completely new experience for organisers and competitors alike, the event proved to be a great success. In all, there were twenty entries, including a strong Irish challenge. The new-fangled foreign import, Dressage, caused much comment, and the standard of Dressage performance was far below that seen at Badminton today. There were, however, a few exceptions, notably, John Shedden and Captain J. A. Collings, both of whom had been sent to Sweden by the BHS in order to gain experience in this type of Event. Captain Collings was in the lead after the Dressage phase, but lost points over the steeplechase course and the twenty-one fence cross-country course. John Shedden, who put in the fastest time on the cross-country, despite bad weather conditions, was the eventual winner on Mrs Home Kidson's horse, Golden Willow. Second was Ian Dudgeon (Ire.) on Sea Lark (the only clear round in the jumping phase), while third was Brigadier Lyndon Bolton on Titus III.

1950. This second Badminton proved to be an exciting affair, by virtue of the closeness of the finish, and was only decided in the final phase of the competition. Captain J. A. Collings was again in the lead after the Dressage, and also rode an excellent cross-country. He was overtaken, however, by the 1949 winner, John Shedden on Kingpin, and also by Captain Arkwright on Minster Green. In the final jumping phase, although Collings had a pole down, his nearest rivals both had two poles down, and Captain Collings (who was to die in an air crash in the following year) won the Event, riding Mrs G. H. Crystal's horse, Remus. John Shedden, who, incidentally, was the first competitor ever to enter two horses at Badminton—Kingpin and Golden Willow—finished in fifth place.

1951. This was the first International Badminton, with riders from Holland and Switzerland taking part. As might be expected, the European riders excelled in the Dressage phase of the competition but, surprisingly, they also did well in the cross-country. The Swiss horses, although not thought to be in peak condition, were better schooled, and they "swept the board" both in the individual competition (Swiss riders finishing first, fourth and sixth) and in the team event—their two teams finishing first and second. The individual winner was Captain H. Schwarzenbach on Vae Victis. Great Britain's honour was saved by a young lady rider, Jane Drummond-Hay, who jumped the only clear round in the final phase, and finished second on Happy Knight.

1952. Jane Drummond-Hay led after the Dressage, but fell behind on the cross-country. This year was a very open competition, being the year of the Helsinki Olympics, so that the potential Olympic riders and horses were not able to compete. Again, the competition resulted in a close finish, with everything depending on the final phase. The two leaders, Brigadier Lyndon Bolton on Greylag and Penny Moreton on Vigilant, each had three fences down and Captain M. A. Q. Darley on Emily Little, jumped clear to take first place. Brian Young on Dandy finished second. Brigadier Lyndon Bolton was third, and Penny Moreton was fourth. (Women riders were already beginning to prove that they could cope with the rigours of a three-day event.) There were also two other happenings which were to affect later Badmintons. For the very first time, Her Majesty the Queen attended the Event and presented the prizes, and the name of F. W. C. Weldon appeared amongst the names of the competitors. However, on that first attempt, Frank Weldon, riding Liza Mandy, fell during the cross-country phase and spent a week in Tetbury Cottage Hospital while his two subalterns from the King's Troop RHA went home to London delighted with themselves for completing the course. That made him start to take the whole thing seriously to ensure that such a situation should never recur.

1953. The Badminton Horse Trials had by now become an established part of the British equestrian scene; from somewhat rough and ready beginnings, the Event was slowly developing into the major international Event we know today. British riders, too, had improved rapidly as far as eventing was concerned. Badminton 1953 was the first ever European Championship, with individuals and teams from Sweden, Holland, Ireland and Switzerland competing. A surprise member of the British team was Major Frank Weldon, on the relatively inexperienced Kilbarry. Major Weldon replaced Major Laurence Rook on Starlight at the last moment. The selectors made this decision in order to let Major Rook concentrate on the individual competition. It was, as things transpired, a very wise decision, for Major Rook on Mrs. J. R. Baker's horse (second in the Dressage) won the competition with ease. Major Weldon and Kilbarry were second, and Captain Schwarzenbach (winner in 1951) finished third on Vae Victis. In addition to taking first and second places in the individual competition, Great Britain won its first European Championship. Once again, women riders did well, and there were three in the first twelve placings.

1954. A memorable Badminton for two reasons. First, the cross-country results were seriously affected by a time-keeping error—an error which, it has been suggested, could well have cost Major Weldon the individual title. Even so, he and Kilbarry were in the lead at the final phase but, unfortunately, he had two fences down and, once again, had to be content with second place. Margaret Hough, who jumped clear on Bambi V, went into first place, and thus became the first woman rider to win at Badminton. Another girl, Diana Mason (on Tramella) was third. Incidentally, the British team went on to win their second European Championship later that year, at Basle.

1955. Second in 1953, second in 1954—it was only a matter of time before the brilliant combination of Major Weldon and Kilbarry took the Badminton title, and this was the year in which they did it. At the request of Her Majesty the Queen, the competition that year was held at Windsor. It was decided to hold the competition in May that year on the assumption that the weather would be more favourable. Unfortunately, it snowed. It was also a European Championship year, with teams from Italy, Germany, Sweden, Switzerland and Ireland competing. In the team event, the British team—Diana Mason on Tramella, Frank Weldon on Kilbarry, and Bertie Hill on Countryman—won their third European Championship, with Switzerland coming second. All of the other teams were eliminated. In the individual competition, Major Weldon, who had finished second in the Dressage behind Diana Mason (who was later eliminated) won easily. John Oram (Radar) was second and Bertie Hill (Countryman) was third. A girl named Sheila Willcox, riding in her first three-day event, finished in thirteenth place.

1956. Although it was only her second three-day event, Sheila Willcox proved herself to be in the very top flight of Event riders, when she engaged in a battle for the individual title with Frank Weldon, now Lieutenant-Colonel. At the end of the dressage phase, Colonel Weldon and Kilbarry were only fractionally ahead of Miss Willcox on High and Mighty. On the second day, both riders scored maximum bonus points, and both went clear in the exciting jumping phase. Colonel Weldon emerged the winner by a mere one and a half points. An Australian, Laurie Morgan (Gold Ross) came third, and Bertie Hill on Countryman was fourth.

1957. Tragically, Kilbarry was killed while jumping at Cottesbrooke, and so High and Mighty, again ridden by Sheila Willcox, became the new star of Badminton. This was a real *tour de force*. Sheila Willcox, the last to go in each phase, swept the board, finishing in the lead at the end of each stage of the Event, and won the competition with ease. The male riders must have received a nasty jolt, since five women finished in the first eight places. Penny Moreton (Red Sea) finished second.

1958. Once again, it was High and Mighty, ridden by European Champion, Sheila Willcox, who dominated the field, so much so that the Event became virtually a one-horse race, with the interest being in who would finish second. Sheila Willcox and High and Mighty, with only ten penalties in the show-jumping phase, won by the widest margin of points in the history of Badminton, forty-seven points ahead of Derek Allhusen (Laurien) who was second, while John Oram (Copperplate) was third.

1959. This was the year in which Sheila Willcox achieved the first Badminton hat trick. It was also the year of the "great rains", when the whole Event was carried out in truly appalling weather conditions. At the end of the Dressage phase, Sheila Willcox was in the lead on Airs and Graces. On the second day, however, David Somerset, riding Countryman rode a very creditable round despite the bad going, and jumped up fifteen places to take the lead. In the final jumping stage, however, David Somerset, going in first, had a fence down, while Sheila Willcox went clear, thus becoming the first person to win three Badminton Horse Trials. Ted Marsh on Wild Venture was third. This year also saw the introduction of Little Badminton, which was used in order to cope with the ever-increasing number of entries (Great and Little Badminton are the names of the two villages). The first Little Badminton was won by Shelagh Kesler on Double Diamond. (In 1966, however, Badminton became a four-day event—the first two days of which are devoted to Dressage—and the Little Badminton competition was abandoned.)

1960. This was memorable as the first year in which Whitbread began their extremely generous sponsorship of the competition. It was also memorable as the "year of the Australians". (Following the heavy rains of 1959, the Park in front of Badminton House had been reduced to a sea of mud. It was, therefore, decided to re-site the course further out in the Park, where it has remained ever since.) This was Olympic year and the Australian team, on its way to Rome, put forward a very strong challenge. After the Dressage, however, it was a British girl who led the field—Anneli Drummond-Hay, riding Perhaps (a horse she had bought for only a few pounds and which she had schooled herself). Bill Roycroft, on Our Solo, scored maximum bonus points on both the Steeplechase and the Cross-Country phases, as also did Colonel Weldon on Samuel Johnson but, at the end of the second day, it was still Anneli Drummond-Hay who led. Unfortunately, she had two fences down on the final Jumping section, and two Australians swept into the lead—Bill Roycroft on Our Solo was first, and Laurie Morgan (the Australian team captain) on Salad Days was second. Laurie Morgan and Salad Days went on to win the Olympic Gold Medal in Rome. Australian riders finished in first, second, fourth and tenth places, and one rider, Captain Darley, Badminton winner in 1952, received a special mention in *The Field* for having completed the Cross-Country course in good time after a very bad fall, with considerable "visceral fortitude". Little Badminton that year was won by Martin Whiteley on Peggotty.

1961. Another year of bad weather conditions at Badminton, resulting in very soft going on the Cross-Country phase. At the end of the Dressage section, Jeremy Beale (Fulmer Folly) was in the lead. At the end of the rigorous second day, however, Olympic medallist, Laurie Morgan, was in the lead on Salad Days (placed sixth in the Dressage), while Harry Freeman-Jackson (St. Finbarr) was in second place. Incredibly, considering the state of the going, Michael Bullen was in both third and fourth places with Cottage Romance and Sea Breeze, and that was, in fact, the final order. In pouring rain, Laurie Morgan went clear in the Jumping section, as did Harry Freeman-Jackson, who finished only four points behind the winner. Little Badminton was won by Peter Welch on Mr Wilson.

1962. This was another "one horse" year, with the main interest being in the fierce struggle for second place. Anneli Drummond-Hay on the great horse, Merely-a-Monarch (who had recently won the first Burghley competition) led in each of the three stages of the Event, and never even looked like being headed. Frank Weldon on Young Pretender, and Michael Bullen on Sea Breeze, both had maximum bonus points on the Cross-Country phase but, in the end, Colonel Weldon and Young Pretender took second place by virtue of a better Dressage score, while only two points behind them came Michael Bullen and Sea Breeze. Penny Crofts (on Priam) won Little Badminton. (Later, as everyone knows, Miss Drummond-Hay and Merely-a-Monarch went on to tremendous success in the world of show-jumping.)

1963. Somebody once said that it is always raining at Badminton and while, of course, this is not strictly true, one could be forgiven for imagining it to be the case. The unusually cold winter of 1962/63 prevented the cross-country course being prepared for a full-scale three-day event. A substitute one-day event was staged, but even this suffered because of heavy rain. However, the competitors battled on in the appalling conditions, and the Event, such as it was, was won by Susan Fleet on The Gladiator from Richard Meade on Barbary.

1964. With the Tokyo Olympics in the offing, Badminton 1964 was regarded as a pre-Olympic warm-up by the large contingent of entries from overseas, France, Germany, Ireland, Switzerland and Denmark. Weather conditions, for a change, were good, and the competition was won by the Army rider, Captain J. R. Templer riding M'Lord Connolly. In seventh place after the Dressage, Captain Templer had an excellent Cross-Country round and was clear in the Jumping phase, finishing 27 points ahead of Jeremy Bingham-Smith on By Golly. Harry Freeman-Jackson on St. Finbarr was third, and Michael Bullen on Young Pretender was fourth. Sheila Willcox, returning to Badminton after a long absence, won Little Badminton on Glenamoy.

1965. This will be remembered for the incredible achievements of Bill Roycroft (Badminton winner in 1960) who, en route to Australia from Tokyo, stopped over to enter three horses at Badminton—a feat which must have required a great deal of organisational skill. Not only that, but Bill Roycroft was placed on all three horses, and had the only clear round in the final Jumping phase, almost winning the competition. However, the winner on this occasion was Major E. A. Boylan (Ire.), the first Irish winner since 1952. Major Boylan, riding Durlas Eile, led after the Dressage section, and retained his lead after the second day, with Sheila Willcox in second place on Glenamoy. Despite incurring 20 faults in the final stage of the competition, Major Boylan and Duras Eile had enough points in hand to win. Bill Roycroft, who had moved into third place with Stony Crossing (which had also been third to Arkle and Mill House in the Cheltenham Gold Cup!) jumped clear, but failed to win. He did, however, finish second on Eldorado and sixth on Stony Crossing. He also, incredibly, finished second at Little Badminton on Avatar. The winner was The Poacher (later to win an Olympic Gold medal when ridden by Richard Meade) ridden by Martin Whiteley.

1966. Cancelled owing to bad weather conditions.

1967. This was one of the few Badmintons to be won by a horse and rider who had never before taken part in the competition—Celia Ross-Taylor on Jonathan. At the end of the Dressage section, the previous year's winner, Major Boylan, was in the lead, but by the end of the Cross-Country phase, both Derek Allhusen (Lochinvar) and Celia Ross-Taylor (Jonathan) were breathing down his neck. A number of German riders did extremely well in the Dressage, but dropped down in the order after the second stage of the competition. The final result depended on the Jumping stage. Major Boylan (Durlas Eile) had two fences down, and was relegated to second place, and Celia Ross-Taylor went clear to win the Event. Derek Allhusen dropped from second to eleventh place, by virtue of a disastrous Jumping round, and in third place was Pollyann Hely-Hutchinson on Count Jasper. (The Little Badminton competition was discontinued.)

1968. This year produced a desperately close-fought affair, with all five members of the subsequent British Olympic team in the shake-up on the final day. At the end of the Dressage phase, Sergeant Ben Jones on Foxdor was in the lead. There were a number of eliminations during the Cross-Country section, but Ben Jones was able to retain his lead, due to a clear, albeit slow, second stage. Jane Bullen on Our Nobby (a former member of the Beaufort Hunt Pony Club), however, scorched round (she was twenty-third after the Dressage) and moved up twenty places into second place. At the final Jumping stage, only one fence separated five competitors—Ben Jones, Jane Bullen, Mark Phillips (Rock On), Richard Meade (Turnstone), and Derek Allhusen

(Lochinvar). Jane Bullen jumped clear to win; Richard Meade, who also went clear, was in second place, and the unfortunate Ben Jones, who had the second fence down, had to be content with third place. Mark Phillips was placed fourth. Later that year, these five riders (Mark Phillips was reserve) won the Olympic Team Gold Medal in Mexico.

1969. A year of disaster for many of the more experienced riders and horses, and one which saw a victory for the youngest competitor to win the Whitbread Trophy—Richard Walker on Pasha (Junior European Champion in 1968). During the second stage of the competition, Bertie Hill on Chicago, leading after the Dressage phase, fell on the Steeplechase course. Another faller was Sheila Willcox who broke her ribs, while Richard Meade (Barbary) suffered his second soaking in two years, when he fell into the Lake, and lost his bridle. Again, as in 1968, the final Jumping stage was extremely close, with the five leading competitors separated by one fence: Richard Walker (Pasha); Mary Gordon-Watson (Cornishman V); Bill Roycroft (Furtive and Warrathoola); Angela Martin-Bird (Grey Cloud). Richard Walker had a clear round, thus winning the Event. Angela Martin-Bird also went clear, finishing in second place; Bill Roycroft was third and fourth; the unfortunate Mary Gordon-Watson dropped down to ninth place.

1970. There were forty-six entries for this competition, including riders and horses from Ireland, Holland, the United States of America and France. At the end of the Dressage section, Richard Meade, riding the Combined Training Committee's horse, The Poacher, was in the lead by 15 points, from Bertie Hill on Chicago III. Times on the second stage were slow, and perhaps the introduction of the fearsome Normandy Bank fence had something to do with this. However, The Poacher was never headed, but Chicago was relegated into third place, when Captain Ronnie McMahon did the fastest time on San Carlos to move up into second place. In the final stage of the competition, Richard Meade and The Poacher went clear to win, and Ronnie McMahon, who also had a clear round, finished second—both competitors ending up with bonus points. Bertie Hill suffered a tragedy when he jumped the tenth fence instead of the sixth, and was eliminated. Mary Gordon-Watson on Cornishman V finished in third place. Not to be outdone by a mere male, Lorna Sutherland entered three horses (thus emulating Bill Roycroft's 1965 effort) and, indeed, she almost equalled his feat in having all three horses placed—being placed fourth on Gypsy Flame and twelfth on Popadom; while her third horse Mrs C. Horton's The Dark Horse, was placed fifteenth.

1971. For the next seven years (six Events) two riders were to dominate the competition—Lt. (as he then was) Mark Phillips and Lucinda Prior-Palmer, both of whom won three Events apiece. Lt. Phillips, like so many good riders, was a member of the Beaufort Hunt Pony Club (one of the instructors being Colonel Weldon). He also trained with Mrs Molly Sievewright at the Talland School. This year saw the first of Mark Phillips's three wins at Badminton. At the end of the first day, he was in the lead on Great Ovation (a horse he owned in partnership with his aunt). Princess Anne (later that year to become European Champion) was riding for the first time at Badminton, and was in second place on Doublet. On the second day, a great many of the competitors came to grief on the Cross-Country course, with Mary Gordon-Watson (Cornishman V), Debbie West (Baccarat) and Richard Walker (Upper Strata) all incurring refusals at different obstacles. In the end, Mark Phillips scored a comfortable victory on Great Ovation, while Mary Gordon-Watson (Cornishman V) was second, with Debbie West (Baccarat) third. Richard Walker (Upper Strata) was fourth, and Princess Anne (Doublet) finished in fifth place.

1972. Another Olympic year, which was celebrated by the inclusion of a fence named the Munich Pen (it is seldom that Colonel Weldon misses a trick). Badminton 1972 attracted a large international field again, with riders and horses from Italy, Ireland, Switzerland and Australia. It proved to be a memorable competition, by virtue of the terrific struggle which ensued between Lt. Mark Phillips on Great Ovation and Richard Meade on Major Allhusen's horse, Laurieston (later that year to win the individual Gold Medal at the Munich Olympics). After the Dressage stage, Mark Phillips was in the lead, closely followed by Richard Meade, Mary Gordon-Watson (again with Cornishman V), Lorna Sutherland (Peer Gynt), and the 1969 winner, Richard Walker (Upper Strata). During the second stage of the competition, Richard Meade recorded better times over both the Steeplechase and the Cross-Country courses, and at the end of the day was slightly in the lead over Great Ovation and Mark Phillips. In the final Jumping test, the competition was not decided until the very last minute, when Great Ovation went clear and Laurieston incurred $1\frac{1}{4}$ time faults, thus giving Mark Phillips and Great Ovation their second Badminton victory—the final scores being Great Ovation 106.6 and Laurieston 107.25. Bridget Parker on Cornish Gold was third, while Debbie West on Baccarat was fourth. In fifth place was a young lady taking part in her first Badminton—Miss Lucinda Prior-Palmer on Be Fair. Incidentally, Richard Meade was also placed seventh—on Mrs H. Wilkins' horse, Wayfarer. In addition to Richard Meade's Munich Olympics individual Gold Medal, the British Team of Mark Phillips (Great Ovation), Mary Gordon-Watson (Cornishman V) and Bridget Parker (Cornish Gold) also won the Team Gold Medal.

1973. This was the first of Lucinda Prior-Palmer's three famous victories. There was a record field of entries—sixty-nine—and if the competition was stiff, the course proved even stiffer. At the end of the Dressage test, Mark Phillips was in the lead on Great Ovation, but he withdrew during the Steeplechase phase. This year saw the introduction of a new FEI Dressage test,* which proved extremely unpopular with the competitors. The Cross-Country course, with the re-introduced Coffin fence, proved to be an extremely tough one. No doubt, Colonel Weldon had designed it with an eye to the forthcoming European Championships at Kiev, but even he could not have foreseen the alternative route taken by Miss Rachel Bayliss (Gurgle the Greek) who actually went under the Stockholm Fence. At the end of the second day, Lucinda Prior-Palmer on Be Fair was in a clear lead and was never headed. Richard Meade (Eagle Rock) was second and Virginia Thompson (Cornish Duke) was in third place.

1974. This time, Captain Mark Phillips completed his hat trick, although not on Great Ovation. For a while it looked as though Captain Phillips and Great Ovation were going to head the Dressage for the fourth year running, but they were then overtaken by Princess Anne on Doublet. Even so, Captain Phillips was lying third, on Her Majesty the Queen's horse, Columbus. On the second day, unfortunately, Doublet had to be withdrawn after a fall on the Steeplechase course, and Great Ovation was retired on the Cross-Country course. On Columbus, however, Captain Phillips had a clear round, within the optimum time (as also did Princess Anne on Goodwill, Chris Collins on Smokey VI, Janet Hodgson on Larkspur, and Hugh Thomas on Playamar). Captain Phillips and Janet Hodgson, who finished first and second, respectively, achieved the unusual feat of incurring no penalties after the first day. In third place that year was an American, Bruce Davidson (Irish Cap), while Princess Anne finished fourth on Goodwill. There was a great deal of fun during the presentation of the awards when Captain Phillips, having received the trophy from the Queen, immediately returned it to her as winning owner, needless to say, to the huge delight of the crowd.

*"In fairness, it must be said that, being an individual competition, the actual Dressage test laid down by the FEI was unpopular, not only with competitors, and was changed the next year." F.W.

1975. Cancelled owing to bad weather.

1976. In all there were seventy entries, a record for this competition, and as it was another Olympic year, there was a great deal of speculation as to who would eventually be chosen to go to Montreal. At the end of the Dressage section, Janet Hodgson on Larkspur was in the lead, closely followed by Aly Pattinson (Olivia), with the twenty-two-year old European Champion, Lucinda Prior-Palmer, in third place, on Wide Awake. On the second day, however, Lucinda put in a brilliant display of fast, economic jumping across country, to go into the lead. After that, there was little chance of her being caught, and she entered the final Jumping stage, with a fence in hand, jumping a safe, clear round, to give her her second victory in three years. In second place, was Hugh Thomas on Playamar, and in third place was Captain Mark Phillips on Favour. Fourth was Richard Meade on the British Equestrian Federation's horse, Jacob Jones. Following Lucinda Prior-Palmer's brilliant victory came the sudden, tragic aftermath, when just before doing a lap of honour, Wide Awake collapsed and died in the arena. The resultant publicity, with unfounded accusations of cruelty, must have caused Lucinda great distress, and lovers of equestrian sports the world over were delighted to see her bounce back in the following year to score her third brilliant victory on George.

1977. For this pre-European Championship Badminton, much stricter qualifications were introduced by the Combined Training Committee, resulting in a reduction in the number of entries—all horses having to be Grade I. At the start of the Event there were forty-seven competitors, including riders from Australia, France, Germany, Holland, Ireland, Switzerland and the U.S.A. There were also changes in the method of scoring in the Dressage test, each movement being marked from 0–10 instead of 0–6 as previously; in the Show Jumping, a knock down or a foot in the water now cost only 5 points instead of 10.

At the end of the first day of the Dressage phase, Miss Janet MacDonald on Anna Marie was in the lead; Hanz Melzer (Germany) on Salut was in second place while Lucinda Prior-Palmer on Killaire was lying third. On the second day of the Dressage, things changed dramatically when Mr Karl Schultz (Germany) riding Madrigal did a brilliant test, incurring the incredibly low score of 28.8 penalty points. Mr Tomi Gretener (Switzerland) on Old Jameson also completed an excellent test. However, Captain Mark Phillips on Persian Holiday put the British riders back into the picture by producing a score of 34.8 penalties. Miss Lucinda Prior-Palmer on her second horse, George, also did very well, ending with a score of 37.4 penalties.

The Cross-Country phase produced a brilliant round by Lucinda Prior-Palmer on George, when she incurred only .25 time faults. In second place was Miss Aly Pattinson on Carawich; Miss Diana Thorne on The Kingmaker was third; and in fourth place was Lucinda Prior-Palmer on Killaire. Captain Mark Phillips unfortunately had to retire on Persian Holiday after breaking a rein. Richard Meade was eliminated when Tommy Buck refused three times at the Quarry Fence. Karl Schultz, who was leading at the end of the Dressage phase, dropped down to 12th place.

There was a considerable upset in the Show Jumping phase when Miss Pattinson dropped from second place to finish fifth in the overall competition. The last to jump, Lucinda Prior-Palmer on George, rode a brilliant clear round to win the Whitbread Trophy for the third time. Lucinda also took third place with her other entry, Killaire. In second place was Diana Thorne with The Kingmaker, while the only man to finish in the first eight was Chris Collins on Smokey VI in sixth position.

BADMINTON WINNERS— 1949 TO 1978

Year	Horse	Owner	Rider
1949	Golden Willow	Mrs Home Kidson	John Shedden
1950	Remus	Miss G. H. Crystal	Capt. J. A. Collings
1951	Vae Victis	Capt. H. Schwarzenbach	Owner
1952	Emily Little	Capt. M. A. Q. Darley	Owner
1953	Starlight	Mrs J. R. Baker	Maj. L. Rook
1954	Bambi V	Miss M. Hough	Owner
*1955	Kilbarry	Maj. F. W. C. Weldon	Owner
1956	Kilbarry	Lt.-Col. F. W. C. Weldon	Owner
1957	High and Mighty	Miss S. M. Willcox	Owner
1958	High and Mighty	Miss S. M. Willcox	Owner
1959	Airs and Graces	Mrs. J. Waddington (née Willcox)	Owner
1960	Our Solo	Equestrian Federation of Australia	W. Roycroft

*(held at Windsor)

1961	Salad Days	L. R. Morgan Esq.	Owner
1962	Merely-a-Monarch	Miss A. Drummond-Hay & Mrs A. Gilroy	Miss A. Drummond-Hay
*1963	The Gladiator	Miss S. Fleet	Owner
1964	M'Lord Connolly	Capt. J. R. Templer	Owner
1965	Durlas Eile (Ire.)	Maj. E. A. Boylan	Owner
1966	(Cancelled)		
1967	Jonathan	Miss C. Ross-Taylor	Owner
1968	Our Nobby	Miss Jane Bullen	Owner
1969	Pasha	Richard Walker	Owner
1970	The Poacher	Combined Training Committee	Richard Meade
1971	Great Ovation	Lt. M. A. Phillips & Miss F. Phillips	Lt. M. A. Phillips
1972	Great Ovation	Lt. M. A. Phillips & Miss F. Phillips	Lt. M. A. Phillips
1973	Be Fair	Miss L. Prior-Palmer	Owner
1974	Columbus	H.M. The Queen	Capt. M. A. Phillips
1975	(cancelled)		
1976	Wide Awake	Miss L. Prior-Palmer	Owner
1977	George	Mrs. H. C. Straker	Miss L. Prior-Palmer
1978	Warrior	Mrs S. Howard & Mrs J. Holderness-Roddam	Mrs J. Holderness-Roddam

GREAT BRITAIN'S OLYMPIC & EUROPEAN SUCCESSES

STOCKHOLM, 1956—OLYMPIC TEAM GOLD MEDAL
Lt. Col. Frank Weldon on Kilbarry; Bertie Hill on Countryman; Maj. Laurence Rook on Wild Venture

MEXICO 1968—OLYMPIC TEAM GOLD MEDAL
Maj. Derek Allhusen on Lochinvar; Jane Bullen on Our Nobby; Richard Meade on Cornishman V; Sgt. Ben Jones on The Poacher

MUNICH 1972—OLYMPIC INDIVIDUAL GOLD MEDAL
Richard Meade on Laurieston

*(one-day Event Senior Stakes)

MUNICH 1972—OLYMPIC TEAM GOLD MEDAL
Richard Meade on Laurieston; Bridget Parker on Cornish Gold; Mary
Gordon-Watson on Cornishman V; Lt. Mark Phillips on Great Ovation

BADMINTON 1953—EUROPEAN INDIVIDUAL CHAMPION
Maj. Laurence Rook on Starlight

BADMINTON 1953—EUROPEAN TEAM CHAMPIONSHIPS
Maj. Frank Weldon on Kilbarry; Bertie Hill on Bambi V; Reg Hindley on
Speculation

BASLE 1954—EUROPEAN INDIVIDUAL CHAMPION
Bertie Hill on Crispin

BASLE 1954—EUROPEAN TEAM CHAMPIONSHIP
Maj. Frank Weldon on Kilbarry; Bertie Hill on Crispin; Maj. Laurence
Rook on Starlight; also Diana Mason on Tramella

WINDSOR 1955—EUROPEAN INDIVIDUAL CHAMPION
Maj. Frank Weldon on Kilbarry

WINDSOR 1955—EUROPEAN TEAM CHAMPIONSHIP
Maj. Frank Weldon on Kilbarry; Bertie Hill on Countryman; Maj. Laurence
Rook on Starlight; also Diana Mason on Tramella

COPENHAGEN 1957—EUROPEAN INDIVIDUAL CHAMPION
Sheila Willcox on High and Mighty

COPENHAGEN 1957—EUROPEAN TEAM CHAMPIONSHIP
Sheila Willcox on High and Mighty; Ted Marsh on Wild Venture; Kit
Tatham-Warner on Pampas Cat; Maj. Derek Allhusen on Laurien

BURGHLEY 1962—EUROPEAN INDIVIDUAL CHAMPION
Capt. James Templer on M'Lord Connolly

PUNCHESTOWN 1967—EUROPEAN TEAM CHAMPIONSHIP
Maj. Derek Allhusen on Lochinvar; Richard Meade on Barbary; Martin
Whiteley on The Poacher; Sgt. Ben Jones on Foxdor

HARAS DU PIN 1969—EUROPEAN INDIVIDUAL CHAMPION
Mary Gordon-Watson on Cornishman V

HARAS DU PIN 1969—EUROPEAN TEAM CHAMPIONSHIP
Maj. Derek Allhusen on Lochinvar; Richard Walker on Pasha; Pollyann
Hely-Hutchinson on Count Jasper; Sgt. Ben Jones on The Poacher

PUNCHESTOWN 1970—WORLD INDIVIDUAL CHAMPION
Mary Gordon-Watson on Cornishman V

PUNCHESTOWN 1970—WORLD TEAM CHAMPIONSHIP
Richard Meade on The Poacher; Lt. Mark Phillips on Chicago; Stewart Stevens on Benson; Mary Gordon-Watson on Cornishman V

BURGHLEY 1971—EUROPEAN INDIVIDUAL CHAMPION
H.R.H. Princess Anne on Doublet

BURGHLEY 1971—EUROPEAN TEAM CHAMPIONSHIP
Richard Meade on The Poacher; Lt. Mark Phillips on Great Ovation; Debbie West on Baccarat; Mary Gordon-Watson on Cornishman V

LUHMUHLEN 1975—EUROPEAN INDIVIDUAL CHAMPION
Lucinda Prior-Palmer on Be Fair

BURGHLEY 1977—EUROPEAN INDIVIDUAL CHAMPION
Lucinda Prior-Palmer on George

BURGHLEY 1977—EUROPEAN TEAM CHAMPIONSHIP
Lucinda Prior-Palmer on George; Jane Holderness-Roddam on Warrior; Chris Collins on Smokey VI; Clarissa Strachan on Merry Sovereign

Bibliography

Letters, Manuscripts and Papers from Badminton House, by kind permission of His Grace, The Duke of Beaufort, KG, PC, GCVO, MFH.

The Badminton Library volumes: *Hunting* and *The Poetry of Sport*, edited by Alfred E. T. Watson, Longman Green & Co., 1889
Badminton World Magazine, 1976
Bailey's Magazine, 1874
Baily's Hunting Directory, 1976
Bell's Life, 1836
Biographical Reminiscences: Lord William Lennox, 1863
British Sports and Pastimes: edited by Anthony Trollope, 1868
Burke's Peerage
Country Life magazine
The 8th Duke of Beaufort and the Badminton Hunt: T. F. Dale, Constable, 1901
English Country Life 1780–1830: E. W. Bovill, Oxford University Press, 1962
The Field magazine
The Formal Garden in England: R. Blomfield
Foxhunting Recollections: Sir Reginald Graham
The Gentleman's Magazine
The Gloucestershire Landscape: H. P. R. Finberg, Hodder & Stoughton
The Greville Diary: Charles Cavendish Fulke Greville, edited by P. Whitwell Wilson, Doubleday and Co. Inc., 1927
Handley Cross: R. S. Surtees, Bradbury Agnew & Co., 1854
Harriette Wilson's Memoirs: by Herself, Stockdales, 1825
Horse and Hound magazine
Hounds of Britain: Jack Ivester Lloyd
Hunting England: Sir William Beach Thomas, Batsford, 1936
Hunting Tours: 'Cecil', Phillip Allan & Co., 1924
Hunting Tours: "Nimrod", 1835
In Nimrod's Footsteps: Daphne Moore, J. A. Allen & Co. Ltd.
In Praise of Hunting: Edited by David James and Wilson Stephens, Hollis & Carter, 1960
Jorrocks' Jaunts and Jollities: R. S. Surtees, Ackermann, 1843
Journale de la Vienne, 1863
Letters: Horace Walpole

Lives of the Norths: Hon. R. North

London Gazette

Lonsdale Sporting Library (New Sporting Magazine), 1832

Memoirs of the 10th Royal Hussars: Colonel R. S. Liddell, 1891

Mr Sponge's Sporting Tour: R. S. Surtees, Methuen, 1853

A New History of Gloucestershire: Samuel Rudder, 1779

Official Guide Book to Badminton House

Official Progress of the 1st Duke of Beaufort Through Wales in 1684: Thomas
　　Dineley

The Passing Years: Lord Willoughby de Broke, Constable, 1924

Ratcatcher to Scarlet: Cecil Aldin, Eyre & Spottiswode, 1926

Recollections of a Foxhunter: "Scrutator", 1861

Recollections of a Sporting and Dramatic Career: Alfred Watson, 1918

Recollections of a Younger Son: Claude Luttrell, Duckworth, 1925

The Reminiscences of Lady Dorothy Neville: 1861

Riding Recollections: G. J. Whyte-Melville, 1878

St. Michael's and All Angels Pamphlet: Rev. R. E. Owen

Silk and Scarlet: "Druid", Winton & Co., 1859

The Somerset Sequence: Horatia Durant, Hughes & Sons Ltd., 1976

Thoughts on Hunting: Peter Beckford, Methuen & Co., 1899

Vanity Fair magazine

Victorian Days: Lady Clodagh Anson, Richards Press, 1957

The Wiltshire & Gloucestershire Standard

Index

Names of horses are in *italic*

Abergavenny, Lady, 144
Acton Turville, 17, 23
Agutter, Tom, 143
Airlie, Lady, 25
Airs and Graces, 166, 213–14, 221
Albert, Prince, 69
Aldin, Cecil, 116
Alderton, 17
Alderton, Thomas, 102, 106
Alken, Henry, 100
Allhusen, Derek, 213, 216, 218, 222–3
Alvanley, Lord, 63
Andrew, HRH Prince, 198, 199
Anna Marie, 220
Anne, HRH Princess, 120, 161, 162, 168, 175, 179, 180, 182, 183, 201, 204, 205, 206, 207, 218, 219, 224
Anne, Queen, 50, 51
Anson, Lady Clodagh, 20, 71–2, 74, 75, 89
Apperley, Charles, *see* 'Nimrod'
Argyle, Duke of, 59
Arkwright, Captain, 211
Arlott, John, 33
Armstrong-Jones, Lady Sarah, 199
Arrago, François, 41
Asprey & Co., 177
Avatar, 216
Avenly, Lord, 63
Avon Vale Hunt, 111, 127, 129, 132, 136–7

Baccarat, 218, 224
Badminton Estate: size of, xii, 75n, 81; Office, 19, 28; workers, 22; farms, 28; finance of, 152
Badminton House: open to the public, 18, 85, 161; stables, 22–3, 178–9, 203; Park, 29–30, 32, 165, 202;

Worcester Lodge, 29–30; gardens, 30–1, 52; Hermit's Cell, 31–2; Swangrove, 32, 50; architecture, 39; purchase from Boteler family, 39; improvements by 1st Duke, 45–6, 47; works of art, 46, 51–3, 54; in time of 1st Duke, 46–7; in time of 2nd Duke, 50; improvements by 3rd Duke, 51, 53; improvements by 4th Duke, 55; in time of 5th Duke, 57, 103–4; in time of 6th Duke, 58; in time of 7th Duke, 70–1; in time of 8th Duke, 76–7; social changes in time of 10th Duke, 84–5
Badminton Library of Sport, The, 73, 120, 128–9; *Hunting* volume, 100, 102; other volumes, 79, 129
badminton, origination of game, 33–4, 161
Badminton village, 16–34; etymology of name, 17; crowds in, 18, 138, 204; houses and cottages, 19, 21–3; St Michael & All Angels church, 19–21, 46, 203–4; original school, 21–2; villagers, 22–4, 88; fire brigade, 23; station, 26–7; cricket, 32–3, 178; during Horse Trials, 178, 180, 204
Bagot, Sir Charles, 65
Bagot, Lady, 65
Bailey's Magazine, 120
Bailey, Sidney, 105, 200
Baker, Mrs J. R., 212
Balch, Charles, 101, 130, 131
Baldwin, John Loraine, 33
Bambi V, 212, 221, 223
Bampton Fair, 210
Barbary, 215, 217, 223
Barker, Marjorie, 87
Barrat, Mervyn, 147

Barrington, Earl of, 70
Bartlett, David, xi, xii
Bath, 6th Marquess of, 154
Bathurst, Earl, 70
Bathurst, Lady Georgiana, 68
Bathurst, Lord, 51
Bayliss, Rachel, 219
Beach Thomas, Sir William, 104
Beale, Jeremy, 214
Beau Brummel, 63
Beauchamp, Mary Lady (wife of 1st
    Duke), 40, 44
Beauchamp, Lord, 44
BEAUFORT, 1ST DUKE OF (3rd Marquess
    of Worcester), 44–9, 96;
    monument in Badminton church, 20;
    avenue, 30; inherits Badminton, 40,
    44; marriage, 40, 44; succeeds as 3rd
    Marquess of Worcester, 40; created
    1st Duke of Beaufort, 40, 46; at Siege
    of Gloucester, 43, 44; petition for
    return of income, 43, 44; becomes a
    Protestant, 44; friendship with
    Cromwell, 44; as MP, 44; support for
    Charles II, 45; appointments, 45, 46,
    47, 49; improvements to Badminton
    House, 45, 47; interest in horses and
    breeding, 46; part in Monmouth's
    Rebellion, 48; opposition to William
    of Orange, 49; death, 49; portraits,
    52
    Duchess, Hon. Mary Capel (formerly
    Mary, Lady Beauchamp), 21, 40, 44,
    45, 46, 47, 96
BEAUFORT, 2ND DUKE OF, 49–51
    monument in Badminton church, 20;
    succeeds to title, 49, 50; marriages,
    50–1; appointments, 51; death, 51;
    portrait, 52
    1st Duchess (Lady Mary Sackville), 50
    2nd Duchess (Lady Rachel Noel), 50
    3rd Duchess (Lady Mary Osborne),
    51
BEAUFORT, 3RD DUKE OF, 50, 51–3, 55
    monument in Badminton church, 20;
    and Capability Brown, 31, 52;
    Swangrove, 32; purchase of works of
    art, 46, 51–2, 53; succeeds to title,
    51; hunting interests, 51; portrait, 52;
    marriage and divorce, 53; death, 53
    Duchess (Frances Scudamore), 53

BEAUFORT, 4TH DUKE OF, 50, 53–5
    portrait, 52; succeeds to title, 53; as
    MP, 54; Jacobite follower, 54;
    marriage, 54; and hunting, 54; and
    art, 54; death, 55
    Duchess (Elizabeth Berkeley), 54, 55
BEAUFORT, 5TH DUKE OF, 55–7
    builds new church, 19, 57; portrait,
    52; succeeds to title, 55; tour of
    Europe, 55–6; marriage, 56;
    appointments, 56, 57, 89; racing
    interests, 57; alterations to House,
    57; death, 57
    and hunting, 57, 102, 103–9; credited
    with invention of, 55, 95, 97, 103;
    breeding hounds, 105–6
    Duchess (Elizabeth Boscawen), 56–7,
    104, 105
BEAUFORT, 6TH DUKE OF, 57, 58–61
    succeeds to title, 58; as MP, 58;
    marriage, 58; appointments, 58; and
    the Harriette Wilson affair, 59–61,
    67–8; death, 61
    and hunting, 61, 102, 108, 109–11,
    124; introduction of the hound prize,
    109
    Duchess (Lady Charlotte Leveson-
    Gower), 58, 59–60, 64
BEAUFORT, 7TH DUKE OF, 58, 61–9
    and the Hariette Wilson affair,
    59–61, 67; military career, 61–3; as
    MP, 61, 64; amateur actor, 61, 64;
    amateur coachman, 61, 64, 66–7;
    socialite, 61, 63–4, 70–1; first
    marriage, 63–4; racing interests, 64,
    67; second marriage, 65; children,
    66; succeeds to title, 67; titles, 68;
    scandal concerning daughter
    Augusta, 68–9; death, 69, 114.
    and hunting, 102, 111–14, 119; by
    phaeton, 69, 86, 114; and the
    Sporting Sweep, 99–100, 113; break
    with Heythrop Hunt, 104, 109,
    111–12
    1st Duchess (Georgiana FitzRoy),
    63–5
    2nd Duchess (Emily Culling Smith),
    65–6
BEAUFORT, 8TH DUKE OF, 69–77
    15th birthday celebrations, 67, 113;
    nicknames, 69, 114; popularity, 69,

75; coaching, 70, 78; military career, 70, 72; 21st birthday celebrations, 70–1; marriage, 71–2; as MP, 72, 117; succeeds to title, 72; racing interests, 72–4, 79, 117, 155; public duties, 75, 90, 118; gout, 75, 126, 127; *Badminton Library*, 75, 100, 120, 128–9; death, 76, 127; reputation for kindness, 125–6
and hunting, 70, 76, 86, 98, 102, 109, 112, 114–28, 136; as Huntsman, 102, 114–17; as Master, 114; hunting notes, 98, 115–17; problems with excessive holloaing, 98, 116; wolf hunting, 118–19
Duchess (Lady Georgiana Curzon), 21, 71–2, 74–5, 125
BEAUFORT, 9TH DUKE OF, 78–80, 83–4, 126, 134, 139
presentation to church, 21; coming of age party, 75; marriage, 75, 78; military career, 78; appointments, 78; amateur coachman, 78; character, 78, 79, 130; death, 80, 84.
and hunting, 102, 114, 117–24, 129–32; passion for, 78–80, 86, 132; as Huntsman, 102, 118, 119, 125, 127, 129, 131; Greatwood Run (1871), 121–3; Greatwood Run (1901), 130–1
Duchess (Louise de Tuyll), 21, 23, 78, 83–4
BEAUFORT, 10TH DUKE OF, 80–91
and this book, xii; affection for, xii, 24; concern for villagers, 23–4, 86–7; involvement with Estate and farms, 28, 81, 133, 163; and cricket, 32; education, 80; military career, 80; titles, 80–1; nicknames, 81, 133, 135; public engagements, 81–2, 88, 91, 133; and Horse Trials, 81, 134, 162, 163, 164, 179, 180, 196–7, 199, 201, 203, 207, 208–9, 210; concern with village, 82, 86; marriage, 82–3; succeeds to title, 84; as Master of the Horse, 88–91, 154
and hunting, 102, 132–42, 144; passion for, 78, 81, 86, 134, 155; hunts hounds first time, 80, 133, 135; hound breeding, 81, 133, 135, 147; concerned with organisation of Hunt,

81; falls, 85–6, 140–1; gives up hunting hounds, 86, 133, 141, 143–4; as Huntsman, 102, 132, 133; birthday meets, 105, 138–9, 156–7; harrier pack, 133, 134; as joint Master and Huntsman, 133, 136; drafting of hounds, 133, 135, 147; hunting today, 134; Eton College Beagles, 135
Duchess of (Lady Mary Cambridge): presents church memorial, 21; concern for villagers, 24, 86; affection for, 24; hunting, 81; marriage, 82–3; and Badminton House, 84; and Horse Trials, 164, 199, 207
Beaufort Spurs, 170
Beckford, Peter, xi, 103, 106
Be Fair, 162, 218, 222, 224
Bell's Life, 61, 109, 111*n*, 112
Belvoir Hunt, 109, 143
Bennett, Jim, 105
Benson, 224
Bentinck, Lord Henry, 124
Berkeley, Elizabeth (wife of 4th Duke), 54
Berkeley Hunt, 105
Berkeley, John, 54
Bicester and Warden Hill Hunt, 105, 133, 134
Bingham-Smith, Jeremy, 215
Binning, Lord, 65
Bleak Hills, 168, 183, 201, 207, 210
Blomfield, R., 31
Bolton, Brig. Lyndon, 211
Bonnie Prince Charlie, 54
Book of the Foxhound (Moore), 96
Boone, Elizabeth, 209, 210
Borwick, Major Peter, 164
Boscawen, Admiral Edward, 52, 56
Boscawen, Mrs Edward, 56–7, 104
Boscawen, Elizabeth (wife of 5th Duke), 56–7
Boteler family, 17, 39
Boteler, Nicholas, 39
Botentout, Lord, 54
Boustead, Mervyn, 53*n*
Bovill, E. W., 99
Bowden-Smith, Brigadier, 163
Boylan, Major E. A., 216, 222
Bradley, Caroline, 204
Brake, Andrew, 210

Brassey, Lt-Col. H. T., 151
Bray, Ronald, 26
British Equestrian Federation, 220
British Field Sports Society, 176, 196
British Horse Society, 162–3, 177, 209, 210; tent at Horse Trials, 176, 180, 196, 201, 205, 208
British Sports and Pastimes (Trollope), 98n
Brocklesby Hunt, 109, 127, 143
Broome, David, 177, 204, 205
Brown, Fred, 102, 126
Brown, John, 80
Browne, Capt. Stephen, 52
Bullen, Jane, 168, 216–17, 222; *see also* Jane Holderness-Roddam
Bullen, Michael, 214, 215
Burke, Edmund, 35
Burke's Peerage, 58
Burlington, 3rd Earl, 52
Butler Challenge Bowl, 171
By Golly, 215
Byng, Hon. John, 97

Calpe Hunt, 118
Calvert, Mrs, 65
Camas Park, 168, 186, 200
Cambridge Blue, 168, 201
Cambridge, Duchess of, 68
Cambridge, Duke of, 68, 70, 71
Cambridge, Lord Frederick, 21
Cambridge, Marquess of, 24n, 82
Cambridge, Lady Mary (wife of 10th Duke), 82
Camden, Ernest, 101
Canaletto, Antonio, 52, 54
Cantillion, Helen, 200, 207
Capability Brown, 31, 52
Capel, Lord, 40
Capel, Mary (wife of 1st Duke), 40, 44
Carawich, 221
Carnarvon, Earl of, 41
Castle Farm, 28
Cattistock Hunt, 136, 148
Cavendish, 1st Earl of, 64
Cavendish, Lady Harriet, 58, 64; *see also* Lady Granville
"Cecil" (Cornelius Tongue), 95, 104, 109, 119
Century of Inventions, A, 40, 44
Chapman, Robert, 39
Charles I, 40, 42–3, 44, 52

Charles II, 40, 45, 48, 90, 96
Charles, HRH Prince, 120
Charlotte, Queen, 57, 89
Cheshire Hunt, 107
Chicago, 217, 224
Chippendale, Thomas, 55
Churchill, Randolph, 42
Churchill, Winston, 132
Civil War, 42–3, 44
Clapham, Diana, 179
Clarendon, Chancellor, 44
Clarke, Tom, 78, 102, 112, 118, 129
Claude Lorraine, 51
Clayton, Michael, 95
Codrington, Sir William, 118
Collings, Capt. J. A., 210, 211, 221
Collins, Chris, 162, 168, 210, 219, 221, 224
Collins, Tony, 105
Columbus, 219, 222
Combined Training Committee, 170, 217, 220
Cook, Col. John, 97
Cooke, John, 144
Copperplate, 213
Cornell, C., 164
Cornish Duke, 219
Cornish Gold, 218–19, 223
Cornishman V, 217, 218–19, 222–4
Cotswold Hunt, 105
Cottage Romance, 215
Cottesmore, 106, 107
Count Jasper, 216, 223
Country Life magazine, 98
Countryman, 154, 213, 222–3
Cox, H. C., 102, 136
Crane, Will, 102, 105–6
Craven, Earl of, 59
Crispin, 223
Crockford's Club, 64
Crofts, Penny, 215
Cromwell, Oliver, 43, 44, 45
Crystal, Mrs G. H., 211
Cubitt, Hon. C. G., 163
Culling Smith, Charles, 63
Culling Smith, Emily (wife of 7th Duke), 65
Cuneo, Terence, 88–9
Curzon, Lady Georgiana (wife of 8th Duke), 70, 71–2
Curzon, Viscount, 70

Dale, T. F., 41, 43*n*, 44, 54, 62, 67, 72*n*,
96, 98, 103, 106*n*, 109*n*, 111, 114–15,
124, 127
Dale, Will, 101, 102, 127, 130–1, 136
Dallas, Major R. J. G., 135, 151–3
Dandy, 211
Dark Horse, The, 217
Darley, Capt. M. A. Q., 211, 214, 221
Davidson, Bruce, 219
Davies, Denis, 176
da Vinci, Leonardo, 46, 51
Davis, R. B., 99
Day, John, 73
de Caus, Salomon, 41–2
de Cinq Mars, Marquis, 41
Delany, Mary, 53
de Lorme, Marion, 41–2
de Tuyll, Baron Carol, 78
de Tuyll, Louise Emily (wife of 9th
Duke), 78
Devonshire Regiment, 48
Dilworth, John, 102, 106
Dineley, Thomas, 47–8
Domesday Book, 17
Dormer, Elizabeth (wife of 2nd
Marquess of Worcester), 41, 52
Dormer, Sir William, 41
Dorset, Earl of, 50
Double Diamond, 214
Doublet, 218, 219, 224
"Druid", 103
Drummond-Hay, Anneli, 214, 215, 222
Drummond-Hay, Jane, 211
Dudgeon, Ian, 210
Dudley, Robert Earl of Leicester, 89
Duke of Beaufort's Hunt, xi, 93–157,
161
kennels, xi; Puppy show, xi, 109;
administered from Estate Office, 28;
Supporters' Club, 32, 81, 147, 152–3,
162; Terrier Show, 32, 147; hunting
the Heythrop country, 57, 103–4,
109, 111–12; lawn meets, 67, 76, 119;
Greatwood Run of 1871, 79, 120–3;
drafting of hounds, 81, 135, 147; list
of Masters, 102; list of Huntsmen,
102; dress, 63, 104, 110, 119; split
with Heythrop, 104; friendship with
Heythrop, 104–5; hound breeding,
106–7, 109, 110, 135, 147, 155;
Beaufort Justice, 107–8; prize for best

reared hound, 109; Royalty out with,
119–20; subscription raised, 127;
Greatwood Run of 1901, 130–1;
during 1914/18 war, 132; during
1939/45 war, 136; staff, 144, 152;
new entry, 144–5; organisation of,
148–51; future of, 151–2, 156–7;
involvement with Horse Trials, 162,
176, 196, 206, 208
Dundmald, 4th Earl of, 51
Durant, Horatia, 29, 32, 41, 46, 50, 58,
63, 65, 69, 96, 119
Durham, Earl of, 106
Durlas Eile, 216, 222
Dyson, Maj. Derrick, 167

Eagle Rock, 219
Easterby, Walter, 143
East Kent Hunt, 148
East Middleton Hunt, 143
Edgar, Ted, 204
Edward III, 40, 82, 89
*8th Duke of Beaufort and the Badminton
Hunt* (Dale), 41, 43*n*, 96, 114
Eldorado, 216
Elizabeth, HM Queen, 23, 27, 88, 89,
154, 161, 165, 166, 167, 168, 174,
182, 184, 189, 196–7, 198, 199, 203,
205, 206–8, 210, 211, 212, 219
Elizabeth, the Queen Mother, HM
Queen, 23, 154, 184, 199, 200
Emily Little, 211, 221
Eridge Hunt, 143
Essex, Earl of, 40
Estcourt, Edmund, 103
Esterhazy, Count, 70
Eton College Beagles, 135, 148
European Three-Day Event
Championships, 165, 168, 212, 219,
220, 223
Evans, Charles, 19
Evans, Major H. H., 25
Evelyn, John, 40

Falmouth, 3rd Viscount, 56
Fanshawe, Capt. Brian, 105
Farlow & Co., 177
Farquhar, Capt. Ian, 105
Farquhar, Sir Peter, 133–4, 141–2
Favour, 220

Fédération International Equestre, 163–4, 170, 171, 186
Felday Farmer, 209, 210
Fernie Hunt, 143
Field, The, 130, 214
Fiennes, Celia, 30
Fitzherbert, Mrs, 63
FitzRoy, Georgiana (wife of 7th Duke), 63
Fitzwilliam Hunt, 127, 143
Flame Gun, 168, 175
Fleet, Susan, 215, 222
Fleming-Williams, Gillian, 179
Foley, Lord, 57, 103
Ford, Richard, 26
Formal Garden in England, The (Blomfield), 31
Foxdor, 216, 223
foxhounds, English-bred, 98
foxhunting: start of, 95–7, 103; adapting to Enclosure Act, 97; for all classes, 98–9; modern, 101
Foxhunting Recollections (Graham), 124
Freeman-Jackson, Harry, 214–15
Fretwell, Mr, 103
Frost, John, 66
Fullerton, Colonel, 129
Fulmer Folly, 214
Furtive, 217

Gainsborough, 2nd Earl of, 50
Galway Blazers, 143
Galway, Lord, 127
Garrard's Co., 177
Garrick Club, 64
Gaunt, John of (Duke of Lancaster), 40, 82, 89
Gentleman's Magazine, The, 61
George, 162, 168, 220–1, 222, 224
George of Cambridge, Prince, 68
George of Denmark, Prince, 48
Gibbons, Grinling, 20, 46, 85
Gibbs, James, 53*n*
Gibson, Rev. T. T., 17, 18, 20, 23–4, 82, 84, 91
Gilmore, Jim, 174, 183, 196, 205, 206
Gladiator, The, 215, 222
Glenamoy, 215, 216
Gloucestershire County Cricket Club, 32
Goathland Hunt, 149

Goddard, Tom, 114
Golden Willow, 161, 210, 211, 221
Gold Ross, 213
Goodwill, 168, 175, 182, 183, 201, 207, 219
Gordon-Watson, Mary, 162, 186, 217, 218–19, 223–4
Goring, David, 141
Grace, Alfred, 33, 122
Grace, W. G., 33, 122
Graham, Sir Reginald, 124
Granville, Lady, 64–5, 66
Granville, Lord, 58, 66*n*
Great Badminton, *see* Badminton village
Great Ovation, 218–19, 222–4
Greatwood Run: *1871*, 79, 120–3; *1901*, 130–1
Gretener, Tomi, 168, 186, 200, 220
Greville, Charles, 64, 68
Greville Diary, The, 64*n*
Grey Cloud, 217
Greylag, 211
Grimthorpe, Lord, 143
Grove Hunt, 127
Guildford, Lord, 58, 66*n*
Gundry, E. F., 148
Gundry, Major Gerald, 86, 87, 102, 219, 131, 137, 141, 146, 148–51, 154, 165, 177, 206
Gundry, Mrs Gerald, 141
Gupwell, Brian, xi, 28, 102, 105, 132, 137, 143–8, 150, 178, 197, 208
Gupwell, Walter, 143
Gupwell, Mrs Walter, 143
Gurgle the Greek, 219
Gypsy Flame, 217

Halifax, Lord, 143
Hambledon Hunt, 136, 143, 153
Hamblin, Charles, 122
Handley Cross (Surtees), 88*n* 102
Happy Knight, 211
Harding, Peter, 91, 196
Harford, W. H., 78
Hastings, Marquess of, 73
Hawkesbury Upton, 105, 156
Hawk Trust, 177
Hearne, Thomas, 49–50
Hely-Hutchinson, Polyann, 216, 223
Henry VIII, 40

Herbert, Lord, *see* 2nd Marquess of Worcester, and 1st Duke of Beaufort
Hermitage or Hermit's Cell, 31–2
Heythrop House, 57, 58, 66, 103–4
Heythrop Hunt, 103–5, 110
High and Mighty, 165–6, 213, 221, 223
Hill, Bertie, 168, 213, 217, 222, 223
Hindley, Reg, 223
Hodgson, Janet, 219, 220
Holderness-Roddam, Jane, 168, 182, 183, 200, 201, 203, 208–9, 210, 222, 224
Holland, Reg, 102, 136–7
Horlock, K. W., *see* "Scrutator"
Horn, Col. Trevor, 163–4
Horse and Hound, xi, 95, 96, 126, 140, 141, 162, 181
Horse Trials (Badminton Three-Day Event), xi, 32, 161–224
Royal Family's interest, 161, 162, 166, 184, 196–7, 199, 203, 205, 207, 211, 212; Olympic Games selection ground, 162, 210; 10th Duke of Beaufort's involvement with, 81, 134, 162; voluntary help, 162, 165, 191; formation of, 163–4; organisation of, 164, 166–7; Trials Office, 164; stabling, 164, 196, 204; spectators, 165, 167, 184, 197, 198, 205; marshals, 165, 167, 197, 200; trade stands, 166, 167, 174, 176–7, 180, 182–3, 191, 196–7, 200, 204, 206, 208; security, 167, 180, 181, 196, 206; veterinary services, 167, 202–3; farriers, 167, 178; Red Cross facilities, 167, 191; radio, TV and loudspeakers, 167, 199, 203; mounted messengers, 167, 200; fence judges, 167; qualification standards, 167; scoring, 169–70; prizes, 170–1; awards, 171; press tent, 174, 175, 178, 180, 182, 183, 189, 196, 198, 201, 204; dress of spectators, 174, 175, 180, 191; Press Conference, 180, 181–2; dope-testing, 181–2; final veterinary inspection, 201–2, 203; Little Badminton competition, 214, 216 *1949*, 161, 162–4, 210–11; *1950*, 211; *1951*, 211; *1952*, 211–12; *1953*, 212; *1954*, 212; *1955*, 165, 212; *1956*, 213; *1957*, 213; *1958*, 213; *1959*, 165,

213–14; *1960*, 214; *1961*, 214–15; *1962*, 215; *1963*, 165, 215; *1964*, 215; *1965*, 215–16; *1966*, 165, 216; *1967*, 216; *1968*, 216–17, 1969, *217; 1970*, 217; *1971*, 218; *1972*, 218–19; *1973*, 219; *1974*, 219; *1975*, 165, 219; *1976*, 167, 186, 197, 201–2, 205, 220; *1977*, 167, 168, 184, 186, 220–1; *1978*, 167–8, 169, 170, 174–84, 186, 188, 190–201, 202–9
Dressage Phase, 161, 165, 171–84, 210; scoring, 169, 171, 172, 220; multiplying factor, 169; definition of, 171; test, 171, 173, 174, 219; time, 172; errors of course, 172; first day, 174–9; dress, 176; second day, 179–84
Speed and Endurance Phase, 184–201; scoring, 169; optimum time, 169, 188–9; map, 187; distance, 188, 189; veterinary inspection, 189
  Steeplechase course, 189; scoring, 169, 188, 189
  Road and Tracks, 188–9; scoring, 188
  Cross-country course, 189–90; scoring, 169, 190; fences, 184–6, 189, *192–5*; course-building, 185–6
Show-jumping Phase, 165, 201–9; scoring, 169, 170, 202
Horton, Mrs C., 217
Hough, Margaret, 212, 221
Hounds of Britain (Ivester Lloyd), 95n
Howard, Mrs S., 209
Howe, Earl, 70, 71
Hudson, Thomas, 52
Hunters' Improvement Society, 171, 177, 196
Hunting England (Beach Thomas), 104
Hunting Tours ("Cecil"), 104
Hutchinson, Albert, 156

In Nimrod's Footsteps (Moore), 138
In Praise of Hunting (James & Stephens), 87n
Irish Cap, 219
Ivester Lloyd, Jack, 95, 96

Jacob Jones, 220
James I, 42
James II, 48, 54

James, David, 87n
Jockey Club, 72
Jonathan, 216, 222
Jones, Sgt. Ben, 216–17, 222–3
Jones, Tom, 101
Jorrocks' Jaunts and Jollities (Surtees), 93
Jorrocks, John, 95, 100, 116
Journale de la Vienne, 119

Kent, William, 29–30, 52
Kesler, Shelagh, 214
Ketch, Thomas, 102, 106
Kidson, Mrs Home, 210
Kilbarry, 165, 212, 213, 221–3
Killaire, 210, 220–1
Kingmaker, The, 168, 200, 210, 221
Kingpin, 211
Kingscote, Colonel, 118
Kneller, Sir Godfrey, 52
Knight, David, 137
Knight, Eleanor, 17–18, 31
Knight, Rupert, 137

Lambert, Stephen, 105
Lambton, Ralph, 100
Langley, Tim, 105
Langston, Mr, 104
Larkspur, 219, 220
Laurien, 213, 223
Laurieston, 161, 177, 218, 222–3
Lavenham Rug Co., 177
Lawrence, Thomas, 52
Leeds, Duke of, 51
Leinster, Lord, 59
Lely, Sir Peter, 52
Lennox, Lord William, 63, 67
Leveson-Gower, Lady Charlotte (wife of 6th Duke), 58
Liddell, R. S., 61
Linley, Viscount, 199
Little Badminton, 17, 23, 28
Lives of the Norths (North), 45n
Liza Mandy, 211
Lloyd George, David, 132
Lochinvar, 216–17, 222–3
London Gazette, 70–1
Long, Charles, 118
Long, Heber, 118, 121–2
Long, Nimrod, 114
Long, William, 102, 108–9, 112, 114–15, 117, 118

Lonsdale, Earl of, 106
Lonsdale, Lord, 82
Lonsdale Sporting Library, 96
"Loppylugs", 140–1
Lovell, Francis, 68
Lower Swell, 104
Lowndes, Selby, 148, 149
Luttrell, Claude, 127, 130
Lyndhurst, Lord, 65–6

Macclesfield, Lord, 49
MacDonald, Janet, 220
Maclberry Co., 177
Madrigal, 220
Margaret, HRH Princess, 27, 184, 199
Markham, Mr, 23
Marlborough Galleries, 155
Marsh, Ted, 214, 223
Martha, 179
Martin-Bird, Angela, 217
Mary, Queen, 23, 24–6, 82
Mason, Diana, 212, 213, 223
McMahon, Capt. Ronnie, 217
Meade, Richard, 161, 162, 168, 177, 183, 201, 207, 210, 215, 216–17, 218–19, 220, 221, 222–4
Melzer, Hans, 220
Memoirs of the 10th Royal Hussars (Liddell), 61
Merely-a-Monarch, 215, 222
Merry Sovereign, 179, 224
Meynell, Hugo, 98, 101
Middleton Hunt, 143
Miller, Col. Sir John, 89
Milne, Parson Jack, 148
Milton Hunt, 109
Minster Green, 211
Mitchell, E. M., 18, 28, 30, 31, 33, 81, 86, 163
M'Lord Connolly, 215, 222–3
Monk, George, Duke of Albemarle, 45
Monmouth, Duke of, 48–9, 90
Montrose, Duchess of, 73
Moore, Daphne, 96, 138, 156
Moreton, Penny, 211, 213
Morgan, Laurie, 213, 214, 222
Morrell, James, 118
Morrison, Archibald John, *see* "Loppylugs"
Moseley, Lt-Col. R. B., 164
Mould, Marion, 204

Mr Sponge's Sporting Tour (Surtees), 100, 107
Mr Wilson, 215

Nash, Colin, 105
National Hunt Committee, 73
Neville, Lady Dorothy, 27
Newcastle, Duke of, 73
New Forest Hunt, 124
New History of Gloucestershire, A (Rudder), 17
Newman, Thomas, 101, 102, 131, 136
Newport, 66
New Sporting Magazine, 96
Niagara Therapy Ltd., 177
"Nimrod" (Charles Apperley), xi, 29, 58, 61, 67, 100, 101, 109–11, 112, 113, 114
Noel, Lady Rachel (wife of 2nd Duke), 50
Normanby, Marquess & Marchioness of, 70
North Cotswold Hunt, 103, 105
North, Hon. R., 45n

O'Brien, Lady Margaret, 41
Official Progress of His Grace the Duke of Beaufort through Wales in 1864 (Dineley), 47n
Old Berkshire Hunt, 105, 118
Old Jameson, 220
Old Sodbury, 17
Old Surrey and Burstow Hunt, 143
Olivia, 220
Olympic Games, 161, 162, 210 *1948*, 163; *1952*, 211; *1956*, 222; *1960*, 214; *1964*, 215; *1968*, 216–17, 222; *1972*, 218–19, 222–3; *1976*, 168, 220; *1980*, 210
Oram, John, 213
Ormonde, Dowager Countess of, 39
Osborne, Lady Mary (wife of 2nd Duke), 51
Ossary, Bishop of, 55
Our Nobby, 168, 216, 222

Palladio, Andrea, 52
Palmerston, Lord, 27
Pampas Cat, 223
Parker, Bridget, 218–19, 223
Parsons, R. K., 32

Pasha, 217, 222–3
Passing Years, The (Willoughby de Broke), 15, 28, 39n
Pateman, Bert, 102, 137
Patent of the Dukedom of Somerset, 43n
Pattinson, Aly, 220, 221
Payne, Philip, 102, 106–8, 109, 110
Peel, Sir Robert, 68–9
Peer Gynt, 218
Peggotty, 214
Penney, Dr Robert, 19, 103
Perhaps, 214
Persian Holiday, 168, 220–1
Peterborough Hound Show, 135, 139, 147
Philip, HRH Prince, 88, 170, 184, 199
Phillips, Flavia, 218
Phillips, Gregory, 138
Phillips, Capt. Mark, 162, 168, 175, 183, 186, 216–17, 218–19, 220–1, 222–4
Phillips, Peter, 120
Phillips, Mrs Peter, 206
Pittaway, Fred, 131
Playamar, 219, 220
Poacher, The, 216, 217, 222–4
Pocock, Bishop Richard, 29
Popadom, 217
Porson, Richard, 110
Portcullis Hotel, 19
Portland, Duchess of, 50
Poussin, Nicolas, 51
Pratt's Club, 64, 74
Press Association, 179, 180
Priam, 215
Prince Regent (George IV), 62–3
Prior-Palmer, Lucinda, 162, 168, 174, 177, 183, 185, 197, 198, 199, 201, 202, 207–8, 209, 210, 218, 219, 220–1, 222, 224
Pytchley Hunt, 100–1

Quorn Hunt, 98, 100

Raby Hunt, 106
Radar, 213
Raglan Castle, 41, 43, 59
Raisons des Forces Mouvantes avec Diverses Machines (de Caus), 41
Ratcatcher to Scarlet (Alden), 116

Reade, Ted, 102, 137
Recollections of a Foxhunter ("Scrutator"), 106
Recollections of a Younger Son (Luttrell), 127, 130
Redesdale, Lord, 104
Red Sea, 213
Registry of Hunt Servants, 150
Reminiscences of Lady Dorothy Neville, 27
Remus, 211, 221
Rescator, 179
Reynolds, Sir Joshua, 52
Ribblesdale, Lord, 39n
Richelieu, Cardinal, 41
Richmond, 3rd Duke of, 35
Ricketts, Derek, 204
Riding for the Disabled, 177, 197
Rochester, A. L., 19, 26, 137
Rock On, 216
Rook, Maj. Laurence, 162, 212, 221–3
Ross-Taylor, Celia, 216, 222
Roycroft, Bill, 214, 215–16, 217
Rudder, Samuel, 17, 27, 29
Rural Crafts Association, 177
Rysbracht, Michael, 20

Sackville, Lady Mary (wife of 2nd Duke), 50
St Finbarr, 214, 215
St Germans, Countess of (Lady Blanche Somerset), 84
Salad Days, 214–15, 222
Salt family, 18
Samuel Johnson, 214
San Carlos, 217
Sartorius, F., 103
Schwarzenbach, Capt. H., 211, 212, 221
Scott, Sir Walter, 59
"Scrutator" (K. W. Horlock), 106, 111–12
Scudamore, Frances (wife of 3rd Duke), 53
Scudamore, Sir James, 53
Sea Breeze, 215
Sea Lark, 210
Seymour family, 43n
Shedden, John, 161, 210, 211, 221
Shipton Lodge, 115
Shire Horse Society, 177
Schultz, Karl, 220–1

Sievewright, Molly, 218
Silk Wood, 95, 97, 103, 117
Smith, Charles, 24
Smith, Charlie, 137
Smith, Francis, 53n
Smith, Harvey, 177, 204, 208
Smokey VI, 210, 219, 221, 224
Somerset, Lady Augusta (daughter of 7th Duke), 68
Somerset, Lady Blanche (daughter of 8th Duke, later Marchioness of Waterford), 75
Somerset, Lady Caroline (wife of David Somerset), 20, 32, 84, 85, 131
Somerset, Lord Charles (son of 5th Duke), 57, 103
Somerset, David (present heir to Beaufort title), 22, 86, 102, 153–6, 203, 213–14
Somerset, Lady Diana (daughter of 9th Duke), 83–4
Somerset, Lord Edward (Robert Edward Henry, son of 5th Duke), 57
Somerset, Edward (son of David Somerset), 91, 154
Somerset, Lady Elizabeth (daughter of 4th Earl of Worcester), 40, 44
Somerset, Lady FitzRoy, 65
Somerset, Lord FitzRoy (son of 5th Duke, later Lord Raglan), 57, 65n
Somerset, Lady Henrietta (daughter of 4th Duke), 56
Somerset, Duke of (Henry Beaufort), 40
Somerset, Earl of (John Beaufort), 40
Somerset, Lord Plantaganet (son of 6th Duke), 58
Somerset, Col. Powlett, 118
Somerset, Lady Rose (daughter of 7th Duke), 68
Somerset, Thomas (son of 4th Earl of Worcester, later Viscount Somerset of Cashel), 39
Somerset, Lord William (son of 5th Duke), 57, 60
Somerset Sequence, The (Durant), 29n, 42, 69, 96
South and West Wilts. Hunt, 118, 129
Speculation, 223
Speculator, 186
Spicer, Captain (senior), 127, 129
Spicer, Capt. F., 102, 136–7

Sporting and Dramatic Career, A (Watson) 73*n*
Sporting Magazine, 111
Stafford, 1st Marquess, 58
Starlight, 212, 221, 223
Starkey, Jane, 168, 183, 201, 209, 210
Stephens, Wilson, 87*n*
Stevens, Stewart, 224
Stinchcombe, Miss, 31
Stoke Park, 75
Stony Crossing, 216
Strachan, Clarissa, 179, 224
Surrey Union Hunt, 151
Surtees, R. S., xi, 88*n*, 93, 100, 102, 107, 110
Swangrove, 32, 50
Swynford, Katherine, 40

Talbot, Lord William, 53
Talland School, 218
Tatham-Warner, Kit, 223
Taylor, Alec, 73
Templer, Capt. J. R., 215, 222–3
10th Royal Hussars, 62–3
Tetbury Furniture Co., (Joke Shop), 177, 180, 191, 198, 204
Thomas, Hugh, 168, 219, 220
Thomond, 5th Earl of, 41
Thornbury, Gilbert, 185
Thorne, Diana, 168, 200, 210, 221
Thoughts on Hunting (Beckford), 103, 106
Thynne, Lady Caroline, *see* Lady Caroline Somerset
Times, The, 68
Tindal, Matthew, 54
Titus III, 211
Tomkins, W., 103
Tommy Buck, 221
Tongue, Cornelius, *see* "Cecil"
Topper Too, 168, 201, 209, 210
Tramella, 212, 213, 223
Trollope, Anthony, 97–8, 103
Trotman, Wally, 120
Troy House, Monmouthshire, 45
Turnstone, 216
Tyrell, Sir Thomas, 90

Unwin, Tim, 105
Upper Strata, 218
Urganda the hermit, 32

Vae Vitis, 211, 212, 221
Vale of Aylesbury Hunt, 105
van Dyck, Anthony, 52
Vanity Fair magazine, 33
Victoria, Queen, 68–9, 90, 113
Victorian Days (Anson), 20, 72*n* 74*n*, 75*n*, 76*n*, 89*n*
Vigilant, 211
Village Gossip, 168, 174, 198, 201, 207, 209, 210
Villiers, George, Duke of Buckingham, 90
Vizard, Mr (the Sporting Sweep), 67, 99–100, 113
von Naumann, Baron, 58
V.W.H. Hunt, 79, 99, 105, 120, 126, 127, 136, 138

Waddington, Mrs J. (Sheila Willcox), 166, 221
Wakeling, Major Arthur, 25
Wales, Prince of (Edward VII), 119–20, 129
Wales, Prince of (Edward VIII), 120
Walker, Bill, 114
Walker, Richard, 217, 218, 222–3
Wallace, Capt. Ronnie, 104–5, 110
Walpole, Horace, 54
Walsingham, Lord, 129
Walters, George, 102, 131
Warrathoola, 217
Warrior, 168, 182, 183, 200, 201, 203, 208–9, 210, 222, 224
Warwickshire Hunt, 105
Waterford, Blanche, Marchioness of, 20, 21, 75
Waterford, 5th Marquess of, 20, 75
Watkins, B. L., 32
Watson, Alfred, 73, 124–5, 128–9
Watson, John, 168, 201
Wayfarer, 219
Weatheralls Ltd., 176
Webster, Clarence, 105
Welch, Peter, 215
Weldon, Lt-Col. Frank, 85, 139–40, 162, 164, 166–7, 175, 180, 181–2, 184–6, 189, 201, 202, 208–10, 218, 219; as competitor, 162, 165–6, 211, 212, 213, 214, 215, 221–3
Wellington, Duke of, 59–60, 62, 63, 64, 65*n*, 67, 68–9, 72

Wemyss, Mr, 102
West, Debbie, 218, 224
West Kington, 28
Westminster, 1st Duke, 90
Westmorland, Earl of, 91
West Wiltshire Hunt, 111
Whaddon Chase Hunt, 105
Whitbread & Co., 162, 170, 179, 181,
    196, 206, 210, 214
Whitbread Championship, 204, 208
Whitbread, Colonel W., 200
Whitbread Grand Stakes, 201, 203
Whitbread, Michael, 179
Whitbread Spring Stakes, 203, 205
Whitbread Trophy, 154, 166, 170, 184,
    201, 221
White, John, 138
Whiteley, Martin, 214, 216, 223
Whyte-Melville, G. J., 100, 126
Wide Awake, 162, 201–2, 220, 222
Wilde, Jimmy, 81
Wild Venture, 214, 222–3
Wilkins, Mrs H., 219
Willcox, Sheila, 154, 162, 165–6,
    213–14, 215, 216, 217, 221, 223
William of Orange, 49, 90, 96
Williams, Colonel, 154
Williams, Dorian, 90, 105
Willis, Alan, 185
Willoughby de Broke, 20th Lord, xiii,

15, 28, 39n, 95, 98, 150
Wilson, Harriette, 59–61, 67; *Memoirs*,
    59–60
Wilts. and Gloucestershire Standard, 82n,
    83n, 86
Windsor, 165, 212
Wootton, John, 52
Worcester, 1st Earl (Charles Somerset),
    40
Worcester, 4th Earl (Edward
    Somerset), 17, 39, 89
Worcester, 5th Earl and 1st Marquess
    (Henry Somerset), 40, 41, 42–3, 44
Worcester, 2nd Marquess (Edward
    Somerset), 40–4; titles, 40; scientific
    inventions, 40, 41–2, 43–4;
    marriages, 41; part in Civil War,
    42–3; in Ireland, 43; and Estate, 43n
Worcester House, London, 44
Worcester Lodge, 29–30, 139
World Badminton Magazine, 33
World Three-Day Event
    Championships, 161, 168, 181, 183,
    185, 210
Worshipful Company of Saddlers, 171
Wray, William, 113
Wychwood, 103

Young, Brian, 211
Young Pretender, 215